3—
1/

THE
TWISTED
THREAD

CHARLOTTE
BACON

voice

Hyperion   New York

To my students at MPS:
as they say in Wolof,
this one's for you.

THE
TWISTED
THREAD

CHAPTER 1

Five mornings a week, Madeline Christopher jogged through the cool air of Armitage, past tidy clapboard houses, below stately maples, down the quiet, shuttered High Street. It was New England at its most pristine. The town had staved off box stores and cul-de-sacs plowed from cornfields; high taxes and strict zoning had allowed Armitage to relegate the Shop 'n Saves and condos to Greenville, a factory town it bordered to the north. Her route used to include it. After living in one of Cambridge's seedier neighborhoods, Madeline had felt comfortable with the body shops. Gradually, and not quite consciously, she'd retooled her five miles so that she traveled down elm-shaded lanes, parallel to porches with Doric columns. One stretch of the run now took her past a reservoir where swans nested, white birds on black water, while the wind chapped her face raw well into spring. A big curve guided her around the Quaker graveyard and then up a steady hill and through iron gates to the plush, orderly campus where she had lived for the last nine months. Armitage Academy, where ivy clung to mellowed brick and lawns unfolded like thick, green pelts. Madeline felt always that she was not grand enough to walk on the marble stairs or through the shady buildings. It was preposterous that schools like this still operated, were available to teenagers, of all people, and even more, that she worked at one of them.

For all its appearance of mannered ease, Armitage was a place of ferocious industry. Forty-five minutes was all she had to herself each morning, and it was the only time she could call her own until late that night. Her day was pared into slivers—four minutes to change before track practice, seventeen for lunch. An intern in the English department, she'd had nineteen years of education, acquiring two degrees and no practical experience of any use in the process. But an M.A., a firm handshake, and the willingness to relinquish one's personal life were apparently all it took to qualify you as a teacher at a boarding school.

Her mother, when she'd seen her at Easter, had placed a thumb between her daughter's eyes and pressed critically at the skin. At first, Madeline thought Isabelle was engaging in some yogic practice—trying to pry open a tightly shut third eye, for instance, as out of character as such a gesture seemed. Then she said, "You know, they're doing Botox younger and younger."

Being responsible for the transmission of American literature to four classes of intelligent, slouching adolescents sometimes struck Madeline as a task more ludicrous than ending dependence on foreign oil. That she was also entrusted with the girls' JV track team, the literary magazine, and dorm duty twice a week in Portland, a residence known, even to teachers, as Potland, just added to her sense of living in a Sisyphean nightmare. *Sisyphean* was a word one of her sophomores had used in an essay; Madeline had had to look it up in the dictionary to make sure it had been spelled correctly. It had been. Grindingly repetitive, relating to the futility of labor.

At least it would soon be over. In ten days, she'd be spending the summer on the Cape, in a house her mother had wrested from her second marriage. The plan was to stay and lend a hand to Kate, her older sister, caught in the throes of early motherhood. Rather self-consciously so, thought Madeline, who had seen Kate, her husband, Nick, and their baby, Tadeo, during the recent holiday.

At twenty-eight, Kate had a Ph.D. in architectural history, a husband, a son, a house, and a dog, which seemed like a lot of having for someone so young. What was more disturbing to Madeline was that all these possessions seemed equivalent to her sister. The house equaled the baby; the degree equaled the husband. This wasn't going to work as a long-term strategy, Madeline sensed. Babies and husbands in general rebelled against being treated like hardwood floors or dissertations, things that could be polished. But for now, Kate's life looked admirably shiny, well appointed, primed for more and more accomplishment. Kate was a graduate of Armitage.

It was Kate, in fact, she had to thank for having a job here in the first place. Madeline had produced a thesis on Flannery O'Connor and a covertly written collection of short stories—well, at least seven, and that was almost a collection, wasn't it? By early last spring, she had also amassed a quiver of rejections from the community colleges where she'd hoped to teach near her boyfriend's medical school. By May, Madeline's prospects for employment had thinned like her father's hair after divorcing his third wife. It was Kate who had bluntly captured the situation. "Face it, Madeline, Owen wouldn't move for you, so why move for him? Put him to the test. Strike out on your own." She was right, of course. Owen had steadfastly and with no guilt insisted that Duke was the only place he was willing to study medicine. And there he was in North Carolina, dissecting Gary, his cadaver, into thousands of tiny bits. Quite happily. With only occasional calls that had, in truth, become so occasional they were almost nonexistent. The question was, would he break up with her by e-mail or by text?

When Madeline confessed in July that even the slimmest of job leads had evaporated, Kate had wangled an interview for her at the academy. Hired in August, as far as Madeline could tell exclusively on Kate's recommendation, she'd had a sudden insight into how these schools functioned. Blood mattered. If she was related to Kate, fantastically successful even by Armitage's distorted standards, she had to be all right. It almost hadn't been an issue that the hem of her skirt had gapped a little and she had tripped coming up the stairs to meet Porter McLellan, the head. It couldn't be that bad for a year, they must have thought. They had Mindy Allison's place to fill; inconvenient of her to be having her fourth child, but there it was. They could make Madeline a last-minute intern, give her a closet to live in, get her to fill unpopular dorm and coaching slots, pay her less than a third what they paid regular teachers, and she'd be grateful in the end to have Armitage on her résumé. A neat trick all around.

The literary magazine—*The Turret*, for the room where for the past eighty years the faculty adviser and perhaps one competent student had thrown it together—had been published; the track team had one last meet, an invitational. Armitage had conceived of the brilliant system of giving exams early, making the last two weeks of school far less burdensome all around. Now all Madeline had to do was finish teaching, grade several tall stacks of papers, survive the stuffy rituals of graduation and reunion, and she'd be blissfully, completely done. Come September, she had a job tutoring high school kids in Boston and an apartment on Marlborough Street to be shared with three friends from college. She also sustained a misty fantasy of finishing her story collection and achieving some vague form of artistic notoriety, but that was far too embarrassing to admit out loud. Beyond that, she had no idea what the future held.

Thinking about all this—Kate, Owen, her decidedly patchy earning potential—had made Madeline run a bit faster than usual, and before she knew it, her dorm swam into view. Normally, at this time of day, especially on a Monday, Portland, a gambrel-roofed building three stories tall on the far side of the Quad, was dim except for the column of lights that illuminated the central corridor. The girls slept in as late as possible before chapel, unless they were up early to finish a lab, nudge a boyfriend out the door, smoke a cigarette, or do any of the dozens of things forbidden in the Major School Rules. They pursued none of these activities in the light, and at 6:50, Madeline expected only dark windows and hush before the day sprang relentlessly forward.

But Portland was ablaze. Every pane shone. An ambulance and two police cruisers, their red, white, and blue lights pulsing irregularly, pasted the faces of the girls clustered at the door with fleeting, transparent tattoos. Madeline discovered herself bolting past the statue of James Armitage, a gunpowder merchant who'd founded the academy in 1820 for the "betterment of boys," and straight toward the students. Strange to have had such ambivalent feelings about them so much of the year and find suddenly that she considered herself responsible for their welfare.

Someone's dead, Madeline thought, and panic jolted through her. She hated this sensation, the knowledge, only half-admitted most of the time, that the world could crack wide at any moment, and that you would never, despite wit, fiscal prudence, or luck, be entirely prepared for what might happen next. Who was it? Maybe Harvey Fuller had keeled over after forty years of teaching biology and almost as many living in the same apartment at the back of Portland. Old enough to have known Darwin, not only teach his theories. But it wasn't Harvey. There he was, spry in a bathrobe of Black Watch, as he spoke to a policeman. Looking, Madeline thought incongruously, as leathery as those oceangoing lizards the naturalist had studied in the Galápagos.

"You're finally back, Madeline. No one knew where you were," Grace Peters scolded, intercepting her before she could reach the terrified girls. And that was the word, Madeline realized: they *were* terrified, tearstained and quaking. Grace, the dorm head, glanced at Madeline's damp T-shirt and shorts, the untied lace of one of her sneakers. Even in the midst of a crisis, Grace, a classics teacher, had managed to find an unwrinkled pair of brown slacks and a neat gray cardigan. She was known to give pop quizzes with breathtaking regularity. Her students regularly scored 5s on AP exams. Madeline couldn't believe she was thinking about iguanas and Grace's reputation, but it was the way the mind worked when frightened, wasn't it? Forming and clinging to ridiculous impressions when least necessary.

"What's going on?" Madeline asked. She could barely breathe.

"Claire Harkness is dead," Grace said, and Madeline saw that Grace was actually as gray as her sweater.

The worst thing possible, every teacher's private horror. A student dying on their watch. And why Claire? Madeline had taught her in Contemporary World Literature the first semester, and the girl's crystalline beauty and complete disdain for the adults around her had awed her. She hadn't quite realized kids like Claire actually existed, though Kate ought to have prepared her. At seventeen, Claire had a composure that Madeline couldn't imagine possessing at fifty, even if her hair had managed at last to stay straight. Claire's last paper—well argued, neatly phrased, but somehow bloodless—had compared ineffectual parents in the stories of Lorrie Moore and Alice Munro. Claire had not been a person whose passion for life bubbled through her, but the girl had a certain fierceness that made the thought of her dead almost impossible to fathom. And how? Suicide seemed unlikely, but even so, Madeline imagined rope, a bottle of pills. The school counselor, Nina Garcia-Jones, had devoted half a day during new teacher orientation to Warning Signs and Appropriate Responses. Madeline tried to remember when she had last seen Claire and couldn't. "What happened?"

"We don't know," Grace said, looking over at the group of girls still huddled in the doorway. Sally Jansen had started to scream that Claire was on the floor and couldn't be woken up. That was all, so far. Grace's phone chirped, and she leaned in to answer it.

Madeline didn't know what to do. Faculty members and students had begun to stream from their dorms to investigate the unseemly commotion with which Portland had started the week. Grace was still on the phone. Was she talking to the police? Claire's parents? What a terrible job that would be. Wouldn't Porter take care of that? Madeline began to walk toward the girls and tripped on her shoelace. She leaned down to tie it, and memories of Claire scrambled around her mind. Her gold hair had flowed in even waves past her shoulders, and on that hair alone, Ned Madison, the dean for college admission, had snorted, she could have gotten into paradise, much less Harvard. He'd had four beers at the welcome picnic when he said it, but it was probably true. That she was a lithe, instinctive athlete, captain of lacrosse, a more than competent student, and a volunteer at the Greenville animal shelter combined to create an irresistible package for most schools. Add to that what was known as a "heavy leg," four generations of relatives who'd gone and contributed mightily to Harvard, and Claire had been a shoo-in.

But in what counted as a rebellious move only at Armitage, Claire had chosen to go to Yale. She'd gotten in early and had done approximately nothing since then in most of her classes. She was close to failing calculus, Alice Grassley had said to Madeline at a faculty meeting. "And while I wouldn't call her a genius, behind that perfect nose she's no dummy," Alice added. Far worse from most people's perspectives, the girl had refused to go out for lacrosse during this, her last year at Armitage. There had been hand-wringing about it at the lunch table.

Grace snapped her phone closed. Madeline stood up, shivering. One of the girls huddled at the doorway started to wail. It was Sally Jansen, a reedy, neurotic senior bound for Skidmore. Others gathered round and tried to hush her. "It shouldn't have happened!" Sally was screaming.

"What's she talking about?" Madeline asked. "What's Sally saying?" From the corner of her eye, she saw Porter, handsome and rugged in a groomed, patrician way. All he was doing was talking to a man in a suit, but even from this distance, Porter gave off a palpable impression that he could handle the job before him. He was almost universally considered competent. Even with her limited exposure to places like this, Madeline knew how rare it was to find someone as respected as he was, especially in an environment where stakes were so small and entitlements so large. Madeline always had a hard time calling him by his first name.

Sally was screaming louder now. "She shouldn't have died. It shouldn't have happened!" Porter appeared to see the girl for the first time. At almost the same moment, he glimpsed Madeline and motioned with his hand that she was to go and deal with Sally. He so rarely noticed her, his brief gesture had the weight of a touch. Just then, Sally broke free and dashed inside the dorm. Madeline felt her own knees unlock as she went to do Porter's bidding. She tore through the door, past police and students, and up the stairs, following the sound of Sally's quick feet.

Claire had been a prefect, and as such had scored herself a large single with an attached bathroom. Sally was lunging toward Claire's room, but two uniformed officers pinned her firmly by the arms. "Slow down, sweetheart," said the older one. "Take it easy," said the other as Sally collapsed in the hallway. The cops were used to Armitage students. These men, large, local, unimpressed with privilege, knew exactly how to handle kids like Sally Jansen, and they frequently did when the more hapless were caught smoking pot in the graveyard or trying to buy liquor in Greenville's package stores.

Madeline panted up the last stairs and went toward the trembling girl. As she did, she couldn't help but glance inside the room, known in the dorm as Claire's Lair. Drawers were open, and expensive clothes were flung everywhere on the dhurrie rugs that she'd used to mask the tile. Her desk was piled with books and binders. A bulletin board was covered with snapshots and Post-its and her acceptance letter from Yale. Madeline could see the school's name from where she stood.

The room of a spoiled girl. A girl who had openly considered herself superior to others and been admired by her peers for her beauty and confidence. A girl whose social connections intimidated most teachers and made stark the gap between the origins of the students and the adults meant to guide them. But none of that had protected her from dying. All of a sudden, Madeline spied Claire, her almost naked body not even six feet away, sprawled on the floor near the desk chair. She was on her back, head tilted to the side. No wound or mark was visible from here; she looked almost as if she were sleeping, but there was no mistaking the absolute lack of life in the angle at which her neck was bent and in the pallor of her skin. The policemen moved protectively in front of the door but hadn't closed it yet, unwilling apparently to alter the scene before photographers arrived. Everything had to be frozen as it had been found. Even Madeline knew that. Still, the cops' wide legs couldn't block her view entirely.

Holding Sally to her chest, trying to still the girl, she couldn't help but stare. It struck her how little she had been around the dead. Americans kept death at arm's length, as if it were a country they would never visit. Yet even in places where mortality was less crudely separated from life, people would be stunned at the extinction of the young and lovely. No one could make Claire Harkness on the floor, her skin the color of a candle, turn into something normal. Sally kept sobbing, Madeline kept holding her. And then she realized something else that was not normal about Claire. It was her breasts. They were full, and rigid with veins, their tips wide, rosy caps. Something about them made her think of Kate. Her sister had been complaining about her newly huge nipples and had to be reassured by several doctors that they would eventually revert to small, delicate pinkness. She had nursed because it was what was best for Tadeo, she said, but after six months, that was it. She needed her body back. At the tip of each of Claire's breasts was a grayish pearl of what could only be milk. One of the officers had had enough of Sally, the crying, and Madeline's sweaty presence and was trying with gentle insistence to get them going. "Miss, take the young lady downstairs now, please," he said.

But Madeline, arms still wrapped around Sally, was rooted to the floor. "No, no, that's not possible. Sally, did Claire just have a baby?" Madeline said sharply, still holding the girl, but lifting her chin so she could stare into the narrow face. "Where's the baby?" Madeline found that she was almost shaking Sally's bony shoulders. Abruptly, a number of details came into focus: Claire's refusal to participate in sports this spring, her low grades, her sickly color the last week, the eerie buzz that had run through the dorm this weekend that Madeline had thought was only end-of-the-year jitters. A baby. And none of the community's adults had even known she was pregnant. Or had they? Madeline's stomach felt as if a stone had landed in it. A girl she'd supervised and taught, and she hadn't noticed. How could she have missed something so obvious? How could she have been so stupid?

Sally, a damp weight, said brokenly, "Miss Christopher, she wouldn't let us tell anyone. She wanted to keep it a secret. She made us promise."

"Sally," Madeline said, more steel in her voice than she'd known she possessed, "I'm going to ask you again. Where is the baby?"

Sally shook her head and could not speak. "I don't know," she finally whispered. "He's gone. When I found her this morning, we looked everywhere, but he's gone. Someone took all his blankets and the diapers. Someone took him. I just can't believe he's gone." She burst into ragged tears again and threw herself on Madeline.

The officers' watchfulness had thickened. The taller murmured into his radio. Almost instantly, Madeline heard the scrape of men's shoes on the stairs. She held Sally close. She wanted to offer some reassurance, to blot away the girl's grief. She understood now why Sally had shouted on the steps and why the girls had seemed not just saddened but so scared. She started to ease Sally to her feet, but

Madeline's mind was charging forward. Claire might have given birth in that room. Where was her child? Sally kept sobbing. Police in uniforms, in suits came swarming up the stairs. One was ordered to take Madeline and Sally downstairs, now, and as he leaned in to help them, Madeline saw that his face was almost as young as those of her students. Sally tottered back to the first floor, and Madeline followed, her hand on the girl's shoulder. As they moved, light poured in through the high windows and dazzled the gold braid on the officer's cap. Above them, radios crackled, cell phones shrilled, men barked into them, voices taut.

The sun spread in hot bands through the stairwell, illuminating long threads of dust floating through the air. It was going to be a beautiful day, green, warm, rich with spring's fullness. With a suddenness that made Sally, the silent officer, and Madeline all jump, the chapel bells began to peal.

CHAPTER 2

F red Naylor was sitting next to Alice Grassley and doctoring his dining hall coffee with a carefully engineered combination of cream and raw sugar. A miniature success with which to start the morning. It was just 6:45, and peace reigned in the elegantly proportioned room. He hadn't realized how much he savored the ritual until Rob Barlow, the dean of students, strode in, saw them both, and came over to shatter the day. Rob planted his hands on their table and said, with a rough attempt at lowered volume, "Tragic news. Claire Harkness is dead. We're meeting at seven fifteen in the Study."

Fred and Alice happened to eat breakfast at the same early hour, and they'd developed a habit of sitting next to each other and trading sections of the newspaper. It was a friendship of sorts, an unexpected one. Alice was at least sixty, bony, exacting, the keeper of minutes at faculty meetings, and best known for the ruthless speed with which she graded calculus exams. Fred was twenty-nine, the painting teacher and boys' soccer coach, and had cultivated a professionally relaxed attitude about almost everything. Nonetheless, he and Alice had grown used to talking companionably together each morning in the hushed, almost empty dining hall, sports pages spread over the narrow table. They were both citizens of what was now called Red Sox Nation, but Alice didn't like that name. "Die-hard fan will do nicely," she said. When Rob approached them, they were about to tuck into a discussion of last night's loss to Baltimore, a five-run lead blown in the ninth inning, a kind of mishap specific to the Sox. But Rob's news destroyed everything. Fred dropped the packet of sugar. Alice's tea spilled an amber river through her eggs. "Do the students know?" she asked Rob. Her face was as pale as the chalk she still insisted on using. Everyone else had long ago switched to whiteboards.

"A few," said Rob. "The ones in the dorm, mostly. Sarah's meeting with them now." Sarah Talmadge was the assistant head: professional, crisp, smart. Exactly the right person to calm a dorm full of panic-stricken girls. Rob was a former history teacher and had a bristling head of brown hair and a square set of shoulders he'd used to great effect as a hockey player and coach. A good person to convey bad news to adults, because he'd be brisk about it, but the wrong choice for kids. Porter McLellan, once again, had made the right decision. Rob stalked off to alert the next faculty member he'd been slated to tell. No doubt he was working from a carefully denoted list about who was contacting whom. Porter was remarkably thorough. It was 6:50. Fred and Alice had a few minutes to gather themselves before they had to leave.

He glanced at the group of Korean kids sitting in the corner where they chatted every morning. Breakfast was an optional meal at Armitage, and only the most dedicated of students got up this early. Jung Lee, a handsome senior, was laughing loudly at something Maya Kim had said. They had no idea about Claire, and Fred wasn't going to tell them. He was desolate at the thought that he would never feel the same about these mornings in Alice's tactful, pleasant company reliving the dramas of their baseball team as these serious children ate pancakes.

Alice was wiping her forehead with a napkin. "Thirty-six years," she said, staring out the bay window through which they could see a broad green bank leading down to the Bluestone River. This Saturday, Armitage was supposed to host a rowing regatta that Fred knew would now be canceled.

"Thirty-six," Alice said again. "I've been here thirty-six years, and in that time only three other students have died. Alex Schwartz, in a car accident. Louisa Harper, of leukemia. One other, in a climbing accident. Kids just don't die here. But this is different. I know this is different, Fred."

Later, Fred would not quite remember how he and Alice made it to the meeting, but he did know that he offered her his arm and was surprised to realize she needed his support. Alice was wrong. Another Armitage boy had died here, but it was before her tenure and almost everyone had forgotten about him.

They took their seats in the Study, a mock Gothic, wood-paneled room off the main hall of Nicholson House, where the deans and Porter hatched administrative strategies on the first floor. The language lab lurked moldily in the basement, and the college counselors had spread themselves out for their embattled work across the second. The Study featured stained-glass panels of Pre-Raphaelite maidens and vaguely Arthurian knights posed among lilies. In the moony glow of these long-haired figures, almost seventy faculty members gathered each week to discuss everything from the curriculum to parents' weekend, benefits packages to student morale. At a regular meeting, a buzz of chipper, sociable talk hummed through the room. This morning, however, teachers folded themselves into their usual seats and refused to meet one another's eyes. It was so hushed Fred could hear a twittering flock of birds in the lilac bush that grew beyond the window.

Then Madeline Christopher rushed in. Fred raised his hand and waved her over. Her disheveled, dark brown hair distinguished her from many of the other teachers and most of the students. One of the first things Madeline had said to him, rather crossly, was "Blondes. Working here's like being trapped in some preppy, unfishy version of Iceland." What had made Fred laugh was that she'd blushed unevenly and gulped "Sorry!" the moment she looked up at him and remembered his own tousled golden curls.

Just yesterday, she was making fun of Mindy Allison and the staggering, Scandinavian braid that swung down her back, calling Mindy and her kids the Happy Elves. Even the baby seemed fantastically cheerful, she complained. Madeline, a grunter in the morning, unfunctional without infusions of caffeine, was going out of her way not to run into them until she'd swilled down at least four cups of the weak dining hall brew. If she could stop grousing about the toothy smiles and the privilege, however, she'd be great at Armitage. He thought she was making a mistake going to Boston. Backtracking, he'd told her, straight to college. "But at least I won't have curfew," she'd answered. Plainspoken and bright, Madeline loved her subject, pushed the students hard, and found they liked what she had to say. She'd done well this year. An intern in Spanish was downed by chronic fatigue in the middle of the first semester, and the other two, in physics and math, were shaky and worn and palpably ready to sprint off campus as soon as possible. But Madeline, against expectation, mostly her own, had thrived. "Jesus," she said under her breath to Fred as she flopped into her chair. "This is the worst. The dorm is freaking out."

Madeline was young enough to swear a lot when she shouldn't and use phrases like *freaking out* unironically. She was wearing baggy gym shorts and a T-shirt advertising Heinz ketchup. Her cheeks were densely pink, and a not unpleasant smell of sweat rose from her. "Oh, sorry, Fred, I'm disgusting," she said, noticing that he was looking at her. "I went for a run, and there wasn't time to change. Fred, it's Claire Harkness. She's dead," she whispered.

A vision of Claire flared in his mind, and he snapped it shut as fast as he could. He didn't want to think about it. Claire had been beautiful, even in a sea of beautiful girls. Friends from graduate school had visited campus a few times, but they stared at the students in a way that made him uncomfortable. One had even asked how he kept it together around all those gorgeous teenagers. He shrugged the question off. You just did, he thought privately. That was your job. You did not give in to temptation. You had your own life, your own relationships. They were just kids, and the lines were firm.

He heard Rob Barlow's words echo through his head again, followed by Madeline's. Claire was dead. He had taught her a few semesters ago and been impressed with her painting and articulate critiques of other students' efforts. Yet there'd been an essential ice to the girl, something calculated in the amount of energy she'd given to her own art and that of others. The students, however, had admired her work extravagantly, praise she had seemed to accept as her due. Girls like Claire were exactly what people meant when they claimed that Armitage was nothing but a den for the upper class, a lair for the perpetuation of entitlement. Claire dead seemed almost impossible to imagine. She had apparently relished the exercise of her particular power.

As faculty continued to gather, Fred noticed as he always did that the air smelled of stale coffee, apples, and newspaper ink. He remembered something Madeline had said early in the year. *The*

New York Times and *The Boston Globe* were delivered daily to this room so teachers could have a snack, and a cup of joe, and catch up on world events in their free periods, an act that she considered a kind of insane optimism. She had read about two headlines all year, she confessed, and Fred had told her that it wasn't that people didn't have time to read as much as the fact that the action that swirled through Armitage started to seem like the only thing that was real. Today, those worlds would intersect. The media would be all over this. Margaret Oliver, the communications director, was pecking at her BlackBerry in a corner, while Stuart Murray, the head of what was now known as the advancement office, muttered fiercely to her. He was the money guy, the one who raised Armitage's millions, vulgar, loud, and none of it mattered because he was the one who brought the gifts and buildings rolling in. Fred wondered how long it would take him to spin or mute the death of a kid from a big donor family.

Porter came into the room then and strode to the dais, where he always stood. It often took a few moments for everyone to stop chatting and turn their attention to the head. But today, their focus was instant, tightened with worry and fear. Porter looked ghastly, Fred thought, even if his voice was mellifluous as usual as he thanked them for arriving so quickly. Not everyone was here, he continued, since they had to make sure that at least one adult was present at every dormitory. Fred noticed the absence of some key people: a dean or two; the head of history; Nina Garcia-Jones; Susie Allen, the athletic director. "I have tried to alert as many of you as possible, but if you haven't heard, I have the worst possible news. Claire Harkness died sometime early this morning." He was right. In twenty-five minutes, on a campus of hundreds of acres, well before the start of the school day, the word had spread with astonishing speed. Fred, a student here before returning to teach after graduate school, had often noted you could leave your dorm with a cold and five minutes later the whole school heard you had pneumonia. Information not only traveled with terrific swiftness, it swelled and grew more dire with its movement. But there was no way to make this more awful. No one reacted as Porter spoke. Even if Rob hadn't reached them, they had indeed heard. They bent their heads and stared more fixedly at the floor.

Then he said, "A student found her at approximately six thirty. But there is more to tell you." He paused. Fred snapped his head up; maybe it could get worse. "Apparently," Porter went on, "Claire had just," and here his voice did falter, "given birth. To a son, we think. But this child has not been found." This announcement stunned them all, Fred saw, although a glance told him that Madeline had already known. She was looking hard at her fingers, which she had knotted into a ball. Chairs creaked, people caught their breaths. Someone stifled a shout.

Porter lifted his hands. "I know this couldn't be more horrifying. We have lost a student. There may have been crimes committed. Armitage will become the scene of an investigation that could take weeks to resolve. The police and the press are already involved." If anyone knew anything about Claire or the baby that they thought would be of use, they were to come to him immediately so they could go together to the police. For the moment, classes and all sports competitions were suspended, as were seated meal and chapel. Probably the prom would be canceled, as well as other year-end festivities. They might have to modify graduation and reunion as well. They would know soon and keep the faculty informed. Teachers should expect, too, that parents would want their children to leave early. They would deal with that eventuality as necessary. He paused and pulled a handkerchief from his pocket to wipe his temples. It was clear he couldn't, for the moment, say more. Then, inside the shocked, restless silence, someone coughed. "Porter," said Forrest Thompson, the chair of English, "what are we going to do instead of having classes?" It was oddly kind of Forrest, intentionally or not, Fred couldn't tell, to offer Porter an avenue away from his distress toward some practical detail.

It worked, and Porter straightened himself instantly, snapping back to headship. "I've spoken with Sarah, Rob, and Nina," he said, "and we've decided that we'll break up into dorm groups. Obviously, the girls who live in Portland will be among the most distraught. And the police will need to talk with them and with the faculty there right away. We'll probably relocate students from that dorm for the rest of the term as well." For now, he continued, dorms would take turns going to the dining hall; he passed out a schedule from a stack of Xeroxes at his elbow. As the practicalities were being handled, he pleaded with them not to discuss the situation with family, friends, or journalists. Discretion wasn't the only issue at stake. "The police have made it very clear," he said. "It's not the academy's reputation that we have to be concerned about. We're looking for a newborn."

Porter usually allowed for a generous question-and-answer period after he spoke. He was very good at allowing people to disagree with him and speak their views without growing threatened himself. He managed the cranks, the bores, and the blowhards with even, thoughtful ease. It was masterful. Fred, whose grandfather had been Armitage's eighth head thirty years ago, had made a study of headmasters and was always comparing them to

Llewellan. Porter was the most astute he'd ever seen. Among other virtues, he had the ability to sense when he was on the brink of turning into a caricature, a hazard for those at boarding schools, where the line between becoming a well-loved campus fixture and turning into a fossil was quite porous. For instance, Porter had spent two years after college as a Peace Corps volunteer in Senegal and for the first few months of his tenure at Armitage had given a hair too many talks that included the phrase *As they say in Wolof*, followed by the delivery of some quaint maxim to illustrate a point he was making. Wolof was the local language in the district where he'd worked as a water engineer. But Porter had soon gotten wind that students were mocking these lapses into tribal wisdom and he had dropped the practice, though he still occasionally referenced it with a self-deprecating smile that only increased his luster: not only was he smart enough to be alert to rumor, he had the confidence to poke fun at himself. Today, however, no shred of that liveliness was visible. He invited no comments this time. He told the faculty that classes in a shortened format would probably resume in the next two days. They were to check their school e-mail accounts frequently. They were to monitor their students with extreme care. When they had more information, they would talk about how to make up for lost time, lost events.

Fred peered at his colleagues. Everyone was chastened. Even Alan Shepherd, a physics teacher who complained frequently that sports—or theater or dance or chorus—cut into the time his students had to prepare for the AP, had the wit not to protest. But Fred also noticed that a few people were staring a little more sharply than usual at Grace Peters. It had happened under her supervision, in her dorm. Claire had been her advisee. And she hadn't known.

She hadn't seen. That none of them had either was, at the moment, immaterial. This situation, drastic as it was, demanded an almost immediate apportioning of blame. Grace's chin was set and hard. She was clearly aware she'd be called on to explain and was girding herself for scrutiny. Readying her script and her defenses. Fred hoped Madeline realized that she, too, was going to come under fire: she lived in the same dorm, and Grace would be looking to shift responsibility off her own back. That's what these places encouraged with their emphasis on perfect behavior, flawless results. When there were slips, minor or extreme, the cost was high and so was the corresponding need to heave guilt elsewhere as quickly as possible.

"That's all," said Porter. "Please get to your dormitories and talk to your students." Nina the counselor would be rotating among dorms to assist teachers and students, and they were bringing in the network of psychologists the school used to help everyone through this first difficult period. Teachers prepared to go, and then, inside the murmur of voices and the scrape of chairs, Janie Marcus, the spindly ballet mistress, asked, "Have Claire's parents been told?" She so rarely spoke at faculty meetings, everyone was startled.

"Yes," said Porter. "Her father will be here as soon as he can from New York. Her mother lives in Paris and will arrive tonight." It struck Fred then that no one envied the head at that moment. And they frequently did. The man earned an excellent salary; he oversaw a school that possessed both intellectual and social prestige; trustees, teachers, students, and alumni all admired him. He'd written well-respected books about educating adolescents, and he helped Stuart Murray raise head-spinning amounts of money for

Armitage's already healthy endowment. His elegant wife and three handsome sons traveled with him each summer to a seaside cottage in Maine and the rest of the year surrounded him with what appeared to be open, plentiful affection. The twins were at Cornell, and the youngest, a senior named Miles, a handsome, lively boy with a quick wit, was well liked by faculty, Fred among them. Next year, he was going to Amherst, as his father had. Porter had been at the academy five years, the same amount of time as Fred, and everyone hoped he'd last much longer. He wore these achievements lightly. Those who didn't approve of Porter could be discounted as jealous, malcontent, or insecure.

But today, no one coveted one ounce of his responsibilities. People started to make their way toward the door. Then Mary Manchester, the librarian, asked in her braying voice, the same one she used to badger faculty about planning their students' research projects six months in advance, "Porter, was Claire murdered?"

"We can't talk about that," Porter said slowly. "Not at the moment." He looked profoundly sad as he said this. Someone cleared her throat then, and the sound somehow released the crowd of teachers, got them moving again. Fred glanced around and saw that the prompt had come from Tamsin Lovell, dressed in a black skirt and blindingly white blouse. Porter's assistant, she had stationed herself below the dais and to the right. She was picking up the extra Xeroxes, her face as always unreadable. Fred looked at the headmaster, who was folding his handkerchief carefully. The gesture didn't register until later, but Porter never folded his handkerchiefs. He always twisted them into balls and stuffed them back in his pocket. Owning these bits of linen was the mildest of affectations, something vaguely French or nineteenth century about it, an impression he counteracted by treating them carelessly. But that ruined morning, Porter took pains to restore the cloth to a square and touched the neat packet as if it were something precious, something easily torn.

CHAPTER 3

I n the woods, where the pines and birches thinned and gave way to a wide stand of beeches, Matt Corelli was running as fast as he could manage. His heart was banging hard as he breathed the warm air, which he thought changed in this part of the forest. The light certainly did, filtering through a veil of lime green leaves. The ground, too, became more treacherous, with a webbed net of gray roots that could send him hurtling if he didn't pay close attention. He had run this route when he was on the cross-country team at Armitage, and even now, fifteen years later, he couldn't make the loop without memories of meets—corded muscles, pumping arms—crowding into the present, though he took the five miles more slowly than he had.

Passing through the beeches, he took the next quarter of a mile at a trot, delaying the return to town, his rented house, the station. The woods were clean, separate, and despite their raft of associations, relaxing. Each morning, he ran past trees that had grown there undisturbed for three hundred years, beholden only to themselves, nature so much more neutral than the troubles humans knitted for themselves. When he finally emerged onto a sidewalk, he turned down High Street, took a left on Elm, and then another left on Concord, before arriving at the shingled bungalow where he'd been living the last two years.

The screen door creaked, and he heard his phone beeping the presence of a new voice mail. It was either his father, Joseph, reminding him for the third time that they were going to have dinner that night, or Vernon Cates, his partner, who rose at dawn and assumed everyone else should, too. Matt ignored the cell and went to the kitchen to get coffee on the stove before retreating to the shower. On a busy but generally nonviolent desk devoted mostly to tax evasion and white-collar crime, Matt didn't have to live anymore with the phone almost sutured to his palm. It was one of the reasons he didn't regret leaving Philadelphia, where he had worked on the homicide squad at a jolting, frantic pace. Distance from gory crisis was one of the reasons he'd returned to Greenville, a place he had to call, no matter how ambivalently, home.

He twisted shut the top half of his Bialetti, the octagonal silver pot in which he brewed what Vernon called his "toxic tar," and placed it on the front burner. When the coffee was ready, the contraption bubbled volcanically, a controllable Vesuvius with which to start the day. An etching of a squat, mustachioed man in a trench coat and fedora, hand raised high and stubborn, decorated the side. An Italian Inspector Clouseau, a picture of unjustified confidence. Matt returned his salute.

Just as the eruption began, the phone rang again, and he guessed before he went to answer it that it would be Vernon. Often merely thinking of Vernon drew him toward you; he had an adhesive quality once he was part of your life.

"Enriquez testimony this morning at nine fifteen, Judge Mack Truck presiding." Matt had an iPhone, a date book, an excellent memory, an aptitude for timeliness, and occasional help from the office secretary, in short very little chance of not being where he was supposed to be. He also had Vernon, who, if he had been an object instead of a person, Matt had decided, would have been a backup hard drive. They had been working together since Matt joined the Armitage-Greenville Police. Armitage didn't have quite enough crime to justify its own force, and it had just enough sense of self-importance to feel in occasional need of protection, so the two towns shared a station that straddled their exact border. Vernon had worked what he called with relish the "paper beat" for the last five years. Most of his and Matt's work arose from Armitage, and Vernon loved dispossessing the men in ties of their suburban certainties.

"I'll be there, Vernon. Early," Matt said, walking back to the kitchen, where he fetched the milk frother from the cabinet. It had been a final, paltry gift from his last girlfriend, Ann, a lawyer who had invested in an impressive array of cooking gear that Matt belatedly realized had served a decorative rather than a functional use. His own spare kitchen held little more than blackened steel pans and a set of worn if excellent knives he sharpened himself. Still, he had kept the frother as a token of the relationship and had grown to like the dense foam and the touch of ridiculousness it added to the mornings.

"Wear the white oxford and the blue tie."

"Got it, Vernon: white oxford, blue tie," Matt said, sipping.

"You should use soy. You're going to kill yourself with all that dairy."

"Shut up, Vernon," said Matt, and he sipped louder, just to annoy his partner, who clicked the phone off quickly as if merely hearing the consumption of a milk product would cause a leap in his cholesterol.

Vernon, like Matt, had been born in Greenville. He had become a cop when he graduated from high school not only because it ran in his blood but because of what he described as "high standards for civic hygiene." He took loitering seriously. Red-light running even more so. He was fourteen years older than Matt, and Matt remembered him at the school crossing, writing ticket after ticket and saying, as drivers protested, "See you in court, ma'am, and might I suggest you arrive there slowly." Back then, he was 230 pounds, all red cheek, gut, and swagger. But he irritated the public so much he was taken off street assignments and put behind a desk, where he picked apart alibis, ran background checks on suspects, and developed his true skills: mucking with patient orneriness around large bureaucracies and discovering discomfiting information stored on paper or in files. There was a personal downside to this transition, however. Vernon's habit of Twinkie and Dorito inhalation accompanied him, and he got even larger. "My time as a blue whale," he called it. His father and grandfather had both been cops, huge and dead by forty-five. Vernon had assumed he would follow the family tradition. "But then came Kathy." He said this, Matt mused, the way other people might say, "And then I won Powerball."

Still sipping coffee, Matt went to turn the shower on. He had been warned that Vernon was more like a burr than a person, but he soon realized the man was merely bored. He needed more and better work to do. Matt had helped him double his load, and together they'd started working three cold cases from missing persons.

The resolution of the second—the discovery of the whereabouts of an old lady named Olive Anderson in the nursing home of a neighboring town—had required celebration. That was when Matt learned about what Vernon called with messianic seriousness his conversion. He had broken an ankle on an icy sidewalk, and Kathy had been his nurse at Armitage General. She had fussed over him, suggested extra tests, found his bone density was low. He had told her his history, and she suggested it wasn't fate that he keel over in middle age. It might have something to do with choices.

Choices, Matt thought. To come back, to stay away. To call someone or not. To admit what you felt or stay silent. The hot water pounded on his neck and back. Lucky water; no free will involved. It would flow wherever gravity demanded. He could have spent an hour there, suspended from his day, but it would be smart to get to the courthouse early and run through details. Matt already had the white oxford out. He had been planning on the blue tie before Vernon phoned.

Clean now, he dressed carefully, and as he threaded the tie around his neck, Matt knew that if someone who looked like Kathy had told him to drink a pint of motor oil, he would have given up on the concept of free will altogether and asked her if two were better. But she had had her eye on Vernon, and she told him to down green tea and kombucha and in the process fell in love with the gradually slimming and increasingly committed vegan that Vernon, spectacularly against type, was becoming.

That was ten years ago. He was now forty-seven and had baked a wheat-free carrot cake for the occasion. He had lost fifty-eight pounds and kept them off. He had married Kathy and produced twin girls, Sky and Shanti. "Don't ask. I may be vegan, but I draw the line at all that woo-woo." Kathy did not, and Sky and Shanti, unimmunized, wreaked havoc at the Greenville Montessori. "They're expressing their shakti energy," Kathy said cozily, indulgence lighting the deep blue eyes that had sent Vernon hurtling down his dairy-free path. "They're hellions, Kath," Vernon said and wrapped them all in long, lean arms. Matt envied his partner his frisky, shakti-infused family. He also envied his lack of ambition, openly expressed, and his pleasure at living, working, and eating locally. "Paris, Shmaris. Look closely enough at anything and all you get is century after century of complication. At least this is complication I belong to."

He had looked at Matt then, and Matt had seen his mouth pucker the way it did before he asked a pointed question. He'd paused, seen no invitation to continue, and said nothing, a rarity in Vernon's life. He had wanted to discuss, Matt assumed, why Matt had ditched a promising career to return to Greenville, and on that topic, Matt had decided, he would remain as silent as he could as long as possible. If he were honest, some of those motives remained so murky it was hard to understand them in private much less admit them out loud.

He sat down then on the queen-size bed, an optimistic purchase. It had not seen much of anything but his own restless sleep since he'd bought it. The phone rang again. He rose from the bed and checked the time. 6:55. He ignored the sound and shrugged on the jacket to his suit. Vernon was probably going to recommend something superfluous, like buffing his nails. While the evidence in the Enriquez case seemed incontrovertible—stacks of doctored tax returns, not to mention a grudging confession—Judge Henry Mack was a stickler, and Vernon was not averse to trying to sway an impression no matter how much the facts stank. For a moment, Matt stared at his closet, which held no clothes but his own. There was something pathetic in all that navy blue, all that suiting.

The phone didn't go to voice mail. It began to chime again. He tied his shoes, and that was when he noticed the sirens, a chorus of them. Abruptly, he knew that all of Vernon's warnings about what to wear weren't going to add up to anything today. Those sirens were too close to Armitage. And more were coming. Police cars, not ambulances, that slight shift in decibel and tone, something anyone whose life edged up next to emergencies would know. Matt flipped open the cell.

"Dead kid. Missing baby. That fucking school on the hill," shouted Vernon. "Why the fuck do you never answer your phone?"

Because, Matt thought, that is exactly the kind of thing I do not want to hear anymore. More of them, sirens, echoing through the green day. He grabbed keys, phone, wallet. At the last moment, he spun the combination to the safe he'd bolted to the floor of the closet and retrieved his holster and gun. He hadn't worn them in days, though it irritated Vernon, who believed that weaponry was just one of the burdens of being a cop. Matt had tried to explain to him that one of the benefits of the paper beat was that the criminals were generally soft-palmed office folk, devious but unaggressive. Vernon didn't buy it. "Snakes everywhere, and last I checked, gun control laws weren't exactly working."

So it was over, the interlude, the almost pleasurable boredom of self-imposed exile, backwater isolation, cases that did not sit heavy on his conscience and unfolded at a poky pace. Weekends spent leafing through the stack of novels and histories by his bed. Dinners with his widowed father, his sister joining when she could. Long runs in empty woods. Vernon's cranky, appealing friendship. Evenings when nothing, happily, happened. Most of all, the gradual accumulation of something close to peace and the wonder of actual privacy. As he struggled to fit the gun into the holster, Matt realized he hadn't really believed this tranquil period would last as long as it had or be as satisfying as it was. Nothing continued unchanged. Not a place on earth was exempt. But what he also hadn't expected, as he slammed the door shut and ran to his car, was that he'd mind the jolt so much, and that it would in fact frighten him.

CHAPTER 4

Later that morning, Jim French thought that he was probably the only person on campus who did not know that Claire Harkness was dead by seven. He'd been underground, and his phone didn't ring at certain junctures in the tunnels that furrowed the earth below Armitage. He had been working contentedly, one of the few members of the buildings and grounds crew who actively liked this rotation. People got spooked down here, though the tunnels were clean and well lighted, built during World War II as an innovation for heating the dorms and, some said, as a place where the students, faculty, and even townspeople could take shelter if Armitage were ever bombed. Jim's father had fought in the Pacific, and his mother had told him that, yes, unexpected as it seemed, a village in the center of Massachusetts had at that time seemed vulnerable to the Germans and Japanese. She never said so, but Jim guessed from the way she spoke that the invitation to share the shelter of the tunnels hadn't been entirely inclusive. The academy would protect its own above anything, she implied when she could be coaxed to talk about those days. She had never been pleased that Jim worked at what everyone in Greenville called the school on the hill. Even at eighty-two, she could summon the energy for disapproval. Her family had lived in Greenville for five generations, and she still occupied the house where Jim and his siblings had grown up. A former postmistress, teacher, and during the war, a worker in a munitions factory, Angela made aging look like a manageable process. Her carriage was startlingly erect, her hands firm, her skin almost unlined.

Still, there was no denying her age; she bore watching. Jim was the youngest of her children and the only one living in the area. Before work each morning, he drove from his apartment to make her breakfast. Each evening, when he was done, he drove back to prepare her dinner. Despite the fact she'd had six kids, or maybe because of it, she was an indifferent cook and entirely uninterested in nourishing herself or others. He, on the other hand, enjoyed the work of making good, healthy food to be eaten in the company of family.

He thought about his mother, her carefully styled hair, her head buried in the newspaper when she wasn't observing the neighbors, and he sighed. Orienting his day around the need to keep Angela fed was hampering his social life. His wife had left three years ago, his youngest daughter was a freshman in college. His mother herself had said she didn't need him so close by, but he knew she depended on him more than she liked to admit. In the summer, he mowed the lawn and tended the yard, and this year, he had hired a high school student to come in three afternoons a week to empty trash cans, sweep, and accompany Angela to the pharmacy, the senior center, or the beauty parlor. Though Angela complained about how little the girl knew about the world, Jim knew his mother liked Kayla, who was polite, kind, and prompt. She even drove slowly enough to please Angela.

He replaced a dead bulb along the corridor, and the dim stretch of the tunnel bloomed with light again. It was warm and peaceful here, the only sounds pleasant mechanical clicks of heating and plumbing doing their jobs. Once in a while, students liked to go roving down here, and if he was in the tunnels, he instantly knew they were there. Something changed in the way air traveled. Even when they were incredibly secretive, something shifted, as if sneaky behavior produced a smell that wicked off them. Last year, he'd stumbled on a gaggle of sophomore girls drinking Diet Sprite and vodka, and he'd had to report the whole shrieking group to their dorm head.

Jim's most impressive bust had occurred in 2004, aboveground, on a night shift one spring, when he nabbed three seniors rolling Marie-France Maillot's '76 Mustang out of the garage. They'd successfully arranged a hotwire and were preparing to take it for a spin. He'd had to turn them in, though he understood the allure of the car and admired the delicacy of the engineering it had taken to make the engine roll over. Marie-France had bought the Mustang for a song when she'd come to the academy in 1977, and she drove the car only to and from the supermarket to buy coffee and cigarettes. Saturdays, she washed and waxed it, and five times a year she had a groundsman change the oil. Recently, she'd even had antique plates put on it. An absolute classic, it was worth probably a hundred times what she'd paid for it. Every time one of the boys saw it, they couldn't stop staring. The ones he'd caught had been summarily kicked out and lucky they hadn't been charged with grand theft auto. Kids from the academy, no matter how you looked at it, received special protection. All kinds of laws didn't seem to extend past the gates.

Most of the time, Jim shooed kids back to their dorms without a word to anyone, much less bothering to call the cops. Cigarettes, he just couldn't care about that. Couples sneaking around to kiss each other. But he'd turn them in no matter what they were doing if they were rude. If they were truly cocky, like that Scotty Johnston, who had once actually tried to bribe him, they didn't have a chance. Then he'd scare them by flicking his large flashlight on and off, like some slick investigator on a TV show. He'd play the whole role: steer them upstairs, get them to fish out their IDs, make them wait against a wall while he called their dorms. The trick was appearing to have no qualms about the consequences. Yet he rarely needed to go so far; most of the kids were quite polite. They at least had been raised to say please and thank you. That they also expected doors to open at their bidding wasn't exactly their fault; their parents had raised them to that, too.

He kept walking down the corridor and took a left at the next juncture, with the intention of going back to the supply room for more bulbs. It had taken him a while to learn his way around the underground network, and even now, if he wasn't paying attention, he could wind up somewhere he hadn't meant to. But this morning he felt alert and relaxed. The list of chores he had to accomplish was long but not impossible. Nancy Mitchell, head of facilities, was a good boss, with a clear sense of how much to ask and when to ask it. Her priorities were clear, too, and he'd never met a person with a firmer grasp on electrical maintenance than she had. She was at ease on a roof, better with heights than Jim himself. She was also very attractive, a fact he was letting himself notice a bit more intently.

Then, at the beginning of the next tunnel, he stopped short. The corridor was black, which it shouldn't have been. He flicked the switch, and still, total darkness. Jim turned his flashlight on, started down the corridor, then stopped short again. He heard something. A scuffle. A tap. Something more than a mouse, less than a raccoon. A very quiet person, if he'd had to guess. A person trying to be quiet.

Fear coursed through his body. That itself was also rare; he'd been here for twelve years and rarely felt more than occasional nervousness, and that was usually around faulty wiring, which still turned up despite extensive renovation. Besides, Jim was tall and solid and lifted weights three times a week after the kids were in study hall. He didn't frequent the school's gym when the girls might be around. He understood without Nancy or anyone else needing to tell him that it was better that a sweating man in workout clothes not spend too much time near students in tiny shorts and tank tops. It wasn't even that they interested him: they looked like his own daughters, pretty yet far too young to be taken seriously. He preferred the gym when it was empty, too, with its new equipment and precise sound system. Perks like this had gone a long way to keeping him these last years at Armitage.

But this was a new situation. His whole body was on alert. He knew instinctively the tunnel was neither empty nor safe. Someone either had just left it or was leaving. "Hello?" he called out, not so much expecting an answer as informing the intruder he'd been detected. Jim even found himself shifting the flashlight in his hand, turning it from a tool used to illuminate into something like a club. Farther off, he heard another sound. The unmistakable *click* of a door in its jamb. The door could only be the one at the far end of the tunnel, which led to Nicholson House. Whoever it was had become aware of him, briefly contemplated a confrontation, decided against it, and made a quick exit. A student? An adult? He had no idea, except that it was obviously someone who knew his way around.

Jim found himself running into the dark, and then he stopped. A door in the side of the tunnel was open, a door he hadn't opened himself. Again, he flicked the switch to no avail. The whole area around him was black except for the cone of yellow his flashlight revealed. If he remembered correctly, the last time he'd been in this room was when he and another B and G guy had dropped off a load of obsolete computer stuff: monitors and printers no longer current enough for students and faculty. At the time, Jim had thought, Looks good enough to me. The equipment was in fact newer than the computer on which he worked at home. It was going to be stashed here, Nancy said, until it got shipped to a local public school as a charitable donation. Tax write-off, his mother sniffed. Better than chucking it altogether, Jim argued.

At first, it looked as if nothing had been disturbed. Then he noticed a crumpled ball that appeared to be a white bedsheet. That might not have been worrisome: he'd caught couples in his time, though he hated when it happened. But the sheet wasn't wrapped around a pair of frightened lovers. It was, however, liberally stained with a dark red slash, which on inspection looked to be dried blood. Crouching there, Jim had a panicky sense that everything was about to fall apart. Part of him was tempted to grab the sheet and stuff it in the incinerator and let it burn along with the rest of the school's trash. The tranquillity of the last years was so hard-won. He remembered his wife's unhappy face, his children's anguish as Carla had announced that she was leaving for good.

But then he thought of Angela. She would never tolerate such cowardice. He tidied the sheet, locked the door behind him, and walked as fast as he could through the tunnel and into the basement of Nicholson House, stopping only to check the fuse box. Someone had indeed shut a circuit breaker off. Snapping it back, Jim watched as lights blazed down the tunnel. He had to call Nancy. Climbing the stairs, knowing the signal would improve the moment he headed up, he checked his phone and found messages she'd left him. It was then that he headed past the Study and glanced through the window in the door. He paused for a moment and took in the faculty, ominously subdued, and assembled at the wrong hour. He knew then that what he'd feared had already happened. The change was in motion, unfolding everywhere.

CHAPTER 5

When Matt first returned to Armitage and Greenville, an irritable tension wound itself into every errand. He kept imagining bumping into classmates and former teachers in the cereal aisle or in line to mail packages. He'd be dressed like an off-duty cop, in jeans and schlumpy shirt. They'd be crisp and natty, New England posh. He'd have stubble; their jaws would be shiny from a fresh shave. On it went, the Armitage clan always having the upper sartorial hand, their cool intact as his wavered, limp head of lettuce in his hands. He spent more time than he wanted to admit devising conversations in which he presented himself in the best possible light as he selected beef and carrots. Kids didn't attend Armitage to become cops, much less cops in a small town, and it would take some finesse to put that decision in context. But gradually, as he bought Cheerios and stamps with no incident and few encounters, he relaxed. The academy was, after all, its own world, contained like a castle by a moat made not of stagnant water but of iron gates, forest, a narrow river, the school's slight elevation above the town, and its own sense of itself. Those inside it ventured rather sporadically into the surrounding area, and those outside rarely gained access, a condition that was about to reverse itself. A dead child, a missing baby. No institution could shut its doors against the scrutiny such disaster invited.

Vernon had called twice more en route, a feat given that Matt was driving fast and had no more than a mile to go. "Meet Angell at . . . what the hell's it called . . . Portland." Like most townies,

Vernon had had little direct contact with Armitage; its names and ways were unfamiliar. To Vernon, the school remained an elitist fortress, quite useless except that it provided jobs and paid a lot to the town in taxes even though it didn't have to. "Noblesse fucking oblige," he said, though he had to admit his pension was the better for it.

Captain Thomas Angell, their boss, shared similar feelings but had hired Matt despite his Armitage diploma and other openly stated misgivings. He had listed them on his stubby fingers as he lounged behind his desk and Matt perched opposite in a flimsy plastic chair. "You did that prep school and Ivy League crapola. Made detective at twenty-nine and are now pissing off superiors who don't understand why you want to go. No history of behaving like an asshole. Why here?" He stared at Matt with small brown eyes. He knew that Matt's mother had just died and Joseph wasn't well but guessed as well the motive didn't end there. "You know what? I don't want to know. Just don't tell me you're in therapy or you're rethinking your decision to be a cop. And when something ugly comes up, you're the one dealing with it." Anything cumbersome—murder, racketeering, drugs—drew state and federal cops in sticky waves, an extra layer of urban attention that was tiresome and frequently screwed things up. Matt had been on the other end of the problem in Philadelphia and knew the scowling faces of officers in Scranton and Lancaster. Their displeasure was often well founded. The keys to most crimes were specific, germane to the place and its particular people. Outsiders often blundered in the unfamiliar terrain and culture. Today, Angell would expect Matt to make good on their initial understanding. The men in good suits and black cars would start streaming in from Boston.

Angell was a deeply local man, rooted in much the same way Vernon was to his town, though he still barbecued and drank beer and far more closely resembled a usual cop. Yet working for Angell had allowed Matt to see the man had many, rather hidden gifts, and one of them was for assessing the talents of his staff and convincing them of the same insights he had. He had, for instance, been the first and only person in the department to grasp and rechannel Vernon's less than obvious virtues.

Just as Matt roared up the hill, Vernon called again and said, "If you forgot your gun, I will kill you."

For the second time that day, Matt said, "Shut up, Vernon." The gun lay in dense, metallic outline against his ribs, a weight where he did not want one. A uniformed kid stopped him at the gate, recognized him, let him pass. The rights of cops, Matt thought. To enter where the public can't, to see what others aren't allowed to. Not entirely dissimilar from the image Armitage tried to craft for itself. A place you couldn't waltz into, a place reserved for the extraordinary. But today the lawn in front of Portland looked as if a tornado had scattered cars there. Below the tires, the lawn had been crushed. Stupid. There could be footprints or tracks that would now be impossible to read. Since the moment of Vernon's call, almost against his wishes, the structure of looking at death was coming alive in his mind again, unpleating like a little-used map.

Matt glimpsed Angell and Porter McLellan on the steps, amid a cluster of uniforms. He had never met the headmaster but knew him from his omnipresence in the alumni bulletin, *The Armitage Record*. If anything, the man looked even more formidable in person than in his photographs; pictures never entirely captured someone's physical force. Porter's was powerfully serious. He stood at least five inches over Angell, who was rubbing the ends of his mustache.

It was 7:10. Students stood in sobbing knots on the steps, by the entrance, on the lawn, and cops and teachers were trying to press them steadily back. Vernon was pacing near the dorm and, the moment he spied Matt, came trotting toward him. Vegan life had been very good for Vernon's heart rate.

"We got unlucky and pulled Norm Parker for SOC. Brought the beauty queen along to take pictures. The kids who found the dead girl pawed all over her, teachers were up there. It's going to be a mess. You look like shit, by the way." He peered at Matt closely and not without sympathy. By instinct, they walked slowly, knowing that, once they reached the building, there'd be no time to share details. My partner, Matt found himself thinking. How funny to have to come back here to find that someone as spirited and difficult as Vernon was just sitting there, eating kale and ripe for the taking. Still, there were limits.

"Thanks, Vern. And you smell like patchouli." Vernon hated being called Vern and he hated hippies, except for Kathy. "Go on," Matt said, and Vernon, momentarily chastened, glanced at his notes. The dead girl's name was Claire Harkness; she was seventeen years old. Hit her head or had it bashed. Bruises on the wrist and neck. Vernon's money was on bashing, but it would be hard to pin it down without good evidence. No weapon at first glance, and she could have smacked herself on the bedstead, the desk corner, a chair. No sign of the baby, which had probably been born on Saturday night.

Matt nodded and glanced around, hearing Vernon's voice as if it were coming in from a distance. It was jarring, the need to match such a situation to this beautiful, insulated place. Sweep away the flashing lights, the cruisers, the hectic pulse of a crime scene, and it was amazing how little had changed. If anything, the campus looked even more graceful than he'd remembered. The trees huge and pruned to elegant fullness. The Georgian and Federal lines of the brick and wood buildings. It astonished him he had once been part of this landscape, had felt even remotely entitled to the shade of its elms.

Vernon said, "She was a queen bee. They're not saying it, but no one liked this girl."

"Boyfriends?"

"No one current. But last year, she went out with a kid named Scotty Johnston."

Vernon pressed on. Claire being dead was almost the least of it. The problem was of course the baby. Gone, missing, no trace. The reason that, even if Claire's death had been an accident, this was still ruinous. None of the adults claimed to know a thing, though some of the girls had been in on the secret. The FBI was about to be unleashed, the whole campus shaken out. Angell was apoplectic. Feds complicated everything, and the captain's temper was fearsome, though they were usually too competent to incur it; his nickname was Devil Dog.

Matt was distracted. He shouldn't be thinking about Angell and his nickname. It was being back here. It altered everything. It even smells the same, the wet scent of cut grass, Matt thought. He could have been eighteen walking across that lawn. A senior on his way to college. About to stretch out his hand and receive his diploma.

Suddenly, Matt said to Vernon, "I want to go to the room. I want to see her before Parker gets his hands all over her." It wasn't exactly that he couldn't face Angell and McLellan. It was the abrupt desire not to exchange pleasantries and put Porter at ease. All he wanted was to get immersed in his job, not tangled in his history on the steps of a dorm whose geography he remembered with uncomfortable precision. Memory sometimes felt like little more than layer upon painful layer of detail waiting for the slightest of triggers to release it. "There's a side entrance," Matt said, and they swerved to the right. Another uniformed kid peered out at them from a frosted window set in the door.

Through the looking glass we go, Matt thought, as he tugged the handle. "Jesus, it even smells rich," Vernon said suspiciously, sniffing deeply. He was right. It was the scent of perfume, real perfume, expensive shampoo, cleanliness, all of it at odds with a girl lying dead on the floor.

"It's fresh, and it's a nightmare." Parker said this without even turning around; he'd heard them coming up the stairwell. He had three men in there and the photographer he insisted on using, a gorgeous brunette who spent a lot more time on her hair than she did on developing her camera skills. Without saying a word, Matt handed Vernon his iPhone; Vernon had mastered the slight delay in its shutter and could produce images of stunning clarity. They'd need supplementary angles captured if Jessica was the only person documenting the scene. Vernon began clicking pictures. The girl glared at him, but he kept right on snapping. "Dozens of people have been in and out of here. It's worse than Filene's Basement," Parker said. "They've touched everything. And no, no weapon and not a lot of blood." Matt and Vernon looked at each other. It would take weeks to sort out the DNA material: in addition, many of these kids were minors and protected ones; they'd all have lawyers. Every scrap would be contested.

"She was a beauty," Parker continued nasally. "My vote would be for crime of passion. If anyone's asking." He was thorough and he was clean, Parker, but he took forever to get results back and was crippling to the prosecution in front of a jury. His voice sounded like a saw on wire, and in a (backfired) effort to loan his field even more scientific credibility, he refused, in court at least, to say anything that could be taken as an absolute. *In the realm of possibility* was one of his favorite phrases. His unrequited lust for that untalented photographer had also more than once complicated their cases. Vernon loathed him.

They weren't going to have the leisure of waiting for Parker's results to come in. Everyone, from the girl's parents to the school, Angell to the feds, was going to want an instant solution, a yearning that might stem from anguish but even more from desire for the quickest and surest of answers to such an anomalous, unseemly event. Claire's death was a hideous twist in the order of a proudly orderly place. It would need to be rectified. It would require fast and thorough explanation.

But as Matt walked around her room and looked at her body, he had an unpleasant feeling that whatever answers he and Vernon would find would actually extend the disruption in the elegant world to which Claire belonged. Girls like this didn't simply have babies that went missing and then slip and bump their heads. Claire had made a cascade of choices for particular reasons, and something had gone completely awry. Most likely, neither adults nor peers had behaved all that sensibly around someone so beautiful. Even dead, she was agitatingly attractive, and that alone was disturbing. Most murdered people Matt had dealt with were scarred or battered, poor and unlucky. A few times, they had been girls as well, but never ones with teeth as straight or prospects as secure. The clothes scattered around the room were of delicate fabrics and colors. The pictures he glimpsed on her bulletin board showed Claire fine-boned and penetratingly lovely, and quite conscious of the power that gave her. In one, she was glancing at a blond boy, her clear physical equal, with both mischief and, more strikingly, arrogance. He wondered if there had been anyone this girl had respected.

Matt looked back at Claire's body, at the angle at which she'd fallen, the way the light spilled with unremitting clarity on her lean arms and the fan of her brilliant hair. As always when he was near the dead, he felt as if he had suddenly separated into two men: one that filled his clothes and moved about with solid physical presence, and another, a kind of watchful abstraction, a hovering awareness that darted and glanced, noticed and responded, trying to weave together impressions that might steer him toward who this girl had been and why exactly she had died. But a third person was observing the scene with him, the boy he'd been at Armitage, the kid who had lived and worked here for four arduous years, the townie who had climbed the hill. The one who would have taken a glance at Claire Harkness and not been able to stop looking, not just because of her beauty but because she embodied all the privilege that whispered through the place: the stretches of beachfront and the inheritances, the naming of the ancestors. The sureness of her right to be part of it all.

Vernon kept taking pictures, and Norm Parker went stolidly about his collection. Matt tried to gather himself into a single being and more or less succeeded. What was apparent as he grounded himself again in the room, the body on the floor, the play of light was that this was a death that had occurred in terrifically specific circumstances. The forensic evidence Parker was collecting might be the bright, shiny stuff that wove it all together, but the solution would start somewhere far more personal and knotted. Matt glanced at Claire's desk and the crowded bulletin board. That alone, all those layers of notes and papers, jokes and photographs, might hold exactly what he was looking for if properly deciphered.

"Vernon, let's get that bulletin board, her laptop, and the contents of that desk into the office as soon as possible. We'll need cell phones, probably computers, too. I want to talk to the head of security, the facilities manager, the IT people. And the boyfriend." Vernon started the chain of phone calls. "After the boyfriend, I want to talk to the dorm parents."

"Some parents," said Vernon, dialing, and in a moment, Matt heard him heading down the stairs. He couldn't help but agree. *In loco parentis*, the promise boarding schools gave to families to watch over their young, seemed to have failed with utter decisiveness in this case. He stood there for another moment, watching Parker and his assistants at their painstaking work. The rustle of plastic bags was the only sound, and the glint of sun on tiny tweezers darted through the room. A silent industry bustled around the girl's still body, which in the warmth had yet to stiffen.

The high window looking out on the Quad. Her own bathroom. Early to Yale. Beautiful and conscious of it. Why had she had the baby? Why had she been willing to put herself through an ordeal that required both secrecy and sacrifice? Who was the father? Who had hated her so much that he or she had been willing to kill? What if, a part of his brain said, Claire had simply wanted the baby and been unwilling to part with what she had made? But even in death, Claire had the look of someone who preserved her own interests above others'. Even so, why had she stayed here? Why had it been so important to remain at school and risk both her health and reputation? What had fueled such a dramatic choice? He crouched down next to her and saw the bruises Vernon had mentioned on her neck and wrists, as if someone had shaken her. He also noticed a red cord circling her left upper arm, a braided bracelet of some kind, the only ornament, if you could call it that, she had on. There was an Armitage tradition tied to it, he felt sure of it, though he could recall nothing specific. It was something about which the girls in his time had become cagey when questioned.

"Later, Norm," Matt said, and Parker grunted a response. He stood and turned to go. In Philadelphia, he had known it was time to leave because, at this moment of an investigation, his entire body used to go heavy with despair at the dreadful information and complete misery he was about to uncover. Murder detectives survived their exposure to drastic violence in three ways. Some created a wide, permanent gulf between the selves that operated at work and the selves that functioned outside of it. Once, Matt had bumped into a colleague in Cape May and hadn't recognized him. The man was wearing a pink polo shirt, cotton candy in one hand, the other wrapped around the brass pole of a carousel horse, spinning to the music of a calliope as if murder had never once occurred in the world. Others immersed themselves entirely in the muck that surrounded them and lived veiled in smoke or the tang of bars, the ink of racing forms darkening their fingers. They carried the job about them in a smudged halo and, to manage what they had to do, became part of it. And the last group, the smallest, tried to find some abstract bridge between the person who looked at murder and the person who didn't. These detectives were the ones who fit the work inside a puzzle that was intellectual, sociological, or cultural and made of their profession a heightened game, wit and mental dexterity the factors that allowed them to survive daily tides of rank news about the kind of harm that people were willing and able to inflict on one another. That, and a caustic ability to laugh at his own foibles, had been what allowed Matt to savor and move forward with the work.

And then the strategies had stopped functioning. Not suddenly, but gradually, dread had grown to replace satisfaction. Discomfort around weapons had been one symptom, and slowly, he had sought out something simpler. Coming back to Greenville had worked in part; he hadn't needed to leave the police altogether. But the news with which Vernon had ripped open the day had brought the uneasiness back. He had to admit that he no longer had the stomach for murder. And then there was this unpleasant feeling to factor in. If he were honest, part of the prickly sensation running through his body now stemmed from schadenfreude, the guilty enjoyment of the misfortunes of others. Walking to meet Porter, Matt remembered that it was a word he'd learned in Mr. Snow's tenth-grade English class, while reading *Hamlet*. The old man had managed to teach them a lot of vocabulary despite his habit of drifting off during in-class essays. There would, Matt confessed with a twinge, be some keen, personal enjoyment in watching Armitage struggle.

Coming down the central stairs, seeing the captain and the head now in Portland's main hall, Matt wondered if Claire had felt this way, too. If something in her had wanted to crack the veneer and draw attention to some polluted corner of someone's history. If rot had been what she was trying to expose with such a dangerous choice. Maybe Claire had found something she could not stay quiet about. But what had it been, and why would she risk so much? A quickening, a memory of desire for the chase, sparked slightly then, but there at the base of the stairs stood Porter, looking up at him. He was drawn but self-possessed, the man whose picture in the pages of the alumni magazine provided such a reassuring image of what the head of school should look and sound like. His hand was on the ball that capped the carved newel post, and he was saying with polite insistence, "Detective, may I speak with you?" and that, though the morning had barely begun, was the last private moment of the day.

CHAPTER 6

I t was ten at night of that awful Monday, and Madeline was finally back in her apartment rummaging in the refrigerator for something to eat. There was some yogurt, a beer, cream for coffee she had to brew as a supplement to what the dining hall made, half a falafel sandwich. She shoved the falafel in the microwave, but even warm, she couldn't touch it. It had been made by Ali Khalid, a Syrian guy who ran a Middle Eastern food stand from a small restaurant incongruously carved out of a laundromat, and it represented the best food available in Armitage. Madeline liked Ali, who told her he had changed his shop's name from Flying Carpet Foods to Al's Snack Shack after 9/11 and could sometimes be coaxed to talk of life in Aleppo, which seemed very exotic compared to her own. Madeline would have been surprised to know that her stories of suburban American dysfunction struck him as just as foreign and that he looked forward to hearing snippets about her unsupervised youth. She usually went to Ali's a couple of times a week just to get off campus. But tonight, her body refused the rich spicing, and she settled for yogurt and flat ginger ale left over from a dorm party.

A horrible day. A shocking day, she thought, sipping the tepid soda. And she had gotten through it and done what had been asked of her. She had rallied in the face of death and had been if not fantastically useful then not a burden to those around her. That might be as good a definition of adulthood as she had yet found, she admitted as she searched for raspberries at the bottom of the yogurt container. The question would be how long she could sustain this posture. Claire's death and the disappearance of her baby were going to unleash a long string of horrible days.

Several disturbing facts had emerged over the last fifteen hours. The first was that Grace was going to engage in a full-on campaign to preserve her own reputation even if that meant sullying the names of those around her, with a special emphasis on Madeline's. That a student was dead and a baby missing seemed almost irrelevant to the classics teacher: it was her position that she was considering above all. The other members of Portland's dorm team—Harvey Fuller and Marie-France Maillot—also had no intention of letting Grace tar them with her scorn or accusations, and combined, they had almost eighty years of experience in managing boarding school politics. I'm doomed if I'm not careful, thought Madeline, swallowing more yogurt. She was going to have to refuse to be naïve. In her first step toward astuteness, she had not immediately called Owen to tell him what was going on, not that he would have much cared. More to the point, she had not returned Kate's call demanding instant response and total disclosure; Claire's death had made national television by ten that morning. Of course her parents hadn't phoned to ask how she was or if she'd known the student. But several friends had, and Madeline had ignored them all. Porter had told them not to talk to anyone outside the school and had been right to do so. Besides, there was, at bottom, nothing more to say than Claire had probably been murdered and her baby was missing. All it made you feel was completely sick. Madeline, who hadn't even liked Claire, had been cowed by her, found herself shaken to the bone and overpoweringly sad. The girl had been young, alone, a new mother. She should never have been so neglected, much less killed.

Madeline reviewed the day's long events while pouring out some more ginger ale. The dorm meeting during which the girls had taken turns screaming, crying, or flailing. Sally Jansen had gotten so distraught that she had to be taken to the infirmary and sedated. Her parents were on their way from San Francisco. Nina Garcia-Jones in a tent-size dress and a green chiffon scarf had occupied the common room and told them that everything they were feeling was normal. She'd swayed and moved her hands in motions she apparently perceived as soothing as she said all this, looking, Madeline couldn't help but think, like a physically unfit interpretive dancer. When she'd finished talking, Lee Hastings, a prefect, a stern girl going to Stanford next year, had said, "Ms. Garcia-Jones, I don't mean to be disrespectful, but there is not one thing about this situation that is normal," and then she had crossed her arms and taken turns glaring at every adult except Madeline, who had been relieved to escape her harsh judgment. There were many students who were far more intimidating than faculty, and Lee (and Claire) had ranked high among these.

Parents, phones, sobbing, usually all three at once, and all of it threaded through with visits from the police—tall ones, short ones, thin ones, fat. Ones in plainclothes, ones in hats. When her mind started to warp horror into Dr. Seuss, Madeline knew she needed a break. But it wasn't forthcoming. Exhausted by eleven, numb by noon, and ravenous by one, Madeline had at last re-treated for ten minutes to the shower and revived herself under the stream of hot water. That was during the confiscation of the computers and laptops, and the discovery that a large percent-age of the girls had cell phones, which they weren't supposed to bring to school. This wave of police activity caused a fresh out-burst of hysteria, and Madeline, feeling she had done her part for

the moment quite manfully, had let Grace deal with this development.

After her shower, she wolfed down a peanut-butter-and-jelly
sandwich and made several cups of espresso, which allowed her to
survive the afternoon. The next three hours had included twitchy,
low-slung German shepherds roaming the corridors followed by
police officers elbow-deep in the frothy contents of the girls' bu-
reaus. Marie-France had tried to block access to her apartment—
arms akimbo, nose high, repeating, "I refuse, I refuse"—until Porter
himself had to be summoned. Madeline had wondered for a moment what Marie-France was so set on protecting in her underwear
drawer, but that thought was profoundly disturbing and she immediately set it aside.

In the midst of this, three other girls, spurred on by Sally's admission, made frantic confessions that they'd also known Claire
had had a baby. They'd gotten her formula, they'd brought her
sanitary napkins. They'd even seen the baby. Madeline kept wanting to shout, Why didn't you say anything to an adult? until finally
she asked, far more delicately than she wanted to, "Why didn't you
tell anyone?" And all of them had said the same thing: "We promised not to." Madeline thought about the four girls Claire had
trusted and realized she had chosen her handmaidens well—none
of them was her social equal. In some strange way, they would all
have been thrilled to do her bidding. And Claire, apparently still
razor clear about her status, even nine months pregnant, had
known exactly how to extract vows no one else would have given.
Madeline had never gone to school with anyone quite as cool and
scary as Claire and had missed that particular aspect of the ways
adolescents could inflict trauma on one another. But it was still
surprising that kids as generally confident as they were at Armitage

could submit to such thorough manipulation. Post tearful admission, the other three went off to join Sally at the infirmary, where FBI officers reinforcing the ranks of the Armitage police scurried after them.

His dorm was alive with cops, too, Fred Naylor had said when he saw her at dinner, toying with some chicken he plainly wasn't going to eat. They'd taken all the cell phones, which had, as in Portland, shown up in staggering numbers. "Have the police talked to you yet?" he asked, and she said yes, briefly, but they had scheduled something longer for the morning and searched her apartment. She didn't tell Fred that in the process she'd discovered the location of two pairs of sneakers and three sweaters that she had thought long gone. She didn't think she'd imagined the look of disapproval on the officer's face, either.

Senior investigators, the ones clearly running the show, had been in and out of Grace's apartment, talking with Grace and Porter, though Porter had emerged to greet Claire's father, who looked, Madeline couldn't help but notice, nothing more than supremely irritated.

The police had also managed to seal off the campus, station uniformed cops at every entrance, road, or gate, and close some of those off entirely. Fred said the woods were full of men, too. The chuff of helicopter wings had broken the tense, hot air all day. A great wave of intent, relentlessly professional searching had consumed the campus and resulted in nothing but prickling anxiety and silence.

Madeline heard a bump in the hall, and it reminded her that she ought to bolt her outside door. It had been impressive to her, having moved from Somerville, that so few people took advantage of her spaciousness out here in the countryside. She'd left her wallet the other night in her car, for instance, doors unlocked, and there it had been the next morning. Students sometimes stole from one another, but there was remarkably little thievery given how vulnerable most rooms and apartments were. Only cameras, AV equipment, medication, and dorm doors after 9:00 P.M. were regularly shut tight. Opening the screen, she sniffed the rich air. It was disconcerting how nature and weather seemed to resist bad news: trees and rivers kept on being beautiful even when horrifying events occurred around them. Sunsets flared red. The world went on doing its best imitation of a livable place. A strategically located spotlight illuminated the grand spray of a still vibrant elm on the Quad. The path linking the dorms snaked through lush, low grass. The windows of the buildings shone gold. She could even hear the burble of the Bluestone River and, past that, the slow hooting of a train as it rolled through Greenville. It looked and sounded the safest of all possible locations for teenagers, a deeply regulated environment that would reassure the most nervous of parents.

Then she saw a boy running at a dead heat from somewhere on the other side of the Quad. She was used to this. A steady traffic of students flowed across the campus at night, as physics labs, Ritalin, and alcohol changed hands. But tonight Madeline noticed a special intensity to his speed as he altered course to head toward Greaves, a boys' dorm. She still didn't recognize him. Tall and blond, but that distinguished him from almost no one here.

She made the door fast and went to call the head of Greaves, Joyce Phelan, a history teacher and field hockey coach. Everyone here had at least three job titles, and teachers were expected to perform all of their tasks equally well, in some sort of crazed imitation of polymaths. Some of them wore this burden more lightly than others. Joyce looked about ready to give it all up and join the circus, and Madeline couldn't blame her.

Usually, Madeline didn't care what the students were doing after hours. She thought it incredible that they accomplished so much given how little they slept and how much trouble they were always courting. They still attended Ivy League schools and won national science prizes and music competitions in alarming numbers. Factored into her laissez-faire approach to enforcing rules was the fact that Madeline, at twenty-five, was only seven years older than most seniors. She remembered all too clearly the desperate need to get away with deceiving adults, the feverish intensity with which she had smoked palmed Marlboros and poured out sips of Stoli from her parents' stash. It was hard for her to situate herself unequivocally on the side of the grown-ups around her most days; they seemed so shorn of liveliness. More troublingly, her personality at times felt uncomfortably elastic, sometimes wide enough to accommodate adulthood, but often more at ease within the confines a child understood. Claire's death was apparently changing that. Madeline knew exactly where she was expected to stand, and she was able to do it.

Joyce sighed resignedly when Madeline finished explaining what she'd seen. "I'll go check it out. It was probably Scotty Johnston. He got taken in by the cops this afternoon, but sadly, they let him go. Thanks, Madeline," she said, before hanging up, sounding not in the least grateful. Madeline could hear her toddler crying and her dog barking at once. Fred had joked that Joyce should get hardship pay for having had to deal with Scotty the last two years, as if he were a malarial or coup-ridden country dreaded by the diplomatic corps. Madeline ushered her thoughts away from Fred. It was a little dangerous to think about him too much. He had looked distraught at dinner, and she had wanted to do nothing more than push away his tray and the pallid chicken and, a bit to her mortification, throw her arms around him.

She heard another noise in the hall but chalked it up to ancient plumbing. Portland was due a renovation of its pipes. Madeline continued to sit on her lumpy futon sofa and observe her small apartment. There were two doors: the one that led to the outside world was the one through which she'd witnessed the running boy. The other opened onto the first-floor corridor in the dorm, a door she was supposed to fling wide while on duty, a signal of "cheerful welcome," according to the faculty handbook.

She lived at the east end of the first floor; Marie-France lived on the west. Harvey occupied an apartment on the second floor, as did Grace. Only Claire and another student, studying in China this term, had had rooms up on the third floor. How many of the girls had known what was going on? Madeline wondered. All of them, she assumed. But apparently they had said nothing to a single adult. She stretched out on the futon, a castoff of Kate's from her graduate school days. Madeline had been absurdly happy to possess such a substantial piece of furniture.

She could understand their not talking to Harvey. No one did that unless she possessed some insatiable interest in mitochondria. Marie-France, too, was pretty off-putting, with her formidable Frenchness and her habit of cutting up apples and pears with knife and fork instead of eating them whole by hand, which she considered an American barbarism. Grace was a little sportier, perhaps appealing to some of the more athletic girls, but rather fierce. She always seemed to have a clipboard in her hands. And me, thought Madeline, they discounted me the moment I stepped on campus. An intern. Less status even than grounds-keepers, who could be cultivated for access to all the keys.

The scuffling resumed a little more loudly, and suddenly frightened, Madeline sprang up and yanked open the door. Hissing in surprise, she found Lee Hastings, Suzy Kim, Portia Hall, and Olu Obodone standing there in a shifting clump. "Miss Christopher?" said Lee. "Can we come talk to you?"

Which was how Madeline found herself spending the evening with four girls in pajamas seated on the floor around her coffee table. She put out cookies and made them tea, which they accepted with grave gratitude. They were Portland's most formidable, apart from Claire. Lee was brilliant; Suzy a superb chemistry student off to Yale; Portia an English girl heading first to Brazil for a year and then to Oxford; Olu a Nigerian heiress bound for Wharton. These girls had possibilities at eighteen that Madeline could barely fathom. Unlike her sister, she'd been addled and thrown off track during her parents' multiple divorces and remarriages. All that domestic turmoil had affected her notions of how much grades mattered, and as a consequence, it was clear she didn't stand a chance of becoming Armitage material. By the time she'd recovered herself, she was ensconced at a private school outside Boston where the head was thirty-three, long-haired, and called Duff-Man or Duff-Meister even by the vice principal. An institution where they started the day with a quasi-Quaker assembly that featured a lot of acoustic guitar and harmonica playing. Teachers often slept through it, and dogs frequently burst in and scampered across the floor. A friend of Madeline's had gotten full credit for an English class by going to women's marches in Washington and memorizing some Adrienne Rich.

A far cry from Armitage, with its assumption of worldly success that students like these girls seemed to treat as their birth-
right. But watching their frail collarbones through their pajama
tops made Madeline aware that they were still teenagers and fantastically inexperienced. They'd certainly never dealt with anything like a classmate dying just a floor above their heads. That
event appeared momentous enough to dislodge their considerable
poise.

"Have the police talked with you yet, Miss Christopher? I
mean, have they really interviewed you?" Lee asked. Being addressed so formally still took her aback. Yet any means to distin-
guish herself from the students was useful. She'd hung on to the
"Miss" for dear life all year, despite all the Jodis and Lilas who'd
taught her in high school. When Madeline shook her head, Lee
said, "You should hear what we know before they do."

It was about what had happened to Claire, of course. They—by
this, Lee meant the four of them—had guessed a long time ago
that Claire was pregnant. Suzy cut in and said they'd suspected as
far back as October, but Claire wouldn't say anything, even when
they found her throwing up in the bathroom.

"But that's not unusual around here," Portia said flatly, assuming correctly that Madeline would know what she was talking about. Bulimia was rampant. Nina the counselor had warned
Madeline early on to pay attention to toilets that seemed to flush
a lot or at unusual times of day.

"She barely gained any weight," Suzy continued. "Only about
ten pounds, and she needed to gain ten pounds. And once she was
through the first part of the second trimester, she felt better." By
March, she'd grudgingly admitted what was going on. She refused
to go to a doctor, but she had stopped drinking coffee and begun to

take prenatals. "We made sure she ate and drank a lot of water," Suzy added.

Second trimester, prenatals. These girls were as comfortable with the terminology as a brood of newly married women. Madeline began to see that Claire's pregnancy had become a kind of dorm project. "Why didn't you tell anyone?" she wanted to shout, as before. But knowing if she revealed anything but studied interest they would clamp the story shut, she simply drank her scalding tea and nodded vigorously.

As if anticipating Madeline's queries, Olu said, very softly, "One of the reasons we didn't say anything was that she told us if we told anyone—parents, teachers, anyone—she'd give herself an abortion." The girls looked at one another then, and no one spoke for a moment. Madeline could imagine Claire saying this in her clear, low voice, and worse, she could imagine her doing it. There had been something profoundly detached in Claire. Madeline might have believed her, too. These girls, socially and intellectually as suave as the dead girl, wouldn't have been intimidated in the same way that Sally Jansen was, however. They weren't Claire's vassals, they were her equals. And still they'd been in her thrall. Or maybe in the thrall of someone caught inside an unequivocally adult situation.

"But there's more to it than that," Portia said quietly and looked at her friends to see if they'd permit her to keep speaking. "We tied the thread with her about the pregnancy, and then she violated the terms."

"The thread?" Madeline asked, wondering if this was yet another piece of teenspeak she'd missed out on.

Lee took up the story. "You know about traditions?" she asked Madeline.

Madeline said, "Well, I know what they say in the faculty handbook," an answer that made the girls exchange tilted, smirking smiles. Traditions were discussed on one page, deep in the document's interior, and referred to as "activities and informal gatherings that students engage in year to year." In slightly sterner language, the handbook noted that hazing and other forms of unacceptable behavior had once been linked to some of these experiences, but any form of harassment was not to be tolerated and was to be reported immediately to the dean of students. But the knowing glance the girls gave one another confirmed Madeline's suspicions. An entire river of activity flowed on below the more obvious daily competitions that animated Armitage.

"Most of them," Lee continued, "are pretty sophomoric: new kids get assigned to older ones and they do things together. Some of the dorms have a history of doing pranks at certain times of the year." There were historic rivalries for reasons no one could remember, like between Dunlop and Cantwell, two of the girls' dorms. "But there's only one or two any of us takes seriously." Lee's voice grew even lower.

"The Reign was the big one. I know this will sound weird. It's something we don't really describe to people outside." Here she did waver slightly. She took a sip of tea and then said, "Claire was the head. She was Robespierre."

"Robespierre?" Madeline asked. "The French guy who cut off the king's head?" When Lee first said "reign," Madeline had thought she meant "precipitation," curious as it sounded. The Head of the Rain? Was it a regatta, like the Head of the Charles? This, however, was immeasurably more disturbing. The name Robespierre conjured a vague memory of a powdered wig, sharp nose, and then, of course, the phrase *Reign of Terror*. The pale napes of duchesses waiting for the slanted descent of the guillotine in the Place de la Concorde. Madeline gobbled another cookie to keep herself from shouting. A secret society called the Reign of Terror had operated under their noses, and Claire, known as Robespierre, had run it? And all this time she thought they were only fretting about getting in early to college.

Madeline knew she had to appear impassive or the girls would stow the entire story and flee. "Go on," she said, sounding only slightly strangled, she hoped. Slowly, Lee began to speak again. Every year, the head of the tradition picked the next one, and "they were always girls like Claire." Which meant, Madeline assumed, beautiful, rich, and terrifying.

"Had she chosen her successor?" Madeline asked, and Suzy shook her head. "That was something that happened the very last day of school. We have no idea who she had in mind. She had stopped talking to us about anything."

That was the problem, Lee interjected. When you belonged to the Reign, you had to secure permission from the others to enact certain of its rituals.

Rituals. Secrets. Permission. Madeline felt goose bumps rise on her arms despite the heat. She had attended schools so ridiculous merely getting students to come to class on a regular basis had been the primary focus of every teacher there. Kids had generally been so sloppy about everything from what they wore to the completion of their homework, they would never have been able to summon the energy, much less the guile required to form a quasi-governmental force orchestrating all kinds of activities without any supposed grown-ups cottoning on. A little more subtle probing revealed that the Reign was basically a way, sometimes a rather frightening way, of establishing the hierarchy of old girl versus new girl, a way to be sure that no one stepped out of her social place and that the powerful remained so. The girls tried to downplay any real influence the group had, though Madeline suspected they and anyone else affected took the whole experience to heart. But there were other aspects to it. A group of girls served as its central committee, and these, too, were chosen every year on the last day of school. All four of the girls in front of her were members, confirmed with solemn, rather prideful nods when Madeline asked.

"And that was it. There are ten of us on campus, with Robespierre in charge. No members allowed to leave, and no one else can join." They sat there on Madeline's less than vacuumed floor and looked at her with their wide, calm eyes. She wondered if their contingency plans might ever include armed insurrection against all the dense adults around them. What would they have been like in, say, Congo, with some rifles, revolutionary theory, and true oppression to motivate them? It was a very alarming vision, and at that moment, she would have thought them capable of anything.

She forced herself to look unsurprised and asked something she hoped wouldn't be seen as too prying: How long had the group been around? Lee shrugged. She thought since the seventies, when girls were first admitted. And it had died out when there were more girls, but someone in the nineties had revived it.

Lee said then Claire had invoked one of the most sacred of the Reign's rituals, which was the making of a braided thread—always red, and braided with a few hairs from the members' heads—that meant those who wore it vowed secrecy for life about a certain topic. Then they were to wear it until it wore off, naturally somewhere outsiders weren't likely to see it. "When you twist the thread with the Reign, you have to vow not to tell roommates, boyfriends, anybody. Even husbands, later."

"And you can't just use it for something ordinary," Portia added, "like going into rehab. It's only for really important things."

Madeline thought rehab sounded pretty important, but she took their point. A few weeks drying out somewhere was numbingly common for kids not only in the shabby schools Madeline had attended but here, where even more money created even greater ease of access to illicit substances. And she could understand that getting and remaining pregnant probably constituted something many teenagers would want to keep secret. She also couldn't help but notice that the list of people not to tell included all grown-ups: parents, teachers, advisers. Yet they were so palpably not useful as confidants they hadn't even merited mentioning.

But the way Claire had invoked the thread had broken an essential rule. "She twisted it with us first, and then she went outside the Reign. She never told us she had done it. She totally abused her position," Portia said accusingly. "She went to Sally, Margaret, Kelly, and Anna, and initiated them without asking us." It still made them angry, these tall, beautiful girls, to have those lesser beings violate their private clan. Or were they upset more because Claire simply hadn't chosen only them to share the secret with?

"We figured it out pretty quickly," Olu said, with a certain satisfaction. "Sally couldn't help but show hers." She almost snorted, and they all shook their heads in mild disgust at Sally's inability to control herself. Still, Claire's betrayal irked them.

"We don't know what Claire told them exactly, if it was any different from what she said to us," Portia said. "Even Sally refused to talk." Madeline did not quite want to imagine what they might have said or done to Sally to get her to that point. The memory of the girl's shaking shoulders, her deep grief, was still ringing through

Madeline's own body. Claire must have been desperate to reach so far beneath her and to have turned so abruptly from her natural peers.

An uneasy stillness settled in the room then. Madeline searched for something that might keep them talking and asked if everyone, even those outside the group—she couldn't bring herself to say "the Reign"—had known that Claire was pregnant and that she had had a baby. It struck her, too, that the girls hadn't needed some clandestine group to preserve silence. That had happened quite effectively on its own.

Most did, Lee said, but there were always a few who were kept out of the loop, and Madeline could guess which ones before Lee told her. Priya Srinivasan, who was fifteen, a math and piano prodigy, probably somewhere on the Asperger's scale, and certainly no one these girls would confide in. And Allison Hartley, who had spent most of the semester either smoking pot or getting caught at it. She'd been suspended the bulk of the last two months and was rumored to be drying out somewhere in the Berkshires. She was also the student with whom Madeline had felt most comfortable. Allison's body was swathed in layers of Indian skirts and chunky wool sweaters, and she had hair that had probably once been blond and was now a mouse brown, dreadlocked hive. But under all those clove cigarettes, Fred had noted, you could still smell Greenwich.

Minus Priya and Allison, however, by this spring, everyone had been aware that Claire was pregnant and had twisted a thread with girls outside the Reign. Still, the question remained. Why hadn't Claire taken the easier route and obtained an abortion to begin with?

When Madeline voiced that concern, Lee said, "This is something we've talked a lot about. I think it was too late by the time she figured it out. A second- or third-trimester abortion is an entirely different kind of procedure," she said sternly. "She just couldn't believe it was true," Lee finished.

Suzy pressed her lips together firmly, then said, "But Lee and I disagree about this." She glanced respectfully at her friend, and Lee dipped her head, acknowledging Suzy's dissent. Again, Madeline sat listening in amazement. The range of the girls' awareness stunned her. They were involved in a secret society of intimidation yet could cultivate a diplomacy worthy of the negotiation of nuclear treaties. All this politic language and astonishingly adult comprehension. Then she remembered that they all had to take Conflict Resolution and do ropes courses through sophomore and junior years, one of Porter's innovations. Perhaps this conciliatory vocabulary had been acquired while hanging twelve feet above a forest floor on a length of nylon. But what was more real to them? The Reign or that? What aspect of their experience said most about who they really were?

Suzy continued, "I think Claire knew from the start." Holding her mug tightly, she added, "I know it sounds unlikely, but I think she wanted the baby. Not like she wanted to be a mother, but she wanted the baby for some reason. And that that was why she stayed in school, too. She refused to go home or leave. Being here mattered to her, but she wouldn't say why."

"And she never said who the father was?" Madeline inquired, trying hard not to put too much emphasis on the question. She even looked away from the girls as she and they considered that that single detail—the paternity of Claire's baby—would be the most important piece of information the girls might have access to. "She never told the group? Or the other girls?"

They all shook their heads, whether in lack of knowledge or in a refusal to divulge it, Madeline couldn't quite tell. "Lee asked her outright, but she refused to say. She just smiled that smile of hers and said we would never force it out of her," Portia said.

"No," Lee confirmed. "She refused. She said it was no one we knew, but of course that's probably not true. She would have told us otherwise. And last year, at least, she hooked up with Scotty Johnston all the time. And a few times she said something about an older man. It could have been anyone, a friend of her father's, a teacher. But she never did more than hint."

The other girls paid close attention as Lee spoke. They'd discussed this issue many times before, Madeline suspected. Yet they kept glancing at one another. They were still being cautious with what they admitted. They did add that, despite Claire's betrayal of the Reign's trust, they had loaned her their brothers' shirts to cover her belly as the pregnancy progressed, though she barely showed. They helped her with homework—"but no one plagiarized, Miss Christopher," Olu insisted, in what struck Madeline as a slightly misguided application of ethical niceties given the circumstances. They returned her library books.

"We weren't there when she had the baby. She was overdue, but we don't know by how much. We don't know where she had him. We didn't even know she'd gone into labor. She just came back to the dorm late Saturday with this baby wrapped in a sheet. But I think she had him alone," Lee said. Madeline closed her eyes for a moment. At some point in the pitch-black night, Claire had staggered up the stairs above Madeline's head with a newborn in her arms. It seemed close to unbelievable.

"She promised she would take him to the doctor on Monday. She was tired and scared, and she promised," said Olu. In the meantime, for the day she and her baby were in the dorm, the real and faux members of the Reign looked after Claire. They fed her, fed him, cleaned the baby, turned up music when he cried, which wasn't often. They organized an almost round-the-clock schedule of care. The last anyone had seen her was Monday morning around 4:00 A.M. Sally, slated to go to her at 6:30, found her dead and the baby gone.

"He was beautiful, Miss Christopher. He was tiny, but he was perfect. A little boy," said Suzy, and slowly, all the girls lowered their eyes. Madeline sat very still, trying to take in the facts of what the girls had done. Of their competence in the face of a situation none of them had ever dealt with before. Of the stern ring of silence they had maintained. Of how much they actively distrusted most of the adults around them.

She got up then to shake herself back to life and to replenish the cookies on the plate. She needed, she knew, to keep them talking. "So you really think she didn't tell her parents?" Madeline asked. Portia looked at her and asked, "Have you met them?" and Madeline quickly realized the folly of her question. They were divorced, like 60 percent of the parents who sent their children to Armitage. But few matched the Harknesses for detachment. Most of the parents loved and pushed their children in equal measure, in Madeline's experience. But Flora Duval was tall, beautiful, and lived most of the year in Paris with her third husband. She'd deposited Claire at school that fall, stayed less than an hour, and left Madeline with an abiding impression of long legs, indifference, and profoundly expensive taste in clothes. Her daughter, Madeline calculated, would have been a month or so pregnant at that point.

The father lived in New York with the second wife and two small children. Just as imposing as Flora, he had missed parents' weekend and had made a brief appearance near Thanksgiving, which would have meant that Claire was into her fourth month at least and no doubt aware of what was going on. Madeline remembered that he hadn't even kissed his daughter good-bye, just tapped her on the shoulder. Where had she spent the holidays? Madeline couldn't recall now, but not with either parent, she thought. Probably with a willing member of her secrecy team. But wouldn't someone outside the Armitage circle have caught on and alerted the school? Madeline, she reminded herself, you didn't notice, either. You had absolutely no idea. What else had she missed this year? What had made her so stubbornly unable to acquire critically important information right in front of her eyes?

Madeline gently asked the girls, "Do you think any teachers here knew?"

Olu shook her head. "We're not sure. Probably not, but we couldn't tell. Claire was really hard to read. You couldn't just ask her things you could ask other people."

Madeline knew what she meant and then, unable to maintain her impersonation of a grown-up, blurted out her last question. "Why did you tell me all this?"

"Claire is dead. It changes everything. People will find out a lot of stuff anyway. We wanted someone to know who wasn't a student. And besides, Claire wasn't like you, Miss Christopher," Suzy said. "Someone you could just talk to. Someone ordinary."

Madeline smiled for the first time that day. She knew what Suzy meant. The comment had been intended as a kind of compliment. She did have something else she wanted to know, but it was nothing she'd dare ask the girls. It was about whether or not

Claire had known her killer. In any case, Madeline was quite sure of the answer. She must have. The dorm was locked from the outside after 9:00 P.M., but kids could and often did let people in from the inside. Alternatively, students and faculty could enter any dorm with the swipe of an Armitage ID through a sensor. Madeline had seen Claire's room: no robbery had taken place; either she'd let the person in herself or he or she had come in on his or her own. Madeline shivered. In any case, everyone here knew everyone else. Community connectedness. It was one of the reasons Armitage was supposed to be so safe, though this revelation about Robespierre and twisting threads and pacts of silence had permanently altered her own sense of the kind of protections the academy offered.

It was midnight. The girls looked exhausted, their tea mugs were empty, but they showed no signs of moving. They were shocked and scared as well. But not, it occurred to Madeline, sad. Not one of them missed Claire. At least they weren't hypocritical enough to pretend that. "Hey," Madeline said abruptly. "I have an idea. Go get your sleeping bags and you can crash on the floor." At first, she regretted her impulsive offer. It sounded like the kind of treat you'd dangle in front of ten-year-olds. A slumber party! She cringed slightly, dreading some sarcastic rejection. But the girls smiled and said yes, relieved for once, it seemed, to be treated like kids. In a few minutes, they returned with down cocoons and pillows and settled in colorful lengths on her floor, fast asleep.

Her hands were trembling with fatigue, but she couldn't go to bed yet. Google cheerfully supplied her with thousands of potential sources to learn more about Robespierre, and she chose one, in rather rickety English, clearly translated from the French, to discover that he had been responsible with his colleagues for taking more than thirteen hundred members of the aristocracy and other enemies of the Revolution to the guillotine. But apparently his zeal or power grew onerous, even for his enthusiasts. And at the tail end of that hot and bloody July, his own head had landed in a basket much like the one which had received that of his former king, and he, too, could be claimed as a victim of the relentless violence of war.

Madeline shut down the computer and slumped at her desk. Was this Revolutionary theme rampant at Armitage? Were there Royalists, Girondists, stormers of the Bastille lurking in the boys' dorms? She was going to have to tell this all to the police, but she was too tired to move. Even so, she sat up for a moment, to look at the sleeping girls. Serious Lee, beautiful Olu, Portia's pristine mouth, and Suzy's lush, dark hair. Asleep, they looked much younger and far more vulnerable. Asleep, they couldn't say things that would change for good how she looked at them and Armitage. She wondered if they knew that the real Robespierre had been destroyed by the very forces he so ardently believed in, and assumed they did. They all took European history. They were good at amassing important facts. Madeline wondered if the grotesque irony had struck Claire, too. And then she was abruptly so spent she went to bed without taking off her clothes, much less brushing her teeth.

The next morning, on her way to breakfast—her run temporarily suspended because no one was allowed off campus—Madeline had to step carefully over the girls' tangled bodies. They were even more lovely in the morning light. She was creeping out the door when it slid from her grasp and smacked the jamb with a bang. But they didn't move an inch, like all children who sleep deeply.

he campus had always been most beautiful at dawn. The sun rose over the river and streamed through a filigree of oak and maple leaves that fractured and spread the light across expansive tracts of grass and beds of flowers. In that scattered golden haze, Armitage wasn't only a place of clean proportions and obvious ease. It could seem the embodiment of a sublime coherence. Matt was standing outside Portland and looking at the window of Claire's room. The panes winked brightly. Her autopsy was scheduled for seven this morning, youth, beauty, and status assuring her a place on the gurney ahead of the victims of a drunk driver, a suicide, and a probable drug addict found near the tracks. Even in death, she was taking precedence.

It was a shade too early to rouse teachers and students. Vernon would arrive soon, and they'd review the list of people they had to talk to and split the next ten hours into listening to stories that would, he hoped, coalesce into something harsh and simple by the day's end. Angry boyfriend. Baby stashed somewhere in the woods. Something Greek and unvarnished about both the feelings and solutions. Coffee was ticking through his bloodstream, making his heart run a bit too quickly. Below an elm, he sat on a bench dedicated to Woodrow "Bully" Loftis, an English teacher at the academy from 1950 until 1995. A career bracketed by Shakespeare and comma splices, hymns and hockey games.

He started to pace the Quad. Uniformed officers were stationed at the doors of several buildings. Muffled squawks from their radios troubled the gauzy silence. A few teachers and students stood blinking on the granite steps of their dorms. It was time for breakfast. Hunger rumbled on, even when students died and babies disappeared. A few boys, rather hangdog, walked down the path to the Commons, ignoring the police, on their way to bacon and omelets.

Matt remembered that tangled combination of sensations. On the morning of his discipline hearing, he had woken both terrified and ravenous. He had not wanted to eat, thought he might throw up if he did, but it proved impossible to ignore the need for food. Eggs, sausage, juice, and coffee. Later, he thought all that ballast had been the only way to prepare for Gordon Farnsworth's stark judgment. He'd been accused of cheating. If he was found guilty, Penn would be notified. It was May of his senior year.

In his time, breakfast had been the best or at least most reliably appetizing meal of the day, and this still appeared to be true. More people were on their way to eat, but everyone he saw was subdued and tired. No Frisbees whirled along the path, there was no boyish jostling. A few obviously weepy girls joined the patchy stream. How many of them had stainless reputations? he wondered. His own had been spotless until that spring, when his roommate of three years, a boy from Beacon Hill named Charlie Pierce, had stolen an essay of his on Lear's madness, and presented it, with a few key revisions, as his own, to the same Bully Loftis on whose bench Matt had just been sitting. Both Matt and Charlie were in separate sections of Shakespeare's Late Plays. Bully Loftis had apparently discussed a few of the more unusual claims—that Lear's insanity was psychedelically induced—with Matt's teacher, Penny Weeks, a severe young woman, unadorned as a pencil. The papers were compared, the boys confronted, and to Matt's total surprise, Charlie claimed that Matt had taken the work wholesale from him.

Three years of covering for each other when one of them was late for chapel, check-in, seated meal. Three years of loaning books, ties, money, personal goods overlapping in that feckless, teenage way, their room more of a raven's nest than anything humans would want to occupy. And it had been a kind of bliss for Matt. A revelation. There was nothing in this secret, separate Armitage existence that had reminded him of his parents' thrift, their self-conscious plotting of a life that steered itself away from Sicily and toward a safe, American perch of normalcy. Charlie had shown him how to have the fun of the entitled. To be careless. To treat money as something that flowed as naturally as the Bluestone. They'd met in Latin class freshman year, and that encounter had led to three years of drinking Charlie's father's bourbon, fantasizing madly about girls, staying up to finish college applications, watching the Celtics. It had led, Matt thought, to a friendship as steady as a bulwark. He'd been chosen, initiated. He belonged.

But at nine in the morning, ten days before graduation, almost exactly this time of year, Matt had watched Charlie's open, mobile face transform into that of a complete liar. In Gordon Farnsworth's office, he had protested and emoted and even cried. It was a performance so convincing, Matt himself had nearly wanted to believe it. Charlie had sobbed, and Matt had had to steel himself against comforting his friend. Then, inside that wrenching sound, Matt understood something with total, sudden clarity.

None of his history with Charlie mattered. His roommate, in a moment of apparent crisis, was content to scuttle a friendship, Matt's reputation, perhaps his scholarship to college. Looking back, Matt knew there had been signs. Charlie often blurred the truth about small issues. He borrowed inconsequential sums of money that were never returned. He hurt girls' feelings more than necessary. Charlie was not just casual with things, he was casual with people. But in front of adults, he maintained an impeccable politeness, great charm, and with all that floppy brown hair and his bright complexion, it was hard not to enjoy him. You felt grudging and small if you didn't always want to forgive him his lapses. And Matt had. Matt had genuinely liked him and, even more, been grateful that someone like Charlie, someone with Charlie's advantages, could find room for him in his handsome, well-appointed world.

Sitting in the stiff chair, his palms sliding on its shiny leather arms, Matt knew it was only Charlie's word against his. There'd be no way to clear his name entirely, and he grasped with sickening certainty the arc of what would happen. Charlie's family had gone to Armitage for four generations. A playing field was named in their honor. Charlie was bound for Yale, where his brother, father, and grandfather had gone. Matt looked at Gordon Farnsworth. They'd let him in on a full ride, the local kid. They'd placed faith in him. They had expected him to fulfill it.

It would have been so easy to bow his head and say, as Charlie clearly expected him to, "I'm sorry." It might have led to the problem being handled in house, without Penn or Yale any the wiser. But Matt hadn't chosen that course. Thinking of his parents' stricken faces as he told them what had happened, he looked at the headmaster and said, "I didn't do it. It's exactly the opposite of what Charlie is saying. He knows it. He will always know it," which was greeted with howls of protest (Charlie) and the slightest of hesitations (Farnsworth). Both of them had been punished, with a letter to Yale that affected nothing—Charlie's parents were paying full tuition—and a letter to Penn, which reduced Matt's financial aid package, a move that then required he take a twenty-hour-a-week job cleaning toilets; it paid better than anything else on campus.

Matt had moved back to his parents' house that morning and spent the last two weeks of school as a day student. He had walked in graduation, assiduously avoided Charlie, grabbed the diploma from Farnsworth's outstretched hand, and promised himself never to come back. He'd never attended a reunion, returned to the area rarely to see his family, and stayed in touch only intermittently with a couple of friends who had belatedly taken his side against Charlie's. From the alumni magazine, which he read against his better intentions, he learned that Charlie had married someone whose last name was Frelinghuysen and that he'd had twin boys.

It was a relief to see Vernon trotting toward him. It wasn't often Matt let himself think about what had happened in such precise detail—Charlie's tear-streaked cheeks, the V of worry between Farnsworth's brows—and it was troubling that the emotions the experience stirred were still so bitter. Vernon, whom Matt sometimes called his personal barometer, looked at him and said, "Caught in your tangled past?"

The light was growing paler. They had an enormously long day ahead of them. Matt should do nothing other than say, "Get lost, Vernon," and start segmenting the tasks they had into manageable pieces. But he didn't. He stopped and looked at Vernon with his red skin and beaky nose, a person who would never fit here, a person he trusted every working day, and said, "There's something I should tell you." They were walking toward Porter McLellan's office; he was first on the list, followed by the girls who had looked after Claire—if they could get access to them— and the teachers in Portland.

Vernon was adjusting the strap of his computer bag. He took all his notes on a laptop and considered Matt's pencil and pad affectations. A patch of sweat showed on his shirt. Heat shimmers were already rising from the freshly cut lawn. "You mean about the shit that went down about you cheating?"

A blend of violation, embarrassment, and admiration mingled in Matt. "You are one tenacious bastard," he said.

"The old biologist told me yesterday, or at least a version." Vernon hoisted his bag up higher on his shoulder, obviously harder than he'd intended, and Matt saw that his partner's primary reaction was hurt. He wanted to have been trusted enough to be told. He would have in his place.

Fuller, of course. And Matt understood Vernon's response. It was what you did with partners. You told. They knew what you ate, how you smelled, when you showered. It was marriage without a bed and bills in a lot of ways, at least the closest he had come to marriage.

Matt looked at Vernon and said, "How long have you known? It wasn't Fuller."

Vernon rubbed the back of his neck and held the door to Nicholson open for Matt. "Okay, but he also cornered me. He and that uptight Latin teacher both saw fit to inform me you had . . . what did she call it? 'A blot on your copybook.'" Vernon sighed. "But you're right. I did my own research on you when Angell said he was going to put us together. The last bozo I got hooked up to had this Internet porn problem. I just wanted to know who I was dealing with. And so, yes, I did a check. Do one on me. You'll feel better. I'm a lot grubbier."

Matt supposed it was fair, and it was certainly Vernon's nature. He even discovered he wasn't particularly surprised. "By the way," Vernon continued, "your credit's better than mine. Anyhow, it came up from a classmate. I talked to a kid you knew. Andrew Morgan."

Andrew Morgan had been in Matt's math class, year after year, and had always been a gossip. "How'd you get him to talk?" They walked up a set of marble stairs with dips worn in their centers from 130 years of feet walking up them on their way to see the head. "On second thought," Matt added, "I don't want to know."

"Pretended I was from the alumni office, trying to get a reunion together. Did he know what had happened to you since high school," Vernon admitted glumly. "I know. It's not legal." He scratched his chin. "Does Angell know?"

"Probably. I tried to tell him when I first got hired. Seemed only fair. But he wasn't interested. Didn't want to hear or, more likely, already had."

They were outside Porter McLellan's office and could see the assistant tapping with sharp-nailed efficiency at her keyboard. It was just seven, but she looked as if she'd been hard at work for hours already.

Vernon thought for a moment, then said, "Less said now the better. It might actually work in our favor. They'll think less of you and let something slip." Matt felt a surge of appreciation for Vernon and his practical ways. "Time for the Grand Poohbah?" he said and tilted his head toward Porter's office. Matt was going to handle Porter and try to see the girls who claimed to have helped Claire. Vernon was off to talk to the security people again and get an update on the search for the baby. Later that morning, they would share the faculty. So far, they'd barely mentioned the child; it seemed clear another body would soon be found, and there were parts of their job that were too dispiriting to dwell on.

In the waiting area, Tamsin told Matt to have a seat and that Mr. McLellan would be with him shortly. He was grateful for the pause. It was unsettling to be back in this room in such different circumstances. The rugs had been changed, the furniture, too, but the overall similarity was notable, and it brought with it an ugly stew of memories. Charlie's histrionics, his own stalking back to the dorm to throw his belongings in a few bags, the teachers who would not meet his eyes when he passed them on the Quad. He breathed deeply and leaned forward to page through a brochure for Armitage. Printed on the heaviest stock, with a glossy blue cover embossed with the school shield, the pamphlet gave off an impression of polished gravity. Inside, he read that classes contained no more than twelve students at a time and were often smaller, especially for mathematics and languages. Paul Revere, Greenville's high school, housed fifteen hundred students and offered instruction in seventeen different languages. But that number was linked not to a desire to "create global citizens," as Armitage claimed in its mission statement, but to the fact that the school had so many kids in need of ESL. Only twenty-four hours had passed since Claire Harkness had died. Small class sizes hadn't kept that from happening, a thought Matt did not quite forgive himself for having.

Porter opened the door then and ushered him into a Persian-carpeted room flush with light and winking brass. The desk at which he seated himself was massive, but such was his own size and seriousness, it took a moment to register the sweeping lines of the piece of furniture. Gordon Farnsworth had been swallowed by its grandeur. Yet something seemed unsettled, in the room or the man or both, Matt couldn't quite tell. He didn't think it was yet another seizure of his own memory; something was emanating from Porter that he didn't precisely grasp. Bookshelves lined one side of the office and bow windows two others. The last held portraits of former heads of the board of trustees, men who seemed indistinguishable from one another, their stately self-regard utterly fungible.

It was the bareness of the desk. Every other surface—the mantel, certain of the shelves, the walls—held the sorts of decorations one would expect in a head's office. Discreet bronzes. Silver cups commemorating some achievement or other. Metal and wood and gleaming glass, polished and subdued. But the desk held nothing. Not a pad, a computer, an orchid, nothing. Yet it had, and recently. Matt could still see the dried smear of droplets that indicated a recent cleaning, which had been thorough but not meticulous. A corner of wood still held a low, barely perceptible fuzz of dust. What had Porter McLellan removed or had removed from that long length of carved oak?

As he settled himself in his chair, Matt ran through what he needed to discuss with Porter. Any dark history around Claire, the faculty in her dorm, the teachers who had had her this year.

"I understand you interviewed Scott Johnston yesterday," Porter began. "But that he's been released pending further investigation, as his parents said." His tone implied he knew what Matt might be dealing with when it came to handling the Johnstons; he even managed to imply that he, too, had been on the receiving end of their formidable capacity for outrage.

What alarmed Matt as he adjusted himself in the overly comfortable seat was how readily he wanted to take Porter's offer of
commiseration. It would have been so easy to raise eyebrows over
the barbed, hysterical wall of protection the Johnstons were trying
to erect around their son. It was clear that this kind of drama was
part of what they considered appropriate parenting, and it was
equally clear that Scotty's arrogance had given them many oppor-
tunities to hone their approach. "It's true Scott's no longer being
questioned," Matt forced himself to say with some terseness. "But
I actually need to discuss other issues with you, Mr. McLellan."

"Of course," Porter said. Quickly abandoning his attempt at
camaraderie, he leaned forward in apparent eagerness to be of any
help he could, in striking contrast to Grace Peters and Harvey
Fuller. Brief interviews had proved two things to be true: they
had no intention of admitting any wrongdoing—Grace had gone
so far as to blame extra loads of committee work for her slightly less
prominent presence in the dorm. And they were going to make a
special effort to remember absolutely nothing useful about Claire
or the last few weeks she spent in their care.

Matt stood then and chose another chair, far less padded, to sit
in. He was going to try something now. It was daring, perhaps stupid, but it might yield the most interesting results. "You're probably
aware of the difficulty I'm finding myself in here. I'm an alumnus,
but not one with a perfect record."

"Class of 'ninety-four, Penn 'ninety-eight," Porter said thoughtfully. "And probably one of our few graduates in law enforce-
ment." He almost managed to make it sound as if Matt had made
a respectable choice, at least in his eyes. And he added that he had
heard from several faculty about what he called Matt's "experience" but didn't see why an event that had never been conclu-

sively resolved should prevent him from dealing effectively with what the school was now facing. They were entirely different situations. "I'm assuming, Detective, if you felt yourself unable to handle the investigation with some degree of objectivity, that you wouldn't be here and that Captain Angell wouldn't have assigned you. And I'm assuming that your familiarity with Armitage will be useful to you."

"Which means, Mr. McLellan, that you and I both understand that what Armitage pretends to represent doesn't always mesh with what happens here."

The man was uncannily good. Matt felt a curious current run through his body, a feeling he hadn't had on a case in a long time. It was uncomfortably exhilarating to be dealing with a potential suspect this sophisticated. Certainly what he'd gone through at Armitage had made a difference in the career he'd chosen; being a police officer had been a repudiation of the cozy world to which Charlie so effortlessly belonged, to the ease with which his classmates expected to move into handsome homes and well-feathered professions. But what had been grueling about his work was how petty most of the crimes were, even those that resulted in murder. This was going to be more complicated than he'd thought this morning, the resolutions more knotty than he'd feared. Porter might well be involved, and he was already delicately, insistently on the offensive, prepared to protect his school, his place.

"By that," Porter answered, "I assume you mean that not only students had issues or concerns to hide. But to discuss Claire first, there was no hint of trouble in her past." Porter leaned back in his chair. "She was a very good student, a respected athlete, and she came from a family with a long history at Armitage." He paused, and his fingers fluttered slightly. Matt realized he was looking for a pen to tap, a restless movement. He was used to finding one on his desk, but that had suddenly been cleared.

"Most of the faculty in Portland and Claire's teachers this year have stellar reputations. Many of them have spent the entirety of their careers here. Even those with less experience have received excellent evaluations." He produced a file and pushed it toward Matt, no doubt expertly organized by Tamsin, that he said included the most recent reports on each of the adults who'd had dealings with Claire. "You can see for yourself that, while they and we all might have been guilty of a lack of observation, there is no reason to suspect any one of them of harboring some motive to harm her or her child." And here, Porter's face darkened and his voice grew softer. "I am sorry to have to caution you about this, but there's nothing for it." He leaned forward a bit more assertively and said, "Last year, a student complained that Harvey Fuller had made her very uncomfortable in class. According to the student, he had stared at her. It sounds mild enough and impossible to turn into an actual allegation of harassment, but she was insistent that he had made her very uneasy. What gave her claim more weight was that another student complained of the same problem first semester."

"But neither of these was Claire," Matt asked.

"No," Porter answered. "Though both were tall and blond and on the lacrosse team with her. She would have been almost sure to know. Students aren't always as discreet as they might be." He looked at one of the portraits hanging in the gloom at the back of his office. "It's one of the most difficult aspects of life at a boarding school. As you know, we live in such close proximity to one another. It's often a case of one person's word against another's. Looks and appearances can be misjudged. I am confident in Harvey's case that nothing untoward happened, but he has been cautioned—not with a letter in his file, merely verbally—to be careful in his dealings with female students."

"Be careful? And with what kind of supervision to ensure that, Mr. McLellan? Who was paying attention to him? It might be wise to be a little more straightforward." Matt was abruptly irritated with Porter's detachment. "We could both probably name three teachers in the last twenty years who'd had relationships with students and were allowed to stay on the job."

Porter grew very still. He might, Matt thought, be remembering not only what had been allowed to happen at Armitage but scandals that had leaked out at other schools. Teachers videotaping boys in locker rooms. Others caught soliciting teens on the Internet. It was galling no matter where it happened, but all the more so at institutions that prided themselves on their impeccability. An actual death, an actual baby eclipsed everything. "I'll be very grateful if that's not the case here, but you should be prepared to find out otherwise."

Porter said nothing for a moment. "What you just mentioned, Mr. Corelli, improprieties between students and teachers, are situations we can't tolerate now. Too much is at stake, for the school, for the students. Even the mildest hints or allegations are thoroughly investigated. That's precisely why I alerted you to my concerns about Harvey." He was impressively calm, even when confronted directly. He was no doubt masterful at board meetings. Matt made a note to get Vernon to check into Fuller's background, an assignment he knew his partner would relish.

Matt took the file the headmaster offered and stood. It was almost 7:30, and he wanted to get to Harvey Fuller even before he talked to the girls. He had had him as a teacher and had never liked the man, too dried up by far, though a commanding presence in

the classroom. It would be interesting to see what he would say
when asked about an entirely different aspect of biology.

At that moment, a tall, extremely good-looking woman entered
the room, and it was clear she was itchily displeased to find Matt
closeted with Porter. "Police," she said with undisguised contempt,
as if what had just happened at Armitage didn't warrant such scrutiny. "They're everywhere." She was broad-shouldered, fit, with a
strong nose and long, dark blond hair.

Porter rose and made a fluent introduction. This was his wife,
Lucinda, but she barely acknowledged Matt. Her fingers in his
were ringed but rough. She worked outside, he guessed. She was
tanned, and fans of wrinkles spread from her eyes. Her hands had
spent time with earth, tools, a garden. He watched her as she spoke
impatiently to her husband. "The boys," she said. "Porter, the boys
need to talk to you. They're not being allowed on campus." She
cast another scathing look in Matt's direction.

"I'll handle it," said Porter. "I'm sorry, Detective. I'll happily
speak with you later."

Matt tucked the file in the crook of his elbow and made his
way out of the office. The assistant again avoided his glance. His
phone chirped with a text from Vernon. "Zilch on phones. Zilch
on baby. Teacher in dorm named Madeline wants to talk to you
ASAP."

Matt walked down the steps and headed toward Portland to
deal with Harvey Fuller and now Madeline, the young teacher
with the messy hair, whom he had just remembered. He assumed
that Porter had given him information on her as well, and he was
curious to see what had been said about her. As he strode toward
the dorm, he realized what was lacking in Porter's office. He and
his wife made a strikingly attractive pair. They had two, three

children, and Lucinda had been distraught about at least two of them not being able to return to the school. Heads came as packages. The full complement of wife or husband, family, dog, all of whose personalities really ought to blend with and mirror what the school said about itself. In the case of Armitage, they had to be as confident and accomplished as they expected their faculty and graduates to be. It seemed ridiculous to reduce the issue to one inadequate word, but their image mattered.

No photos. Porter's desk and office ought to have been littered with photos. Lucinda's face was abruptly familiar to Matt. He'd seen her often enough presiding over parties in the alumni magazine. But in her husband's office, where she would naturally have assumed pride of place, there was no sign of her or of their children.

CHAPTER 8

t had been a long time since Fred had broken in anywhere. Prying open his father's liquor cabinet all those weekends when he was a teenager should have counted for something, but he'd forgotten how fear accompanied the transgression. And he had to admit that rooting around in Armitage's archives carried heavier consequences than filching booze, even forty-year-old Scotch.

It was early Tuesday morning, and he was in the tunnels below Nicholson House with a set of keys he'd persuaded one of the dimmer B and G workers to loan him on the pretext of needing to get into the gym. He didn't feel right about taking advantage of the slight edge of power that faculty had over staff. Nor could he persuade himself that the ends justified the means. Still, it was what he had done and what had led directly to groping in the dark at such an hour. He was also ashamed to admit that he was using the distracting furor of Claire's death and her baby's disappearance. No one was remotely interested in what the art teacher was up to at the moment.

The fistful of keys must have weighed close to two pounds, a circular mass of spiked, dull bronze. Quite effective as a weapon if you slipped the individual bits of metal between your fingers and made a fist. One of them had to be a skeleton. Fred held a penlight between his teeth and swore softly as he slipped one after the other into the lock. Finally, a key clicked to the right and he heard the tumblers slide into place. The door opened and released the pleasant staleness of old paper, the unmistakable funk of libraries, into the corridor. Fred slipped inside and pulled the door to as gently as possible. Why were archives always underground? What was it about history that required it to be buried? Institutions loved preserving what had happened to them, especially when it was flattering, but even so these rooms were always stuck somewhere damp and inconvenient.

From an earlier, legitimate visit, Fred knew the walls were hung with photographs of Armitage from another day: early hockey teams; classes from 1912, when only twenty boys a year graduated, all of them bound for colleges even the best students would kill now to get into, a berth secured merely with a letter from the headmaster, in brutal contrast to the heavy dossiers of achievement required now. Even so, maybe those old guys deserved their spots at Princeton and Yale. Their faces were full of stern dedication to duty, boys who would serve in the great wars. Most long dead. But Harvey Fuller could probably name the raw-faced teenagers in those faded pictures and also list the four or so students who had chosen military service as their career since Korea. Although he wasn't technically the archivist—that job belonged to an ancient local alumnus named Samuel Briggs—everyone leaned on Harvey to pluck out the most telling details of the school's past. When people spoke about institutional memory, they usually meant something rather abstract. In Harvey, this idea had condensed in an actual person, like a toxic nugget of musk.

It was not useful to have his mind wander toward Harvey at the moment. A memory of the man's face—he'd been Fred's teacher— triggered guilt, and he felt enough at odds with himself as it was. He wasn't sure where he should start looking, though he knew the papers he was after wouldn't be in the actual files for the 1950s; nothing was officially on record about the incident on which he wanted information. He wasn't even entirely certain that the papers of former heads were kept here. But he'd confirmed that they weren't in the library, and without exciting the suspicions of Mary Manchester, no small feat. Mary had doggedly guarded the card catalog in the basement out of some dragonlike loyalty to the old ways, though the heavy drawers took up space Porter wanted to use for new computers. She'd recently lost the battle to have them saved indefinitely, but Fred had found and pocketed the card he needed before the movers could come. The manila rectangle had merely said, "Papers of a personal nature, correspondence 1954–1955, archives," and had no Dewey number attached. The handwriting was like no other he had seen in the catalog, delicate but firm, and that fragile, human trace was what he was looking for now.

Though the room was compact, Fred realized it contained an enormous amount of material. Bound volumes lined one wall, file cabinets another, and low shelves the two others. He felt a twinge of despair. It could take months to sort through it all, and he didn't want to spend months on this dubious project. He flashed his light around the room and saw with a start that he'd briefly illuminated a picture of his grandfather Llewellan Naylor. He edged closer to the photo, taken, its typewritten caption said, in 1953. In it, Llewellan looked exhilarated. He had his arm around the shoulder of a student and was smiling into the lens, looking straight at the camera, his strong teeth a blinding slash of white, his hair dark and curly, the very image of confidence, intelligence, good humor. A person worthy of trust.

Fred thought about his grandfather, who had died last year, and knew with a flush of shame that Llewellan would have been enraged that Fred was rooting around in these old papers, searching for the details of a story that might well turn out to be wholly false. But that was wishful thinking. Fred's intuition was uncomfortably certain that something deeply unpleasant could indeed emerge about his grandfather. Llewellan had been a dominant force in his life, the presiding male. Fred had acquired the deepest, fiercest lessons from him, and to search seriously for flaws in a powerful mentor was to invite betrayal.

Fred started with the file cabinets, opening the bottom drawer, his hands slipping with sweat, his teeth clenched on the penlight. The headings on the cardboard files were handwritten, in curling penmanship, in what was probably India ink. "Admissions," "Assembly programs, 1941." The wrong years, the wrong writing.

As he flicked through the contents, Fred thought about the man named Malcolm Smith, whose visit this April had prompted his descent into the archives. Not finding what he was looking for, Fred shut the drawer for the 1940s a little more sharply than he'd intended. Smith had had squirrel-bright eyes, rounded shoulders, tweedy clothes, very much like most of the graduates who wandered back to stroll the campus and engage in diluted versions of the competitions that had stirred their lives as young men. Smith had sought Fred out, claiming to want to observe an art class and the work of current students. "He's an artist," said Sarah Talmadge, the assistant head and an admired colleague. "Sorry, Fred. Would you mind? I know it's a bit of a drag, but he's an alum." Fred and Sarah, old-school Armitage, knew better than to offend any former student. Big gifts could come from unexpected sources, and it was always wise to court them.

Besides, Fred honestly didn't mind. Unlike some of his colleagues, sensitive to the point of paranoia, Fred didn't really care who observed him. He was confident in the classroom, a natural.

As a teacher, he had nothing to hide. When it came time for his annual evaluations, he tended not to notice Porter or Sarah or whoever had been slated to write up his report sitting in the corner of the room. Malcolm Smith had produced a sharply different effect the moment he stepped in the studio. In spite of the old man's silence, something in his presence was obtrusive. Fred could feel Smith's eyes on him as he discussed two-point perspective with his ninth graders. He couldn't shake the unease he felt when the old man took his hand and looked searchingly in his face. Searchingly, but not kindly. "You look like him," Smith said firmly. "You look very much like your grandfather."

It was something people who had known them both commented on frequently. Apart from their hair color—Fred was blond and Llewellan very dark—they shared not just similar bones but similar voices and even mannerisms. Bizarrely, Fred's father seemed to have been passed over genetically, as if nature had known the son's personality wasn't quite worth replicating. "You knew my grandfather?" Fred asked, guessing Smith was the right age to have been at Armitage during Llewellan's tenure.

"Oh yes, indeed," said Smith. Students were inspecting their easels. In these beginning classes, Fred considered it his job to get the kids to like art. Not just looking at it but making it. To that end, they began most classes with a free-drawing assignment. He played a piece of music, Xeroxed a poem or a joke, gave them an image or a quote to work from. The students enjoyed the space he allowed them, this easing into the period, especially since the classes were often the first of the day. Today, the assignment was to think about their favorite place on campus and try to re-create it from memory, using perspective. They were working in charcoal, and Fred could hear the soft scratch of the sticks on the large pads of paper.

"Were you a student of his?" Fred asked Malcolm Smith, fumbling for more information. What did he want, this man?

"Not exactly, in that none of us was. As you know, he didn't teach," Smith answered. "But I was here when he was headmaster. He was quite a personality, your grandfather."

"He was," said Fred with more warmth than he intended. He could tell Smith had something harsh to add. Usually, when these old guys figured out who Fred was, they wanted to regale him with stories about his grandfather's savvy handling of young boys. Scrapes they found themselves in that he helped get them out of. His swiftness on hockey skates the years the pond froze before it snowed and they could all sweep out across the black, bubbled ice. The worst thing former charges ever said about him concerned his radically off-key but enthusiastic singing and the battle that Higgins, the organist, had ineffectively waged to keep him silent during Christmas services. Apparently, Llewellan always answered that God would rather hear himself praised than not, even by someone with a tin ear. Well-worn, harmless anecdotes.

But this man clearly felt differently about Fred's grandfather. What he had to say was not going to be wedged inside a cheerful anecdote. Just then, however, a student asked a question about how to achieve shadings in charcoal. Fred took his time explaining, hoping Smith would take the hint and leave.

He did not. The moment Fred had finished with his student, the old man was back at his elbow, whispering savagely, "He wasn't what he seemed, Llewellan Naylor. You might want to learn more about the events of the winter of 1955. You might, Mr. Naylor, need to revise your opinion of your grandfather."

Fred's first reaction had been rage. His memories of Llewellan were banked in clear, clean light: the man had taught him to fish, swim, pitch a tent, hike a mountain. He'd been a bearer of practical wisdom. Not kind. No one ever described Llewellan as warm. But present, firm, and above all, strong. Intelligent and strong. So much more effective than Fred's father, Harrison, the son so weak he couldn't even pass his looks on to his boys. It was for Llewellan that Fred had come to Armitage as a student and returned to it as a teacher.

"What do you want to say, Mr. Smith?" Fred asked, keeping his voice low. The students were busy working, and if they sensed tension, they'd immediately start staring.

Smith gave a terse, smug smile. "I'll let you discover the particulars for yourself, Mr. Naylor. You might want to find out what you can about a student named Edward Smith, my older brother. The Class of 1955. No longer a contributing alumnus. He died." Then he turned, as quickly as it was possible for a man of sixty-nine to turn, and left the studio.

"Who was that guy, Mr. Naylor?" asked Quinn Foster at the end of class. "He gave me the creeps," she said, and Fred silently agreed.

Worse than the creeps, he thought. He'd been malevolent. Some acid ball of memory had been roiling inside him, rotting his stomach until he'd needed to spit up the whole, vile mess. He had probably planned this moment for years, deciding finally that Fred was the person he was heading toward, waiting until he couldn't stand it any longer. Fred shook his head, trying to clear it of such targeted hatred. But Smith's ploy had worked; the man had gotten his attention.

For the first week after Smith's visit, Fred had tried to forget about him and the story he brought. But as April wore on, he found himself increasingly distracted by the idea that Llewellan had been involved in something shameful. Slowly, and with deeply assumed casualness, he began to search for traces of Edward Smith. He first ran a quick Google search, but the name was so common that even with keywords like "Armitage" attached, nothing useful emerged, and Fred decided that he would start with sources closer to home. He looked then for Edward on the wooden plaques that listed the names of all the graduating seniors for each class, boards that ran down the walls of the dining hall and the many long corridors of the school: rosters of boys from distinguished families, many names crowned with Roman numerals. But Edward's wasn't there. Fred's next attempt to locate him centered on the yearbook for 1955, but Edward barely appeared in that, either. He had no senior page; no announcement mourning his death had been published; and Fred found him only once, in a sea of white faces in a photo of the Glee Club, which must have been taken early in the fall. Yet in the book for 1954, to Fred's concern, he discovered far more evidence of Edward's existence: there he was, a short boy with a wide smile, a junior in Greaves, a member of the chorus and the theater club. He appeared as well in the books for 1952 and 1953, his only pursuits apparently music and theater. In 1952, he had played Ophelia, and on page 73, Fred found a picture of him in blond braids, arm thrown dramatically over his brow.

By the end of April, Fred had started looking in academy records, and his worry increased by small but measurable degrees. A thorough examination of admissions files had shown nothing. Every other student who had graduated from Armitage in 1955, and several who had made it only through their sophomore or junior years, had their records intact. But Edward's papers were nowhere to be found.

Fred enlarged the scope of his search, fitting the project in with growing unease on weekends or late at night when not on duty. Malcolm was amply documented. A good student, top of his class, won the art prize. Went to Brown. From Providence, Rhode Island, living now in Little Compton. A painter of more than competent if rather boring landscapes if the pictures on the Web from his gallery were to be trusted. Married, though no children appeared to have attended Armitage. No record, even of his having come back for reunions or having given a cent, though the development people guarded their information zealously and Fred might be wrong on that front. The Smiths had money, but none of it appeared to have filtered down to the academy.

It had taken weeks of rather clandestine work to gather even that much. And still, news about Edward was hard to come by. Then Fred had unearthed the library card with the distinctive handwriting. The archives were what was left, apart from combing Google or Porter's office, where Fred assumed some of the more sensitive material that heads had access to was still kept. And breaking into Porter's office was something he couldn't face. He felt a queasy parallel between himself and Malcolm Smith; he was beginning to understand what it might be like to live with a noxious obsession, and it had been only a couple of months. Opening the next drawer in the cabinet, marked merely "1950s," Fred was visited with a brief panic that what he found out was going to change him in ways he would not find comfortable.

As an artist, he was supposed to savor difficulty: it was supposed to feed his work, keep him productively off balance. As a teacher with a safe, pleasant job, this prospect horrified him. He wondered for a moment what side of his personality would win out: the part that could spend ten-hour days in the studio week after week, painting with both wild focus and abandon, or the part that happily traded Sox gossip with Alice Grassley while nursing a cup of coffee. Knowing exactly how the year would progress in step by measured step. But that wasn't true, he told himself. Look how this year was ending. Then, toward the back of the file, he found a folder marked with the same handwriting that graced the old catalog card. He was on the brink of grabbing it when he heard a sound.

Footsteps, unmistakably. Someone was walking down the tunnel. And not exactly stealthily. He had to move fast. He wouldn't examine the folder tonight. And he couldn't risk being discovered in this room. Slipping out of the archives, dousing the penlight, and pocketing the keys, Fred cocked his head for an instant and followed the sound of the retreating feet.

Trotting slightly to keep up, Fred rounded a bend and saw, without a huge amount of surprise, Scotty Johnston. "Scotty," he called, "slow down." He saw the boy's back tense, the flicker of doubt run through his body as he decided whether to bolt or be caught. But Fred knew what he'd decide; he'd coached the boy since his freshman year, and he was more familiar with Scotty than he cared to be.

Scotty was the captain of the varsity soccer, squash, and crew teams. He was going to Harvard, as had his brothers, father, uncles, and grandfather, a thicket of relatives just as blond, tall, and self-assured. That he was also a major smoker of pot, probably a dealer, and almost universally disliked by the faculty hadn't prevented his acceptance. His erg scores probably had something to do with that. He was a moderately good student but an absolutely brilliant athlete. Magically, the marijuana had yet to diminish his performance. Six foot three, broad at the shoulders, the owner of blue eyes and a tapered waist, Scotty Johnston was catnip to girls and rowing coaches. Easygoing when it came to judging character, Fred had found that, after four years of exposure to Scotty, he had come to loathe him. With a prickle of discomfort, he was looking forward to what could be referred to in only the most technical terms as busting Scotty's ass.

But he wasn't prepared for the grin on the boy's face. "Hey, Mr. Naylor. Nice night for a little B and E. Find what you were looking for? Good move to score the keys from Jackson. Easiest mark in the crew."

The only solution was to hit back as sharply as possible. A classic soccer move. Look up the midfield, then strike for the goal just when the goalie thought you were going to send the ball to a fullback. "Whose word carries more weight, Scott? Mine or yours? Ms. Phelan's been looking into that midnight raid when you were caught running to Claire's dorm. Anything to do with that situation? If I were you, I'd be careful about leveling accusations right now." Joyce had sent out an all-faculty e-mail late Monday night, letting teachers know that Scotty had been seen hightailing it back from Portland. Fred had also heard that Scotty had been questioned by police that afternoon, but not about the outcome of that interrogation. People were being tight-lipped about their conversations with the police, maintaining a level of discretion unusual for Armitage's population, who traded gossip with the vigor and expertise of village women.

Fred would never have predicted what happened next. A look of pure panic ran across Scotty's face, and he looked as nervous as any scrawny kid on the first day of school. He charged past Fred and back down the tunnel. Too surprised to follow, Fred heard Scotty's quickly moving footsteps and then the slam of a door.

Heading in the direction that the terrified boy had come from—it had been Claire's name, Fred was sure of it, that had sparked the fear—he went looking for traces of what Scotty might have been up to. As soon as he got out of the tunnels, he'd call security, and all of it would most certainly mean more trouble for Scotty, both with the school and perhaps with the police. He'd have to come up with some excuse about why he himself had been down there, but there was nothing for that. Satisfying his curiosity about what Scotty had been doing here would take only a minute. Touching the handles of the doors that lined the tunnel, Fred found them uniformly cool until he reached one about a third of the way down: the knob was warm, as if recently palmed. Opening the lock with the skeleton key, Fred was surprised to find himself in a storeroom with a lot of old computer equipment. He was even more surprised to find that the plastic roof and screen of a monitor near the door was almost hot to the touch. Someone, probably Scotty, had taken some care to unplug it and try to hide the cords below some plastic sheeting, but Fred guessed that he had been using this outmoded Mac. Fred looked more closely in the beam of his penlight: yes, he wasn't imagining it. The computer had been wired for dial-up. A few weekends before, he had gone to Connecticut to help his mother at last change hers over to a faster service. For some reason, Scotty Johnston had wanted to use the Internet without resorting to the school's network.

CHAPTER 9

Tuesday morning, Madeline returned from breakfast to discover that the girls were no longer nestled in their sleeping bags on her floor. They hadn't straightened anything up but had managed to leave a short note, signed by Lee, on the coffee table. "Thank you for your hospitality, Miss Christopher." Madeline had bumped into the tall, skinny police officer on the way back from the dining hall and asked to talk to him or one of his colleagues as soon as possible. The news about the Reign of Terror and Robespierre, as adolescent as it all sounded in the safety of daylight, was sure to be significant. He had assured her he would send someone to speak with her right away. But by the time Madeline stepped back into her apartment and glanced at Lee's note, Grace had pounced, saying, "There you are," as if eating breakfast were something to be ashamed of. Grace looked a wreck, her eyes red not so much with grief but with anxiety, the skin drawn around her small, sour mouth. They had to supervise the removal of the girls from the dorm, she scolded. The poor things were traumatized and had to be escorted to other rooms for the remainder of the year. The ones who stayed, of course. Quite a few were already being packed up and whisked home, where their parents could make sure nothing could happen to them, now that Armitage had been revealed as a dangerous and scandal-tainted place.

"Sarah has reassigned everyone," Grace said and shook a list in front of Madeline's nose. "Would you please take this copy and go see if you can help them out?" It was the lot of the intern to be treated as the dorm head's personal servant, and Madeline had no option but to agree. She brushed her teeth first, as if proper dental hygiene might be useful armor when dealing with teenagers unstrung by death and horror. If anything, the girls were more distraught than the day before. The reality of Claire's killing and the stark fact of the baby's disappearance were growing clearer to them, as was the loss of their cell phones and laptops. Madeline frequently had to pause and let one of them sob on her shoulder between bouts of stuffing duffel bags with lingerie that would have made most starlets blush. She really ought to have spent more time in their rooms this year; it was disconcerting to discover so much about them so late in the game and in such dreadful circumstances. For instance, their ironclad belief in beauty as a protective agent. "Claire was so pretty," one mousy freshman kept saying, as if the girl's looks alone ought to have prevented her death.

Throughout, Madeline tried to listen for whispers about Claire, the Reign, anything that might have led to her murder. But the girls weren't just hysterical, they were frightened. No one said much of anything; they just sniffled, zipped, and gravely accepted Madeline's help as they pulled together their luxurious belongings and prepared to move. The morning rolled on: illegal tapestries were unpinned from the walls; beds were stripped; washing machines whirred. It was the activity that would have spun through the last days of school in any case. Just now it was accelerated and broken up with fits of tears and the bulky presence of police, who were still roaming the halls and poking around in Claire's room, which they had sealed off with what seemed to Madeline an ungodly amount of yellow tape printed with CRIME SCENE down its garish length. The girls worked quickly. They were eager to be gone.

Occasionally, Madeline spotted Grace sitting on an overstuffed suitcase, but she didn't catch a glimpse of Harvey or Marie-France, who either hadn't been asked or, more likely, had simply decided that offering such assistance didn't befit Armitage's senior faculty. At noon, Grace allowed her twenty minutes to get lunch, a reprieve for which Madeline was grateful. She sat at her usual place in the Commons and looked around for Fred. It would have been deeply reassuring to talk with him about this Robespierre business. As both an Armitage graduate and a more experienced teacher, he might have light to shed on it that would render the whole thing a little less ghoulish. But Fred was nowhere to be found, and to Madeline's surprise, it was Lee Hastings who came up to her. Lee grasped a tray that held mostly raw vegetables, a meager roll, and what was obviously skim milk, gray and watery. Madeline's own plate was home to a slab of corned beef and onion rings. How was it possible that these teenagers always had the upper hand, even when it came to nutritional choices? Weren't they the ones who were supposed to have all these unchecked appetites? Madeline asked Lee to sit down, pleased to have the company.

But Lee declined with a short nod and Madeline felt a slight sting of rejection, noting even so that these were the tactics by which Lee and Claire and their kind worked. An invitation that you allowed yourself to find gratifying, followed by a sliver of rejection that left you dangling and uncertain of anything except their power to wound. Lee had something to add to her curt dismissal. "Miss Christopher, please don't take this badly. But Olu, Portia, Suzy, and I were talking. We would really prefer it if you didn't say anything to anyone about what we told you last night." What was interesting, Madeline thought later, was that Lee expected Madeline to do her bidding. Or at least she gave every impression of expecting that,

even if she knew her request was irrational at worst and at best unlikely to be fulfilled. For a moment, Madeline experienced a craven
desire only to please this tall, commanding girl and had a direct
taste of what it would be like to be subject to the girls of the Reign.
Yet her next response was unequivocal and, she thought with some
pride, grown-up. Picking up an onion ring, she said, "Lee, don't
be ridiculous. You know I can't possibly do that. It's not because I'm
that eager to expose your"—and here she struggled for a word, since
her first inclination had been to use the phrase *freaky cult*, substi-
tuting the more benign *group*—"but you and I both know it might
have something to do with Claire's death. And anything that can
help the police find out what happened has to be discussed." She
met Lee's glacial gaze with only a mildly pounding heart and
watched the girl stalk with her irreproachable lunch back to the
table she had secured with Portia, Suzy, and Olu. Madeline ate her
whole platter of corned beef and went back for thirds of sweetened
iced tea, all as they watched and whispered from their perch three
tables away.

When she got up, she felt their cool stares follow her. Thank
God, she thought, it's the end of the year. I could never have lived
with this for more than a few weeks. On her return to the dorm, she
helped move five sophomores to a few vacant spaces on the other
side of campus. They'd looked a little like refugees, toting laundry
baskets full of clothes on their heads. The image was slightly marred
by the fact that the clothes spilling from a single container cost
more than most Kosovars spent on an entire house.

Madeline did not encounter Lee and her coconspirators for the
rest of the afternoon, and by four, she was back in the now-empty
dorm. Grace, to her relief, was occupied elsewhere. Her phone was
beeping with new messages. More from Kate and one from a man

with a deep voice who said his name was Matt Corelli from the Armitage Police and he understood she wanted to speak with him. He had stopped by, but she hadn't been in. Could she please get in touch as soon as possible? She rang and was slightly relieved when the call flipped instantly to voice mail. It was blisteringly hot, and she went then to take a shower but discovered that she was entirely out of shampoo.

Well, that would be easy enough to find. She doubted the girls had packed with complete care and guessed that in their showers she'd find some partially full containers of Pantene she could scavenge. She took a shopping bag with her so she could hide her ill-gained booty should Grace be stalking the halls. But the first-floor bathroom was unusually clean; the custodians must have come through already. The second floor, still unscrubbed, held a treasure trove of bath beads and conditioners that claimed they'd do everything from giving your hair volume to boosting your self-esteem. Pretty impressive claims for a detangler, Madeline thought as she guiltily plucked the bottles from the shower stalls, reassuring herself that (1) she would actually finish off these products and not waste them and (2) she'd recycle all the containers. Still, she felt rather furtive as she crept out of the bathroom and down the hall with her rustling bag full of wickedly perfumy smells.

Then she heard someone walking behind her. She paused and realized the sounds were actually coming from the third floor. Someone was up there and about to descend the staircase. Madeline hopped into an empty room along the corridor, not wanting to be caught with her stash. She guessed it was the police, collecting, checking, investigating, whatever it was that police did, but she had the door cracked to peer out at whoever passed. To her total surprise, it was Harvey Fuller, and he was heading down the hall, back to the far wing of the dorm where he lived. He was going at a tremendous clip, body bent forward, head lowered, and Madeline got an impression of deep strain. She was intensely relieved as well that her childish instinct to hide had been a useful one. Harvey would be just about the last person she would have wanted to greet with armfuls of the girls' shampoo.

Still, it was extremely disconcerting. The only reason he could have had to be up there was to look at Claire's room. And what would draw Harvey Fuller there, and why would it have so upset him? What was really unusual, thought Madeline, was that she had never seen Harvey experiencing any kind of emotion before. It was too much to think about all at once, and she wanted to call the detective again.

Madeline sneaked back to her apartment, put her new assortment of goodies in the bathroom, and chose something peachy called Afternoon Storm for her hair. Just as she finished showering, she heard the phone ring and, still streaming with water, ran to grab it. It was Matt Corelli.

He was in town, he explained, and wouldn't need to return to Armitage until later this evening. Would she mind coming in to meet him in the next hour or so? "But won't I have trouble getting off campus?" she asked. He'd take care of it, he said and asked, a little sheepishly, if she'd mind meeting him at Ali's. He hadn't had a chance to eat all day.

"I love Ali's," Madeline said and thought that she was actually going to look forward to speaking with this polite man who also appreciated falafel. They arranged to meet at five, which gave Madeline a few minutes to check e-mail and otherwise catch her breath. Porter had written several all-faculty notes, alerting them that classes lasting no more than forty minutes would start again on Thursday. Memorial services for Claire were being planned, with one taking place tomorrow on the Knoll at seven in the evening. Grief sessions were being held in the wellness center. Sports practices would also resume on Thursday, not with any intent of sending students off to competitions but because physical release was an important part of healing. Blah blah blah, thought Madeline. Porter was usually crisper than that, less prone to cliché. But perhaps fear and shock were enough to rob even the most articulate of originality.

Madeline then ignored several e-mails from Kate, who'd resorted to another means of communication since her phone calls were going unreturned, and wrote one to Fred that said, "How are you holding up? I stole all the shampoo the girls left behind. Need to talk to you about something weird." By then it was 4:45, and she glanced out at the weather. Gigantic thunderheads had massed in the west, and although she would have preferred to bike down to Ali's, since it was less than a mile away, she decided to take her car in case it poured.

The detective was already there, standing in front of the laundromat. They had met very briefly the morning Claire died, but Madeline had assumed he had a lot more significant people to talk to than the intern. But as he shook her hand and held her eyes, she was conscious of feeling important. He was good at that, she guessed, making people feel at ease, making people feel listened to.

As they entered, Ali was shouting into a cell phone in Arabic, and he motioned to them to sit down on the bench that ran in front of a row of washing machines. Ali hung up at last. "Sisters," he said, shaking his head. His youngest, at eighteen, had decided she wasn't going to go to university and would instead marry a barber in Damascus. "A barber," he said. "What kind of life is she going to have with a barber? And without an education. Anyway, what can I get you?" It was peaceful here, too early for the dinner rush or a horde of people wanting to wash their clothes after work.

Matt ordered a falafel and shawarma sandwich, and Madeline ordered two, one for now and the other one probably, too. Ali jotted down their orders and said he was glad to have some police protection, with everything going on up there. He pointed upward with his hand, implying the sprawl of the academy. Matt laughed, and the sound had an unhinged edge to it. Madeline guessed he hadn't had much occasion in the last two days to find humor in many situations. But it was funny. If anyone was less in need of police protection in Armitage or Greenville, it was Ali Khalid. He was tall, powerfully built, and moved around his tiny kitchen with caged grace. They watched Ali heat up the oil and start to shape the chickpea patties from a tub of tan batter. His phone rang again, and he was speaking loudly in Arabic as the falafel began to fry.

"I wonder something," Madeline said. "I wonder how running a falafel stand inside a laundromat in a small Massachusetts town stacks up against life as a Damascene barber?"

Matt looked at her. "Remember, he's an eldest son. He sends everything he makes back home. He's got six, seven sisters and a mother who's a widow." Then he asked Madeline if she knew that Ali lived with an elderly lady in town and did all her yard work in exchange for rent.

"How do you know all this?" Madeline asked.

"I'm a cop," Matt said. "People have a bizarre habit of talking to us." And Madeline thought it wasn't that he was a policeman; more, it was the way he did his work, paying attention with a strict, almost unnerving intensity.

Ali clicked off his phone, shook his head, and did something deft with some pita. "Any progress?" he asked, and Madeline could see that the detective knew better than to answer right away. What Ali was really doing was preparing to tell him what he himself thought about the events of the last couple of days. Reporters were all over the place, Ali said. They'd even tried to interview him, but he wasn't going to have any of it. "I'm legal, man, but I don't want them anywhere near me." Ali's papers were indeed legitimate, Matt told Madeline. "I know. I had to check them myself."

Ali smiled bitterly. "The Patriot Act. But I got lucky." He had had the astonishing fortune of receiving a green card in the lottery. "First and last thing I ever won," he said as he ripped a length of tinfoil from a roll mounted on the wall. "I didn't even have to bribe anybody. No one could believe it. My family's known for never winning anything."

It struck Madeline for the first time that people beyond the academy would be affected by Claire's death and her baby's disappearance. They were acts with a far wider echo than she would have suspected. She had purposely not read newspapers or looked at the television; this kind of event would instantly reach those media, and their creators would milk the ugliness for only the most sensational of details. It was an entirely different thing to live through it, to have known the person involved, to be implicated. Ali looked chastened, bewildered almost that this small town could manage to produce something so unabashedly final and violent. Students had stopped coming and, of course, faculty, Ali added. He thought, however, that the girl who died had been in sometime the last month. "No way I would have known the poor thing was having a baby." It had rained all of April, so she would have been in some big poncho. "Anyway, if she's who I think she is, she was skinny, sickly. But all those girls: they look exactly alike, like they're about to die from hunger. Impossible to tell them apart." Ali gave them their sandwiches, accepted their money, returned their change, then slid two wet bottles of lemonade over the counter. "Drinks on the house tonight. You two look tired."

They thanked him and went outside. The chemical tang of fabric softener wasn't pleasant layered with chickpeas. Thunder growled, but the rain hadn't yet arrived. On the bench in front of the plate-glass window, they dug into their sandwiches for a moment, and then Matt said, "Well, I should probably ask you what you were doing the night before Claire died. And I know you've got things you'd like to say. Just let me finish this bite and get my pencil out."

"Your pencil?" Madeline asked.

"I know," Matt said. "My partner thinks it's weird, too. But writing makes me think more clearly. Typing puts me to sleep. And I'm the only one who can decipher my own penmanship. Keeps information out of the wrong hands." He looked at her again and said, "I knew I recognized you. You run around town in the morning. You don't tie your hair back."

"Yes," she said and thought she would have to stop wearing those baggy shorts. She had no idea anybody had noticed her.

"You don't look at anything but the road when you're out there. You run like it's necessary to you." His eyes were very deeply brown.

"Well, if you taught up there, you'd need something that was totally your own for a few minutes a day, too," Madeline said, and then she took another enormous taste of lamb.

He reached into a pocket and opened his notebook. Madeline had had a long night on Sunday, she admitted. She wasn't on duty, hadn't heard or seen anything unusual in the dorm, though she had remembered thinking the girls were abnormally quiet. Between midnight and one, she had finished correcting some papers about Emily Dickinson and then confessed that between one and one thirty she wrote but didn't send an e-mail to a man who was probably her ex but who at one time had agreed to be her boyfriend. And then, she said, "I basically passed out until the alarm rang."

Matt noted then he was only thirty-three but past the age when he could get by on four hours a night day after day. She could tell he wanted to tell her that that kind of bounce didn't last, but he restrained himself. "So," she said, "I've got no way to prove where I was between midnight and dawn, since I didn't even send an e-mail or make a phone call." But just as she started out on her run a little after six, she'd nearly been run over by the Barfmobile. She'd been listening to music on her headphones, a little too loudly, and she was sleepy.

"Excuse me, the Barfmobile?" Matt said, pencil raised above the pad.

"Oh, of course you wouldn't know about that," Madeline said. "That's what we, I mean Fred Naylor and I, call Betsy Lowery's car. She has these four kids who get sick in their station wagon all the time, and it's just not the best idea to get too close to it. Or get run over by it, either."

"Do you have any idea where she was going?" Matt asked then, clearly still digesting the idea of the Barfmobile.

"No," said Madeline, chewing a piece of her hair, something she did only when she found someone attractive. "Maybe she was heading up to the CVS to get some milk or Benadryl. She looked totally out of it, honestly. Maybe it had been a late night for her, too."

Matt made a note and asked, "And then?"

And then she'd come back from her run and Grace had found her at about 6:50 and she'd learned what happened. That was when Sally Jansen had flipped out and she had actually seen Claire. Matt said, "So you're the person who realized that Claire had had a baby."

"Oh, that," Madeline said, flushing. "Well, it was her breasts. My sister, Kate, she had them, too, I mean of course Kate has breasts, she's a woman, but what I mean," she said, growing more and more flustered, "was she'd just given birth, too, and her nipples spread like Claire's. So that's how I knew. Oh no, I am just going to shut up right now."

But she didn't and for the next ten minutes kept talking between bites of her sandwich. It was tonic to discuss what she'd been thinking, to share impressions of her colleagues and students. About Claire she said, "She sort of terrified me. I mean, she lived part of the year in Paris. She was seventeen and spoke perfect French. And I'll say this, too, because I'm sure it's not something you're going to hear from most people, that although Claire was beautiful and intelligent, she was not someone I would ever describe as kind or even pleasant." Not, Madeline added, that that would justify someone wanting to hurt her or take her child. Madeline told Matt then about the evening that Lee and her friends had spent with her and discussed Claire's role as Robespierre and her apparent transgression in including people like Sally as her secret keepers. Matt wrote all the while she spoke but didn't appear overly taken aback.

"Did you already know about this?" Madeline asked, slightly disappointed. The thunder was coming closer and the sky was darkening.

"No," he answered, looking up at the clouds. "But that group was around when I was at the academy. I'm not surprised it's still operating or that Claire was involved. She was the type of kid who always ran it. I've already talked to the girls you mentioned, but it's complicated. Many of them are minors, and most of them have their parents with them. They're reluctant to discuss anything." Sally, in particular, he said, had a ring of doctors and lawyers around her it might take weeks to break through.

Madeline nearly choked on a piece of cucumber. "You went there? I had no idea."

Matt smiled and said, "Yes, I went there."

She tried to mask her reaction by taking a big sip of lemonade, but she thought it was pretty clear the next thought darting across her brain was, And you're a cop? She watched him notice that, too. "And then I went to Penn, and no, I know it doesn't make sense to take an education from Armitage and head into the seamy world of police work. But it's what happened."

"Well, you probably had your reasons," Madeline tried to say as gamely as possible, but then she realized something else. "You're the one who must have told them to search the forts." Out in the woods, students had for years built makeshift clubhouses in which to drink and smoke, and they tried mightily to keep the locations secret. Even if all that was out there in the swampy reaches of the forest was a few pieces of plywood, they considered them sacred. "Well, that was a great idea, though the kids were upset. As far as they're concerned, the forts are their property."

"We did, I mean, I did, too," Matt said.

"Oh, and there's another thing," she said and nearly spilled the last of her lemonade. She told him then about Harvey Fuller, about how he had been on the third floor and, even more strangely, how he had appeared to be in pain. She had been on the second floor, she admitted shamefacedly, because she'd run out of shampoo and the girls had left a lot of it behind.

"Harvey Fuller was up there? When?" This alarmed him, she saw. This was something he hadn't actually known. He began to shift on the bench, to crumple the remains of his meal and look around for a trash bin. She watched as he altered in front of her from a kind of confidant to a police officer. It was time for him to go.

She stood as well, but before he left, she had something she wanted to ask him. "Mr. Corelli, this isn't about the investigation, but it's something that really worries me. I just feel so bad that I didn't know about Claire. That I wasn't there to help." A few fat drops of rain began to spatter the hot sidewalk. They both noticed, but Matt slowed down for a moment, and neither of them moved to seek shelter. It actually felt refreshing, Madeline thought.

"It's not that unusual for people not to notice," he told her. "Which might be hard to believe, but it's true. It's a pretty well-documented phenomenon, a mixture of something like that being exceptional for a certain community and the person actively trying to deceive that community."

"It's true, I guess," Madeline admitted. "She went to sort of unimaginable lengths to hide it. And for some reason, she wanted to stay at school. That's what I can't figure out." Still, Madeline continued, you'd think an outsider, one of these curriculum consultants they were always hiring, someone, might have noticed. "Or," she finished, "one of us who was actually there, who might have been even a tiny bit more observant or brave."

"Madeline, it happens all the time. In smaller ways, usually. But people just don't see what they don't want to." The rain was gathering force, and they could no longer pretend to ignore it. She wanted, she realized, to ask another hundred questions about everything from his time at the academy to the case. Then the biggest worry won out, even as the shower began to turn into a cloudburst. She blurted, "The baby. I keep thinking about that baby. Do you think he's still alive?"

Matt held the door open for her, and they entered the steamy warmth of the laundromat again. They put their trash in a barrel loaded with empty packets of Tide, and although Matt was clearly impatient to get going, the rain was so intense it seemed wise to wait for a moment in front of the window.

"I don't know," he said. "I really hope so," he added. His phone beeped, and he made himself busy for a moment examining the text. The storm pounded the storefront. Finished with his message, Matt asked, "Do you need a ride?" and she said, "No thanks, Mr. Corelli. I've got my car."

"You can call me Matt, Madeline," he said, and he gave her his card. "Please phone anytime."

"Thank you," she said, and together they waved good-bye to Ali, busy now with a new customer, and dashed into the heavy rain. Matt ran toward his car, and Madeline darted in the other direction. She was soaked in seconds and sat breathing heavily in the driver's seat, letting water sluice off her body before she fully grasped what was on her dashboard. There was a note, written in scarlet ink on white paper, that said, "You have the right to use terror to crush the enemies of liberty." On it was a spool, an old-fashioned, wooden kind, and the thread that was wrapped around it glinted red, even in the low, gray light of the storm.

CHAPTER 10

Kayla was never late, Jim thought, but today she was behind by fifteen minutes. Maybe it was the rain. It was Wednesday afternoon, and it was still pouring. The rain that had started the evening before had yet to let up. Fortunately, Angela had lain down after lunch and was taking her time getting ready. Jim sat waiting on the porch, looking for Kayla's car down the neat street. Over the years, this area of Greenville had slowly grown more respectable. People who aspired to Armitage but couldn't quite afford it—newlyweds and young professionals fleeing Boston's impossible prices—had moved to this section of town with its large bungalows and big maples and begun to make it an area where people prided themselves on the neatness of their hedges and the freshness of their paint jobs. Angela accused them of boosting taxes. Jim sighed. At least property values were increasing. He even liked the new neighbors. They put in native species; they didn't use pesticides; they picked up after their dogs. In the winter, the young couple next door often shoveled Angela's steps before he could and were smart enough to always call her Mrs. French instead of Angela.

Kayla wasn't from this part of Greenville. She and her large family lived in what was still known, with literal and figurative exactness, as the other side of the tracks. Jim had never seen her house or met her mother. He'd met the father, however, a Cape Verdean who worked in one of the old cotton mills converted now into a factory for fabric spun from recycled soda bottles. Kayla's mother was Brazilian, and they spoke Portuguese at home. He'd found all this out from the guidance counselor at Revere, an old friend he'd approached when he wanted to find someone to spend time with Angela in the afternoons. "I need someone extremely reliable," he'd said, and the counselor had joked wearily, "And you want to hire a teenager?" But she'd immediately suggested Kayla Teixaido. Old beyond her years. Smart and ambitious. "We're going to try to get her a scholarship. But in the meantime, she needs the cash. And a chance to get away from home."

When the girl came to interview for the job, her father drove her. Jim had been impressed. This was parenting he understood, a father wanting to know the people his daughter worked for. Making sure his girl was safe. The father's English was a little uncertain, but he wore a very clean polo shirt and drove an old, spotless Chevy that Kayla said her brothers waxed every week. How many brothers do you have? Angela asked. Six, she said, but she was the oldest and the only girl. Jim and Angela had exchanged a brief glance and hired her on the spot.

She dressed in tight jeans and T-shirts, but nothing too revealing. She pulled her long brown hair back into a neat ponytail and wore discreet jewelry. She was respectful with Angela and even read the books that she gave her, reporting her opinions as soon as she finished. *Pride and Prejudice* was too long. And you knew they were going to end up together. She liked *The Great Gatsby* a little better; it confirmed her suspicions about rich people, who always turned out bad as far as she could tell. When Jim asked Kayla what she wanted to be, she said, "A lawyer. My dad says no one's better at winning arguments than I am, and at least I should make money at it." Jim laughed. Angela was wasting her time on literature with Kayla. In blunt contrast to most teenage girls, Kayla was immune to romance and stories. She was someone attuned to and deeply capable of handling practicalities. He had assured the girl's loyalty with raises given every two months. She now earned twelve dollars an hour, more than twice what he told Angela he was paying. His mother's sense of the minimum wage was frozen somewhere around 1980.

Kayla had rewarded his generosity: she brought Angela books she thought his mother would like, found her a cheaper and better hairstylist, and even convinced her to get her toenails painted. It had been in February, during a grim two-week stretch of sleet that kept the skies gray and the roads slick. Angela had been broody and cantankerous. But one evening, Jim had returned from work to find his mother and Kayla listening to Tommy Dorsey records and drinking tea. "What's the occasion?" he asked as the crooner's voice swayed around the living room. "Look," Kayla crowed. And Angela had shyly revealed her feet, which were gnarled and blue with old veins and fresh, shiny dollops of coral polish on the nails. "Now put your socks on," Kayla scolded, "you'll get cold," then she bent down to pull the warm red socks, her Christmas present to Angela, over his mother's newly sparkling toes.

At dinner that night, he said, "You got your toes painted, Ma." He was touched by Kayla's obvious affection, but still surprised Angela had been coaxed into such an indulgence. Angela had for so long frowned on such fripperies. When his own daughters got their ears pierced at thirteen, she had been horrified. "We're not in the old country anymore, Angela," Jim's ex-wife had said. It had not been a wise comment to make, though it would have been hard to repair the relationship between Carla and his mother at that point.

"Kayla said her friend ran the salon. She said she would clean the footbath for me personally. With bleach. And she did." Angela had eaten some green beans and stared at some indeterminate point over Jim's shoulder. "She's a good girl, Jimmie. I like that girl." Every two weeks since then, Angela and Kayla had made a stop at the nail salon. Sometimes, they even went to Starbucks afterward and got lattes. "Lattes, Ma?" Angela waved her hands and said, "Low-fat, Jimmie, low-fat." Kayla, in short, had been a godsend. He was glad she was only a junior. They would get to have her with them for another year before she went off to college.

Today was a pedicure day, which made it even more unusual that Kayla was late. Angela was getting ready for the outing, finding a pair of earrings that would match a new shade of polish she wanted to try. Jim checked his phone to see if the girl had called and he hadn't gotten the message. He usually wasn't here on a Wednesday but had felt the need to check in with his mother. The last few days had been so unsettling, and he wanted to be sure certain routines were in place. Finally, he saw Kayla's old Nissan come around the top of the block. Her wipers were set a notch higher than they needed to be, which gave him the impression that although her car was going as slowly as usual, she was holding herself back from going fast. "I'm so sorry I'm late, Mr. French," she called up to him through her window the moment she parked in front of the house. She opened the car door, large handbag on one shoulder, ring of keys in her hand. Darting through the rain, she said, "One of my brothers was sick this afternoon, and I had to help my mom get him to the doctor."

Jim dealt with teenagers on a regular basis; he'd raised two girls, and he saw and talked to all those kids at Armitage. He was almost certain Kayla was lying. Her hair was damp, too, as if she'd just jumped out of the shower, though she might merely have been caught in the downpour.

"That's okay, Kayla. I hope he's all right."

"Oh, he'll be fine," she said and shoved the keys in her bag. "How's Mrs. French?" Jim sensed that the change of subject was calculated. She was doing her best to scramble to safer ground as fast as possible.

"Doing well," he answered slowly, wondering if he should say something to the girl. A direct approach certainly wouldn't work, but maybe he could try something oblique. "She's looking forward to getting her toes done."

"Is she ready? Should I go and help her?" Again, Jim got a sharp feeling that she wanted to get away from him quickly. From his occasional visits during the afternoon, Jim knew the routine was well established. Kayla would either wait on the porch or in the living room until Angela was fully prepared for her outing, the understanding being that Angela didn't require actual assistance getting ready, that Kayla was merely a companion and not a helper.

"No, she's in good shape. She'll be down in a minute. She napped today, and she said her hair was a mess." They both smiled. Angela was terribly proud of her still glossy hair, which she had set in fat, abundant curls every week. It had to obtain absolute smoothness before she'd let herself be seen in public. Kayla sat nervously in one of the rockers on the porch, her hands in a lump on her lap, her bag in a lump on the floor. They could hear Angela singing to herself, probably some Sinatra. Looking at Kayla, Jim realized just how young she was. Her skin was a light coffee color, absolutely flawless.

"Maybe you could get her to listen to something a little more current, like the Beatles or Simon and Garfunkel," Jim joked. "You can get her to do anything."

Kayla's shoulders grew a little less tense. "I'll try, Mr. French." She probably would, too, thought Jim. She had a fairly literal mind and took all her responsibilities seriously.

"Just no hip-hop," he added. "It might not be good for her heart. And I don't think I'm ready for it, either."

The girl smiled and seemed herself for the first time since she'd arrived. There was a long pause, and then, all of a sudden, Kayla leaned forward and said, "Hey, Mr. French, what's it like up there?" And she tilted her head in the general direction of the academy. It wasn't an idle question, which didn't surprise Jim. There was nothing idle about Kayla. He didn't even think she was asking about the murder. She'd meant the question more generally.

He took a breath to start to answer her, but she interrupted him. "I mean, what are the kids like. Are they, I don't know, nice? Are they stuck-up?"

What was the honest answer? Many of them were indeed stuck-up. It was the very word he used himself to describe them, though he supposed the more sanitized term would be *entitled*. Sure of themselves, cocky, spoiled. Those were also words that could label them. But some of them, even some of the richest, weren't that way at all. Some of them were genuinely polite, well brought up, and intelligent. Others, despite wealth and privilege, were sad, lost, even deprived, not so much of material support but of parents who knew anything about them. But what should he say to Kayla? Was she looking for some connection that allowed them, from Greenville, to look down on the snobs? Or was she genuinely curious? He felt protective of the academy, especially when it was so exposed. Then he decided Kayla deserved as close to the truth as he could get.

"Sometimes," he said. "Some of them don't deserve the education they're getting. They think things will always go easily for them. That they'll always get their way. Some of them have a lot of money, but they don't have much more than that, especially parents who think twice about them. And some of them are nice kids, smart kids. I don't know, Kayla. They're a mixed bag, like people everywhere."

She was listening hard. They could hear Angela making her slow, careful way down the stairs. It was one of the only ways you really noticed her age: the slight warble to her voice and this, the hesitation in dealing with steps.

"But they get into trouble just like everybody else," said Kayla and hoisted her bag to her shoulder. "Mr. French, please take off half an hour of my pay this week. I was late, and I shouldn't have been."

"Okay, Kayla," he said, "if that's what you want." Once before, there'd been confusion over her schedule, and that time, too, she had been scrupulous about the money to be docked from her weekly salary. He had tried to add it on anyway, and she had noticed and returned it.

As she went to greet Angela, Jim got the distinct impression Kayla hadn't been talking just about Claire. There'd been no judgment in her voice, just a sad confirmation of news she already knew.

CHAPTER 11

"Could Roderick Charles please get a haircut?" Madeline asked Fred. The chaplain had a bushel of black frizz he wore tied in a leather thong, and tonight it sprang out like a broom at the back of his head. It was early Wednesday evening, and the rain had finally ended, though humidity lingered in a smothering quilt. It was an appropriately sticky atmosphere for what was about to come. The entire school had gathered for a quasi-memorial service for Claire on the Knoll, an area reserved for just this sort of event: outdoor performance, the more New Agey of celebrations. Once a year, the school's pets were blessed here, by the same Roderick Charles, chaplain, in flowing robes he claimed to have worn while ministering to the Sioux. But to Fred, the connection between Plains Indians and the dozens of chocolate Labs who constituted the vast majority of the pet community at Armitage remained obscure. He had thought for sure that Roderick would cancel the event after the time Dewey, Mary Manchester's Jack Russell, nearly took his nose off. But unfortunately, not even pain and plastic surgery had persuaded Roderick to forgo the ceremony.

Now he cleared his wide throat in preparation for welcoming the community to the service. "How did Roderick ever get hired?" Madeline had asked Fred early in the year during a talk in which he quoted Kahlil Gibran to vast excess. "He's an alum," Fred had told her, "and his father basically owns Ohio. He predates Porter." That apparently was enough to earn Roderick a role on campus, though his work was augmented by an ecumenical and far more serious complement of rabbis, a Buddhist or two, and a couple of Episcopalian priests. No one took Roderick seriously. He was rumored to be on Porter's list of Faculty Not Asked Back, but his fate wouldn't be known until the last few days of school, when all such departures were aired at another Armitage institution, Last Tea.

The wind was blowing, heavy and warm. "No," said Fred, thinking about Madeline's question. "Roderick's entire personality lies in that hair. Not happening."

"Well, he ought to chop it all off," Madeline said crossly and picked at a scrap of food on her shirt. "I'm fried and I'm cranky, Fred. I'm sorry. I don't mean to be rude. Roderick's doing his best. This is just all really hard." Fred had missed seeing Madeline the past few days and wanted to ask her about the e-mail she had sent. Madeline was not particularly dramatic; if she said something was weird, it probably was. She looked out of sorts, and he was visited with a desire to wrap her close.

But there were a lot of good reasons why that was not a good idea—all of their students watching them; the event's sad occasion; and news of his own he wasn't quite prepared to share—and he distracted himself from Madeline's shoulders by looking at the crowd. Students stood in the first ring nearest Roderick, with faculty in a second, taller circle around them. They were clutching the tapers that the chaplain had solemnly placed in their hands as they'd arrived, though matches had yet to be provided. All of us, thought Fred, look beaten up. Even the kids had hollows beneath their eyes and were glancing cautiously about one another. Then Roderick started booming away at them, and Fred saw that Madeline was trying to pay attention.

The chaplain was holding forth about the sanctity of life, and reincarnation was probably to come; it had been cropping up a lot more in his homilies of late. He'd been to India last year, on what he insisted on calling a pilgrimage to some of the great places of the spirit, and the visit was having lingering effects.

But then Porter arrived behind him and discreetly displaced Roderick at his makeshift podium. Roddy the Shoddy, as the kids called him, looked like he was going to pout, but what was there to do? Porter was the head. Porter could do as he wished, and that was what made him stand out. Behind him stood Lucinda, his wife. She was rarely in the mix at the school, though this kind of gathering was required if anything was. Often, she claimed her burgeoning landscape gardening business kept her occupied, but Fred knew better. At a faculty Christmas party one year, with perhaps half a glass of wine too much in her, she had told Fred they had let go of the staff that had come with the job, the accoutrements that would have lined their lives with a nearly royal level of privilege. A limo and driver, a valet, a cook. Lucinda had consented to help from a housekeeper once a week because the house was so large, but rejected everything else. "Who do they think he is?" she'd said to Fred. "Some bishop?" Fred thought that even that level of assistance bothered her; she didn't like people prying into their closets or peering under the rugs. Having access to intimate details when they shouldn't. After years at independent schools, living in such closeness to others, she guarded her family's private lives with the wariness and weariness of a politician's wife.

Fred, with his background as a kid who'd grown up in the shadow of Armitage, understood Lucinda with more sympathy than most. She had a reputation for coldness, but he thought it was more self-protective than that. He wondered if Porter had ever wanted to do something else, as Lucinda clearly had. If Porter had ever wrestled with leaving this cloistered world. Fred doubted it as he watched Porter lean to light a candle and then pass it to Roderick to start the chain of light around the circle. The man had had his ambitions and he had doggedly pursued them. From everything Fred knew about him, Porter had discreetly and persistently chased a prestigious headship for years, working his way through administrative posts at just the right sorts of schools, earning a reputation for excellent leadership, the ability to manage crises, raise money, recruit and retain good teachers. When the opening came at Armitage, he'd been the natural choice. How much had Lucinda been part of that choosing? What had her feelings been? Maybe it had come down to practicalities. Porter's position meant, among other things, that her three boys would basically have a free education at one of the country's best schools. That alone would have made the position hard to turn down. Where was Miles, their youngest? He often stood with his parents at this kind of event, even when he could have mingled with kids his own age. They were a close family, and Fred was surprised not to see them together at such a moment. Maybe Miles was keeping his head low for the time being. There'd been an incident at a recent lacrosse match, his coach had said last week, during which Miles had pegged a player on the opposing team with unnecessary aggression and been ejected from the game. Still, if anything could pull a family together, it would be something like Claire's death.

The tapers flickered into brightness around the Knoll, just as the sun was going down. Many of them went out as soon as they were lighted, given the fitful wind. Roddy's had spilled a great quantity of hot wax on his large hand, and he was hopping from foot to foot in pain. Porter did not hold a candle once he'd passed his on. Lucinda stood close behind him, also candleless.

He said to them, "Thank you for gathering tonight. We are going to have a service for Claire at her parents' request in the chapel this Sunday, so right now, I want to say only a few things to you. First, thank you. Thank you for being brave in almost unimaginable circumstances." He paused and looked around, and so did Fred and Madeline. The girls who had been in Claire's dorm had their heads bent, Fred noticed. "But look at those boys from Greaves," Madeline whispered. Fred had already noticed. They were restless and mobile. Something was stirring them up. With a beleaguered air, Joyce Phelan hissed something that made them stop, except for Scotty Johnston, who glared at Porter with what looked like personal malevolence. Porter appeared not to notice, however, and went on, his hair blown back from his forehead. "I need you to understand that we don't know yet what happened. Or why. And that all of this will take years for us to accept. It has changed us in ways we can't imagine." What mattered now, he said, was that they do what they aspired to do at the school, which was to act as a community. To treat one another with respect and care. And to remain both courageous and flexible. "I can't even guarantee you a proper graduation. It will depend on what happens in the next few days. All I can promise is that I will do my best as your headmaster to support and sustain you. I ask you to provide even more important support to each other. We must in this moment sustain one another. You will face other difficulties in life; you may have already faced them—but this will be among the most important. It will matter how you behave, and we are here to help you do your best."

They were listening; they were all listening. Even Scotty Johnston had grown still, though he continued glowering in Porter's direction. Then one of the programs caught fire and had to be stamped on until it flared out. One of the girls in Madeline's dorm read a poem about grief by Edna St. Vincent Millay that made Madeline sniff with some scorn.

Finally, a girl named Beatrice got up to sing a song a cappella, and Fred braced himself for the discomfort of cracked and faltering notes, unachieved high Cs. Madeline turned to him and cringed slightly. They shared this fear of unaccompanied singing, to which boarding schools seemed attached despite the fact these performances so often went awry. They had nearly fled a wobbly rendition of "The Circle Game" in chapel a few weeks ago. But this girl, a freshman he had never seen, turned out to have one of the purest voices Fred had ever heard, and in spite of himself, he felt his throat tighten with the sadness of "Amazing Grace." A group of girls began to sob on the other side of the Knoll, and the boys had their heads hung low, to keep people from seeing their faces.

To distract himself, Fred forced himself to watch the crowd and noticed a couple of details that seemed out of place. First, Tamsin Lovell was standing to Porter's left and a few people behind. Curious: she rarely turned out for after-hours events. As it was, she was well away from Lucinda, who was rumored to loathe her. What was interesting about Tamsin, and why he secretly would have loved the chance to paint her, was the completeness of her composure. Tamsin had an English accent that made most Americans back off in submission, a pair of sharp black eyeglasses, and a manner so precise as to be almost abrasive. She had a horror of what she dismissively called office banter. She staved off chaos with perfect diction, an immaculate understanding of boarding school etiquette, and strongly protective sensibilities toward Porter. Fred knew this about her because he'd tried to be friendly with her, with, it had to be admitted, the ulterior motive of attempting to find out if she were single. She was attractive, curiously sexy in a prim way. But she had rebuffed him and everyone else who'd come knocking, and he'd long ago given up anything but watching to see what she had up her sleeve.

Tonight, she herself was scanning the crowd and kept glancing over at Scotty Johnston. Sarah Talmadge had once told Fred that Tamsin had the best reference letters she'd ever seen. So glowing they had made her suspicious enough to call each writer to confirm the accolades. Tamsin had been with Porter for three years, and Fred wondered if he would be lucky enough to keep her around for much longer. She had real abilities. Work as a secretary wouldn't satisfy her hunger much longer, nor would life in a small New England town. What Tamsin's goals were, however, he couldn't exactly say.

The other thing Fred noticed was that those two police officers were there. The tall, scrawny one with a rather disgusted look on his face and Detective Corelli. His expression was far more difficult to read. He, like Tamsin, was watching the crowd, paying particular attention to the faculty. His face was harder than Fred had first thought, but that might have been the light, which was fading. The night was growing cooler. Beatrice, fortunately, had reached the end of the spiritual. Roderick was bustling back to the podium. Porter looked wrung out. Lucinda was already turning to leave. Then Fred saw the dark officer's eyes rest on Madeline and watched, with some degree of worry, how much more relaxed his face suddenly became. "Ow," said Madeline as she zipped up her jacket. "Somehow I managed to scrape my thumb." She untangled herself and obviously had no idea the officer was watching her. But the man kept his eyes on her, even as the other policeman leaned down to talk to him. He nodded in response to his partner's words but kept his eyes trained on Madeline.

"Come on, Fred, let's get out of here," she said, still oblivious, as the students dispersed in ragged little knots. "I can't bear another minute of this," a feeling that Fred at that moment wholeheartedly shared. How callous of me, he thought, to be worried about a rival for the affections of a woman to whom I haven't even declared myself. Claire is dead, her baby is gone, but my mind is somewhere else entirely. "Hey, want to meet at Mackey's around ten?" he asked, and she said, "Just what I was thinking. I'm going to run screaming naked into the Bluestone if I don't get out of here," a very distracting image.

"Think there'll be police or reporters down there?" she asked. "Ah, who cares? We can wear disguises in case they're staking it out." They both knew this was unlikely. Mackey's was so local most locals didn't know where it was. Still, it was a good instinct. They needed a break. The gloom and anxiety that had descended over the campus had agitated everyone; tempers were fraying. Despite the tumult of the investigation, there was still no news about how the process was moving forward. Fred saw the pair of cops walk slowly toward Porter, cornering him yet again.

Madeline had a hard time understanding Fred's pleasure in this life, and Claire's death and the horror it unleashed had only compounded her misgivings, he guessed. Even when students weren't dying, there were Saturday classes, and if you coached, you often had to travel most of that day to some dreary corner of New England with your football or tennis players, and by evening, you were worn to the bone. Dorm duty, teaching, sports, the endless exhortation toward excellence, it was enough to drive a lot of people straight back to day schools or out of teaching altogether.

Yet despite all the work and the mounting fatigue as the year drew on, this world was what Fred knew, where he had prospered, and what, he had to admit, he liked. The slow, awkward mastery of perspective his students reliably gained each semester; the increasingly crisp plays on soccer fields on fall afternoons; the clear, orderly flow of days. Even when his mind was tugged toward Edward Smith or Scotty Johnston, not to mention Claire, he could look at the school's world and feel grateful to be part of it, especially now there was the possibility of not staying. That was another reason he'd wanted to talk to Madeline in a slightly more secluded setting.

It had started to rain again by the time he convinced the cops to let him off campus and arrived at the bar. Madeline's beat-up Camry wasn't there yet. He had begun going to Mackey's, a bar on the border of Greenville and Armitage, with a colleague who had later taken a job as a dean at another boarding school. He'd tipped Fred off to the place in the same way that kids handed down keys to dorms or copies of old exams. Information that let you survive somewhere because you possessed one or two of its secrets. At Mackey's, he never ran into anyone from the academy. Cheap beer, good burgers, Sox and Pats on the tube, no hassle. Basically, no Armitage, just regular life. Sometimes Fred went alone, to be reminded there were other ways to live than at a privileged institution; sometimes he roped in a few young colleagues smart enough not to make a big deal over a great hangout. They had a good time, and never drank enough to be in trouble with the police, hangovers, or locals. A safe release, jealously guarded.

Fred was happy to find the bar almost empty. Until he sat down on a stool and let his shoulders slump, he hadn't realized how tense he was. He ordered a draft Guinness and knew Madeline would do the same. They shared a taste for dark beer. Only three other customers loitered in a booth. Business might pick up a little later—the Sox were playing on the West Coast tonight, and the game started late—but it could trickle along like this all evening. He wondered how the owner, whose name was Bill Price, not Mackey, managed to make a living.

No one smoked in bars anymore, which made tranquil ones good places to think. There was a lot to stew over. Claire's death. Her missing child. He had heard nothing, and students often talked to him. But this they had kept entirely to themselves. He and his roommates had harbored a Maltese puppy in their room for a year and only revealed it the day of graduation to a combination of outrage and laughter. Bonger had lived with Fred's family afterward, had his name changed to Quincy, and was still toddling around his parents' house. But stashing a small animal in a dorm room was nothing compared to hiding a pregnancy and a child. He caught the Greenville guys staring at him and felt momentarily self-conscious. One glance was all it took; they knew instantly where he was from, but there was little more weight to the look than that, even with all that was happening up at the academy. This was what he most appreciated about Mackey's. Everyone's business remained private. People came to brood, chat with friends, drink the good draft beer. He sipped his Guinness and waited for Madeline.

She arrived with her usual gustiness, slamming the door without quite meaning to. Briefly, the men in the booth swiveled to assess the noise and the fact of a woman in their bar; with their usual disinterest, they turned away, though a bit slowly. She looked pretty tonight, flushed and dark-eyed. "Hey," she called, "sorry I'm

late. Got accosted by Grace Face. And it's raining hard again."
Everyone had nicknames, usually not just one but several, often
nonsensical, sometimes mean-spirited, sometimes incredibly apt.
Scary Mary, for instance, suited the librarian perfectly. An acid-
tongued math teacher named Marcus Lyle was known as Mr. Vile.
Fred didn't know what his was and hadn't heard one for Madeline,
either, though he knew they'd been dubbed. Everyone was. It was
prudent to be unaware of some things.

"What did she say?" Fred asked after making room at the bar
for Madeline and helping her with her raincoat. "This coat is
about nine times too big for you."

"I know," she sighed, gesturing to the bartender to order her
Guinness. "It was my dad's. I've had it forever. It'll have to shred
before I admit it's had its day." Even disentangling herself from
a cloud of damp khaki cotton, she was so vivacious. It was getting
harder and harder to ignore that. But what had emerged between
them first was good conversation. They liked talking to each
other. He badly wanted to tell her what had arrived in his in-box
today. He might, with more beer in him, even tell her about looking in the archives for information about Llewellan. Madeline
could be trusted with dark moments in people's characters; she
confessed her own with such disarming, attractive frankness. "As
for Grace, she told me she didn't think it was an appropriate time
to go and amuse myself. We had the students to think of. Then
she got all purple when I told her I realized that, but that there
weren't any students left in our dorm, so who could it hurt if I got
off campus for a while."

Fred smiled. He could imagine how well Grace took that, but
then Madeline jumped and grabbed Fred's arm. "Oh, my God,

this just happened, too. I bumped into Joyce Phelan in the parking lot and she said Scotty Johnston got taken in by the police again."

Fred was ashamed at the flush of pleasure that coursed through him, at both Madeline's touch and at the news she'd just relayed. But he was also surprised. That wasn't right. Scotty was too controlled for killing and too oriented toward his own success. And Fred had this intuition as well. The boy had really been in love with Claire, not that that would prevent someone from doing fatal damage in the grip of red rage. But Scotty had been solicitous of the girl, a quality distinctly lacking in the way he treated everyone else. Fred had seen them together last spring and been astonished at the gentle way the boy helped her get up from the lawn, touching her outstretched hand with unfeigned care. Fred knew, too, that he had far less information than the police and that boyfriends were more often than not the culprits in these cases. The dark detective seemed intelligent, although there were rumors about him, too. Another Armitage student gone wrong.

Madeline grabbed a plastic menu, glanced at it, and politely asked the bartender for a burger, medium rare. "What do I know, but I don't think he did it. I think he's really bad news, but not a murderer." She slurped her beer.

Fred said, "Ditto," and then told her what he had seen on the Quad. Madeline agreed and sipped more beer. "He used to stare at her in chapel," she said. "But almost everyone did. Fred, can you believe we didn't notice? These days, people are so proud of being pregnant; women wear Spandex to show off their bumps, and here was Claire, tucking herself under boys' oxfords to hide hers. If she had much of one. Porter looks devastated."

"I know," Fred said and spun a cardboard coaster on its edge. "He's taking it personally. But everyone else looks like they're"— and here he searched for a word—"shuffling. Dodging blame."

"I know," Madeline said morosely. "And that's what's eating me. All this rhetoric about honesty and responsibility, and here they are, kids and adults, subtly not honoring one bit of it." It was what got her every time, Fred knew. The contradiction between Armitage's lofty mission and the far more political and practical aims of the students and their parents. But there's Porter, he'd say, and Sarah, and that brilliant kid from the South Side and this one from Guatemala, and she would agree and say, I know, but I still can't quite justify all the self-congratulation. She slumped a little further. The smell of her grilling hamburger rose from the small kitchen. The group of three men in the booth ordered another round. "And then Claire. She did something really unusual. She wanted to deceive everyone around her, but she kept that baby when it would have been a lot easier not to. Fred, what I can't help thinking is that she was operating with some strange if misguided notion of integrity."

"I know what you're getting at, Madeline, but Claire was darker than that. Meaner. She was up to something," Fred said.

"That's for sure," Madeline and told him about her visit from Lee, the Reign of Terror, Claire's transgression, and then the spool of thread and the Robespierre quotation that had shown up in her car. She tried to sound jaunty about the whole thing, as if treating it all like a prank would make it less menacing.

"That is really creepy, but I don't know much," he said. "The girls clammed up about it. It was something they took really seriously."

Madeline's burger arrived with a full complement of fries, which she hadn't ordered but accepted anyway.

"Did you know anyone involved?" Madeline was listening very carefully, so absorbed she wasn't even nibbling at the fries.

"Everyone knew who the Robespierre was, but that was about it," Fred said uncomfortably.

Madeline finally picked up a potato and munched it. "Maybe Claire actually dying really frightened them. Maybe they realized they were going to be uncovered—who knew what Sally and those other girls were going to say—and they decided to act preemptively." She ate another fry, paused to plonk out the ketchup, and added, "With me, the intern, as their confessor. They had to know I'd have to divulge what they'd said. But that quotation." Madeline shivered. "That is really unnerving. It means they've been watching me. I've been locking my windows since."

"Have you told the cops?" Fred asked, thinking of the detective who had been looking at Madeline. He sounded a little sharper than he meant to.

"Yes," she said, "I talked to the police, but not about the thread in the car. I'm hoping they get bored with trying to intimidate me and find someone else to bother. But I did think about telling Rob or Sarah."

Rob Barlow, the dean of students, blocky and desperately by the book, was ostensibly the person she should turn to. But neither of them thought for a moment that he'd respond effectively, which left Sarah Talmadge, a person everyone liked and respected. She was absolutely the person to tell, but after a moment, Madeline shook her head no. "Poor woman. She's totally overwhelmed right now. I'll talk with her about it later. And maybe they'll stop."

For a moment, they were silent and focused on the fries. They were salty, greasy, bad for you, and entirely delicious. "I'm ravenous these days," Madeline said, tucking now into her meat. "I feel a little guilty about it. It seems wrong. Victorian heroines lose their appetites when dramatic things happen. I'm just the opposite. I start to chow down. It is so good to get out of there." She ate another fry and peered at him. "How are you, Fred? You're hunched over like someone might try and steal that Guinness," she said and made a false swipe at his mug.

He batted her away playfully, but she was right. He was feeling self-protective, scrutinized, not sure what was next. Without quite meaning to, he blurted, "I got some interesting news today. Seems sort of wrong to be excited about it, given everything going on, but I am." A friend from graduate school had written, he explained. He needed a roommate in a Williamsburg loft, starting late June. It was unbelievably cheap. If Fred could get permission from his dorm head, he was going to go down later this week.

He looked at Madeline. She had stopped chewing. Was he wrong or did she look downcast? She put down her burger and nibbled the wan pickle. That was definitely a sign of distraction. Madeline always gave him her pickles. "And?" she asked, crunching away.

"And," he said, "I'm thinking about it." He'd saved enough the last four years to take the loft, live frugally, and not work for a year at anything but his painting. Although teachers at Armitage weren't paid an enormous amount, it was possible to stash rather a lot of money when rent and food were covered. How these schools explained away all that unaccounted-for income to the IRS was anyone's guess. Still, he'd squirreled away some cash.

He'd done the math this afternoon, and there was no way to avoid the data. Having not spent much on anything but clothing, Saturday nights at Mackey's, and a few vacations, he had enough. A year wasn't long, but it was a lot better than trying to cram in his art during weekends, vacations, summers. He'd have to go and see for himself, and arrange for a leave from the academy, but the loft looked gorgeous from the pictures his friend had sent. Madeline, he noticed with a certain pleasure, continued to chomp on her pickle and stare in the mirror over the bar. Its surface was mostly covered with decals and stickers for the Patriots, Celtics, and Sox, but Fred could still make out the disconsolate cast of her mouth.

"Oh, Fred," she said, "you should do it. Get out of here. You know you should. I look at people like Forrest Thompson, and I think, Wow, he probably used to be a nice guy. But he stayed too long and he turned into a . . ." Here her hands started to flap and she dropped the half-eaten pickle. "A wing chair. He's a wing chair. Not a person anymore, but something stuffed." She noticed the pickle then and said, "Look at that. I was so upset I was eating a pickle. That never happens.

"You probably don't want this now, but here it is," she said, tossing him what was left. Then she ordered another Guinness. "You may have to drive me home tonight, Fred. But what I'm thinking, very selfishly, is this. Jobs are designed to drive people insane. It is just how it is. I know," she said, holding up her hand in protest, "I haven't had many of them. But I'm aware of this. For instance, things would have been a lot worse this year if we hadn't played faculty bingo."

Faculty bingo was something that Fred and Madeline had come up with one night in October at Mackey's. It consisted of a grid with Porter's initials at the center and a random scattering of initials belonging to other faculty members in the rest of the squares. If someone on your card spoke during the faculty meeting, you crossed off the name. You could, they'd agreed, provoke someone to talk with a bogus question, and it was delightful to see how teachers swelled with pride when asked to elaborate on, say, the value of the physics AP or an extended period for volleyball. When you achieved a row, you staged a coughing fit that meant you had won.

It was juvenile. It was beneath them. It was hilarious. In any case, it had whiled away quite a few dull Friday afternoons. Then, after Christmas break, Harvey had nearly caught them, and they'd given it up. Madeline continued, "Sarah was hinting that she needed to see me. She might ask me to stay on. That's what I think is going to happen at least, and, Fred, if you're not here, it just isn't as interesting. And after all the flak I've given you all year about this place, here you are thinking about going and I'm contemplating staying. But, you know, I like talking about poetry all day. Where else but a serious classroom would I get to do that? And I like a lot of the kids. A lot of them care about learning. There's something pure about all that effort. And it's better than what's waiting in Boston." She blushed hotly. "It seems horrible to be thinking about our futures after everything that's happened, and I'm really being selfish because if I'm honest I don't want you to go and enjoy yourself and do art and have a ball in New York because . . ." Here she stopped and ate another mouthful of burger to keep herself from saying something more revealing.

Because they both knew she had been about to say "because I'm going to miss you," and this was certainly not the time to be embarking on something as delicate as discussing feelings that might be mutual. Fred burned with happiness. But it was so confusing. There was nothing much either of them dared say right now. He drank down a gulp of Guinness, Madeline gloomily ate fries and ordered another plateful for them to share. Gradually, he became conscious that the men in the booth were speaking a language other than English in a soft, lilting rhythm that might have been Spanish but wasn't.

"Portuguese," said Madeline, having noticed that Fred was listening to them. "My mother lives near New Bedford, and when I visit, all you can get on the radio are Portuguese stations. That's what those guys are speaking." Fred looked at the men a little more closely. Cape Verdeans, perhaps, workers in the last of the Greenville mills. They were neatly and simply dressed and drinking Budweiser from bottles. All of them had on Red Sox caps and appeared to be watching the game. Often, Fred and Madeline would stay out long enough to hoot Boston toward victory, but that wouldn't happen tonight.

Fred was about to ask Madeline if she wanted to go back when the door to the bar swung open with almost as much violence as it had when Madeline arrived. A girl with long hair flew in and brought with her a gust of hard rain. She glanced around the room and found the three men at the booth. Darting over to the oldest of them, she spoke rapidly in Portuguese. Then the girl happened to spin around and see Fred and Madeline looking at her. There was no reason they shouldn't have; she had burst in so suddenly. But when she returned their glance, all that filled her face was terror. For some reason, she was frightened of them. She ran out of the bar as fast as she'd arrived, followed by the man she had spoken to so urgently. He threw a few bills on the table, murmured what was probably an apology to his friends, and turned to follow the girl without casting a look at anyone else. Fred saw that Madeline was staring at the door, and she was frowning. "Do you know who she was?" she asked.

Fred shrugged. "Never seen her before. But she was pretty upset to see us. How about you?"

Madeline pulled on her baggy raincoat. "No," she said. Fred asked Bill Price for the check. He and Madeline fished out the money each owed. Passing him the cash, Fred asked the owner if he knew who the girl and the man were.

Bill said, "No clue. He and his buddies come in once in a while to watch baseball. Never seen the kid before." He wiped down the bar, cleared their plates. Madeline had eaten every fry.

Outside, the wind blew loudly, whipping Madeline's raincoat into a series of tan sails that threatened to fill and whisk her off to the next county. She waved to him, said good-bye. They wouldn't talk tonight; the weather was too disturbed and their moods as well. There was no sign of the girl or the man.

Fred didn't sleep well, tossing as he thought about the Brooklyn loft, Madeline and the spool of thread, the wild fear in the girl's eyes. He thought, too, about Llewellan and Edward Smith until he finally slept near dawn and dreamed in what he later remembered as the hiss of Portuguese.

CHAPTER 12

I t was the third time that Matt had sat in a room with Scotty Johnston, and each time he liked him less, which was quite astonishing given that he had really disliked him the first time he met the kid. Scotty looked a great deal like his father. Tall and aggressively fit, with a shock of blond hair, a lean jaw, and blue eyes notable for their lack of humanity. What a trait to pass on, Matt thought, contempt for the human race. If you really felt it that strongly, it would be hard to choose to have children, who would also be forced to deal with all the inferior people occupying the world. But Mr. Johnston, as he frequently reminded Matt and Vernon, was the father of four boys, which was very different, Vernon had noted at one point, from saying you had four kids you really cared about.

They had chosen the smallest, most claustrophobic interrogation room. Vernon and Matt were tall, but Scott and Mr. Johnston were of the looming sort of huge, and the room felt clammy and tight. The white walls were scuffed, the plastic chairs deeply uncomfortable, and the fluorescent lights gave you a new feeling for the word *institutional*. The décor, such as it was, was intended to remind everyone that outside the day was beautiful, hot, and clear after the rainstorm. How much more pleasant it would be for Scott to simply admit what he knew and get back outdoors to enjoy this gorgeous Thursday morning. Vernon lounged on a chair, almost getting it to the point where it tilted on two legs into the wall. Matt's chair remained firmly grounded, but he knew how Vernon felt. It was hard to take the self-important bluster of the man in front of them entirely seriously. Yet it was also very clear that in his tightly bunched fists Scotty was holding on hard to quite a bit of necessary information.

"Scott, Mr. Johnston," said Matt, trying to sound equable. "We know Scotty has been through a lot. By all accounts, he and Claire were close. And we don't want to interrupt his return to classes." Was this laying it on? Vernon lifted an eyebrow, but Matt thought he could probably get away with it. Irony was a quality to which neither of the Johnstons appeared susceptible. Perhaps that, like their height and Nordic coloring, was genetic. "We also know," he continued, holding up a hand to block the oncoming train of protest Mr. Johnston was about to release, "that none of our discussions are taped, recorded, or otherwise on record because Scott is a minor until September. But Scott knew Claire better than anyone, and we feel it's important to be sure we understand her from his perspective."

That quelled the elder Johnston for a moment and allowed Matt to ask, "What about the Reign of Terror? Were they involved in all this?" Vernon pursed his mouth; he'd had the group explained to him and added it to a growing list of reasons why he'd never send his own girls to private school. Mr. Johnston merely looked confused, as if wondering what the French Revolution had to do with Claire's death. But the question appeared to alarm Scotty not at all, and for once, he just answered. He shifted his large shoulders forward and said, "No. Claire was sick of them all. Sick of all the stupid shit they got up to." Matt wondered when parents had stopped minding if their children swore in front of adults. His own father, Joseph, had slapped him in the face once for swearing in a parking lot after Matt slammed his thumb in the car door. Even extreme pain didn't justify that kind of slackness.

"And what kind of shit did they get up to?" Vernon asked, still tilted, arms behind his head.

Scotty shrugged. "Idiotic things like telling girls what they could and couldn't wear. Where they could sit in the Commons or the library. Claire could have cared less. She didn't want to be Robespierre. But if they pick you, it's hard to refuse. They tried to boss her around, tell her what she had to do as head, but she didn't listen. It pissed them off." Mr. Johnston was clearly not following a word of this, though for the moment he refrained from barging into the conversation.

"Enough for them to kill her or take her baby?" Matt asked. Since Madeline had told him on Tuesday about the possibility that the Reign was involved, he had tried to corner each of the girls she'd named, as well as the new recruits Claire had initiated. But three of the four new ones were still under a doctor's care; the fourth had been whisked off campus. Of the other girls, two had had their parents retain lawyers and two had left early, citing stress.

Scotty shook his head. "No, I don't think so. I don't know how it happened, but I don't think it was them." His eyes looked glazed, and he hunched farther forward. Claire's death, its utter realness, kept striking him at unanticipated moments, Matt suspected.

"So who does, Scott?" Vernon said. The front legs of his chair hit the linoleum with a clang, and he stood up slowly to his full height. "That's what we need to find out. More precisely, what we need is for someone to tell us who fucked Claire. Because my guess is that the same guy who fucked her also killed her."

No one in the room, probably not even Scotty, expected what happened next. In a flash, the boy stood, grabbed the desk where he was sitting, and hurled the entire sizable piece of furniture at Vernon's head. It was mostly plastic, but some of it was steel and it came very close to connecting with Vernon, who, lucky for him, had excellent reflexes and got out of the way. The desk crashed into the wall, and its metal legs vibrated as if it were an ungainly, robotic insect stuck on its back.

"Shut the fuck up!" Scotty shouted. He was standing, dark red in the face and neck, chest heaving, hands open and ready to grab. Matt stood as well and walked deliberately to the other side of the room to right the desk. Vernon adjusted his tie, quite collected given that a large piece of office equipment had just been flung at him. "Just shut the fuck up," Scotty roared.

For once, Mr. Johnston appeared subdued. He went over to his son and tried to comfort him, but Scotty swatted away his father's hand. "Let's go home, Scott," Mr. Johnston urged, and Scotty screamed, "No fucking way. I am not going anywhere but school." His volume was impressively constant.

"We'll let you resolve Scott's destination," Matt said, "but please tell us where we'll be able to find him. We'll need to talk with you both again sometime soon."

Vernon and Matt went slowly down the hall toward their office. Vernon was sending a text. "What are you doing?" Matt asked.

"Getting you some lunch. We're taking twenty minutes outside before we go back up there. Your turkey sub will be here momentarily. I even got you Diet Coke," Vernon said, though he shuddered slightly as he admitted that detail. He reached into the short fridge he had brought in from home and took out his brown-bagged meal.

The office icebox was a far too scary and carnivorous environment to which to entrust his clean food.

Matt smiled, and they headed toward the parking lot and the picnic bench there to wait for Matt's sandwich. "What I like about you, Vernon, is that, for a vegetarian, you're not that judgmental." The temperature was verging on uncomfortably warm, and the leaves of the linden trees had unfolded to their full, heart-shaped green. The air was flecked with insects. Still, it was a far better idea to talk outside the station. Vernon dusted a yellow jacket off his sleeve. "I'm a vegan, not just a vegetarian, and you're wrong. I am totally judgmental. But that doesn't mean I don't know what you need to function."

They sat at the picnic table. Vernon was glancing into the paper bag and removing a series of complicated little glass pots with tight lids that Kathy had assembled for him. Unsnapping a lid, Vernon peered in and said "Quinoa" without a lot of enthusiasm. There were days, Matt knew, when despite his most recent statement, it would have been quick work to steer Vernon toward a cheeseburger. Nonetheless, he gamely started to munch away on his whole grains, and Matt said, "Delicate choice of words back there. Scotty remained so relaxed, so in control."

"I think he broke the desk. Can we send a bill to the father?" Vernon asked. "I was actually very proud of the fact that I resisted the temptation to arrest him for harassing an officer."

"Yes, that showed real strength of character. And I think it was a move that allowed us to learn some interesting things. One, Claire didn't take the Reign of Terror seriously but the other girls did. Why was that?"

Vernon shrugged. "She was already queen of the world, the real Marie Antoinette, and she didn't think they could do anything to her." He began to eat some celery sticks. "Your lunch is here," he said, looking behind Matt. A uniformed officer had brought it out, and Matt thanked him and gave him the cash needed to pay the delivery kid at the entrance to the station. "May I point out another benefit to the meat-eating life?" Matt said. "It's a lot less noisy." Vernon made no effort to stop crunching his pale stalks.

Matt unwrapped his sub and popped open the Diet Coke. After a sip, he said, "There were two other items. Scotty said he didn't know how she had been killed. How it had happened. But he didn't say he didn't know who had done it. And he had no intention of going home. He plans to stay put." He ate some turkey and looked at the brick cube of the station. People passed in front of windows, a human hive of industry tracking clues and mapping patterns and looking just as primitive as the bees beginning to huddle around his soda. FBI in their shiny shoes clacking up and down halls. If anything, Matt had more faith in the efficacy of the insects. Vernon took off his jacket, folded it under his head, and stretched out on the bench. Matt did the same on the opposite side and immediately felt better. It was good to be horizontal, and the overhanging edge of the table provided some relief from the sun.

They both knew this reprieve was limited. But it was necessary to take short breaks, think through things aloud, and plan small, concrete next steps. They didn't need, however, to discuss how much they didn't know, a point the media in every form had insisted on making repeatedly. Even after three days of exhaustive searching, the case had turned up remarkably little hard evidence. The laptops and phones were still being scanned but so far had revealed nothing. These kids, savvy as they were, must have realized how easily traced all these electronics were. This might be the rare case that didn't have an Internet shadow, though Claire could have had and probably did have accounts under assumed names that they hadn't yet found. Scotty was stonewalling, an effort that almost everyone at Armitage had joined him in, along with the doctors and lawyers and parents intent on preventing access to their sensitive charges. The autopsy results had yet to be completed, and the one alluring clue, a bloody rag a handyman had found in the basement, was still at the lab. Norm Parker was taking his usual endless amount of time. The computers that the art teacher had told them about in the basement had already been removed by the time he told the cops; they'd been hauled out the next morning to Paul Revere, glad for the donation of barely used technology. All the rain had made it difficult for a complete search of the campus to go forward, and it had wiped out remnants of footprints and smells. As for the baby, it was so disheartening that it was almost better not to think about it. Despite calls coming from New Jersey to the Bahamas, the FBI had not found one viable lead. For all intents and purposes, the infant had disappeared. Matt looked over at the government cars. The black vehicles the federal agents preferred winked in the steaming lot. They were everywhere, but they were facing the same slow slog as he and Vernon.

Vernon had draped his arm over his eyes. "You asleep?" Matt asked.

"No, just getting my dose of vitamin D and thinking about all the people we have to see up there today." He ticked off the names. Harvey Fuller, who had yet to account for why he'd been skulking around the third floor. Claire's parents, who were doing quite a job of being both antagonistic and incredibly unforthcoming. Scott's adviser and dorm head.

Vernon's phone beeped with a text. He raised himself partially and looked at the screen. "Lady named Betsy Lowery needs to see you and only you. Urgently. Who the hell is she?"

"The Barfmobile," Matt said and explained the phenomenon of the stinky car to his partner. He reached up for the Diet Coke, nearly inhaled a bee, then finished off almost the whole can. When he was done, he sank back into the gloom below the table. He had been trying to pretend that he had not had a headache for three days, low and deep in his skull, in almost precisely the same place where Claire had sustained the blow that killed her.

"We could use backup," said Vernon, his eyes draped again with his arm. "Lots of people up there. And we need to make some progress or Angell is going to destroy us. Oh, and I forgot. We've got a meeting tonight with the headmaster, too." Vernon sounded weary. Neither of them had been off for more than three hours since Monday morning.

"It's local. It's worse than local. Some of those kids know exactly what happened," said Matt to the underside of the tabletop, through which bright lances of sunlight were streaming.

"But that does not tell me precisely why you're so unwilling to let a few uniforms help with the interviews," Vernon prodded. "I have my guess, however," he added.

"Which you are now pleased to share with me." Matt knew what was coming.

Still speaking with his arm over his eyes, Vernon said, "You're worried some townie won't get it up there. You think they're not going to pick up the nuances and that the snobs will walk all over them. You think you've got that angle covered."

Matt sighed. It was partially true. Armitage was hard to translate if you hadn't experienced it. He knew exactly how the people up there talked about the town, the police, the villagers of Greenville, conversation that ranged in tone from polite acceptance of the fact that people of different origins actually existed to open disdain.

"Vernon, will you uncover your eyes?"

"No," said Vernon.

"All right," said Matt, still lying on his back. "To a certain extent you're right. But it's not because I think the townies will screw it up. It's because I do actually understand it there; I lived it. It doesn't mean I liked it. It doesn't mean I approve of it. And I don't think, despite it all, we're far off. More of us will scare them worse. More of us means they're surrounded. We need to make them feel that we're barely watching, that we're as incompetent as they hope."

Vernon said nothing for a moment. And then he commented, rather darkly, "You may not have liked it there, but it doesn't mean it didn't have its influence on you."

"Point taken. Give me two days," Matt said. "And can we please think now about Claire? She's the key; we know she is."

Vernon finally uncovered his face. "All right. Two days, and then we ask for help. And now I'm hot and want some cold water. We talk Claire inside."

They pulled themselves off the bench and took the remains of their lunch back to the relative cool of their office, where Vernon spread out his files on Claire. He'd found out that second semester she had taken a reduced load. A calculus class with Alice Grassley, biology with Harvey, physics with a guy who wore the thickest glasses you'd ever seen, and an English course with another geezer. "And she switched them all around just before she started in January. She knew what she was doing. She was going to plant herself in the last row in classes that were relatively large and run by old bats or the blind." She had also, Vernon explained, missed just the number of assignments she could: not so many or so frequently as to cause comment but far more than she ever had before. Her grades, too, had slipped a lot, but everyone had said the lapse was blamable on senior slump, a kind of academic mononucleosis. Grace was Claire's adviser, and she and Harvey were old and practiced collaborators. They were the last people to badger a girl who was in early to Yale and whose family endowed squash courts and scholarships at Armitage. In fact, when Alice Grassley, the teacher of the one course in which Claire had made really no effort, started to complain, Grace and Harvey told her to stuff it. At least that was the story from Alice, who was, according to Vernon, a sharp old gal and a Sox fan. Grace and Harvey had of course denied it all.

Scotty was in three of Claire's classes—physics, English, and biology—but he'd been planning on taking those since the year before. Otherwise, all four of the girls Claire had trusted to care for her were in at least one of the courses with her. Thread or no thread, she had done a good job creating her network of co-conspirators.

Scotty had emerged time and again as the person students and teachers named as the possible father. Although Matt and Vernon sensed that Scotty had an extremely flexible notion of truth, they thought he was in this instance telling it. Scotty hadn't seen Claire all summer; it was hard to refute the fact that he had spent almost three uninterrupted months in Canada training with an Olympic rowing coach. "Timing," Matt said to Vernon. "It's the timing."

"Yeah," Vernon said, "I'm doing the numbers for the hundredth time. By *timing* I assume you mean when she got pregnant and with whom. The girls say the baby was late. Most likely, if we can count on her having regular periods, she got pregnant over the summer, in early or mid-August. That chronology means she could have slept with anyone from the pool boy at the father's house to some French guy on a barge."

"On a barge?" Matt asked. Vernon, with his aggressive notions about staying true to one's roots, had sometimes curious notions about life in other countries. But Matt took his point. Claire had spent August shuttling between Paris, Long Island, Maine, and New York, visiting her parents and friends. Her mother and father admitted that, even when she was home, they hadn't seen much of her. "She kept her own counsel," Mr. Harkness said with stunning lack of necessity. Those who had hosted Claire said that she had seemed much as usual: distant, self-possessed, and poised. No one said, What a tragedy, though they all mentioned what a shock her death was. And no boyfriends in particular had been noted. No, she hadn't been dating anyone, just seeing her half brothers and sisters when she'd been in New York and France, the parents both insisted. Then again, both were forced to admit—the father with anger, the mother with regret—that they hadn't always been available during the day to see what she had been doing. East Hampton or Damariscotta were more likely possibilities; the friends had been classmates from Armitage, the parents entirely vague about how the girls had spent their time. Just out, they kept saying. Doing this and that. You know. Teenagers. Impossible to keep track of. The other issue had been speaking with the actual friends. One was on a semester program in China, the other volunteering at an orphanage in India.

"There's a reason she stayed. She was planning something. An exposure, a scene," said Matt. "There's an Armitage link, something very specific." The shameful burst of schadenfreude that had graced the start of the week had faded; maybe its remnants were what was causing his headache. However this was resolved, it was going to be very, very unattractive.

Rearranging his papers, Vernon suddenly asked, "Why'd you leave murder?" And before Matt could respond, he said, "There's a connection, bear with me." Vernon went on, "The guys in Philly, they were surprised you were going and pissed, like What's wrong with us? What I'm saying is, it's personal. I don't know. A bad relationship. A bad case. Your mother died, and you wanted to be close to your father. You missed the clean air of the country." Vernon was readying his laptop now and zipping open its container to receive his notes. "You didn't broadcast it. But you probably told someone, and so did this girl. There is probably one person she let in because she had to be human. She had to be, though they talk about her like she's Athena."

"Athena was ostensibly a virgin, but I take your point." Vernon grunted and said nothing more, but Matt was impressed that he had gotten so much on the mark. It had been a case, a thirteen-year-old girl, raped and killed by her father. A family from South Philadelphia. Workable forensic evidence and even a confession that had taken a year to coax out, and then the entire case collapsed when a lawyer got the confession retracted and the mother wouldn't testify. Finally, what he hadn't been able to stand was that, in murder, you only saw and dealt with the end. You weren't part of anything that wasn't irrevocable.

Vernon sorted through papers and was preparing to close the laptop case when his phone rang. "Kathy," he said and went into the hall to talk to his wife.

Matt walked over to Claire's bulletin board and examined for the fifteenth time the array of notes and photos and papers that the girl had pinned there. But Vernon's comment had unmoored him slightly, and he was abruptly back in Philadelphia, in the middle of that part of his life. He had spent twelve years there, the first four at Penn resolutely avoiding people like Scotty Johnston and wondering what he could do that would keep him away from that kind of world for the rest of his days. Then, senior year, a cop had come to talk to his urban policy class, and within the span of an hour, he had made a choice, exercising an openness of mind he'd first discovered at Armitage. But whatever that man had—some sort of cool mixed with intensity; a grasp on some of the world's true, dark workings—Matt wanted it. Something direct, clear, and difficult. A job that wasn't based at a desk, wrapped in a million different words and not a scrap of social nicety. Something no one would have expected of him, certainly not his parents, who had dreamed of law school and clerking for a famous judge, public service, something sleek and admirable. But he had seen that cop, another Italian, and listened to him describe what cops did and meant to big cities as all the blond girls took notes, and he'd known precisely where he was headed with all his fancy education.

And despite his parents' disappointment, police work had at first seemed like exactly the right choice. He had begun in burglary, which was full of people behaving with both courage and terrific stupidity and meanness. Those early years, when he had worn a uniform and then with a speed that irritated his colleagues moved to murder and become able to wear a suit, had had a kind of drama that made his daily life a blend of confessions, scuffles, and satisfying if often partial successes. He had never been bored and felt grateful to have work in which he felt filled to the edges of his own skin, even though, according to his father, he had turned back the immigrant's clock.

And then, over the course of a few bad years, he had felt the beginnings of the decision's drawbacks. There'd been a series of gruesome cases that had gotten twisted in mistrials and plea bargains. Yet another relationship had ended with nothing more substantial than a milk frother. His mother had gotten ill and very quickly died. He had felt confidence begin to leak from his bones. Vernon had been right about it all, even Matt's telling one person, his sister, Barbara.

Whom had Claire confided in? He riffled through the notes on the cork again and looked at her small, neat handwriting. Whom had she trusted? Scotty, but she had held the upper hand in that relationship. Every photograph of them together betrayed that, and all the witnesses had confirmed it. Not her parents. Not her siblings, who were all half brothers or sisters, and quite a bit younger. Not her teachers. Not her peers. Then who?

Vernon came in. "Kath says hi, says you're coming to dinner when this is all over."

"Vernon," Matt said, thinking of something he had finally understood about the bulletin board. "Claire didn't take French this year, did she?"

"No," said Vernon, as he stooped to put what was left of his lunch back in the fridge. "She'd tested out. Nothing left for her but an independent study, and that would have brought too much attention to her. Why?"

"But when we looked through her books and notebooks in her room, wasn't one of the binders labeled 'French'?"

Vernon straightened up and noticed a particularly persistent yellow jacket on his shirtsleeve. He walked over to the window and carefully blew the insect into the breeze. "Maybe it was from last year. Why does it matter?"

"Because," Matt said, hastily gathering his phone, notepad, keys, and sunglasses, "she wrote in French all the time. It's all over the bulletin board. She preferred it to English. And she may not have told somebody what was going on, but she might have written it down. I want to see that notebook."

"All right," Vernon said, a little skeptically. "It should still be there. Unless, for reasons unknown, Harvey Fuller has decided to nab it."

They walked quickly through the station, both because of Matt's desire to find Claire's notebook and because they wanted to avoid conversation with anyone asking how the case was going. As they opened the door to the parking lot, Vernon said, "You know, you're braver than I am. I never even tried to do something like murder in the first place. Knew it would ruin me. The problem with seeing is you can't unsee." They blinked in the bright light as they hurried toward Matt's car. "By the way, when this case is finished, you should ask out that Madeline girl. She's a keeper."

"Oh yeah? I think the art teacher has his eye on her already." Admitting that he'd noticed Madeline and her potential suitor caused Matt a certain pang.

"Art teacher? You're worried about competition from an art teacher?" Vernon said. They settled into their seats, strapped themselves in, and headed up the hill. Matt realized his headache was gone. Maybe it was the Diet Coke, but more likely, it was this: the eerie way that present life, the sheer force of it, kept walking right alongside disaster. Turkey sandwiches and death, bad memories and bees, Vernon advising him on romance just before they went to investigate a murder. The relentless forward motion of experience that made it hard for anything to stick, even bad headaches. "So you're my partner, my confessor, and now my yenta?"

"You need all three," said Vernon, jabbing a finger at him.

Claire's room was as they had left it, the books and binders in a rough row on the lower shelf of her bookcase. Matt stepped past the yellow tape and quickly found the one dedicated to French. As Vernon had speculated, it was from last year. On the first ten pages were clearly notes taken in a literature class. Assignments were written down, page numbers were marked. She'd done a precise caricature of Marie-France in the margins. Quotations from Baudelaire covered another page. He was just about to turn to Vernon and admit defeat when he opened a page at random in the middle. Suddenly, Claire was writing in dated, single-spaced paragraphs: 10 Octobre. 14 Octobre 2009. He tried to decipher the French, but his languages had been Latin and Spanish. "Vernon," he said, "I think we've got something here." He knew that all the plans to see Harvey, Betsy, Porter, Claire's parents, and all the others they were slated to speak with this afternoon would have to be put off.

"You understand this?" Vernon asked.

"No," Matt told him, "but I know who will."

Marie-France greeted them at her door with a cigarette in her hand. "I know I am not supposed to smoke in here," she said, "but who is going to stop me?"

"Not us, Miss Maillot," said Matt, "especially when we have a favor to ask you. Could you help us translate this?"

Marie-France let them in, and Matt saw Vernon, despite his disapproval of the tobacco, admiring the large window boxes filled with rosemary, oregano, and thyme. The windows were wide open, and though the smoke was an acrid, lingering presence, the room itself was full of the colors of the French south. A yellow and blue tablecloth. A bowlful of lemons. Handsome botanical prints of sunflowers and lavender. A comfortable white sofa that she invited them to occupy. She herself was narrow and tall, with gray hair pinned in a tight chignon and skin deeply damaged by cigarettes and sun. But at one time, he suspected, she had been pretty, and her eyes were dark brown and full of inquiry.

"As I said, Miss Maillot," Matt said, "we have a favor to ask you." He showed her the notebook, turned carefully to the pages with which he wanted help. But she leafed through it from the beginning, finding, as Matt had hoped she would not, Claire's rude drawing. To his surprise, she took a deep draw on her cigarette and laughed, exhaling smoke in a raucous, twisting cloud. "Claire," she said. "I taught her for three years. She was a little *méchante*, that one." She looked up at them. "A little mean. But she spoke the most beautiful French. She spoke like a native." Matt understood for a moment how Marie-France had survived here for so long. She just didn't take any of it particularly seriously, except for her own subject.

"You were Spanish," she said to Matt, still remembering— and disapproving—after all these years, as if the pursuit of any tongue but her own was an affront, an indication of reduced intellect. Matt could imagine how she'd taken the introduction of Mandarin to the curriculum.

He said yes. Her reputation had been too formidable for someone like him, and again she laughed and it was like listening to a dragon. "She wouldn't pursue the independent study," Marie-France said. "I know why now. Stupid girl." Blunt words tinged with tense regret. She continued turning the pages. "I would have helped her. It has happened before." She turned another page and said, "What no one understood about this girl is that she was angry. She had every advantage in life, but no one took her seriously.

I tried, but she had given up on adults. This is what you want, no?" she said and showed them the dated passages. Matt said yes and watched the woman read. She ground out her cigarette and did not immediately light another one, a rarity, he guessed.

"It's a journal, or part of one," Marie-France said, still looking at the pages. "Notes she wrote. I will translate them for you. There are only three or four pages and then she stopped." She glanced up and said, "It will take a bit of time. I will send them on e-mail. Can you give me your address?"

Matt nearly said, "You have e-mail?" thinking that someone who still hoped French would return as the lingua franca would have shunned such an innovation. But he jotted his address on a card and passed it over to her. "Is there anything you can tell us now?"

For this, Marie-France did stop and light a cigarette, and when she had it tucked into her fingers, she said, "She doesn't say who the father is. That's what you're looking for, of course. It's about this girl who was helping her. Rosalie Quiñones. A new girl here this year. She didn't last." At this, Marie-France blew out a perfect cone of smoke and looked at her flourishing beds of herbs.

"What happened to her, Miss Maillot?" Vernon asked, and for the first time, Marie-France looked directly at him.

"I am not sure. But if Claire was telling the truth, it had to do with those ridiculous girls and their group. Robespierre," she spat. "An abomination. Grace will know." She tapped ash into a clam-shell. "No, don't bother talking to Grace," she said, rising. "She will tell you nothing. Talk to Sarah. She will be honest. And I will get the notes to you within an hour. You can download them on your phone, no?" she asked, and her smile was tilted. What was interesting was how delightful it was to hear her say *download* in that undiluted accent and how effortless it was for her to flirt well into her sixth decade.

"Jesus," said Vernon as they walked down the stairs. "She could teach a class on how to stay true to your native culture in the midst of infidels. Now I never have to go to Paris."

CHAPTER 13

Madeline made it to class about thirty seconds before her students arrived, relieved as she left her apartment to find no more emblems of the Reign of Terror on her doorstep. She was off to teach the sophomores, her favorite kids, who for some reason had thrown themselves into American poetry with a fervor most teenagers reserved for online chatting and Cheetos. Porter's instincts had been right; it was better to start up the routine again. He had ridden through a wave of protest from parents and faculty, arguing for the cancellation of the remainder of the school year. He'd stated that sending students off without giving them even a short time to come to terms with their shock and grief would backfire. The emotional consequences were too extreme, he said, not to mention the financial ones. Those, he was quick to point out, would not redound to the school; the time to return deposits was long past. Despite the hit to their wallets, quite a few parents were withdrawing their children for the end of the year and the next. Even by last night, the campus had indeed seemed emptier—the lines in the dining hall were thinner, and there were leftover strawberries for once. The kids who had stayed had a grim set to their faces, evidence of a kind of courage of which Madeline wouldn't have thought them capable. They were going to tough out a difficult situation. She'd thought such cosseted children uniformly allergic to that degree of discomfort.

Madeline looked at the kids flopping into place around the oval table. They seemed relieved to have something to do other than

mope about the dorm. Emily, Carter, Max. Stuart, Eddie, Corde-
lia. From all around the country, all around the world. In this high-
ceilinged room ringed with wispy spider plants and curling posters
from Stratford-upon-Avon—as the intern, Madeline didn't merit
her own classroom and she shared her digs with Forrest, the English chair—she had coaxed them into reading a wide variety of
work and writing experimental sonnets. But today, she realized
with rising panic, she had almost nothing prepared for them.
Merely getting here had taken all her effort. "Why are we talking
about poetry when this tragic thing has happened?" she asked
them. Better to admit to the horror than to hide it, she'd assumed.
But they looked at her, blank and more than a bit confused. And
then she launched into the ways that poetry could teach you to
structure thought and language and expounded on its ability to
provide succinct, precise ways to capture feelings. Her hand motions were getting bigger and bigger, which was always a bad sign; it
was not an effective teaching tool to imitate someone waving sema-
phores from the deck of an aircraft carrier. Then she found herself
pressed up against the whiteboard, a marker clutched in her fist,
and absolutely nothing to write there, so she rubbed her nose and
said, with open desperation, "Well, that's what I was thinking about.
How about you?" And Emily, a delicate redhead, raised her hand
and offered tentatively, "Poetry is beautiful. And focusing on something beautiful when you're really sad or upset puts the hard thing
into perspective." So they spent the rest of the period reading and
discussing the poems they loved most in their Norton anthology.
"That was nice, Miss Christopher," Emily said on her way out, as if
Madeline and not she had been responsible for salvaging the class.

　　During her next class, Madeline let the juniors write in their
journals for twenty minutes and then discussed a handout on a fi-

nal, short analytical paper on dramatic structures. They looked gray but grateful for the full complement of work she'd dumped on them. At least they had something to complain about collectively.

At lunch, she avoided the stares of Lee and Olu, and noticed that they sat with a few other imposing girls at a table near the front of the room. They must be what's left of the Reign, Madeline thought, and though she was grateful that Portia and Suzy had decided to depart early, there were still enough of them remaining to cause more than a little trepidation. She was very happy that Sarah Talmadge sat down next to her.

The assistant head was compact and dark-haired, with an alert, sensitive face. Porter had hired her three years ago, and she, like her boss, was someone faculty and parents liked and respected. She worked hard, made difficult decisions fairly, and was utterly unpretentious. She had spent years at Armitage as a math teacher, gone to another school for almost a decade as a dean, then let Porter lure her back. What Madeline most admired in her, however, was that she managed to take her work seriously without losing a lightness of touch, a sense of humor that made her enjoyable to know. The best kind of grown-up, Fred said, and Madeline agreed. "I won't pretend this is a social call," she said now. She was drained, Madeline saw, and the skin on her face looked fragile. "I've got a couple of things to ask. First, can you set up an appointment to see me early next week? I want to talk to you more concretely about next year. I know it seems jarring, but we've got to keep focused on what's ahead, too. And I have a big favor to ask." She hadn't touched a single one of the carrots on her plate, and Madeline doubted she would. The fish she had served herself was congealing in sauce. But Sarah pressed on. Claire's parents were badgering the school for a chance to look at her room. Someone from the dorm needed to be there, just at the beginning. Would she mind?

Madeline gulped and said, "Really? Why me?" Sarah looked at her and said, "Grace is entirely preoccupied with the police right now. As for Harvey and Marie-France, well, they might not offer the most reassuring presence." She explained she would also come by, as soon as her 3:30 meeting was done. The parents wanted to be there at 4:00. "Okay," said Madeline, wishing that Sarah looked a little less tired; she badly wanted to talk about this Robespierre business with her. Sarah's thanks were genuine, and she lifted her tray and hurried off to her next task.

Madeline got up to take her own tray off to the conveyor belt and knew that Lee and Olu were watching her. They were certainly not through with her yet, but what precisely they had planned and why they were bothering was unclear. In spite of her desire to appear nonchalant, to actually saunter, Madeline scurried past them.

She limped her way through track practice and found herself back at the dorm, hot and smelly, with only five minutes before Claire's parents were supposed to arrive. She didn't want to greet them with wet hair or miss them altogether and chose instead to daub herself with a soapy washcloth. She dragged a comb through her hair and made sure there weren't visible spots on her skirt. She plunked herself down on Kate's old futon and waited, thinking that was the word she associated most with her parents. Waiting for her mother to pick her up from school. Waiting for her father to come by on one of his infrequent custody visits. Waiting for someone to call and tell her which parent she was going to spend Christmas with.

At least, Madeline thought as she chewed her nails, they didn't pretend that they'd done the most stellar of jobs in raising their children. "Darling, people just had babies back then. There wasn't all this *choice* the way there is now," Isabelle had said. As if nothing she had done had led to being pregnant the two times it had taken to produce Kate and Madeline. As if she'd woken one morning to find herself large-bellied and about, as she often put it, to "descend into motherhood," as if parenting were no more than a dank basement in which she had to fold endless loads of laundry. Madeline's father hadn't exactly embraced his familial duties, either. Despite a solid career as a trusts and estates attorney, he had recently blown his fourth marriage, as heartbroken and reckless as Britney every time it didn't work. Fortunately for him, the lawyerly side had kicked in early enough in these relationships that he'd managed to protect his assets before getting scalped by Deborah, Helene, or Jemima. The Hurricanes, Madeline and Kate called them, for the emotional if not financial wreckage that they caused. Unlike Madeline's mother, her father seemed to know how babies were made and had resolutely avoided having any more since his girls had been born. The Fool for Love, Kate and Madeline called him, often shortened merely to Fool, though most people called him David. Still rakishly handsome, he was nursing the end of his latest union in Aruba. Isabelle was apparently happily settled with her third husband, a bland, rich man named Harry who carved decoys as an avocation. They lived on the coast of Massachusetts and cooked ornate meals to impress others with their kitchen equipment. Their stove was so powerful Madeline had singed her eyelashes the last time she'd tried to use it. Madeline sighed. What was there to prevent her from making exactly the same mistakes?

What if marital haplessness was in her genes? How much choice was involved anyway? Owen was indeed breaking up via text, the end of a relationship captured in digital attrition, and she couldn't even keep her eyelashes on.

On her saggy sofa, checking her watch—Claire's family was now fifteen minutes late—Madeline was also observing the arrival of a deep funk that always came when thinking about her parents. To distract herself, she thought instead about Matt. When she had told Grace about her conversation with him at Ali's and mentioned how nice he'd been, Grace had sniffed, "Well, it's true he graduated from Armitage. But in slightly dubious circumstances. It's a wonder he came back here at all. I'm surprised they've let him be involved in this situation," but said nothing further. Madeline had been startled by the idea of dubious circumstances surrounding Matt, though she remembered with some shame her surprise at finding out he'd been part of this place. Peering through the blinds, she guessed that the detective's uneasy relationship with Armitage couldn't stem from something as bald as academic incompetence. He appeared smart enough to have done well here; he looked like a good athlete, too, and he was handsome, not the way all those blond, patrician boys were, but Mediterraneanly. Dark, with brown eyes.

She checked her watch again. Despite their insistence on needing to see Claire's room, the parents were now almost half an hour late and Madeline had gnawed her nails down to bloody cuticles. She had class prep to attend to and needed to organize her thoughts about what she hoped to accomplish during the last few days of school. It was becoming increasingly apparent to her that her groovy education had fostered in her a reactionary desire to give a lot of tests and grade numerically.

Finally, she saw a Mercedes pull up in front of the dorm. Her father could have recited the make and model, but all Madeline knew was that the car barely made a sound and moved almost as lithely as an animal. Claire's mother, Mrs. Duval, got out and tugged her pashmina shawl around her shoulders. It was real pashmina, most definitely unrelated to the one Madeline had bought for five dollars from a nice Nigerian man on Newbury Street one weekend. Even from a distance, Madeline could tell Mrs. Duval's would never pill. The father shut the door on the driver's side and stood by his former wife for a moment. Madeline caught her breath. They still made a gorgeous pair. The only people Madeline had ever seen to whom the adjective *well heeled* could be applied with total aptness. There was no way to know from this distance what their expressions were; they both wore sunglasses that wrapped around their faces. They weren't here to do any actual packing, either. Some assistant would be allotted that particular task. They were here only to witness where their daughter had died.

Madeline hadn't realized until that moment precisely how frightened she was of dealing with these people. But she was discovering an unexpected ability to live alongside unpleasant emotions and to continue to do what was expected of her. Having been gravely disappointed along the way by people and institutions, she had developed rather strict personal standards about comportment under pressure. Still, she couldn't help but imagine Claire's mother rolling her perfect black stockings up her perfect lean shins. How could she have bothered?

"Mrs. Duval?" Madeline said as she walked out to meet Claire's mother, her hand extended like a little banner. "My name is Madeline Christopher. I cannot tell you how sorry I am for your loss."

Claire's mother said, "Thank you." She looked at her former husband, who was staring fixedly at an oak tree.

"Flora," he said in a tone that Madeline recognized. A touch weary, a touch exasperated, yet lined with some small confidence in its ability to exert moral suasion. A note that contained the tiny dose of proprietariness that might be tolerated in an ex-husband. The note that David had used with Isabelle on the rare occasions when he and his former wife needed to provide what he called, with an astounding lack of irony, a "united front" for the children.

Flora Duval, it was abundantly clear to Madeline, was long past being able to stand even the slightest hint at old allegiances. What she needed was a clear destination and an immediate task, and although Madeline was only twenty-five, she was the only one there to provide that. She put her hand on the older woman's and was surprised at the strength of Mrs. Duval's returned grip. "Are you ready to go to Claire's room?" she asked, and Mrs. Duval nodded.

The dorm was empty now, except for faculty. Madeline had been surprised at how she had relied on the girls to provide her with a sense of safety, a padding of voices and bodies that she missed only once they were gone.

The mother's heels and the father's wingtips jarred noisily on steel risers. They climbed in silence, and then, when they reached the entrance to Claire's room, the mother stood stock-still. She tore open the crime scene tape, took off her glasses, and walked slowly through the room, her fingers trailing the surfaces of the desk and bedside table. Traces of the powder the police had used to dust for fingerprints had left grayish smudges on the windowsills, Madeline noticed. She had thought that it was stuff that existed only on television shows or in mystery novels, but apparently not. The furniture had been rearranged: the bed pulled from the wall, the armchair positioned at a new angle to the window. Matt Corelli had apparently confiscated the contents of the desk and the crowded bulletin board, with Claire's Yale letter and its photos and Post-its.

It was the first time Madeline had been back in the suite since she'd seen Claire's body. She didn't know how this was possible, but something of the girl flickered through the space. As if she were wondering what they were going to do next, watching them with her cold little smile. Madeline fervently hoped that she was the only one to experience this discomfiting feeling. "Did you see Claire?" Mrs. Duval asked, looking now out the window. "After she was dead?"

"Yes," said Madeline, edging herself toward the door, the memory of Claire's bent neck and taut breasts springing uncomfortably back to the front of her mind, though she had tried hard not to revisit that image. The father had sat down at Claire's desk, his gaze still unreadable. He hadn't removed his dark glasses, although it was far dimmer indoors than it had been in the thick, bright light of the courtyard.

"This is our fault, William."

Madeline felt her heart seize slightly, and she made the subtlest of motions, as if to duck out as discreetly as possible. She wanted nothing more than to dash from the room before a scene could be played out in front of her. Claire's father apparently felt precisely the same way. "You may leave now, Miss Christopher," he said. But Mrs. Duval raised an imperious hand and said, "No. Madeline can stay."

"Flora," Mr. Harkness said, standing, though his eyes were still concealed behind the shades. For the first time, Madeline heard something waver in his voice.

"Shut up, William. Just shut up," Mrs. Duval said softly, her fingers now propped on the pillow on Claire's bed, which had been stripped to the mattress, its sage green duvet no doubt being examined in some police lab.

Someone coughed just then, and they all snapped their heads to look toward the open door. Madeline thought it must be Sarah, discreetly announcing her arrival. But she was stunned to find Porter there.

"Hello, Porter," Mrs. Duval said, tears running openly down her face now. "Although I consider myself guilty here, I'm also holding you responsible for this." She made her comment almost conversationally. "I am going to want to know about everything that happened. And I want my grandson back."

Only afterward, when Madeline was back in her apartment, shaking having migrated from her hands through her whole body, would she be fully aware of what Porter had said and done next. He had stood there at the edge of the room, his whole tall body crammed inside the frame, an expression running across his strong face as if someone had slashed his jaw with a straight-edged razor.

"I understand, Flora. I accept that responsibility," he'd said. And then Mrs. Duval had started to sob, and it wasn't her former husband or Porter to whom she turned but Madeline, who held the slender woman as she grieved for her daughter. She would never have guessed that such ragged noise could emerge from someone that beautifully groomed, but she held her and listened to the echo of her cries through the building, where the sounds were free to travel, unimpeded now by the gossip and merriment of girls. It was why, Madeline knew, as she held the elegant woman, she had bothered with the stockings. There was a chance that such fine silk might contain all that regret.

By five, Madeline was finally back in her apartment. Sarah had left a message and said with a note of real apology that she was sorry she couldn't be there; her meeting had run far later than expected. Would Madeline call her to check in when she had a chance? There was also a call from Fred, and ones from Grace and then Kate. The last message was someone breathing heavily before clicking off. More Reign nonsense, Madeline guessed, but she looked longingly at her bed. Could she wrap herself up there for a few minutes to digest what had just happened? Madeline shivered as with the advent of a flu, remembering how fragile Mrs. Duval had felt and how her perfume had smelled of freesias.

Madeline wondered why Claire's death had struck her with such grounding force. She had survived her parents' divorces, her haphazard education, life as the unfavored child, and emerged amazingly cheerful and quite competent. The death of a girl whom she hadn't liked seemed an odd thing to unmoor her. That was bothering her, as were two other things she'd noticed in Claire's room. First, why had Mrs. Duval spoken to Porter as if she knew him, not just knew him as the headmaster at her daughter's school but knew him for real, as a man? The second thing was that, when Madeline had seen Claire's room the morning the girl died, she had noticed that the long mirror usually on the back of the door had been removed and placed near the window. But it wasn't there now. Had someone hung it back in place? Had the police done that? If not, who?

Madeline steeled herself and went back up the stairs to see if her memory could be believed. The mirror, beveled and un-smudged, was hanging where it had when Claire was alive: on the back of the door that led to the hall, without a single mark on its bright surface. She wondered if she'd imagined its different placement and quickly turned to leave. She was still troubled by the sensation that something of the girl remained, even considering the tack-pocked walls, the mattress and its institutional blue ticking. And in spite of the investigative remnants—the tape and the powder—as bare and impersonal as if a new student might arrive any day. As if nothing of consequence had ever happened there.

She ought to have supper, but for once Madeline wasn't hungry. Instead, a cold shower and a hair wash with some of the new shampoo she'd acquired from the girls was the most appealing option. In the cool stream of water, she chose a brand that said it was made with coconut and awapuhi, substances that would strengthen the shafts of her hair and make her scalp tingle with vitality. When she went to pour a dollop in her hand, however, something curious happened. Water pounding on her back, she tried to shake the bottle and get it to cough out enough shampoo for her to wash her hair. But the neck was blocked. Madeline turned off the shower and tried to pry at the container. Finally, she snagged a nail on what felt like a plastic bag. It was a Ziploc, sealed tight, and it came out slimy with pearlescent goop. But that didn't mask the fact that it contained a note. Those girls, Madeline thought, those horrid girls. They even got inside my bathroom. Dripping liberally on the tile, heart clanging away, Madeline opened the baggie. But the note wasn't addressed to or even aimed at her. It said, in the same scarlet letters that had graced her own message, "Terror is a by-product of virtue, it is nothing less than swift, stern, and unbending justice. MF: Remember what happened to RQ. You're next." MF? RQ? Who were they? Madeline grabbed a towel and daubed her face dry. Then she knew. MF was Maggie Fitzgerald, that mousy freshman who had been so stunned someone as beautiful as Claire could die. The seniors were harassing her for some reason, perhaps to do with Claire. And RQ had to be Rosalie Quiñones, Maggie's former roommate and a local girl on scholarship, who had withdrawn in November. Madeline, caught up in her own first-semester angst, had barely known who the girl was and had no real idea why she'd gone. Now she wondered if the Reign had been responsible for Rosalie's abrupt departure, too.

As she dressed, she planned to call Sarah and then Matt. This had gone too far. But then she had another thought. It was time to go see Sally Jansen at the infirmary. She'd probably be barricaded in a room behind her parents and a bevy of nurses, but it was worth trying. Sally might just tell her about Maggie Fitzgerald and Rosalie.

Although everyone called it the infirmary, the low, graceful building that had once been the school's stables was technically known as the McFarlane Wellness Center. Health was no longer enough. *Wellness*, with its emphasis on spiritual as well as physical vigor, was the new ideal, though the term made Madeline feel dreadfully inadequate. Inspired by a course she'd taken on Buddhism, she had tried several meditation classes, sponsored by her own college wellness center, and done nothing more than fidget and then fall dead asleep in all of them. Once she'd woken snoring, only to find the instructor looming over her, raising his enlightened eyebrows.

Inside McFarlane, therapeutic hush prevailed. Large ficus trees flanked the front desk, at which, for the moment, no nurse fussed with paperwork or answered phones. Perhaps it was time for a shift in staff. Madeline peered at the whiteboard that noted which rooms were occupied and saw that Sally was supposed to be in Room 12. Trotting down the hall, carpeted in a soothing blue, Madeline sniffed at the combined scents of antiseptic and lavender. She knocked on the door of Room 12 and, when no one answered, cracked the door open. But Sally wasn't there. Heading back down the hall, she found herself in a room that billed itself as the solarium. Filled with potted plants and lofty windows, it was making an earnest effort to create a sense of sunny peace. And in one of its cavernous chairs sat Sally Jansen, curled like a dry leaf inside a fleece blanket.

When she finally noticed Madeline, she jumped the way surprised cats do, and Madeline startled along with her. "I thought you were one of those nurses coming to give me another pill. Sorry, Miss Christopher."

Madeline pulled up an ottoman and sat down next to Sally. The girl, close up, looked even worse than she had from the corridor: skittish and anemic, with red eyes and lank hair. "I'm not supposed to talk to anyone," she said, looking not at Madeline but at some point of the soothing vista that the wide windows offered. "My parents told me not to get involved." But her mouth was quivering, Madeline noticed, perhaps with the advent of tears but also as if a million words were waiting there, ready to be spilled.

"Where are they, Sally?" Madeline asked, aware she might have no more than a few minutes until one of the girl's protectors descended.

"At their hotel for a little while. They want to take me home. We have tickets to go back to San Francisco tomorrow." She wrapped the green fleece more tightly about her narrow shoulders.

"But you don't want to go, do you?"

Sally shook her head no. "I want to find out about the baby. I can't leave until I know what's happened to him." Her eyes began to glisten with tears, and her mouth quivered even more.

"Sally, of course you don't have to talk with me. But I want to ask you about the Reign. I think it's important. It might have something to do with why Claire died." Madeline was using her firmest teacher voice, although she tried to keep it low and almost casual. But both she and Sally knew their time together was limited. Madeline heard voices down the hall and worried that they were getting closer.

If Sally was concerned that Madeline knew about the group, she didn't show it. Maybe she assumed the adults in the community were more aware than they actually were. "Claire was trying to change it. Make it less exclusive," Sally whispered, apparently grateful for the opportunity to talk without being monitored. "I mean, she was in a bad situation, and she needed help. She knew we'd give it to her. But she also wanted to make it what it used to be, something nicer, more supportive." Sally leaned forward in her fleece cocoon and continued to talk as quickly as she could. The Reign had been getting really bad. They were hazing again. Did Madeline remember Rosalie? When Madeline answered "Yes," she said, "They—Lee and Portia and Suzy, mostly—tried to drive her out. But she fought back. And Claire protected her. But then something really bad happened, Miss Christopher. I don't know what it was. But Claire was furious and then Rosalie was gone. That's when she asked us to be part of the Reign and to twist the thread with her. And we took care of her. We gave her prenatal vitamins and made her stop drinking coffee." Sally sniffed, but even that couldn't hide the pride she still felt at having earned Claire's recognition. Claire might have used her, but at least she hadn't been cruel. Another nuance of the adolescent social hierarchy that Madeline hadn't realized existed and a facet to Claire's personality she would never have guessed at. Sally's color was improving. Every adult around her was trying to silence her, but all she wanted was someone to talk to.

Madeline said, "I'm confused. Lee told me that she had done a lot of the work of looking after Claire."

Sally shook her head. "Claire didn't want anything to do with them anymore. They just wanted you to think that. Me and Anna and Margaret and Kelly, we did most of it. Claire wanted us to help, not them."

There was more, Sally said in a rush. The Reign had been picking on Maggie, and Maggie and Rosalie had been close. There was some connection there, but Sally didn't know what it was. The voices were indeed getting louder. Clearly, someone was now at the reception desk.

"Sally, one more thing," Madeline said, leaning forward. But the girl interrupted her. "You want to know if Claire told us who the father was. She didn't. She never said. Just that it was important she have the baby at school. That it would change things here." Then she continued hotly, "Claire wasn't like everyone thought she was. She wanted to know about our families. She wanted to know if we were close to our parents. If we had brothers and sisters we liked and talked to."

Madeline sat up straight. That was interesting, yet another layer to Claire. "She did? And what did you say?" By "we," Madeline assumed Sally meant the other girls with whom Claire had broken tradition.

Sally gave a small shrug. "Well, of course we are. I mean, my parents would do anything for me. We all had families like that." She looked a little bewildered, as if unable to imagine any other possible reality. "Claire said we couldn't tell them about the thread or about her, but she wanted to know all about them. About what we did and where we went on vacation and if anyone had told us about our periods and stuff like that." Now Sally blushed a little and looked flustered. "She wasn't as mean as she looked. She was even kind of lonely," Sally started to say, and then a light clicked on in the hallway and Madeline knew she had to scamper out of the McFarlane Wellness Center or face either Sally's parents or some fearsome nurse.

She quickly thanked Sally and zipped down another corridor that branched off the solarium. Fortunately, it held the school's meditation room, and Madeline gratefully opened the door. No one could accuse her of any wrongdoing in here, and it was a better option than the cleaning closet that had been the other choice. It was far less cramped, too, and rather inviting, with its low Japanese cushions and creamy wall color. Even so, merely being around the suggestion of meditation made her both restless and drowsy. Still, Madeline sat for a moment, trying to reframe Claire in her mind, propping what Sally had said about her next to what she had known, all of it having to fit somehow with those chilly, disturbingly handsome parents. None of it made sense. All of it had to be discussed with the police.

She rose, conscious of gnawing hunger. After slipping out of the infirmary without encountering anyone other than a cafeteria worker delivering meals to some sick children, Madeline had a quick dinner at the Commons. There were few teachers around and not many students. Her silverware echoed off the edge of her plate. It was a bit disappointing, she thought as she chewed some rather tasteless pasta, that Porter hadn't made more of an effort to be in the dining hall this drastic week. Unlike his predecessor, she had been told, Porter and his family had made a habit of eating with teachers and faculty. He and Lucinda and Miles had often been the humming center of a lively dinner table. If Armitage needed anything right now, it would be the compelling presence of its head and his handsome family. Fred, who was teaching the boy this semester, had said he hadn't seen Miles in class. Apparently he was now staying with his parents.

She didn't have time to think about that, she reminded herself as she deposited her tray. She had some schoolwork to finish, and she had to call the detective. She also needed to find out a lot more about Rosalie Quiñones and Maggie Fitzgerald. But she also knew she didn't have a lot of energy left tonight; she could already feel exhaustion trickling into her muscles. Then she reached her doorstep and shock pulled her back to full attention. What was lying there? Madeline squatted down to examine the small white twist of fur. A mouse. A dead mouse. And at first, she thought it was an offering from Virgil, Grace's cat and an unusually resourceful hunter for a male. He had left her a chipmunk and once a small gray squirrel. But Virgil tended to gnaw the heads off of his prey, leaving only mangled stumps low on the neck. This wound was clean, sharp, and precise, and the mouse was white, not wild. A creature bred for a lab. It was then Madeline saw a smaller lump on the doorstep: it was the mouse's head, complete with pink nose and now-stilled white whiskers. Looking more closely, she saw the mouse hadn't merely lost its head: it had had it surgically removed. The word, Madeline thought, was *guillotined.*

CHAPTER 14

Marie-France was as good as her word. Matt was hurrying across campus on his way to knock on Harvey Fuller's door when his phone pinged with a message. He stopped in the shade of an elm to read it as students, freshly showered after sports, made their way to the library or the Commons. The campus was bathed in tender early evening light and looking unusually benign. It was a small file, Marie-France said, and she didn't think it would be very useful. It provided, she wrote, a "picture of the distress of Claire, but nothing about the question of the paternity."

The gist of what Claire had written concerned her intense morning sickness and the fact that a girl, a freshman named Rosalie Quiñones, had helped her. Rosalie had apparently had an older sister in much the same situation as Claire, and she knew how to keep the nausea at bay. Saltines and ginger ale, weak tea and lots of rest. Rosalie was competent, Claire wrote again and again, competence apparently a quality Claire admired. Her sister, too, had decided to keep the baby. Claire had expressed appreciation for someone else making a similar choice but noted darkly, "My reasons are probably different than hers." Matt paused for a second. It was hard to read more than the most cursory e-mails on this tiny screen. What of this would be admissible evidence if this case ever came to trial? Vernon had been skeptical from the start. "Start thinking settlement today. These kids will never see the inside of a courtroom, much less a jail." The DA, a nervous man sensitive to the point of idiocy on the divide between Greenville and Armitage, had hardly pressed the parents of the students involved. To a degree, Matt took his point. No one wanted to be on the wrong side of an argument when the academy was involved. The school's own lawyers, a polished team from an old Boston firm, had made their insistent presence known within minutes of Claire's death.

Matt forced himself back to Marie-France's translation. Rosalie continued to be helpful but reported to Claire that girls were out to get her because she refused to remain cordoned to certain tables in the Commons. She didn't like the view, she told Claire. "I told her to get used to it. This was how it was, for almost everyone here. But she was stubborn." A bit later, Claire noted that she had talked to "other members," among them, presumably, Olu, Lee, Portia, and Suzy. "And they wouldn't relent. But Rosalie said she knew something that would get them kicked out. Something they would always be ashamed of. She wouldn't tell me what it was. I told her to. I told her she had to. And she finally did, and it is as disgusting as they are." What had it been? Matt checked his watch. There was so much to do. He should have been at Harvey's twenty minutes ago.

Then, Claire wrote, "They did something disgusting to Rosalie. She left today. I can't really blame her, but she just left. Like everyone else. But they won't tell me what they did to her. It's over with all of them. I am starting over." That meant, Matt assumed, that Claire had severed her connection with the other girls and felt free to break with tradition altogether and choose new members. It was practical, Matt saw—Claire needed help to support the choice she had made to stay at school while pregnant—but it was also political. She had finished with the nonsense of the Reign. The entries had spanned a period of three weeks, from mid-October to early November. "Find Rosalie Quiñones," he wrote in his notebook and quickly forwarded Marie-France's attachment to Vernon. Vernon texted back: "Nothing else in any of the other notebooks. Autopsy results coming in later tonight."

Matt sighed and went as fast as possible to Harvey Fuller's apartment. The man had a lot of questions to answer, given how much was happening in his dorm. When the biology teacher answered his door, the air trapped in his apartment made its way for a moment into the hallway. Its smell spoke of extreme neatness, but it was also stuffy. Clean without any of the positive associations of that word. It was rare for a person's living space to reflect so little of his character, but Harvey Fuller possessed an abrasive plainness, as if he had sheared off unnecessary edges in everything from his speech to his quarters. Even the backs of the drawers in his kitchen would be scrubbed according to a strict schedule, Matt guessed. He had had him as a teacher and remembered Fuller's spartan lab. It was curious that the man was a biologist and not a mathematician: for someone who considered himself an authority on life and its origins, he was almost devoid of animating spark. His hair was colorless, as were his eyes, a shade that wavered between gray and brown without settling on either, the only indecisive notes in his personality. He had barely aged in fifteen years; his skin was slightly drier, his eyelids a bit more crinkled. He even wore the same style of eyeglasses, horn-rims that had been outmoded for several decades but were now enjoying a resurgence of popularity, giving Fuller an anomalous whiff of hipness.

Matt had learned what he knew of genetics and evolution, Mendel and Darwin, from Harvey Fuller, and for that he was grateful. But of all the teachers he had had while at Armitage, none had caused him the unease that Harvey Fuller had. It was the unblinking stare, the impression he gave of remembering even the scantiest details of your history that made Matt uncomfortable. If he were honest, he had to admit that he had sometimes called upon memories of Harvey Fuller when he was interrogating suspects. That precise command of information, the creation of a mood of icy authority, had proved helpful with all manner of liars. Harvey had created, whether it was accurate or not, an impression of austere integrity.

Which was why it was odd, Matt thought, to find himself almost entirely certain that Harvey Fuller was not telling the truth about what he knew of Claire Harkness. He'd taken the proffered seat, a thinly upholstered armchair, and found himself looking at the walls, pristine white and covered in matted prints and watercolors of coastal scenes. Matt remembered that Fuller owned a cottage in Maine, where he repaired without fail every summer. When he'd been a student, the joke had been that it was never officially spring until Harvey changed from wide-wale cords to khakis.

Fuller's pants now, Matt noted, were without a wrinkle or a stain and neatly cuffed. But he plucked at them as he answered every question Matt asked, revealing a nervousness his voice did not. Yes, he had taught Claire twice. Last year in AP Biology and this spring, in an elective. "An excellent student—she scored a five on the AP, as a junior—but that's quite common here." He knew her, of course, from the dorm as well. He had duty Monday nights, as he had for the last twenty years, and would see her when she came to let him know she was back for the night, as all students were required to do. Those encounters were brief. Claire was not, Fuller said, a chatty sort. Matt couldn't imagine even the most talkative and sociable of girls wanting to chat with Mr. Fuller. Why had he been allowed to live for so long in a dorm? And a girls' dorm at that? Especially after the incidents that Porter McLellan had mentioned. He could have used his seniority to request one of the freestanding houses coveted by anyone who'd survived more than five years living with students, but he'd chosen, as he primly acknowledged, to stay in the same place the last eighteen years. It suited him, he said, with an affronted air, implying he considered it beneath him to be interrogated about anything at all. He had already reminded Matt that he'd answered exactly the same questions before.

He hadn't seen much of Claire all semester, he insisted. Monday nights, for a few moments, and perhaps at the biweekly dorm meetings, and in class, of course. But she always sat at the back of the room and he at the front. "I've got labs to correct, Detective. How much longer do you think this will take?"

Matt found his jaw tensing. A child was killed in your dorm, he wanted to say sharply to the older man. This isn't an investigation into some prank. You might have seen something. You might be willing to be helpful. Matt leaned forward in his chair and said, a little more pointedly than he intended to, "Mr. Fuller, did you notice that Claire was pregnant? Did she or any of the other students tell you?" You taught her when she was about to give birth, he was thinking. Did nothing give away the fact something had changed?

Fuller's face contracted slightly. "I'm not in the habit of observing the bodies of my students, especially my female students. It's something that tends to be frowned on in my position. We stay focused in my classes on the tasks at hand."

In spite of himself, Matt flushed, even as he remarked that Fuller's fingers were hard at work smoothing out a nonexistent crease. He tried another tactic. "What can you tell me about Rosalie Quiñones?"

"Rosalie was a student of only moderate talent. She simply couldn't manage the workload. I sat on the admissions committee last year, and I argued strenuously that we not accept her. I don't think it's fair to invite students of not quite adequate intellect here. It's a recipe for failure." He paused to adjust his pants again.

"And," Matt asked, "what about a group known as the Reign of Terror?"

"That group died out years ago, around the time you yourself graced us with your presence here. They are no longer functioning. The academy no longer tolerates such idiocy."

For an unpleasant moment, Matt thought about how satisfying it would be to deck Harvey Fuller. But this was exactly what the older man wanted, for Matt to lose his composure. Again, a shift in angle was necessary. "There's another concern, Mr. Fuller. You were observed coming from the third floor of the dorm two days after Claire died. What were you doing there? I'd also be interested if you had any idea who the father of the baby might have been."

"Who saw me?" Fuller sputtered, and Matt knew he was thinking of the recent accusations, of Porter's warning. He was suddenly intensely vulnerable, and that thinness of skin triggered something Matt had never seen in Harvey Fuller: a boiling rage that masked, he guessed, an all-consuming fear of jeopardizing what he held most dear—his position and authority at Armitage. "That ridiculous intern? That girl who can't keep her hair combed? Claire was my student. I was doing nothing more than registering the fact that she was no longer here. I touched nothing." The biology teacher looked as if the air had left his lungs. His skin turned a deeper shade of gray. "And as for the father of her child, I have no idea whatsoever. The genetic evidence hasn't been made available to me," he went on in an attempt at jauntiness that the sudden deadening of his complexion belied. "Isn't that something the police should be able to figure out on their own?" He was standing now, a furled flag, his cold composure restored. He walked toward the door and opened it.

Matt stood in the corridor and caught his breath. He wouldn't see Fuller again without Vernon; it had been foolish to think he could handle the man alone. On the other hand, if Vernon had been there, Fuller might have been that much more cautious and not let slide the fact that he was most certainly hiding something. All that plucking at his pants. He had been lying about the Reign, Rosalie, and knowing the identity of the baby's father. It was time to secure a warrant to search that apartment. If nothing else, it would give Matt satisfaction to disrupt Harvey's obsessive tidiness.

Vernon called then and said that Betsy Lowery was driving him nuts. Matt had to go over and see her now. But he expressed true pleasure when told to get working on the warrant for Harvey's place and on finding a girl who'd been harassed by the Reign, Rosalie Quiñones. Once again, Matt was filled with gratitude that he had had the luck to stumble onto Vernon as his partner, and then he started to walk across campus toward Colebrook, the sprawling Victorian that housed most of the freshman boys and the Lowery family.

They lived on the first floor, which gave them access to a fenced-in yard, where a low, shrieking cyclone of dust announced the presence of the kids who inhabited the Barfmobile. Most of the faculty mothers worked hard to keep up appearances: well-cut hair, trim figures even after multiple pregnancies, polite smiles, and children schooled to reflexive good manners from infancy. Careful women, alert to their husbands' positions, the status of certain students; the need to be friendly and circumspect in equal measure. Betsy Lowery had none of these qualities. Her hair, brown and gray and wiry, flew about her shoulders. Her figure, disguised by a sweatshirt and baggy jeans, was lumpy with unshed pounds and unexercised muscle. But her face was open and genuinely friendly. And the children, when called from the yard, were scruffy but sweet: all but the littlest shook hands and said hi and stood there squirming in the dish-strewn kitchen until their mother released them back to their play. "Four kids in four years," she said, sounding at once proud and profoundly tired. "I wouldn't change it for anything, except more sleep and my body when I was thirty. Oops. Should be more cautious talking to the police, I guess," she said and offered Matt some coffee.

He expected hers would be good—she actually needed it—and he was right. They were in the kitchen with the door open to the yard. So far, the kids were whooping with the pleasure of children returned to sun after heavy rain. The two oldest were girls, five and six, and they took care of the two youngest, a boy and another little girl. "I've got about three minutes before someone bumps a head or an elbow and starts to scream," Betsy told him. It was almost time to get dinner on the table. People started drinking now not because it was the end of the workday, she sighed, but because that was when children most reliably fell to pieces.

Betsy had been a biology teacher before she married Stan, a chemistry instructor, and had given up the classroom entirely when the kids came. It had been hard to accept the transition at first; she had loved the students. They were so smart and they worked so hard.

Usually, Matt let people talk, but this piece of information surprised him. "You were a colleague of Harvey Fuller's?" he asked. It was hard to imagine Harvey countenancing the hiring of a woman like Betsy, so full of messy life. Her lab was probably funky with overgrown experiments. Fuller would have been sure to be on any job committee; Matt was amazed someone like Betsy had been allowed to slip through.

Betsy looked somber. "Oh, yes. And it was one of the reasons I wanted to stay in the department; the students needed an alternative perspective, in my view. I didn't know how bad it was going to be. Harvey was on sabbatical the year I came. Otherwise, he would never have let someone like me in. I actually got the kids to keep science journals. And worse"—and here she fluttered her hands in the air—"got a compost bin going in the classroom."

She paused and looked out a little more closely at the children. The littlest had pulled a truck away from the oldest girl, but so far, protests weren't forthcoming. "No," Betsy mused, "Harvey had no patience for me. Although I have him to thank for introducing me to Stan—he had us over for dinner one night and we hit it off. I had barely talked to Stan before that. I think Harvey did it on purpose, knowing that I liked and wanted children and that Stan did, too." She gave a shrug then that was close to a shudder. Her disgust was real, Matt thought.

"But Harvey's not what I wanted to talk to you about, though God knows I could do that forever. He's a fascinating case to me. This is what's bothering me, Detective." She looked at him full on, her eyes hazel and remarkably pretty. "After Claire died, things exploded, as you can imagine. Students in complete distress, parents calling constantly, police everywhere. There was total chaos, and Stan and I did nothing but deal with that for the next two days. And then last night, I woke up and realized that something had been bothering me about the morning her body was found. I got this sickening notion I ought to remember something." It was hard to overemphasize just how much lack of sleep eroded short-term memory, she told Matt, and she spent all day trying to recall it. "And when I did, today, I didn't want to call you at first. I knew I had to, but I didn't want to. I think my mind was actively trying to suppress it. I think you'll understand when I tell you.

"The morning Claire died, I was driving to CVS. Nathaniel had a fever, and we were all out of Tylenol. I was heading past Portland, and I nearly ran over Madeline Christopher. She was listening to music on headphones, and perhaps she hadn't heard me. She's a sweet girl, but a little addlebrained sometimes. But really it was my fault because I was thinking about what I'd seen before that, since it was so unexpected. I am almost positive I saw Porter McLellan heading away from the dorm. He must have left from the back entrance. He was walking quickly, along the edge of the woods. I only saw him from behind, but I think I recognized his jacket, this shabby thing he wears though Lucinda keeps telling him to get rid of it."

Matt put his coffee down. "Was he carrying anything, Mrs. Lowery?"

"No," she said. "At least as far as I could see. As soon as I remembered, I immediately thought of that, too. No, I think his hands were by his sides. He was walking quickly. Mr. Corelli, what struck me was this: I could almost swear that this person was crying. It was his shoulders. They were shaking."

"What time was this, Mrs. Lowery?" Matt was already moving toward the door, his hands twitching for his phone.

"Six ten," she said. "The car has this clock with a very large LED display. I don't know why, but that stuck in my mind."

"Could anyone else have seen him from that angle?" Matt scanned his memory to try to recall the windows on the back side of Portland. At least three faculty apartments would have views on that side, and who knew what the girls had glimpsed.

"Madeline was running, and the others would be Grace and Harvey. And I am sorry to say this, Mr. Corelli, but I don't think that either of them would have necessarily found it prudent to notice Porter at an inconvenient time." She looked sad and confused, caught in a welter of allegiances. Then, from the yard, a scream went up. But it was only that, as Betsy predicted, one of the children had fallen and banged a knee, and in the next moment, her disorderly kitchen was full of shouting kids. As he thanked her and made for the door, Matt caught a glimpse of the wound Betsy was tending to, the small red flag of scraped flesh. Dialing quickly to speak to Vernon, he heard her soothing voice tell the hurt child that she would be fine, that everything was all right.

"Jesus," Vernon said when Matt explained what Betsy had told him. "I'll call the assistant and get him as soon as we can." But then Vernon called back almost immediately and said, "Autopsy results in, and that pathologist is actually making himself available on the phone. I'll meet you up there. I've got dinner for you. Kathy made extra soba noodles. And we should go see the wife right away. The English bitch wouldn't let us change our appointment. We don't see McLellan until seven forty-five."

At a bench outside the library, Vernon met Matt and said, "No more shit food for you." Matt was surprised to find how tasty the meal was and admired the fact that Kathy had even included a pair of chopsticks for him. His wife was worried about the impact of all the adrenaline on their systems, Vernon explained. The buckwheat in the soba noodles was supposed to offset that toxic rush. No matter what its physical effect, it was wonderfully soothing to eat something wholesome. As he sipped in the slippery pasta, Matt talked on the phone to the pathologist.

Claire had been incredibly lucky, the doctor said; there were no complications; she had delivered the placenta cleanly and hadn't even completely torn herself up in the process. Someone most likely had assisted her. She had been rather undernourished but overall healthy. A pity, he'd permitted himself to add. She'd been a beautiful girl. Built, too, for babies.

At least she hadn't dumped her child in the trash the way some of these girls did. Didn't Matt remember that case in Holyoke? All too clearly, Matt said. But if Claire hadn't harmed the baby, where was he? There was still absolutely nothing that pointed to his whereabouts. Angell was starting to be furious not only with them but with the federal agents, too.

As for the wound that had killed Claire, it was going to be hard to use it to prove murder. Blunt trauma. From the bedpost. She had landed on it, and it had hit at a particularly vulnerable spot at the base of the skull. Having just given birth, with her entire vascular system still rather dilated, probably hadn't helped, the doctor noted laconically. There were also some bruises on her arms, wrists, and near her neck. Whether they were sustained at the time of death or during birth, it was hard to say. "Women can get pretty banged up having babies." Abruptly, Matt realized he couldn't keep eating. Besides, as Vernon told him with an ostentatious tap at his watch, they needed to go and visit Lucinda.

Matt had seen her only rarely in his four days on campus, and when they found her in her kitchen, she seemed rooted there. Despite the evening's warmth, she was wrapped in a sweater. When they asked her where she had been early in the morning on Monday, she said, glancing at the far wall, "I was asleep. Porter was probably walking the dog. It's what he does every morning. Just confirm it with him," and then she turned from them in dismissal, though it was clear that she was doing nothing other than gripping a mug of tea that had long ago grown cold. The dog in question, an Australian shepherd, was lying protectively at her feet.

"Buy it?" Vernon asked Matt as they left.

"No," he answered. "Betsy Lowery said nothing about a dog, but it's more than that. She wouldn't even look at us." Matt dialed Betsy's number, and again the woman came through. "That's exactly why I didn't think it was Porter at first," she told Matt. A chorus of squabbling voices could be heard in the background as she spoke. "He didn't have Gretel with him. She's always leashed. Last year, there was a ruckus about dogs on campus raised by Harvey Fuller, of course, and they started enforcing the leash law again. Porter's the head; he had to use one."

It was almost time for them to meet Porter. Tamsin had designated the Commons for the appointment. As they walked into the dining hall, Vernon turned to Matt and said, "You have to wear black tie when you ate here? Use the good silver?" The opulence of the surroundings was irritating Vernon the way the memorial service on the Knoll had: all this rigid attention to appearances. Even in the dim light, it was obvious that the dark-paneled room where the students shuffled in for breakfast, lunch, and dinner was grandly designed, with a bank of windows along one side, chandeliers hanging icily from the ceiling, and parquet floors so highly polished they, too, gave off a sheen. Empty, it echoed, and Matt grew conscious of how full of glinting light it was, even in the settling darkness. When he had been a student here, all he'd been attuned to was where his friends were sitting, where the girls he

liked might be, which teachers were eating where. To most adolescents, the array of one's social connections was the most important kind of architecture there was. He wondered now which
tables had been reserved for the Reign and which for the girls
they deemed inferior.

Vernon walked over to the coffee bar. "Green tea. They even
have green tea," he observed, and he made himself a cup. "I will
not get you coffee. If you're going to pollute yourself, you'll have
to do it on your own."

But Matt didn't need the coffee. Betsy Lowery's reluctant and
slightly belated revelation that she'd seen Porter leaving Portland
at a critical time had given them something slim but real to follow.
Vernon wandered back to their table. "Why did he want to meet
here, you think?"

"Library too public. Even his office. Everybody walks by and
sees the lights. And he doesn't want us at the house with the wife."

Now slurping his tea, Vernon said, "So who was it? Someone
who looked like him? Another big guy with dark hair? And why is
the wife lying, and what's he going to say?"

Matt didn't answer Vernon, distracted by an appetizing smell
of grilled meat that lingered in the room. He'd heard Porter had
made the food better and paid the cafeteria workers more than
they'd ever earned before. But students now washed dishes and
helped to cook the food they and their peers ate. There was an
organic farm where spectacular lettuces and herbs were grown.
The headmaster had also implemented a policy that required
students to work around the school and in the community. They
tutored in Greenville schools. They had cleaned up a stretch of
the Bluestone that ran between Greenville and Armitage. Some
faculty thought Porter's notions of service highfalutin—"we're

not a commune," Grace Peters had sniffed. Some thought of it as yet another layer of padding the kids could add to their college applications. Others admired Porter's ideas and believed it was good for the more insulated of the students to get a sense of how the rest of the world worked, not to mention eat healthy food. A far cry from stern, humorless Gordon Farnsworth.

"You like this guy," Vernon said sternly, smacking his mug on the table. "I have to admit, I'm impressed, too. He almost makes you feel"—and here he swept his hand out to encompass the glimmering room—"that all this means something. Adds up to something other than simply revolting excess."

"You're almost right, Vernon. I am very close to liking him. He's worth talking to. And that's exactly the effect he has. But it's a problem."

"You don't want him to be involved," Vernon said. "But he is."

Matt looked at him. "He has some good history on his side, too." Matt asked, and knew the answer in advance, if Vernon remembered the case a year ago when an Armitage kid had been caught selling speed and date-rape drugs on campus. In direct contradiction to usual procedure, and apparently in the face of opposition from the board, Porter had insisted that this student face charges. He had even written a letter to alumni saying that he would not countenance the breaking of federal law in such a dangerous realm and that, by hiding behind a cloak of privilege and conducting its own form of discipline, Armitage was cheapening what it had to offer and not providing the protection to its students that it claimed. The kid, who was a serious dealer, was now in a juvenile prison.

"That never happened when I was here. Armitage kids got bailed out. They still do, when we catch them trying to buy beer.

But for the big things, McLellan turns them loose. So why isn't he on our side this time?" But Matt stopped talking because Porter had come in. They heard the creak of the wide door and saw him tall and lean on the threshold.

He walked over, shook their hands, and immediately started with an apology for meeting them so late in the day and here in the Commons. "And I'm glad to see you've found the coffee, Mr. Cates."

"Green tea, Mr. McLellan. That's all he drinks," said Matt. They settled at one of the round tables, Vernon with his laptop flipped open.

"Yes, students requested it, and we began to stock it. If you're going to ask them to work so hard, you've got to feed them properly," Porter said.

"It might have something to do with the amount of tuition you charge them, too," said Vernon. Matt realized his partner was only wedging himself without much difficulty into the role of townie antagonist, but the tone almost made him flinch.

Porter said nothing for a second and then laughed. It was a real sound, unexpected in the crystal-spiked dimness, and it took them both by surprise. "You're right, Mr. Cates. It's got a lot to do with that tuition. Which is absurdly high and out of reach of almost anyone in the country, although it's also true that every Armitage student, no matter his or her need, is subsidized. It costs a lot, what we provide. But it's correct that we deal with an elite, and we help propagate that elite. It's an accurate claim, and one I wish weren't quite so true. Still, it's not the only thing that can be said about Armitage and places like it. Because we have money, we can make it possible for students with no means whatsoever to attend and have access to one of the best educations around. An authentic one, with balance and humanity and intelligence in it. And I am still confident that we provide that." He didn't glance at Matt; he didn't need to. Matt had reaped exactly those benefits. It was why he would have chosen to attend Armitage again, in spite of everything that had happened there.

Vernon glowered at his screen, typing something furiously. It was always disappointing to have his bait refused.

"Mr. McLellan," Matt said. "We need to ask you something about the morning Claire died. Could you tell us what you were doing then, from the time you woke up to the time you called the police at six thirty?"

Even in the low light, it was possible to see that Porter had gone entirely still, but he wasn't, Matt sensed, surprised at this new line of discussion. Up to this point, his position had been only that of the authority who needed to be briefed. Yet if he resented this shift in their attitude toward him, he gave no overt sign. "Of course. I woke at five thirty. I got dressed and checked e-mail; there were a number of issues heating up before the next board meeting."

Having spoken to the head of the board, Colson Trowbridge, Matt knew about some of them. A controversial proposal, Porter's, to allow same-sex couples to live together in faculty housing and another, from Sarah Talmadge, to require students to spend at least part of a semester abroad and not only, as Trowbridge put it, "somewhere clean, like Sweden." Porter, according to Trowbridge, didn't seek out fights and was good at brokering alliances where least expected. They rarely turned him down, though what he called the gay faculty problem wasn't likely to be an easy sell.

"Then I walked the dog, which I usually do as Lucinda sleeps later than I do and Gretel gets impatient," Porter went on. He stared out the window down toward the Bluestone.

"Is that where you walk her, Mr. McLellan? By the river?" Matt asked. If he answered yes, this would contradict Betsy Lowery's information; the river was on the other side of campus from Portland.

"No," Porter said slowly. "I was looking at the river and thinking of a prank the seniors played last year. I'm sure you remember those, Detective." In spite of himself, Matt found his own mind alive with the time boys in his class had led a cow into this dining hall, a cow that had been suddenly overwhelmed by its circumstances and responded the only way it knew how, which was to go berserk and then head charging through the plate-glass window that led to the wide green expanse at which Porter was looking. Explosive sound, shards of glass, flailing black-and-white hindquarters. Indelible.

Vernon had stopped typing and was about to interrupt, to pull Porter back to the question at hand, but with a tilt of his index finger, Matt stopped him. "The faculty woke up and couldn't find their dogs, and then this incredible howling rose from the river and everyone ran down to see what was happening. The students had loaded every dog they could get their hands on, including Gretel, into rowboats. It was a protest about the leash law. They claimed they were going to find new homes for all the animals who couldn't walk around on campus anymore. They liked the roaming dogs. It was the faculty and parents who didn't. But Gretel doesn't like boats. Since then, she doesn't want to walk by the river. I walk her in the woods. Not far from Portland."

"Did anything unusual happen with her that morning?" Matt asked.

Porter paused, looking at his hands. "Yes, now that you mention it. She had slipped her lead. I was looking for her." His voice was soft now.

"What were you wearing, Mr. McLellan?" Vernon asked.

"I don't recall," he said more confidently and glancing up again at them. "I don't pay much attention to what I wear. Lucinda is always trying to clean me up. Make me look more like a head of school, whatever that means." He plucked at his handkerchief and folded it. "Is there anything else? I'm afraid I've still got a great deal to do tonight. May I ask if Scott Johnston is with the police again?"

"You're welcome to ask, Mr. McLellan," said Vernon, "but there's nothing to say at this point."

"I understand," he said and rose. He shook their hands and left. It was time to get back to the station, but Vernon went to refill his green tea. "He's talked to the wife."

"Yup," said Matt and flexed his hands. "And he's lying about the dog. I saw the leashes hanging in the kitchen. The kinds they use are almost nooses; there's no way she could have slid out from one of those. Let's check with the neighbors." Remembering Betsy's assumption that Grace Peters and Harvey Fuller would claim blindness when it came to protecting Porter, he didn't think it likely the neighbors would have much to say, and their excuse might well be plausible. As in his day, the head's residence was surrounded by a dense hedge of privet that gave the large white house an unusual measure of privacy.

Vernon rubbed the back of his neck and held the door open for Matt. It was starting to drizzle again. "More goddamn rain. So bad for my tomatoes." The head's house loomed into view as they squelched along. They stopped for a moment, and the tall lamp-posts gave off a pinkish glow that the puddles on the walkway reflected in a thousand broken disks.

But it was then they saw, through a window on the second floor, a woman in profile. It was Lucinda McLellan, and she was shout-ing at someone. Her face was contorted, and she was obviously very angry. Matt glanced at Vernon to see if he noticed the same thing. "Can't hear a thing, can you?" Vernon said. "The dog could have been barking its head off and you'd have no idea. Who's she yelling at? Can you see?"

But Matt couldn't, and whoever was at the receiving end of Lucinda's rage was wisely staying at a distance from her. "Shall we knock?" Vernon asked. Then, just as they were walking to the door, it opened briskly and Tamsin Lovell came out of the house. She barely glanced at them. "Mr. McLellan's not in," she said. "He's at his office." She put up her umbrella as she spoke, making it impos-sible to see her face. But her voice, Matt noted, was unperturbed. If she had been the person Lucinda was screaming at, she seemed to have taken it remarkably in stride. "Good night," she said, pulling the door tight behind her and picking up a large duffel bag that she had left on the step as she opened her umbrella. She hoisted it to her shoulder and set off down the path, toward, they assumed, a parking lot.

"What was in the bag?" Vernon said, looking after her.

"It didn't look like something she would carry. It looked like something you'd take to a hockey rink," Matt said.

"It did, indeed," said Vernon. Just then the door opened, and Lucinda strode out, both taken aback and exasperated that they were there. "Porter's not here," she snapped. "I have no idea where he is." She stepped past them and walked down the path.

By the time they got to the parking lot to see what Tamsin was lugging with her, the assistant had left. And when they drove to her house, a trim bungalow on the outskirts of Armitage, they found it dark and shuttered with no car in the driveway.

CHAPTER 15

Jim woke from a dream of roofs collapsing and buildings whose windows were all broken. The digital clock blinked 3:14 Friday morning. It was the phone. The phone was ringing and his heart began to pound—there was nothing about phones ringing in the middle of the night that did not mean an emergency. He lurched toward the extension and heard Angela's frightened voice. She wasn't breathing right. Her heart hurt. She had called the ambulance, and he needed to get there right away. She'd done everything in the right sequence, she even sounded fairly at ease. Yet Jim felt nothing but the purest fear flow through him. "I'm coming, Ma, I'm coming. I'll be right there."

He dressed in seconds, grabbed his wallet, his cell phone. His charger was in the car; he'd need to be in touch with his siblings, with Nancy Mitchell. Driving over to his mother's, he prayed he wouldn't run into any cops. But maybe they were distracted at the moment. Maybe speeding drivers meant nothing when there were a baby and a killer to find. They weren't saying it was murder, but what else could it be? The streets were empty. Few lights shone from houses, and it was hard to see with the rain that poured down. His windshield wipers dragged across the glass; in the turmoil that had seized the campus, he'd forgotten to change them.

At Angela's, he found an ambulance, its harsh lights wheeling in the wild night. The nice neighbors, the young couple next door, were shivering in bathrobes on their porch, watching with concern as men in blue jumpsuits and yellow slickers tramped in and out of the house, walkie-talkies squawking. When they saw Jim, they waved and the husband shouted, "Please, Mr. French, just let us know if there's anything we can do." He waved back, too distressed to speak but grateful his mother was surrounded by people who cared about her. Kayla. That was another person he would have to call once they knew what was going on.

In the living room, he saw Angela on a stretcher, an oxygen mask clamped to her face. What struck him most was how pale she was. Her face was white as paper, and wrinkled, as if someone had balled up a sheet and tossed it carelessly into the trash. A woman paramedic was at her side, monitoring her pulse and the oxygen flow. Angela's eyes were open, and they were sharp, wet, and round with fear. Her fingers fluttered toward Jim, registering his arrival, and though she couldn't speak, he saw her gratitude, her relief in the movement of her hand.

"How is she?" he asked the woman, as he knelt by his mother, touching what he could of her arm. She'd gotten her nails done. Kayla had persuaded her to add manicures to her indulgences. She sported frosted pink polish, and it looked glamorous in spite of her pallor, her bathrobe.

"We're taking her to the hospital to find out. Are you her son? Are you Jim?" He said he was. "Good. She was worried about you getting here in the storm." She adjusted the oxygen flow and made ready, with the help of a colleague, to roll the stretcher out to the ambulance. "He's here now, Mrs. French," the woman said gently. "You'll see him again at the hospital. Just a few more minutes."

She looked so tiny lying there in the jumble of tubes and bags. Her hair, she would have been horrified to know, was in disarray around her shoulders. The driver motioned to his colleagues to hurry up. The woman turned to Jim and said, "Follow us there. She'll be in the ER. They know she's coming."

But before leaving, he wanted to make sure the house was locked and the lights were out. Very old habits of order asserted themselves, and he even spent extra time balling up the wrappers and Band-Aids and cotton balls the paramedics had strewn about in their haste to stabilize Angela and get her off to the hospital. He made her bed, smelled the fresh cleanness of her sheets, and hurried down, conscious of the need to see his mother again as soon as possible. A passing car briefly made the glass on the framed photos lining the stairwell dance with a thousand shards of brightness. Then it rolled on and Jim could no longer see the smiling faces of his relatives.

Driving fast through the rainy streets, he didn't care if cops spotted him. He didn't even think about cops. What he thought about was his father's death five years ago. When he'd locked eyes with his mother, he guessed that they'd both been thinking about the whole experience. About the sudden pain that had seized George's face and arm, the trip to the same hospital, his dad's initial improvement and then the final collapse. The day his father died, a Thursday in May, forty-eight hours after his first heart attack, Jim had known that his marriage to Carla was going to end. She couldn't mask the fact that she was put out at having to take care of the girls that week and that she'd have to miss her history final. Once the girls were in primary school, Carla had returned to college, reigniting a love of learning that had eventually outdistanced her love of almost anything or anyone else. She was working now in Boston, at the Museum of Fine Arts. She had never been happier, something she made sure to remind him of every time they spoke.

But at least she had been there. Now, driving through the familiar streets at an unfamiliar pace, Jim realized there was no one he would call for such support. There was no one he wanted beside him as he navigated these next critical hours. But then, pulling up to the ER of Armitage General, he realized he was wrong. He wanted to talk to Nancy Mitchell. He would have felt happy if Nancy were there.

Inside, he quickly found the insanely young doctor who was in charge of Angela's case and learned that his mother was on an EKG machine; they were reading the results now, but it looked like she had had a mild heart attack. They'd know more soon from the blood work, and the best thing he could do was to sit down and wait. The young woman looked tired but competent, her hair in a blond twist on her head, pinned with a single take-out chopstick. Angela's arrival had probably interrupted her dinner, ordered a few hours ago from the Happy Palace down the street. Jim did not ask if his mother was going to be okay; doctors never answered that question, trained as they were to steer all information toward the factual, the known, the unsueable.

But the young woman smiled at him and said, "Mr. French? I wouldn't worry too much. Sit down, drink some water. I'll be here all night. We're doing everything we can." Jim took her advice and watched the thin parade of the sick stumble through the doors. Parents with asthmatic kids, old men with bad diabetic reactions. A fender bender. Closer to dawn, he called his brothers and sisters, alerting them to what he kept calling the situation. There were gasps of worry, promises to come as soon as possible, polite expressions of gratitude for what they called being there. Jim knew he was fulfilling his role at last; the reason for which he'd stayed so long near his mother was finally becoming manifest. Slowly, the week would fill with his gathering family.

It was six in the morning. He had reached everyone. His head was blurred with sleep and he had just folded his arms to make a bumpy pillow for himself when the young doctor came to talk to him. "First results are in, Mr. French. It looks like it's what we thought: a minor heart attack. She's resting now, but she's out of immediate danger. We got there in time." There was genuine warmth in her touch. She was new enough to her profession to believe in its most pristine possibilities. He was grateful to her. He couldn't remember her name, but he was grateful to her. "I don't want you to bother her now. She's in cardiology for the time being, and you can see her when she wakes up. Get some rest."

Sleep proved impossible, and he paced until 6:30. Angela was always awake at first light. A few minutes later he found himself by her side, with the yellow sun pouring in through the slats in the closed blinds. The storm had finally cleared. His mother was still sleeping. Her arm was threaded with tubes, and nurses padded in and out in what seemed a constant, soft-footed procession. Bleeps and hums came from the monitors clocking her vital signs, but any fool could see she was better than she had been.

He sat there and held her hand with its frosty nails. She breathed steadily on. He knew someone else he could call this time of day. Nancy. Like Jim and his mother, she was an early riser from both habit and preference. She answered her cell on the first ring. "Jim?" she asked, and he knew he wasn't mistaking the mixture of alarm and concern, affection and worry. "What's wrong? What's happened?"

It was his mother, he explained. She was in the hospital. A heart attack. It looked like she was going to be fine, but he would need to stay here for the day. "I'm sorry; it's a bad time to be out." He'd be back as soon as he could. One of his sisters would be here soon from New York.

"Where are you?" she asked. "Armitage General? I'm coming now." And she did. She was there in fifteen minutes, her hair fanned out around her shoulders; she hadn't paused to put it in a braid or to comb it fully. She didn't even have her ring of school keys with her. But she was there, with a bunch of daffodils. Pulled, she said, from her garden, but real flowers, the right kind, not chrysanthemums wrapped in foil. "Jim, I was just so upset," she said. "I know how close you are to your mother."

She sat down next to him and looked at Angela, and very tenderly brushed a tendril of hair from her forehead. "She's still so beautiful. How old is she, Jim?"

"Eighty-two," he said but almost absentmindedly. He was looking with amazement at Nancy. Here she was in her jeans and her work shirt, and he had never seen a more attractive woman.

"You look alike," Nancy said and then reached for his hand and held it for a moment. What startled him was that her palm was just as callused as his, as bumpy with work. Jim thought about Nancy and was aware of how little he truly knew of her life. She was single, but whether she was divorced or not, he had no idea. He didn't think she had kids, but she was good with them. All he really knew was that she loved her job and that she kept the school in lovely shape.

He thanked her for coming, and she dropped his hand and sat there in a slightly awkward silence. It was almost easier to turn the conversation toward the crisis of the moment, toward Claire and what had happened to her baby. It was so sad, Nancy said, and the worst was that she felt responsible. As if she ought to have put in measures that should have protected the child. It was almost impossible not to feel this way. The horror of what had happened was glaring, and all the people Jim liked or respected seemed somehow to feel they ought to have done something to prevent it. Nancy frowned and pinned her long hair with a clip she pulled from the pocket of her jeans. "I keep thinking about this, Jim. I want to believe that someone from outside got in, killed that poor girl and took the baby, but it doesn't add up." The reasons were these. As they both knew, she said, there was no sign of any door to Portland being forced open. Nor had the window locks been pried wide.

A new system had been installed within the last year that allowed students and faculty to swipe their IDs as if they were credit cards through a little box attached to each major entrance. The system recognized each person as the holder of an Armitage ID, and the door clicked ajar. But these cards weren't coded to individual users; it would have added another hundred thousand dollars to the cost to make the system that specific, and the board of trustees had decided against the extra expenditure, Nancy said. Why would it be that important to know where each student was at every moment of the day? Wasn't that an invasion of privacy? What was the point of storing all that information? Jim remembered that Porter had argued for the extra cost, saying it kept kids safer, but he'd been narrowly defeated. And now, Nancy said ruefully, if he had had his way, we'd know exactly who had come in. "Or even prevented this from happening, because anyone aware of the process would understand how easy it would be to track the flow of people in and out of the dorm. But that just underlines the fact that it was someone who knew about the loophole and used it." She said what had already been emphasized multiple times by multiple people: these kids were very smart and knew how to press on the slightest of advantages to gain what they wanted. In addition, the issue obvious to them both was that Claire had known her killer and either hadn't been worried to see the person or had pulled the door wide herself.

The other issue she had thought a lot about since Claire's death, Nancy told Jim, was security cameras. The students spread these rumors that the whole campus was under surveillance. It was an image that suited their needs as adolescents for drama and intrigue. But the truth was, she said, leaning earnestly toward Jim, and she'd said the same thing to the police, "We don't have a single one. One of the reasons I took this job," she said, "was that I was going to have a chance to focus on what mattered to me. Taking care of beautiful old buildings. Trying to be a good manager. I wanted to help them get their wiring and their safety standards up to snuff. And I like kids. I like being around them. I didn't want to be a part of some school that was mostly a police state." But this had changed everything.

All of a sudden, exhaustion overcame him. Jim could have gone to sleep right there. It was Nancy's presence. Someone else was watching. He could relax. She noticed and said, "Coffee time. I'll go get some. I think your mother's waking up."

She was right. Angela was stirring, and soon after Nancy had walked off to the cafeteria, she woke up. She was clear-eyed but tired. "Jimmie," she said. "I am so glad to see you. At least I know I'm not dead."

The spring sun spilled through where it could. The sterile room was almost cheerful, it was so full of tender morning light. But then Angela said, "Jimmie, remember to tell Kayla not to come to the house. But I want to talk to her, Jim." Her nails flashed in the sun. What was so pressing about her need to see Kayla? He was about to ask his mother more when Nancy came back with a trayful of pastries and coffee and a smile on her face.

"Who's that?" Angela asked.

"Nancy, my boss," Jim said. "She brought these, from her garden," he added, gesturing to the daffodils. He'd found a plastic vase molded to resemble crystal, but the flowers, exuberant and fresh, almost masked the ugliness.

"Very pretty," said Angela, but she was looking at Nancy, not the flowers, when she said it. "Everything's changing," Angela sighed. "I'm never ready for it. But it's always changing."

Nancy smiled at Jim and signaled that she'd be leaving. He raised his hand, miming a telephone call.

"She likes you. Finally, someone who likes you." Angela sniffed. "I want some coffee."

"Ma, you had a heart attack," he protested.

"I know what I had and I want some coffee." She sat up cautiously and reached for the cup. "How'd she know I like mine with milk and sugar?" she asked, having taken a careful sip. "And since when did they make decent coffee at a hospital?"

"Because that's how I take mine, too," said Jim. But when he thought about it, he realized he hadn't told Nancy that. She must just have been watching. She had been paying attention during all the other times they'd taken breaks together.

The young doctor came in then, without the take-out chop-stick in her hair this time, and ushered Jim out, but not before giving the coffee an accusing look. He waited in the hallway. His head was dense with fatigue, but he was alert enough to remember the exact texture of Nancy Mitchell's hand in his. He sat down in the waiting room, surrounded by the clamor of the hospital, the ringing of phones and elevator doors, and tried to relive the feeling of her strong hand.

CHAPTER 16

Admittedly, the mouse and its surgically severed head had frightened Madeline. It was Lee's handiwork, she suspected. As the department's prize student, Lee would have unparalleled access to the bio labs. And the department itself was pleased to possess a complement of instruments and animals more impressive than most universities'. The academy's apparent need to aspire to the status of colleges was something Madeline had always had trouble understanding. A rival school had just raised funds for an electron microscope, and Armitage was jealously trying to marshal the means to build one for itself. But did high school students really need to investigate the world of subatomic particles quite so thoroughly? Couldn't they wait until they were graduate students in physics, just like everybody else?

It was easier to think about this than to figure out what to do with the poor creature Lee had sacrificed in her campaign—quite successful, Madeline was forced to confess—to intimidate the intern. Finally, she settled on rolling it gently in a paper towel and then placing it in an empty tub that had once held hummus. Sealed, the mouse went into the trash barrel outside the dorm. Then Madeline did two things: she left a long message with Sarah Talmadge and another with Matt Corelli. She thought about calling Fred, too, but decided against contacting him until he'd made a choice about Brooklyn. There was just so much vulnerability a person could stand.

Returning from dinner, Madeline had thought that it would be an early night. But finding the mouse on her doorstep had kindled a nervous energy that she knew would not allow her to work or rest easily. Instead, she investigated the rest of the bottles she had scavenged from the second-floor bathroom but found no other Ziploc bags that contained threatening notes. Then she checked her watch and realized she still had a while before study hours were over. She could probably find Maggie Fitzgerald and see what she had to say about Rosalie, the Reign, and other facets of boarding school life that had escaped Madeline this year. Scanning her memory, she remembered that the girl had relocated to Fallows, a dorm two over from Portland on the Quad.

Each dorm had a dedicated study hall; a nice idea, thought Madeline, except that they were uniformly dispiriting, with their bald lighting and threadbare chairs. Few students used them, preferring the comfort of the common room, their own bunks, or the whispery sociability of the library. But in Fallows's bleak basement, Maggie was bent over an open textbook detailing the history of ancient Egypt. Madeline did not think she had interrupted the amassing of critical details about the building of the Great Pyramid. Maggie was clearly paying no attention to the lines of text in front of her. Fortunately, she was also the only person in the room.

"Hi, Miss Christopher," the girl said. "Why are you here?" She wore tiny round spectacles, and her spine seemed unusually limp. It didn't have much to hold up, that was true enough, but even so, Maggie's body had very little vital energy about it.

Madeline pulled up a chair next to her. "To talk to you, actually," she said, assuming a direct approach would be fairest. "I want to ask you about Claire, and those girls in the dorm"—she still

couldn't bring herself to call them the Reign without sarcasm—
"and also about Rosalie."

Maggie took a sip from her can of diet iced tea. She was delicate to the point of translucence and had need of even the empty
calories that regular iced tea would have supplied. "Did you know
there are some people who think that the Pyramids and Machu
Picchu were built with alien technology?" She played with the
tab on the can as she spoke.

Madeline smiled and said, "No, I had no idea about that. But
I don't really believe in aliens. Do you, Maggie?"

The silver tab broke off in the girl's spindly fingers. "Nope. I
think life is creepy enough on this planet without inventing
people from outer space." She looked up then, and Madeline was
struck by the directness of her gaze and the narrow ferocity of her
face. She had been the girl who kept saying about Claire, "But she
was so pretty," as if beauty were all Claire had needed to invoke
to stay alive.

Maggie dropped the tab of the can into the drink, and Madeline hoped she'd be careful when she took her next sip. She closed
the textbook and something shifted in her face. She appeared to
reach a decision. Taking a pen from the desk, she scribbled on a
page in her notebook, tore it out, and said, "Here is Rosalie's number. She might talk to you. She doesn't live too far from here. But
I can't. I promised not to." Here her voice began to fray slightly.
Fallows's basement smelled damply of laundry and lint. What an
unproductive atmosphere in which to try to learn anything.

Madeline leaned forward. "Are they hurting you and other
girls, Maggie? What are they doing to you? I can help you stop
them if you want. I promise to help." Madeline was surprised at
the depth of her concern and the intensity of her response. But I

shouldn't be, she reminded herself. They've been trying to scare me, too, and they've done a pretty good job at it.

"They don't do it directly, Miss Christopher. Well, mostly," Maggie said softly, lowering her voice. "They just like to let you know they're watching," she said. "They create a climate of fear. They try to make themselves like the pharaohs. They want to appear invincible."

A climate of fear. It sounded like a phrase from Orwell. Though clearly on loan from another source, the phrase was quite accurate. "Maggie, did they hurt Claire?" But Maggie was looking around her now, as if talking about the Reign might call them out. The girl shook her head and wouldn't say more. "I've got to go, Miss Christopher." She gathered her books into a flimsy tote bag and scurried from the room. A slightly larger mouse than the one Madeline had found on her doorstep. And fortunately, she still had her head on.

Madeline glanced at the piece of paper. A local area code. As Maggie had said, the Quiñones family lived nearby. It wouldn't be that hard to find out exactly where, and it was only 7:30. Madeline went back to the dorm, dialed, and a woman, sounding weary, answered on the third ring. When Madeline asked to speak to Rosalie, she merely bellowed, "Rosie, it's for you," and then the handset clanked on a counter.

Madeline barely remembered what Rosalie looked like. Short, dark-haired, slight. She'd given off an air of seriousness. And then, before Thanksgiving, she was gone. Madeline vaguely recalled Grace saying something about her not cutting it, or some other expression that meant Rosalie just wasn't Armitage material.

When she answered, Rosalie sounded bored, but as Madeline made her nervous introduction, she could sense the girl slowly standing taller, straighter, listening harder. All of a sudden, she said, "I know who you are. I know what you want to talk about. Can you come over now? It's like twenty minutes away. We can meet at Antonio's," a pizza place on the main street in her town, she explained. She lived in Westerfield, a factory town much like Greenville as far as Madeline knew. Rosalie gave her directions, said she'd be there in a half hour, and that Madeline should order the sausage roll. It was really good.

This is foolish, Madeline told herself, I shouldn't do this, as she started her car in the drizzling rain and rolled toward the great iron gates that surrounded Armitage. The police officer still stationed there gave her ID a thorough looking over, then ushered her on. Driving through the gathering dark toward the highway, Madeline wondered if Lee and her cohorts actually had the steel in them to kill a classmate. Her hands tightened around the steering wheel, and sweat ran a bit down her neck as she realized the answer was yes.

She found the town easily. It could have been Greenville that she was exploring, though an even seedier, less prosperous version. The sidewalks of the main street were lined with empty stores plastered with For Rent placards that Madeline guessed had been in place for months if not years. The lampposts weren't the period wrought iron that lined the brick streets of Armitage but the tall, buzzing variety that fit better along interstates. Several of them had dead bulbs. No one was out, which you might be able to blame on the weather, but even on a clear evening, Madeline suspected, the streets would be close to empty. Below the canopy for a discount shoe store lurked a group of boys in slouchy jeans and tank tops, their hands propped on the handles of their bicycles as if they hoped the battered ten-speeds would turn magically into

Harleys. Madeline found Antonio's easily. It was one of the few businesses still open, and its red-and-white marquee swung in the stiffening wind.

Rosalie was already there, perched in an orange booth, a neatly folded compact umbrella on the tabletop. She had a can of Coke and what looked like one of the sausage rolls she had recommended in front of her on a paper plate. With sudden clarity, Madeline remembered her on the first day of school. While almost all the other girls had sported expensive jeans and flimsy T-shirts that nonetheless cost forty dollars apiece, Rosalie had worn a blue skirt and a long-sleeved shirt, something almost dowdy about it, practically Amish in its sobriety. Poor thing, Madeline had thought at the time, she's missed the code, not quite realizing that it might be something far more basic dictating Rosalie's style. Maybe those plain clothes were all her family was able to afford.

Now Rosalie greeted her with a rather severe nod, in keeping, Madeline felt, with that modest choice of dress. Madeline ordered a sausage roll and a Diet Coke from a man in an apron vivid with the stains appropriate to his work. When her food was hot, she went to join Rosalie, whose own roll remained untouched.

"Thank you for seeing me," Madeline said. "I'm sure you've got schoolwork you need to do. I won't take up much of your time." She thought it best to approach Rosalie frankly. The girl looked so stern sitting there, her hands folded one on top of the other. She was wearing, Madeline saw, a uniform. A shirt with a Peter Pan collar and a gray cardigan, buttoned at the neck. But the clothing only reinforced the impression of primness. Most of that emanated straight from Rosalie and her squared shoulders and serious face, which was now coolly assessing Madeline.

Then Rosalie shrugged. "I get my homework done in twenty minutes most nights." Her school, St. Patrick's, was hard for Westerfield, but nothing compared to Armitage.

It seemed best to get right to the point. "You know what happened to Claire," Madeline said, "and what I'm trying to figure out is if those girls, Lee and her friends, were involved somehow."

The girl took a sip of her drink and a bite of sausage roll. "So you're the detective now?" Madeline noticed that Rosalie hadn't once addressed her by name. She flushed a little. It was decidedly unlike her to take on such a responsibility and to involve herself so directly in difficulty. It must be one of the ways she was stuttering toward adulthood. And why should it take this particular form, sitting across from this dark, plain girl in a pizzeria in a close-to-derelict mill town?

"No," Madeline said, "it's not exactly that." And she explained what had happened with Lee and the other girls after Claire's death. The way they had confessed the existence of the group then demanded silence, and then the signs that they were watching that had arrived in the last few days. She even talked about the Ziploc bag with the threat that targeted Maggie, though it meant admitting she had taken the leftover shampoo.

Rosalie considered this and said, after another bite of sausage roll, "They set you up. When Claire died, they knew the Reign would come out. They didn't trust Sally and the others to keep quiet, so they went on the offensive. They told you and then started to intimidate you. But they figured no one would listen to anything you had to say, and in the long run, they'd be safe. No one would look too hard. You were new. Anyone new, they thought they could scare."

Madeline digested this stark assessment of her status at Armitage and then said, "Rosalie, this all started long before Claire died. What happened? What did they do to you and why did you leave?"

For a moment, Rosalie said nothing. Madeline was conscious of sounds coming from the kitchen as the man in the apron started scrubbing a pan and the boys on the bicycles rolled past, hooting at a joke one of them had made, apparently oblivious to the rain. "I didn't flunk out. I had really good grades. Even from the hard teachers. That's what they said, but you can check it. It's not true." Madeline believed her. Her shrug of indifference at the mention of homework, the strict glitter in her eyes, the fact she still wore her uniform even though it was almost 8:30 at night.

Madeline said, "I understand." She took a bite of her own roll and was amazed to discover it was delicious: flaky and light, the meat gently but well spiced. She watched Rosalie's face and saw an expression travel across it that was similar to the one Maggie had worn when she decided to give Madeline Rosalie's number.

"I figured out that Claire was pregnant. It was October. She was throwing up in the bathroom and she was crying. She was the same color as my sister when that happened to her." Rosalie said her older sister had had a baby, and she knew the signs. "I helped her out. Got her food she could eat. And she tried to protect me."

"From Lee?"

Rosalie, in spite of her considerable composure, looked pained at the memory. "Yes, but they all do it. Make a list of where you can sit in the library and which tables you can eat at in Commons. Paths through the woods that are off-limits. Stuff like that. And you have to do chores for them. Go to town and get them snacks. Clean out their closets." Rosalie scratched a bite on her arm.

"And I said I wouldn't do it. I said they couldn't treat us like their maids. I said I didn't go there to be some servant to rich kids. I said I'd tell Miss Peters and they laughed, and I said I'd tell Miss Talmadge and they laughed even harder." They didn't really think, Rosalie said, any adult could stop them. They felt they were that good at hiding their tracks, and the girls they bossed around, Rosalie said, almost liked the abuse of power, because it made them feel a part of things. "Some of their sisters had been in the group, and those girls were the worst. But even the new kids tried to make each other do what the older girls wanted."

Madeline was nodding like a maniac, saying nothing, hoping Rosalie would just keep talking. And as with Sally, confession did appear to offer her a kind of relief. But then her face hardened. "And Claire was on my side. Because I'd helped her. Because my sister didn't give up her baby, either. Because Claire was sick of them, too, and tried to tell them to stop picking on kids." And then something else had happened. An accident.

Another customer came in, an elderly man with a cane and a raincoat. The owner entered from the kitchen, his hands cloaked in a damp towel. The old man ordered his food, eased himself down in a booth, and opened a newspaper. Somehow, the presence of another person in the otherwise empty pizzeria made it that much more lonely. Rosalie lowered her voice even further.

"There was this freaky kid at my old school. One of these jerks." Her eyes moved to the street, consciously or not, Madeline couldn't tell, to the boys drifting on their bikes through the gathering twilight. "He used to IM me, and I never answered. Made fun of me for leaving here and going to Armitage. Said I thought I was better than the kids here." She took another sip of Coke, and her face implied that she knew she indeed was better than the other kids or at the very least smarter. "But one day he sent me these pictures. And I recognized people in them. It was them." They took showers in the same bathrooms, Rosalie explained, and in some of the pictures, you could see parts of their faces. And they mentioned Armitage in the captions. The photos were from a website called Rich Girls. Rosalie was almost whispering. Kids took gross pictures of one another, usually on cell phones, and sold them there. "And they were on it."

"Except for Claire?" Madeline asked, her head spinning with yet another way in which the students she had lived and worked with for the last year continued to shock her. There were another thousand questions to ask, but it was also becoming clear what these girls really didn't want exposed and why Claire and Rosalie had been such threats.

"No," Rosalie said, shaking her head. "She wasn't part of it. I don't know how the pictures got there, but they were real. You could tell who they were. It was disgusting. I didn't want to tell Claire, but she knew I was hiding something and she made me. And she told them we knew and that they had to lay off the new kids and me in particular." Although they were physically rooted in this shabby restaurant, Rosalie was clearly reliving those days. She wouldn't meet Madeline's gaze, and her voice had almost disappeared.

"Rosalie, Maggie was your roommate. Did you tell her, too? And who was your adviser?" Madeline was still reeling with the knowledge that these sophisticated girls had done something so demeaning to themselves. Nor could she imagine having the audacity or skewed confidence at seventeen to want to expose her body to the stares of millions. It was another way of sensing her own adulthood: awe at the presence of alien worlds and experiences that people younger than she belonged to.

Rosalie said yes. "Maggie's a lot weaker than I am. She needed something to fight back with. I told her not that long ago, when they started to get worse. And my adviser was Mr. Fuller," she added with obvious disdain. "Perv." The girl glanced at her watch. She didn't appear to have a cell phone. She was going to need to get going soon, she said.

"Just a few more questions, Rosalie," Madeline said and pitched forward so that the plastic rim of the table cut rather sharply against her ribs. Again, she could have lobbed a hundred more queries at Rosalie, such as why did she call Harvey Fuller a perv? To Madeline, he appeared as sexless as one of the frogs over whose dissection he presided each year. "Did Claire tell you who the father of her baby was and why she decided to keep him?"

"No," said Rosalie. "But you know what? I never asked. That was her business. All she said was that she had to have the baby and that it was going to change what everyone thought about Armitage. And why wouldn't she want to keep her baby? It's the right thing to do." Barring Rosalie's strong philosophical stance on the topic, it was much the same thing Sally Jansen had said. Claire had felt that her baby would shift everything at Armitage, but no one understood why.

"One more thing, Rosalie, and then I'll drive you home, if you'd like a ride, of course. Why, if you had something like this against Lee and the others, did you leave? Did they keep harassing you?"

Rosalie didn't answer immediately. She got up, put her soda can in the trash—no recycling bins were offered—and threw away the remnants of the sausage roll. The old man had finished his slice of pizza but was still leafing through his newspaper. The scrubbing sounds in the kitchen had started again. The place smelled of spilled soda and old cheese. "They posted one they said was of me. They used my name. That boy I told you about showed it to my parents, and the next day, I had to withdraw. I didn't tell Claire what had happened, but she might have figured it out. I was too embarrassed. But then they spread the rumors that I'd had a break-down, that I'd flunked out." Madeline wanted to reach toward her, but Rosalie stood up, her hands in fists, her arms tense in her St. Patrick's sweater. "I didn't want to come back here. I am going to be a doctor. But my parents said that was it. They never wanted me to go there in the first place. They said, good riddance, let them do evil things. They said, say nothing. Leave with your dignity. You're coming back where you belong."

Madeline stood and cleared her own food away, too ill at ease to save the sausage roll. She asked Rosalie, "Are the pictures still up there?"

Rosalie said wearily, "Of course they are. Once something's on the Web, it's almost impossible to get off."

Madeline inquired again if she might give her a ride, and the girl looked out at the rain and at the boys rolling up and down the sidewalk and gave a quick nod. She was very good, Madeline felt, at assessing risks and potential dangers. Madeline felt a kind of awe at Rosalie's steady awareness of who she was and her sureness of direction. She believed Rosalie when she said she was going to be a doctor. The girl was silent except for providing Madeline with the briefest of directions about how to reach her home. It wasn't far. Madeline braked to a stop on a side street in front of a modest frame house with a porch light on. A dog barked from inside. Madeline could see its indistinct outline through the glass door.

"Rosalie," Madeline said just before the girl leaned over to open the door, "I know you don't want anything to do with Armitage anymore, but I'm still worried that Lee and the others were involved in Claire's death. Do you think you could tell the police about this?"

Her response surprised Madeline. "They already called twice today. I am not talking about this to anyone else. I'm done." The dog's barking gathered force. How had the police heard about Rosalie, too?

"Then why did you see me?" Madeline asked, genuinely taken aback.

"Because," Rosalie said as she stepped onto the driveway and into the rainy night, "you should have noticed. You should have seen something was wrong. You were there."

Madeline sat still, her heart making unsyncopated thumps as she watched Rosalie walk up the steps to her house, not bothering to use her umbrella. The door opened, and the dog, tail flailing, and a young woman came out, a baby on her hip. Madeline kept watching as she saw Rosalie, with evident pleasure, take the child from its mother and hold it close to her chest. The dog wove happily around their legs. Then all of them went in and someone quickly shut the door. A moment later, the porch light snapped off, leaving the drive in a gray gloom.

Finding her way back to the highway, Madeline found herself going far more quickly than she ought to have. Rosalie was right, she kept thinking. I should have noticed. If I'd been less ham-fisted and less worried about myself, I would have. She was almost weeping, she realized, but that still didn't mean she wasn't heading straight to the Armitage police station to find Matt Corelli.

The young man in uniform at the front desk told her she was in luck. A minute later, Matt was walking down the corridor, saying, "Madeline? I'm so sorry I haven't called you back. Are you all right?" with such genuine concern she thought she might burst into tears. He steered her toward his office, and fortunately curiosity got the better of weepiness as she realized this was the first time she had ever been inside a police station.

Matt poured her a glass of water, sat her down in a comfortable chair, and asked her why she was there this time of night. For a moment, Madeline sipped and looked around, trying to gather some of the threads of the story. The room held two desks, both very neat, a small refrigerator, some computer equipment, and several of these well-padded chairs. It could have been an office anywhere, and it even had a rather large window, though the view was only of the parking lot.

"I thought," she said, "it would look a lot more English and nineteenth century in here."

"Oh, that's downstairs, where we keep the criminals. We reserve the mold and chains for them," he said, and she thought again how disconcerting it was to discover what a good man the detective obviously was. Still, his clear concern made it that much easier to talk about the Reign of Terror, Sally, Maggie, and Rosalie. It took a rather long time and was also rather embarrassing to admit that she had been set up, taken advantage of because she, too, was new and unskilled in the ways of managing at Armitage.

"Rich Girls?" Matt said. Madeline had thought that work as a police officer would have inured him to such realities, but apparently not.

"I know," Madeline said. "It's revolting. But I don't think Rosalie was making it up. It can be checked, of course," she went on, but she didn't want to suggest they look at it together. That would be far too awkward.

While Madeline had been talking, Matt had taken notes, asking questions only to clarify times and the spelling of names. He'd obviously already known something about Rosalie; the girl hadn't been lying about being contacted by the police. Madeline didn't get the sense that, despite his uneasy reaction to the name of the website, he was tremendously surprised, either, though at the end of her story, he said, "Would you ever have thought Claire capable of or interested in protecting others? Because what you've told me suggests that she was far more compassionate than most people have implied."

"Yes," said Madeline, leaning forward and in the process spilling a bit of her water. "I'm just glad that wasn't cranberry juice like it usually is," she added as she tried to mop up a damp spot. "This protective streak she apparently showed toward vulnerable kids. Her disgust with the Reign. And then all this interest in families. Wanting to know about them."

"Thanks, Madeline," Matt was saying now. "Thanks for coming down here. What's even better is that you got these girls to talk to you. They saw us coming and they ran." He was escorting her, he said, to the parking lot. Now that she'd done what she had set out to, Madeline could actually notice how sleepless he looked.

"Where's your partner?" she asked, thinking someone ought to be around to support him. Off putting his kids to bed, Matt said, but he'd be back pretty soon.

They stood in the lot for a moment, despite the unsettled weather. She was suddenly reluctant to say good-bye to him. The thought of being alone in the dorm all night wasn't particularly appealing, either.

"Madeline, if they get up to something very bad or you're frightened in any way, call me, please," he said.

She thanked him profusely and got ready to head off. "Thanks again for your help," he said kindly. "See you on campus." He stood there as she slid her car into reverse. She got the feeling without his saying anything that he was close to knowing what had happened. That he was aware of how it would end and that, in spite of himself, it made him sad.

etting off campus was surprisingly easy; the police had been told faculty could come and go, though a uniformed officer peered at Fred with ostentatious suspicion before he waved him through the gates. It was only ten in the morning on Friday. The shortened classes Porter had devised meant he was finished exceedingly early, and a quick chat with his dorm head had secured him time off until the next morning. What a relief it was to be away, to be on a highway going somewhere other than Armitage. The weight of the last days began to lift when he crossed the state line into Connecticut, and by the time he reached New York and saw the city's spires glinting, he was almost buoyant. Fred even found a parking space without much trouble, between a battered pickup and a spotless Mini Cooper, a pairing that seemed to summarize the gestalt of the neighborhood quite neatly, then located the building one block over. He stood on the sidewalk and looked at its five gray stories and nondescript door decorated with the usual urban hieroglyphics. A smell of asphalt and baking bread wafted through the air. As un-Armitage an odor as he could have imagined and, to his surprise, strangely nourishing.

Fred rang the buzzer, trying to dampen his hopes, wishing for a moment for an easy way out. But the space was perfect, raw and open, with excellent ventilation. The building was an old lighting factory, with high windows, higher ceilings, and inspiring views of Manhattan and the river, which glinted richly in the warm spring light.

His friend Hal was delighted to see him, and they stormed back into good conversation as if it had been days and not months since they'd last seen each other. But most of all, with an abruptness and intensity that rattled Fred, his desire to make paintings returned. He looked at Hal's tall canvases in the unsparing light and thought, I want to do this again. The smell of paint and turpentine he was used to. Those permeated his studio and his own skin and had come to seem emblems merely of his job and grading, the mechanics of school. But smelling them here in a working studio, and seeing paintings, real paintings, in the process of being thought over, studied, and created—that was exciting in a way that made his skin prickle. Separate from Armitage, he realized how much the academy's daily routine had helped him suppress that longing. There simply wasn't time to experience it, much less express it. It was folly, he knew suddenly, to think that he could achieve much as an artist simply by painting in bits and pieces, with the cushioned net of Armitage right below him. He had lived a bit long without risk. He had lived a bit long without being his own authority, deferring to the older, wiser assertions of the institution that had done so much to form him. But what was holding him back? He was young, with no dependents, and this was the moment to step out into the air and see what happened. Within ten minutes of talking to Hal, the fantasies began to unroll: heated discussion with other painters, parties where they fought about influence and meaning, openings rife with gallery politics and gossip.

And then there was the lunch Hal threw, and some of the dream wove into real life. For food, there weren't just cold cuts and sliced tomatoes, but juices of exotic fruit and champagne and all kinds of pastries and spreads that apparently existed only in small, exquisite shops all over New York. Instantly, the talk was sharper. And then there were the women. Alluring, smart, well dressed, quirky. Dangerously attractive. All urban edge and irony. Most of them lived in the building, which held artists on every floor, creating in every medium you could imagine, which accounted for their availability in the middle of the day. None of them, Fred suspected, were tied down to jobs so mundane they required you to be there on Friday at one in the afternoon. He didn't mention Armitage; he didn't want to hear what they'd have to say. Claire's death was still all over the news—they'd certainly recognize the name and have pointed questions and comments. Today, he wanted no connection to that life, that place. Today, he was happily untethered. And there were plenty of other topics available. Through the haze of talk and smoke, Fred watched the women and the artful tilts of their wrists and smiles, and they watched him back.

When the guests left, he and Hal sat in the midst of the mess, flutes half-golden with champagne, knives smeared with tapenade, some piece of spiky jazz still playing. Fred leaned back on the sofa. "Well?" Hal asked, and Fred said, looking straight at him, "Yeah. I'll do it. Yes." Hal smiled. "I knew the minute you walked in." They rose and began to clean up the party's remains. Fred left at five, telling Hal that he would have to arrange for leave from Armitage and then he'd be back down by the first of July.

Driving to Massachusetts, he kept telling himself he was going to launch himself back into what everyone at Armitage called the real world, real life. He needed to say it aloud, to the windshield, to the dashboard, to be sure he actually meant it. Painting in New York, living in Brooklyn. All through the journey, he tested the coal of ambition that had sparked into being in the city and began to trust it because, even in cool, verdant New England, it wouldn't fade.

It was barely nine o'clock when he got back. The officer at the gate had changed but performed the same ID check, as if he and his colleague had learned it at exactly the same time. The dorm was subdued, and his dorm head said he'd missed little. The police had still come up with nothing. "I'm glad you're back, Fred," he'd said, and Fred had given him a guilty smile.

He looked around his bedroom and felt a sudden pang of loss at the thought of leaving that small space behind. Its low eaves, the meager double bed into which he had only very occasionally managed to lure a girlfriend—the presence of thirty curious teenage boys had definitely hampered his romantic adventures. He kept thinking of the loft. The light that had poured through it. The sense, fragile, preposterous, and vital, that art still mattered to the people he had talked to. He stopped pacing and looked around. He was indeed going to leave. It was the end of that period of his life, the end of a self-imposed monasticism. Even Armitage in crisis wasn't enough to hold him. Even the disruption that he'd cause his dorm, his department couldn't persuade him otherwise. His loyalties, he had to admit, were more flimsy than he'd realized. Llewellan would have been horrified. Not even that Fred would choose art, but that he would let Armitage down at the last minute. Llewellan had waxed grandiloquent on the need to honor commitments and be a man of one's word. Fred could imagine his leonine head and a frown across his wide brow. He would have reminded Fred that he had signed a contract and that such an act should still mean something. And it did. But this was a truly unusual opportunity. He felt in himself a small but decisive shift away from the man who had done so much to shape his sense of what was right and good. He also had to confess that not even Madeline, whom he liked more and more, was making him regret the longing to go. If something were going to evolve with her, it would have to withstand his need to return to painting.

His body surged with energy. He couldn't sleep, even though it had been an incredibly long day. He nearly called Madeline but thought better of it. This might be the night, however, to return to the tunnels and the archives. No one would be down there. He tried to push the idea aside and failed. All he had to do was locate that one file. Thank God he had that scrap of handwriting to hold on to. If the records had been computerized back then, he'd have almost nothing to go on. He felt a momentary tug of sympathy for people like Mary Manchester and those who fought to preserve the old ways.

He rummaged around his desk and found the old catalog card and the skeleton key he had guiltily copied a few towns over so as not to bump into anyone he knew at the Greenville Agway. He grabbed his Maglite and headed off to the tunnel entrance below Nicholson. The grounds were profoundly still, and no moon hung in the sky. The air was heavy and warm, and only Forrest Thompson was out, walking his ancient greyhound on the far side of the Quad, too distant to be spoken to. But seeing Forrest and the old, stiff animal only reinforced the rightness of his choice. Fred had known it was Forrest and Milton from the sheerest fraction of a glance; that was how familiar he was with this environment. They implied, that silhouette of dog and man, what happened when you stopped running.

The tunnels were even warmer than the grounds, almost stifling. He paused at the bottom of the stairs that led to them and listened, head cocked. Scotty Johnston was the last person he wanted to run into at this moment. But there was nothing, barely even the chugging of machinery. The tunnels were full only of stale air and darkness.

He crept down the hall, fingers trailing the wall, knowing that he had to turn to the right and that the door would be the first on his left in the new corridor. After a moment's struggle with the flashlight and the key, he slipped inside the small room, which was even hotter than the hallway.

It smelled, as before, of stale paper, suppressed histories. Heading straight to the filing cabinet that he'd had to abandon thanks to Scotty, he felt a flicker of fear run through his bones. For a while, he discovered nothing but manila folders with typed labels from the 1940s, though the dates were gradually heading into the next decade. And then he saw it again: that strong but delicate hand. "Files of a Personal Nature, 1950s." It was at the back of the cabinet, at the farthest recess, in a brown accordion file. It might even have been placed below the other papers and only with the pressure of Fred's searching and rearrangement of folders been thrust partially upright.

Pulling it out and training his flashlight on the label, he placed it on top of a dusty table piled with yearbooks from the 1960s. He didn't dare turn on the lamp there in case someone saw the line of brightness below the door. Even the flashlight was a risk. For a moment, he imagined wildly what he would do if he were caught. There'd be nothing for it but to tell the truth, and the truth would sound absurd. And it all depended on who caught him. A random police officer on patrol as part of the investigation into Claire's death or one of the academy's security guys. Fred realized he actually didn't have it in him to bluff much right now. Admitting nakedly what it was you wanted apparently made it harder to lie about other activities as well.

Fred opened the old file and pulled out two manila envelopes, each sealed with a disk of red cardboard and a short length of red string. The first held the entire record of Edward Smith's life at Armitage Academy. With one hand on the flashlight, and the other sorting through the papers, Fred saw that someone had bothered to preserve all the material he had been looking for: it had indeed been confiscated and compiled somewhere else. Edward's application for admission; a letter from his father saying how much he wanted his son to have the benefit of the best education available in America if not the world; a recommendation from an eighth-grade teacher of Edward's who praised his "sensitive way with language and his innate politeness." His reports from Third, Fourth, and Fifth Form. The letters from the head of his dormitory, Francis Clapham, telling his parents that Edward was a "model Armitage boy, except for a rather marked disinterest in athletics."

But then, Fred saw, the tone changed, and he saw, too, the first instance of Llewellan's involvement. In December 1954, there was a letter from the father, saying that Edward had returned for Christmas break senior year in an overwrought state that at first his parents attributed to too much work. "Our boy is delicate and takes things much to heart," the words read. "But when we were able to settle him, he told us something very grave, Mr. Naylor, about certain masters at Armitage," and he then named three men whom Fred had known as a child. Three men who had served Armitage collectively for more than one hundred years. Men for whom dorms were named. Men to whom the yearbook had been dedicated, often multiple times. Men who had formed the very image of what it was to be part of the academy. The letter went on: "Knowing that you would never allow what Edward was implying to occur at your school, may I request a meeting at your earliest convenience to discuss the situation?"

His pulse quickening, Fred suddenly knew what had happened. Without bidding, the image of Llewellan returned. Llewellan yanking his arm back to the exact position necessary for him to make a perfect cast. Llewellan throwing him in the waters of Rangeley Lake to teach him how to swim. Llewellan telling him over and over how important it was to be a man able to face the greatest challenges of life with courage. Llewellan, who wouldn't stand for weakness even in his dogs and called unathletic men, without fail, nancy boys.

Llewellan's reply was brisk. The carbon copy was blurred with age, but again, whoever had preserved these files had done a meticulous job of it, placing this letter between two gossamer-thin pieces of archival paper. Such a meeting was not possible, Llewellan had written. Mr. Smith was suggesting something that simply wouldn't be tolerated at the academy. In addition, he, Llewellan, had taken steps to speak with the masters Edward had named and found that they were men of "impeccable, even stainless character and eminently suited to the teaching of young boys." He went on to suggest that Edward see his doctor or improve his diet or "as he has so often been exhorted to do here at Armitage, involve himself in purposeful physical activity."

As he read these words, Llewellan's voice began to boom around Fred's brain. Suddenly, his grandfather's presence was everywhere. Fred could almost feel him staring at his back from the photograph that hung on the other side of the room. In spite of the stuffy heat, Fred began to feel a creeping chill. He forced himself to continue. But that folder was empty.

The next held mostly clippings from the *Globe* and other Boston newspapers. A boy had been found dead in a room in the Bay State Hotel. He had hanged himself. No identification was found with him, but he had apparently signed in with a false name. Police were investigating. The date was February 20, 1955. Subsequent articles said only that the boy's name had been discovered but was being suppressed because he was a minor. Even an editorial on unsupervised youth that the case apparently sparked had been included. There was no further notice from Armitage, no claim made or connection stated. No program of a service that the school had held for its dead student. Nothing. Edward's inconvenient existence and even more inconvenient assertions had been more or less erased. Except that they hadn't. Someone, somewhere, had seen fit to hold on to this dark corner. Fred found two final notes. The first was from Edward's father to Llewellan, and it said only "I will not forgive you for my son's death and neither will the Lord. May you and your family suffer as I and my family have." And then, finally, a tiny, handwritten note on Armitage notepaper that said, in the now-familiar writing, "I felt strongly that this incident should not go unremarked and have preserved and collected these documents against the express wishes of my employer, Mr. Llewellan Naylor. For that I may be blamed, although I hope the wider light of history will forgive me. Naomi Beardsley."

Fred was shaking as he put the papers back into a semblance of order. He could barely tie the fraying black thread that held together the accordion file. A secretary. A woman who had worked in Llewellan's office. She had seen what was hap-

pening and had had the courage to gather the evidence and in
her own, private way preserve it.

And all of it accounted for Malcolm Smith's rage. His desire
to hang that rage like a heavy, spiked wreath around Fred's neck
and make him feel the shame of his grandfather's neglect. For
that is what it had been, Fred felt sure. Most likely, at least one of
the men that Mr. Smith named had molested Edward or worse.
For all Fred knew, all three could have been involved and their
abuse had driven the boy to suicide. He stood and looked at the
file. The flashlight, on its side on the table, cast a fragile cone of
brightness over all of Armitage's dusty, complicated history. He
knew he could simply stash the file again and let someone else
discover it years or decades from now. He knew, too, he could destroy it. But that wasn't really an option. Naomi Beardsley, with
her careful insistence on documenting what she felt to be an unbearable wrong, had changed that. She had been as brave as she
could be in the circumstances, and she had done what she could
to right an injustice. Who knew what she had been risking? She
hadn't been brave enough to go to the newspapers or the board.
Nor had the family apparently taken any legal action to avenge
their son. But maybe those were different times, and women and
boys seen as weak would be told, as Llewellan had told the parents of Edward Smith, to buck up and get on with it. They
wouldn't be seen, heard, responded to. They would instead be
told that what they were and what they'd been through simply
wasn't true.

Standing, his legs shaky, Fred picked up the file and tucked it to
his side. Malcolm Smith couldn't have known about it. He probably had no idea who Naomi Beardsley was. But he had known
enough of the original story to want Fred, Llewellan's scion, to bear

its burden. Why had he waited until this spring? Did he have a ter-
minal illness and feel it was his last chance to speak out? More
likely, it was something deeply personal that Fred would never be
able to understand. But now Edward's brother could see what had
happened laid out before him. Fred would send the folder to him
tomorrow, from the academy's post office. He turned off the flashlight then, grateful for a moment for the room's encompassing
blackness.

He almost didn't care about making noise anymore but was
still sensible enough to be happy that he met no one once he'd
risen from the tunnels. The file seemed light pressed against his
ribs, though he had to set it down as he crossed the bridge over
the stream leading to the Bluestone. He unhooked the skeleton
key from his ring and tossed it into the flowing water, glad to be
rid of it. The queer stillness in the air had continued. Not even
Forrest and Milton were out now.

Back in his apartment, Fred saw that it was only ten o'clock.
How astonishing that news that could change your life could un-
fold so quickly. He laid the file on his desk, and now, in a room
filled with regular light, he saw how faded it actually was. More
than fifty years had gone by since Naomi Beardsley had done her
careful, secret work. And now Malcolm Smith was going to have
his vengeance. Fred snapped on his computer and opened a new
document form. "Dear Mr. Smith," he wrote. "I do not know why
you chose me or chose the moment you did to come and find me,
but your visit worried me enough to look into what had happened
to your brother. What I found was this, gathered and saved by a
woman who worked, I believe, as my grandfather's secretary. I do
not know if any of this information will make a difference to you or
in any way console you. But these files rightfully belong to you and

your family. Again, I know it can't come as consolation for your loss, but for what my grandfather did, I am truly sorry."

He was utterly drained. But he had one more letter to write: his resignation from Armitage. Not merely the request for the leave he had thought would serve as the compromise position between the year in Williamsburg and the safety of his job at the academy. Knowing what he did, he couldn't stay and couldn't return. When he was done, he went into the hall and found some cardboard boxes left in the recycling bin. He assembled them until he was too tired to move anymore and looked at their brown emptiness, waiting to be filled with what he would take from this part of his life.

CHAPTER 18

Matt woke *before the sun was up and forced himself to go for a run.* Cases like this were wretched on the body; no one let themselves rest, and everyone but Vernon drank far too much coffee. No wonder cops tended to look fifteen years older than they were, haggard and worn. It came from being hunched over emergencies all the time. His joints felt stiff and cramped, but it was a good idea to limber up before meeting Angell at nine at the station. Matt thought about how much had shifted in less than a week. He had slipped his cell phone in a pocket of his shorts and even stopped to answer it when it rang, despite the fact he was in the beech grove, the most beautiful part of the loop, and just at the moment when his muscles had finally released. He had not, he realized, as he leaned in to talk to Vernon, seen Madeline, though the woods were no longer off-limits. Nothing had turned up there, despite the dogs, the men, and all that tense and thorough searching.

"Nowhere to be found," said Vernon by way of saying hello. He was referring to Tamsin, who had not returned to her bungalow the night before. Lucinda, when they'd returned to question her last night about the bag, had said that Tamsin brought it with her. Lucinda had no idea what had been in it. She'd been at the house working on something Porter had asked her to take care of. That late at night? "She's always on duty, Tamsin Lovell," Lucinda had answered spitefully.

And when asked if she and Miss Lovell had had a disagreement, Lucinda had responded, "Of course we did. I didn't like her. I was always disagreeing with her." And then her phone had rung, and she had slammed the door in their faces and gone off to pick it up. Fortunately, at the station, they'd found a young officer eager to be a part of something as real as a murder investigation who had asked if there were anything he could do. Which was how he found himself watching Tamsin's house until Vernon went to relieve him at dawn.

Matt walked through the filtered light that came down through the canopy of rough-edged leaves, listening to Vernon. "She's got lilac bushes that she trims, window boxes full of hyacinth. She's like something out of Beatrix Potter, except I get the strong impression she's an unpleasant character."

"Vernon," Matt asked, "did you go into her house?"

There was a pause. "No," he finally admitted. "But it was close." Matt was pouring with sweat and for the first time in a week felt like he had actually breathed. "And now," said Vernon, "I'm going home to have some breakfast with the kids. I'll see you down at the station." The young cop had tried to offer him a jelly donut. "I nearly yielded," Vernon confessed.

"But you didn't," said Matt. "Go home and have some bulgur. You'll feel better."

"Fuck off," Vernon said, quite cheerfully.

Matt snapped the phone closed and walked the rest of the way out of the woods. It was only seven, but he was planning to go to see his father. His sister, Barbara, was in town; she had no Friday classes, and he hadn't done more than exchange a hurried hello on the phone with her in days. Once a month, she drove over from the Connecticut college where she taught art history to keep an eye on them both, she said. Come for breakfast, she'd urged. I know you can't stay long. Just a few minutes.

Besides, his father was good preparation for Angell. He started in the moment Matt walked through the door. "Barbara," Joseph shouted, "the man of the law has arrived," and continued to sit in his large armchair and fiddle with the plastic tubing that led from his oxygen tank to his nose. Barbara sailed out of the kitchen and gave her brother a hug. His sister, lean as a deer, dark-haired, dressed in something black and architectural that probably cost a fortune in Tokyo, had her hands wrapped around a dish towel that did not match the sharp lines of her dress. "Hi, baby," she said. "How are you?"

"Good to see you. You cooking?" he asked a little cautiously.

She snorted. Barbara's idea of a good meal was Diet Coke with a side of lemon. She was, however, an ace at cleaning up, and she'd been setting the table and putting away dishes from the night before. "I'll leave the food to you. I've got coffee on. Go say hi to Pop."

Joseph was still tinkering with the knob on the tank and didn't look up at his son until he was finished. "So what's going on up there? No arrests? No baby found?" Above everything, Joseph hated incompetence, inaccuracy, vagueness. Matt remembered last year's Thanksgiving, the first without Ella, his mother, and how they'd limped through it with help from a very expensive Barolo and Matt's cooking. The rich smell of dark meat had hung in the air, and Joseph had been unable to stop talking about the bad books kept by the Massachusetts Registry of Motor Vehicles until Matt had said to Barbara in the safety of the kitchen, "Can you hospital-ize someone for obsession with irrelevant details?" And she had said, "We can try," and they had cackled for a minute until they went into the dining room and saw Joseph staring out the window, his hand twisting a napkin to knots.

"Good to see you, Pop," Matt said. "It'll break today or to-morrow," he added, surprising himself. Both he and Vernon had sensed that this was so; that something critical would happen, but he hadn't realized just how confident he felt about it since he had no real idea of why Claire's death had happened as it had.

"What about the baby?" Barbara asked, bringing coffee.

This at least was decent, and they all sat down near Joseph, who continued to fuss with the knobs on his tank. "Barb, this is the part that's strange. Mostly in these cases, there's a clear sus-pect. A boyfriend, an uncle, a babysitter. But no one and everyone is involved here. No overwhelming physical clues, no confessions, no leads that pan out."

"And who thought it would happen in this backwater," Joseph said, "and that you, Mr. Big City Cop, would be dealing with it?" It was a favorite theme. When Matt had told his father that he had taken a desk job in the Armitage-Greenville force, Joseph had said, "Sentimentality. Lack of ambition. What is this? Some *Little House on the Prairie* moment? *Roots* meets Massachusetts?" He'd waved his hand dismissively. "Matthew, I am old and worn-out, but I do not need you here. I have Fabiola"—his tyrannical visiting nurse—"my practice, a lot of old geezers just like me, and your meddling sister one state away." Barbara, who'd been visiting, had said, "I heard that," over the clamor of the vacuum that she'd been running in the next room. Everyone in their family had impossibly keen hearing. Matt sometimes thought that it was his most curious advantage as a cop.

"Oh yeah?" Joseph had called. "Then you'll hear this, too. It would please me to see the two of you get on with your lives." The vacuum stopped and Barbara came in the room. "Pop. We have lives. And we are using them to stay awake."

Matt had smiled. He and Barbara had always been close. She had supported him when he'd left Armitage under a cloud; he had been her biggest ally when she'd gotten her Ph.D. in art history. When he had stayed in Philadelphia "to chase hooligans," she'd been his staunchest advocate. And when she had finally admitted to her parents that the beautiful blond from Sweden with whom she shared a house was her girlfriend, he had been in this living room, holding her hand.

"Bah!" said Joseph. He loved them both helplessly, they knew it, even if their choices mystified him. As he often said, "One kid a gunslinger, the other a professor teaching children to look at pictures of naked people." Barbara's most popular course, unsurprisingly, was The Nude Through the Ages. "If you come back here, don't pretend it's for me. It's your own business what you're here for."

Joseph had been right, of course. His mind was admirably lucid, floating easily from his accounting practice (small but still percolating) to his garden, backgammon game, and book club. That his body was slowly refusing to accommodate his still flexible intelligence was a fact he tried to treat as a trifle, an inconvenience. The wicked gap that Ella's death had left was something they steered around as if it might swallow them all. Thinking of his mother now made Matt bite back the sharp retort he felt ready to make.

Instead, he kissed his father's head and went to make omelets. He didn't stay more than half an hour, though he had been happy in the bright dining room, surrounded by what was left of his family. But Angell had called the meeting for nine and would probably start early. Barbara saw him out and gave her head a tilt in the familiar direction, up the hill, toward the school. "Bringing it all back?"

He stood in the threshold. "It's like a physical slap, walking around that campus. It just jolts me, the memories. The smells. And it's hard to believe I was part of it and that the old guys still hang on to everything that's happened." He paused. "I keep wanting to think I'm different. That I'm not like them. That I might have gone there but I'm not of it. But that's not entirely true. And now they're vulnerable and I feel like protecting them."

She got it, she said. Her thesis had been called "The Ambivalence of Patronage in Renaissance Italy."

"You glad you took the job?" she asked, holding open the door. Since he'd returned, she'd asked him that almost every time she saw him, as if taking his spiritual temperature.

He paused. "No. But that doesn't mean it's not what I should have done." He looked at her more closely. "What's up?" he asked, then, "Inge?"

Barbara looked down, suddenly unwilling to meet his eye. "She's not certain about having a baby. I think it's time." She frowned and said, "We'll talk. Hit the road."

He promised to come to Connecticut to see her when the case was finished. She said, "Go get the evildoers, honey," and shoved him out the door, trying to smile.

On the way to the station, he couldn't stop imagining her lovely face. She was the one he told everything. That same Thanksgiving, Matt had mentioned to Barbara his doubts about continuing in Philadelphia. He'd confided in her about Ann. He had heard the entire paltry story come out as they shared a glass of wine on the cold screened porch, their breath arriving in rounded puffs of fog, their voices low so as not to wake their light-sleeping father. She had listened and then said, "Don't walk entirely. There's a reason you do what you do. Could you get a job here?"

"Greenville?" he'd objected. "Why here?"

"For Dad. For me. For you. It's peaceful. It could give you a place to think. It's an idea," she said and swallowed the last of the wine. "I miss Mama," she said, and he had held her until they were so cold their hands and feet began to go numb. He kissed her good night and said, "No one has a better sister." She laughed and answered, "You've got one thing right at least."

He was still thinking about her when he pulled into the parking lot and saw Vernon pacing there. "How are the kids?" he asked when he saw his partner's face. Vernon shrugged. "Screaming, crying, Daddy, don't leave, blah blah blah." He turned toward the back entrance of the station. "And that is why I do white-collar crime, because white-collar criminals are nine-to-fivers, just like me." Matt could imagine the scene. The tearful girls, Vernon's guilty crankiness spilling over everything. "We finish this this week," Vernon said, "and then you stop drinking coffee and I take my personal days."

"We'll finish," said Matt. How, he wasn't sure, but it was nearly over. But he wasn't the one to start the meeting, which was chaired by a black-browed Captain Angell and attended by three tall men from the FBI who looked like bricks, and the rest of the ragged team as they sat around the laminated table in the conference room, tubes of lights buzzing their nasal song overhead.

One of the bricks discussed how not a single one of the more than four hundred serious leads about the baby's whereabouts had led to a single concrete outcome. The sheet they had found in the tunnels had been used by some handyman to staunch a cut someone had gotten repairing a pipe. Norm Parker's forensic evidence was muddy, slow in coming, going to be very hard to use. Autopsy results ditto. A case could easily be made that Claire had slipped and gotten those bruises in labor. Another of the bricks discussed Scotty Johnston ad nauseam. They had grilled his supposed friends, but he had no one he'd really confided in. They were all scared of him. No roommates. No one wanted to live with him. Still, in spite of his parents' urging that he come home and rest from his ordeal, he had stubbornly insisted that he needed to stay to finish out the year. "He's in the midst of it, and his lawyer won't let him say a thing. His attorney's hourly is a thousand dollars. It's hopeless." Rosalie Quiñones refused to talk. Stymied all around. And the DA practically brokering settlements already. A mood of gray and total gloom descended over the table.

Matt looked at the men gathered there shuffling their papers and picking at the foam rims of their cups; the surface of the table was flecked with the stray white crescents. He felt impatience surge through him. "No, it's not," he said. He described what Betsy Lowery had seen and how Porter had reacted to their questions. He talked about Harvey Fuller and Tamsin Lovell. He told them about Claire's French diary again and passed out Marie-France's translation. He told them in even greater detail what Madeline had learned from Sally Jansen, Maggie, and Rosalie, and the group that called itself the Reign of Terror. And he shared his own view on what might have happened.

They were listening, he could tell they were listening. Even the bricks couldn't pretend that they didn't hear him. As he spoke, he saw Vernon watching him with a combination of admiration and suspicion, but Matt continued to talk with articulate clarity, outlining what he felt needed to happen and how the case should proceed from here in a concise and orderly way. He didn't speak long. He didn't need to. He saw Angell lean back and saw as well the relief on his face. Matt was living up to his end of their agreement. Over the next few minutes, they allotted tasks, and then, earlier than expected, he and Vernon found themselves in the warming light of the parking lot, the sun making the puddles steam as if they were miniature hot springs.

Vernon began to applaud in slow, heavy claps. "Bravo. Did you mean one word of that?"

"I hope so," said Matt as he walked toward his car. "We going in mine?" They were off to talk to Porter.

"Sure," said Vernon. "You have a better CD player." But he wasn't finished. "That's what those places do," he went on. "They make you very, very good at sounding like you know what you're talking about. They make you sound like you're in charge." He opened the passenger side of Matt's car. "What was scary was that you sounded like him. You really did." And Matt knew that he meant Porter, because that was exactly who had flashed through his mind as he'd been speaking, laying out his version of the case. A man who to all appearances had everything under control. A man people trusted with what was deepest to them.

"What I am having trouble squaring with myself," Vernon said as he fussed with his seat belt strap, "is if I'm jealous or merely seeing things accurately. I could have used a better education," he said. "And I wanted to learn to play jazz piano."

"Jazz piano?" said Matt, and he started the car, then realized he needed sunglasses. Pausing to put them on, he said, "I can see it, Vernon." And he could. Vernon loved everyone from Charlie Parker to Coltrane, and he had a loose grace and impossibly wide, long-fingered hands.

"They teach that up there?" his partner asked.

"Of course they do," Matt said, slowly accelerating.

"But even if I had the money, I wouldn't send my kids," Vernon said. "I don't believe in what they've got. I don't want it. I don't buy it." He readjusted his seat belt. "Do you? Do you really?"

Matt had braked at a stop sign and paused to look at his partner. What was there to say? What could he tell Vernon now other than he'd tried to take what was best from Armitage and step away from what was less appealing. But could anyone do that? Could you participate in a place like the academy without being of it in some essential way? "Vernon, the short answer is that there isn't one. Privilege exists. It's real. It's unjust. There's no way to reconcile that with poverty or lack of opportunity. And I profited from it."

Vernon chewed on that for a moment and said, "You're proud of what you got up there."

Matt considered Vernon's choice of words and said, "Yes, I am."

Vernon appeared to think about that for a moment, then said, "That authoritative-voice business. Where's it from?"

"It's a WASP thing, I think," Matt said. "They're masters at it. That and real estate they do really well. Comes from centuries of being the only show in town."

"I've seen it in movies, but I didn't know it actually happened," Vernon said and slumped as far as it was possible for someone tall to slump in a bucket seat. "It's goddamn creepy," he added, and with that, they drove up the hill and through the iron gates, down the light green corridor of maples to begin Porter McLellan's day on a very, very difficult note.

CHAPTER 19

Late Friday afternoon, Jim followed Nancy down the tunnels that led to the main furnace for Nicholson. For some reason, the great black beast had been switching on and off since last Saturday night, sending waves of heat through all the offices, despite the fact that it was almost eighty degrees outside and obviously well past the season for piped-in warmth. Nancy had reached him at Angela's, where he was staying while his mother recovered. She had insisted on being released from the hospital by lunchtime, and her doctors had reluctantly let her go. "I'm sorry to ask, but no one knows Big Bob like you do, Jim. Would you mind?" They'd had a tech look at it, but the problem wasn't resolved. Jim hadn't minded at all; in fact, he was looking forward to seeing Nancy again as soon as possible. And Angela herself looked relieved to have him gone for a time. She'd sleep, she said. She was tired after that inedible food in the hospital. She had almost laughed then and sent him off with a wave of her hand.

Still, Jim had driven with more enthusiasm than he really thought was seemly to go to fix the faulty furnace. They all had names, which was silly but useful. You could say, "Bob's acting up" or "Bertha's at it again," and everyone knew exactly what you meant. And even though Claire had died, her baby had disappeared, and his mother had suffered a heart attack, the daily work of making the school run smoothly still had to continue. Stop for a moment, and cracks started to run through everything. Jim sometimes wondered if anyone—teachers, kids, staff—had any idea how much time, money, and effort went into keeping those lawns fresh and all those buildings painted. To keep everything looking as prosperous as possible. Porter knew, Jim thought appreciatively, as he followed Nancy's trim self down the tunnel. Last year, at a gathering to thank people for work well done, Porter had said that Armitage could get by without him, deans, and most of the teachers. But what it couldn't function without were employees like them, with solid practical skills and a serious work ethic, people who cared about what they did and didn't shirk the tasks before them. "Thank you," he had said, "for making us look so good." It had been moving and it had been genuine and Jim knew it made a difference to everyone he worked with. Porter knew all their names and used them effortlessly. Afterward, Nancy had said, "That Porter is one in a million." And Jim had agreed.

They heard the overactive machine before they found it, and in the small room where it was clanking away, it must have been 110 degrees. Sweat sprouted instantly on his forehead, and he noticed that Nancy was turning a bright and pleasing shade of pink. Jim opened a box of tools and got out a wrench. He suspected the problem was a faulty temperature gauge; something had fooled Bob into believing it was actually close to freezing upstairs. Nancy watched him open up the main workings. He and she were in accord that, even though these old systems took some coddling and maintenance, they were still better made than most of the new stuff on the market and worth every cent of extra work it took to keep them going.

There it was. The gauge had gotten stripped and was exposed to the air. No wonder it had gone wonky. He'd need some other supplies to replace the actual wiring, but for now, a few layers of duct tape, a resetting of the system, and a little luck were all that was necessary to make the whole system function properly. Poor secretaries. They were probably worried about what the unusual heat would do to their computers up there.

Jim turned around then and saw Nancy looking at him. "What?" he said, thinking he'd done something wrong.

She shrugged. "It's just that you do your work well. I appreciate it." But there was something else. It was that she'd been looking at him with another, far less abstract sort of appreciation. She turned to go, but he said, "Nancy?" and before he was quite aware of what he was doing, he walked over to her and gently put his hands on her shoulders and kissed her.

In the boiler room. What a place for a first kiss. Which was exactly what she said when he stopped kissing her. "The boiler room? What are you, some die-hard romantic? Couldn't you just wait until Saturday night like everybody else?"

"No," said Jim, "I couldn't," and he kissed her again. His boss. But at the moment, none of it—their professional relationship, his dirty hands, the impossible heat—seemed to matter much at all.

Out in the clear light of the afternoon, they had grown shy as teenagers and found excuses to hightail it off in opposite directions, both of them, Jim suspected, grinning madly. That was what was wonderful about a kiss. It was terribly revealing about compatibility, and this one had been quite confirming.

He went to the workshop and got the tools he needed for a more conclusive repair to Big Bob, finished the job quickly, and made it back to Angela's by six. She was fast asleep, and he surprised himself by turning on her computer and doing a search of graduate schools in management. Maybe Angela had been right. Maybe it was time to set his sights higher and do something other than labor with his hands. He was good with people, he felt. It was something Nancy told him all the time.

Around seven, he started cooking dinner: sautéed chicken, peas, even fresh baked rolls, whose smell he hoped would arouse his mother's appetite. But Angela only nibbled at the food before her. He found himself watching her hands: when she got too lean, her rings rolled right off the joints. Briefly, he felt some chagrin at his own buoyant mood and experienced instead the return of worry over his mother. Angela continued to push around the peas on her plate as if arranging them in a geometric puzzle. Spearing one now, she sighed and said, "I know I should eat. But I can't stop thinking about that poor girl."

Poor girl? Who was Angela talking about? "Do you mean the girl who was killed? Claire?" Jim asked. In a tone that was a little blunter than he usually allowed himself to be with his mother, he said, "I'm surprised, Ma. I didn't think what happened up there mattered to you."

Angela acknowledged his skepticism with a flutter of her fingers. Usually, his mother could be counted on to rant about Armitage. She was unconscionably proud of the achievements of (most of) her children, all of whom had gone to public schools. Two lawyers, a doctor, a banker, and then Jim. A handyman, a divorced handyman. And the only one left in the area and probably the best parent among them, he said in his own silent defense. He wondered, a bit sharply and, he knew, inaccurately, if Angela could even name all her grandchildren; it was the graduate degrees and the colleges, all attended on scholarship, that she committed most firmly to memory. This concern of hers about Claire, a girl of what she would be sure to consider disgusting privilege, was decidedly unlike her. "I know, Jimmie. I don't like that place and I think it's time you found another job. But she was very young and she died. That's different. And then there's the baby. What do you think has happened to the baby?" His mother was indeed worried. She slowly spun her three gold bangles, something she did only when agitated.

"They're not saying." Ever since the murder and the baby's disappearance, he had barely mentioned the whole mess, fearing it would draw Angela's scorn. She had referred to the events rather obliquely and with her familiar disdain for the doings of the rich. They'd mostly skirted the topic, for which Jim was grateful. He hadn't wanted to recount the feeling of invasion and shock, how the students and faculty were skittering around the campus. If his mother was following what was going in the papers or on television, she was doing so privately, and after a brief mention at dinner each night, they'd stowed the topic as if it were something unsightly. And then she had gotten ill. But suddenly, fresh from the hospital, she was taut with concern.

"They've released some statements, all about ongoing investigations," Jim said carefully. He himself had been a little disappointed at the terseness of Armitage's response. All Porter had said to the staff was that Claire had died and that they were searching for a newborn who had disappeared in "suspicious circumstances." Jim had thought that the head would handle it with a little more finesse, but he wasn't going to give his mother anything else to fuel her long-nourished resentment of the academy.

Angela glanced at the clock and said, "It's time for the news." She watched the show on the public station that aired at 8:00 and not the blond bobbleheads on the major networks. She went in to seat herself in her armchair, and instead of staying in the kitchen to wash dishes and listen to music, avoiding the day's events, Jim joined her. As she listened to reports of carnage in Iraq and Afghanistan, he watched her. Her face had grown veiled and tired. But then a repeat of the local segment of the broadcast came on, and there was Armitage displayed across the screen. It struck Jim how alien it must look to outsiders. The beauty of the grounds. The grandeur of the buildings. How gorgeous it was. You might do anything to be part of it, and you might feel terribly small if you weren't. Then Jim sat up even straighter. The earnest reporter had managed to get on campus with his crew, and he was standing in front of Greaves. Jim wished he had Nancy's list of repairs for the next day right in front of him. He could have sworn that the window he was supposed to fix was on the second floor, to the right of the main corridor. But the cracked pane he spied on the screen was on the third floor and to the left. He said nothing to his mother, who was staring at the television, though clearly not paying attention to the story unfolding in front of her.

She snapped the set off and announced she was going to bed. "These drugs make me tired. I'm going to turn in early." She rose stiffly but refused help with a cross look and slowly walked upstairs. Jim did the dishes and was mopping the floor when the phone rang. It was Kayla, obviously startled at hearing his voice. She had hoped, he realized, only to speak to Angela. But she gathered herself and told Jim she was sorry but she wouldn't be able to come by for the next few days. She hoped Mrs. French would understand, and she was looking forward to seeing her soon. Jim thought about mentioning Angela's heart attack and his mother's desire to talk to Kayla, but he decided not to. The girl sounded so tired. Instead, he said he understood and thanked her for calling, knowing that the news would disappoint his mother.

Angela called from her bedroom, "Who was that, Jimmie?" and when he went upstairs to tell her that Kayla wouldn't be coming back until at least next week, his mother's face crumpled. But when Jim asked if she wanted to talk to Kayla herself, Angela said no. "She's got her reasons, I'm sure of that," his mother said, making much of polishing the lenses of her already spotless glasses. Jim came close to offering to take her to the nail salon and Starbucks himself, but Angela would have refused. It was Kayla's company and the atmosphere of serious fun she brought with her that made all the difference. It was having a girl around and not her fussy old son. It was a friendship where none had been expected. "I want to sleep now, Jimmie," his mother said and sat on the smooth white coverlet of her bed.

Dismissed, Jim returned to the kitchen and started to pace. There was nothing left to clean, and he was too restless to sit down. He realized that the person he actually wanted to talk to was Nancy. It was just nine fifteen and not too late to call; he could check with her about that crack he'd seen in the window of the dorm. She answered on the first ring and was clearly happy to hear from him. Listening to her voice, he thought instantly of the boiler room's steamy warmth.

"Where am I catching you?" he asked, and she confessed that she was still at work. There was so much to do, what with graduation so close and Claire's memorial service coming up on Sunday. It was getting harder and harder to get home at a reasonable hour. "Sorry, Jim. I don't want to complain. How's your mom?"

Despite their encounter in the basement, they settled easily into conversation. About Angela and her testy frame of mind. About the impending visit from Jim's sister Andrea, who would be driving up this weekend. She would come, Jim told Nancy, to make sure he still knew he was the youngest in the family, though given that he was fifty, it was news she didn't really need to reinforce. Two years ago, Angela had broken her ankle, and Andrea had made the same trip. Within moments of her arrival, his sister had looked askance at the steep stairs and glanced suspiciously at Angela's car keys hanging on a kitchen hook. By the end of her visit, she had arranged a conference call with two other siblings and everyone had started to mention assisted living with not such studied casualness. Angela and Jim had fended her off, but this time it might be different.

"My brother tried the same thing with my dad," Nancy said thoughtfully. "But Dad was as stubborn as your mom sounds, and he died eight years later in his own bed."

"And my mother is not only stubborn, she's competent," Jim said.

"Like you," Nancy said, laughing, and even though she was his boss, even though their school was in the midst of a crisis, he stopped, gathered his courage, and asked her out to dinner. "Yes," she said with obvious enthusiasm. "Absolutely," and despite their kiss, they both seemed to get terribly shy and he switched the topic to work, ostensibly the reason he had called in the first place.

He told her then what he'd seen on the TV. "Oh, you saw that," Nancy said. "No one knows how the reporter got in, but security whisked him off pretty quick." She paused and then said, "You sure it was the third floor? I'll go check it out and call you back."

To pass time until Nancy rang him, Jim settled in to watch a *Nova* show about Ernest Shackleton and his miraculous feat of rescue on Antarctica. He vaguely recognized the narrator's voice and knew that when he read the credits at the end he'd be disgusted with himself for not realizing who it was. When Nancy called back, ten minutes later, he switched the sound to mute and watched the grainy photographs of Shackleton's crew roll steadily across the screen. "You're right, Jim," she said. "It's the third and the second. The one on the second comes from a Frisbee. The kid who did it was really sorry and offered to pay. The one on the third looks different, like someone threw something at it, a rock or stone. And it's Scotty Johnston's room."

"Big surprise," said Jim. "I'll fix it first thing and see if I can figure it out."

"And there's something else," Nancy said. Jim listened and kept looking at the pictures of the dogs on the ice and the serious men in their peacoats. "Porter just texted me to ask to have the locks changed on his and Tamsin's offices. Could you handle that to-morrow morning?"

Jim waited before he spoke. He could hear that Nancy was walking across the campus, to her car, he hoped. It was close to ten. "Why does Porter need the locks changed?"

"I don't know," she said softly. "Seemed odd to me, too."

"I'll get to it right away." Looking at Ernest Shackleton on a ship near South Georgia Island, Jim said, "Go home, Nancy. You need to take a break." He himself felt abruptly tired and knew the next day was going to be a long one.

"Thanks, Jim, for everything," she said, and he didn't think he was imagining the energy in her voice. She liked him, this woman liked him. And he liked her back. It was uplifting, even in the midst of all that was happening. "Nancy," he said, "when this is all over, remember you agreed I could take you out to dinner?"

"Just as long as it's not a restaurant in a basement," she said, and he laughed and promised her that it would be somewhere well aboveground. They wished each other good night, and Jim hung up feeling more alert than he had in a very long time.

He then crept down the hallway to Angela's room. She had fallen asleep with her lamp on. She barely moved as he pulled the book from her hands and tucked the blanket under her chin before clicking off the light.

He slept in his old room downstairs, which his mother had converted to a study of sorts. Her books and files lined the space, and all night he dreamed of librarians with fierce grins and rings of keys. When he woke at 4:30, he knew instantly he was up for good. He looked silently in on Angela and, for a few minutes, sat by her side and watched her breathe, the way he had his girls when they were babies, as if they needed his presence to remember to keep pulling air into their lungs. Then he showered, dressed, made his bed, and ate an egg and coffee. He did his dishes and laid a place for Angela at the table. He wrote her a note saying he was leaving early but would be back by three. "Call if you need anything, Ma."

Even after all this activity, it was only 5:30. But he couldn't read or sit still, his mind caught in a fruitless circle of topics that rolled from Angela to Nancy, Kayla to Claire, and back again. The only solution was motion. He backed up his car as quickly as possible so as not to wake his mother and drove off to campus as the sun was rising over the edge of the green hills.

The morning was utterly tranquil, and this early, not even the dog walkers or the most masochistic of runners were up yet, much less anyone else on his crew. The shop smelled of oil and well-used tools, warm metal. He found what he needed for the locks at Nicholson and gathered a few other tools. He liked his work. He liked that he got to do it on his own and that no one really interfered

with him because he was good at it. He could do it for years to
come. But Armitage was changing. Looking at the barrels of the
new lock he was about to load in the old doors of Nicholson, he
knew that the intuition he had first had the morning he'd learned
of Claire's death was coming true. Nothing would be the same afterward. And as he shouldered his satchel full of tools, he knew,
too, that, for the first time in a long time, this job wasn't going to
be quite enough to satisfy him. You old goat, he told himself, part
of what you're saying is that you want to pursue this woman. And
that you don't want to be dating your boss.

He almost laughed as he walked from the shop across campus
to Nicholson. Well, it was respectable as far as motives went, and
his mother would certainly be happy that he would consider leaving the academy. But he wasn't going to say anything to anybody
until he had something else in hand. As for what might possibly
replace working at Armitage, he had no idea. Going back for a
graduate degree kept tugging at his mind.

He had just arrived in front of Nicholson and stood for a moment looking at its stained glass, its third-floor turrets. For all the
silly flourishes of its architecture, it was the school's center, the
setting in which its most important decisions unfolded. It was
where the board met, the faculty gathered, where students were
disciplined or expelled, where teachers were hired or let go. Finally, he walked into the long dark hall and stopped still. He had
always liked this first scent of Nicholson, its smell of school: soap
and paper. The hall was wide and dark, the marble floor smooth
and polished. The whole structure was so firm and solid, crafted
when materials were better, when workmanship took time and
everything from tools to bricks was made by hand. The slates on
the roof had been shaped by chisels well over a hundred years

ago. When the tiles needed work, Jim always marveled at how well formed they were, how delicate the edges of each one were. The work had required remarkable care, time, attention and had been done with the intention of making it last.

Slowly, he headed toward Porter's office and climbed a short flight. When he had first been hired at the school, caring for these stairs had been one of his jobs, but Nancy had pulled him off janitorial detail and given him tasks that let him use his real skills as a carpenter and a person who could fix almost anything.

He paused on the landing, put his satchel by his feet, and looked out over the Quad, thoughts of Nancy intruding though he was trying firmly to keep her out of his mind. He hadn't felt this way about someone since when? It was funny how it had sneaked up on him. He hadn't, he had to say frankly, felt exactly this way about his wife. He had married Carla because she was pregnant, a decision he'd never regretted because it resulted in his lovely eldest daughter. And he had loved Carla, but it had never felt natural with her. Every speck of their marriage felt earned and built. With Nancy, there was an ease that it had taken years to achieve with Carla. But it terrified him, too. And nothing beyond a kiss in the basement had actually happened yet. They hadn't even had a real first date.

It was time to get started. Porter's office was at the far end of the corridor, and Jim crept down it noiselessly. He had chosen his shoes for years for their ability to move without a chorus of squeaks or slaps along hallways and tunnels, which meant picking footwear with rubber soles. He could wear loafers in another life or running shoes or clogs. The thought was enough to make him smile, and then he heard a voice coming from the end of the hall.

It was someone speaking rapidly and loudly, and at first he couldn't place it because he'd never heard this person speak in anything but a moderate, steady tone. It was Tamsin Lovell, and she was yelling at someone on the phone. And it wasn't just yelling, Jim realized; this woman whom he'd always thought of as composed and immeasurably dutiful was shouting. Initially, Jim thought she might be in trouble, but then he heard the anger in her words, and moving lightly along the corridor until he was just outside Porter's office door, he heard the words themselves.

"Colson, you don't understand," Tamsin cried with blind fury. "I have the boy, I have him." Her voice was ragged, shattering. Jim heard the whir of a machine as well as the frantic rush of Tamsin's words.

The person on the other end obviously tried to interrupt her, but she cut him short again. "Colson," she said. Tamsin's rage flowed on: "You have to help, Colson."

Tamsin had to be talking to Colson Trowbridge, the head of the board. An influential Boston lawyer, an alumnus, a generous donor for whom the new athletic complex was named. Jim had often been the one in charge of preparing the boardroom for meetings, and he had seen Trowbridge on several occasions over the years. Tall, well groomed, the man had seemed the embodiment of clubby success. And self-confidence that bordered on arrogance.

She said she had the boy. Was she talking about the baby? She was trying to get Trowbridge to step in to help somehow. Just as he was about to turn back down the corridor, to flee from whatever was happening in that room, Jim's cell phone chirped, its signal for a low battery. In his distraction last night, he must have forgotten to plug it in. Tamsin paused, slammed down the phone, and the door flew open. She wore running shoes, athletic shorts, and a T-shirt.

Her hair was in a ponytail, and she was flushed and breathing hard. Jim understood instantly that she had chosen an outfit that would give her a reason to be seen on campus so early in the morning. But she hadn't expected to be caught here. And then the humming sound that had seemed to come from the office appeared to be rising from his own head, and it was the sound of pure fear. Because Tamsin, as she ran at him, was lifting high a fire extinguisher, ready to smash its red bulk at his skull, and then he realized where the sound really came from. A shredder. She was running a shredder. But then he saw her bared teeth and the shiny cylinder and then nothing at all.

CHAPTER 20

Track had just finished for Saturday afternoon, and Madeline wondered again why they were bothering with sports. The students need the exercise, Grace had insisted. It kept them busy and tired after class. It kept them out of trouble. Madeline wondered what kind of trouble Grace might be worrying about after the worst that could happen already had, though she allowed that tuckering teenagers out to whatever degree possible was most likely a good idea. The last three days, her group of athletes had thrown itself into punishing rounds of sprints and difficult cross-country runs. Still, she thought, all this activity is certainly not good for me. Dealing with troubling encounters with students and discomfiting news about their extremely extracurricular activities had left her more addled than usual. She was dreading leaving and returning to the dorm. God only knew what she'd find on her doorstep next. In addition, last night Owen had had the grace to send not a text but an actual e-mail saying that things seemed to have petered out between them and he was ready to move on. Meaning, Madeline thought, that he already had. Amazing how a computer screen could give off a whiff of new girlfriend, but it did.

Approaching her apartment, looking forward only to the coldest shower, she saw something else that wasn't good for her. Kate, her sister, had manipulated her way past security and onto campus. Her baby was in her arms, and he was screaming.

"Tadeo," Madeline shouted, glad in spite of herself to see the little boy. "Hi, baby, stop crying! Auntie Madeline is here!"

"Oh, God, Madeline, you're disgusting. You're getting sweat all over him," Kate complained. But Tadeo immediately stopped wailing and snuggled instead into Madeline's arms. Even in the few weeks since she'd seen him, he'd grown. Kate, however, was the same as always: beautifully turned out and apparently immune to the effects of high humidity. A diaper bag that managed to be elegant was slung over her shoulder, and smooth dark blond hair flowed down her back. She wore a topaz necklace and unwrinkled linen pants and shirt. It dawned on Madeline that Kate was all in white. She had a just-nine-month-old baby and she was in spotless white. Yet Madeline, without a single child in tow, couldn't wear a white T-shirt to breakfast without spattering cranberry juice in a crimson plume all over herself. Fred had pointed that out last week, and she had wanted to deck him. Thinking of Fred, where was he? She hadn't seen or heard from him since his trip to Brooklyn, which was not a good sign.

Tadeo, Madeline was glad to notice, took after her. He was covered in a fine layer of rice cereal and yogurt and needed nothing more than a dip in the tub. Madeline fished out her key from her shorts pocket and ushered them all inside. Fortunately, no signs from the Reign were immediately present. "I can't believe you let them put you in this dump. It's tiny," Kate said. She collapsed on the futon sofa, and Madeline was glad she'd cleared it of her laundry this morning, depriving her sister of one more thing to criticize.

She ignored Kate and went straight to the bathroom. Tadeo was pulling on her necklace and trying to bite it. "Are you teething, little man?" she asked him.

"Glor," he said, apparently meaning Yes, and it sucks. Drool streamed in twin rivers from either side of his mouth. Oh, how she loved this baby, his physical completeness, the seemingly poreless skin, the clear fire of his dark eyes. He was just beautiful. He gnawed some more on the silver chain.

Kate had been astonished that Madeline wanted to be present at his birth. "Not in the room or anything," Madeline had assured her, though she'd secretly hoped that her sister would invite her to be right there. She had always wanted to see a baby being born, and this one was going to be her nephew. "Just nearby, so I can help. So I can meet him right from the start." She thought that would be nice, sisterly, auntly, something she should do when Isabelle and David so clearly weren't capable of it. Kate had grudgingly agreed to have her at the hospital, and for that, Madeline would always be grateful. When she'd met Tadeo for the first time, he looked more like a large plum with a thatch of black hair than a person, and still, she'd been overwhelmed with joy and surprise, conscious of a deep, abiding mystery she had no idea existed. Kate and Nick had been too exhausted to notice that Madeline wept as she held the swaddled baby, welcoming him to the world.

Now, as she let the water seep into the tub, making sure it was only tepid, Madeline thought of Claire's baby. He would be about a week old. He would need constant care, constant feeding. Warmth and of course love. Where was he? Why hadn't they found him or any trace of him? Madeline couldn't say "body." She refused to admit to herself that he might have been killed, too. Tadeo, squirming in her arms, said, "Glahglahglah."

She unpeeled his onesie from his sticky body and took off his diaper, too. He sat with pleasure in the warm water and splashed it with fat hands. Madeline gave him her washcloth to play with and hoped Kate wouldn't ask when the last time was Madeline had actually cleaned the tub.

But that was too much to hope for. Kate was standing behind her, drinking a glass of water. She actually had one for Madeline in her other hand. Just when you were ready to write Kate off altogether, she'd do something that made you not quite hate her anymore. "Thanks," she said now, "but when was the last time you cleaned that tub?"

"This morning, with my toothbrush," Madeline said. "He's happy, Kate. Let him be." That was new, she thought. I never talk back to Kate. Perhaps death and harassment were firming up her inner strength. To her surprise, her sister didn't come up with a retort. Instead, she flipped the lid down on the toilet and sank onto it. Tadeo noticed her, said, "clom," and kept splashing happily when he wasn't sucking on Madeline's washcloth. "You're so good with him," Kate said. "You get him." To Madeline's horror, Kate was crying.

"Kate?" she asked, propping the baby up a little more firmly.

She was having a hard time, she said, but even when she cried, Kate's complexion didn't become mottled and her mascara didn't run. She wanted to apply for a tenure-track job in New York, but Nick didn't want to leave Boston. The baby couldn't sleep through the night. Nick was working a lot, and even with the nanny, she was just tired all the time. This was the worst of it: he wanted lots of kids. She didn't think she wanted any more. It was too hard. She was desperate to get back to a job. Work was so much easier than parenting. "Madeline, it's just so hard." She started to sob. This time, her mascara really did run. And Tadeo started to scream in earnest.

I'm getting good at this, Madeline thought, this being graceful under pressure. She scooped the baby up and bundled him in a towel. One arm around Tadeo, she used her other hand to pull Kate up from the toilet and to wrap her close. Her sister was shaking and crying so hard, she couldn't speak. This was worse than Madeline had realized. Somehow, she maneuvered everyone out to the living room, settled Kate on the futon, got Tadeo diapered, and from Kate's handsome bag fished out a bottle that she microwaved. Between hiccups, Kate said, "You're not supposed to do that," and Madeline said, "Shut up, Kate," and did it anyway, because what the baby needed was food and reassurance and the chance to sleep. He conked out in a couple of minutes, and she laid him on a towel on her futon and turned a fan on low so he wouldn't get sweaty and hot again. Then she refilled Kate's water glass and said, "What's going on? You're a basket case," thinking this was the first time she had ever had reason to use that word in relation to her sister.

"I want to leave Nick," Kate sniffled. It was the job issue and the kid issue and maybe they'd just been too young and they'd outgrown each other. The baby sighed in his sleep and kicked out a leg. Madeline took in the dumpiness of her environment. The old throw pillows, the inch of ancient coffee in the percolator. The piles of final papers she needed to correct by Monday and the battered copy of Norton's anthology of American poetry. Her sneakers smelled, and frankly, so did she. Most days, a list like this was enough to give Kate a strong advantage. But Madeline felt something welling up in her, something powerful enough to sweep away her sister's cosmetic superiority.

"No," said Madeline firmly. "No. You have to try harder. You said you would do this. And if you can't, you can't just walk away like it never happened, as if Tadeo wasn't there. You have to do better than that. You have to do it for the baby. And you know what? You have to do it for Nick. Kate, he's a great guy. You're lucky to have him." Madeline had always liked her brother-in-law. Despite being handsome, smart, and rich, he was also a nice man. Despite every opportunity not to, he'd resisted self-importance. "I'll help you, Kate. I'll be around all summer. I'll give you time. You can get counseling. You can work it out."

Kate blinked at her. She took a deep breath. She was returning to her usual state. "I don't know what I want," she said, and her voice wavered. The baby stirred. He would be awake soon. Madeline fetched a clean suit from the diaper bag.

"How did you get on campus?" she asked her sister. "And why are you here?" Now that Kate had stopped weeping, Madeline could ask what had brought her sister out from Boston.

"I told the police I had to meet Porter, and then he happened to be walking by the gate with his dog," she said. "I said I wanted to check on you. He owes Nick a favor; one of his twins has an internship at Nick's firm this summer."

"How does Nick know Porter?" Madeline asked. Nick hadn't gone to Armitage, which at first had seemed to count against him during his courtship of Kate. Slipping Tadeo's leg through a hole in a fresh onesie made Madeline reflect that it was a lot easier to dress a sleeping baby than one who was wide awake.

"We saw him last summer up in Castine, where he has this little house. He was there with his kids. Nick sailed with them a few times. That's when I met that girl who was killed. She was up there, too."

Tadeo turned over in his new suit, stuck his bum in the air, and sighed again. "Glarr," he added sleepily.

"You met Claire?" Madeline asked.

Kate said, "Yes, in August. It was one of the things I wanted to tell you, but you kept not returning my calls." She glared at her sister. "Or e-mails. She was a beautiful girl. She looked just like her mother." Flora, Kate explained, had come to Maine to get her, supposedly, though Claire had obviously been taking care of herself for years. Kate thought there was another agenda at work. One night, they'd all had dinner at Porter's house, but Lucinda wasn't there. "I think Flora and Porter were old flames," Kate said, wiping away all traces of her tears, more herself now that there was some gossip to distract her. "They seemed comfortable together. I got the sense that, if Lucinda had been around, it wouldn't have happened at all."

Then Tadeo woke and Kate looked at her watch and said she guessed she should get back. Madeline, still thinking of what Kate had said, helped her sister gather her things. At the threshold, Kate said, "I know I told you about it. That's when I found out Porter was going to hire you. After you'd gotten rejected everywhere else."

Madeline remembered now. She'd been struck by the casualness with which her sister mentioned eating a meal with the headmaster. Probably Kate had mentioned Claire and Flora, too, but what had registered was the ease with which she spoke of Porter, the way she had waltzed into his house.

Tadeo was in that blissful post-nap mood where he was neither hungry nor sleepy. He was being, simply, a sweet and loving baby. "You're so lucky, Kate," Madeline said. She meant it mostly about Tadeo, but the remark encompassed everything: Kate's confidence, her degrees, the potential of her career, her marriage. "Work it out with Nick," she said as she held the door open.

Looking slightly less disconsolate, Kate sniffed. "I'll try. Please don't tell Mom or Dad about this."

"Why would I do that?" Madeline asked, truly curious. She never told her parents anything of consequence. Isabelle and David had each called once since Claire's death, to make sure she wasn't going to be arrested imminently, as David put it. "In need of legal counsel?" he'd asked, and she'd reassured him that no, indeed, she had all her bases covered. She even held herself back from saying, And if I did, you'd be the last person I'd ask.

"I don't know." Kate shrugged. "Just in case."

"Wait a minute, Kate. There's something else." Madeline had no desire to tell her sister about what had been going on, but Kate would certainly know about the Reign, and perhaps she'd have some useful information. Kate was ready to go but waited impatiently just outside the door, jiggling Tadeo on her hip. Madeline asked, "When you were here, did they have this Reign of Terror thing? Complete with Robespierre and all this silliness about who could sit where?"

To Madeline's concern, Kate's face grew closed and haughty. She shifted Tadeo protectively to her other side and said, "I'm afraid I can't talk about that."

"Oh, God," Madeline cried, "you were one of them. Of course! I should have known! Kate, how could you? They're dreadful, these girls. Do you know what they do to each other?" Madeline was going to bluster on, but Kate said, coolly, "You have no idea what you're talking about," and started to walk away.

"Kate, how could you have been a part of it?" Madeline called after her. But all her sister said was "Phone me when you've pulled yourself together," in her usual, infuriating manner that implied she had cornered the entire market on composure. Madeline was left standing on her doorstep staring at the slim, retreating figure of her sister. Kate slipped across the Quad and past Greaves to where she'd parked with her usual irreverence for rules in the faculty lot. It seemed a miracle or some dark joke that she and Kate were related, Madeline mused, anger still ticking through her at her sister's lack of total disclosure, her invocation of thorny silence, a pact that apparently trumped family loyalty. Madeline was glad Kate was gone, despite the fact she had taken Tadeo with her. She went to take a shower and was letting her frustration with Kate sluice off under the flow of water when, abruptly, she began to sputter. Spinning the taps shut, she lurched for a towel. What Kate had said struck her the moment she'd rinsed the shampoo from her hair: Claire had been with Porter and his family in August and the girl had returned to school in mid-September, most likely already pregnant.

Just then there was a knock on the door, and Madeline jumped and nearly fell she was so jittery. Pulling on some clothes that at least looked clean, she got to the door and saw Sarah Talmadge standing there, arms folded across her chest. "Sarah," Madeline said, "I'm so sorry. I just got out of the shower."

"Don't worry, Madeline. I'm the one who should be apologizing to you, for not getting back to you and then barging in like this." She looked even more wan than she had when Madeline had seen her earlier in the week. "Could I come in for a moment?"

Madeline offered Sarah water or coffee, and the assistant head gratefully accepted water. "Well, there's a lot to talk about, but why don't you start?" She sat on an armchair and settled in to listen.

Madeline flopped on her futon and leaned in to describe what she had learned about the Reign of Terror, Claire, Sally, and Rosalie. Sarah listened with some of the same concentrated intensity as the police officer, and she shared as well his apparent lack of surprise.

But before she spoke, she took a long sip of water. "We've been wanting to get rid of this Reign business for years. Porter and I and a few others have been looking into it for a long time. Unfortunately, as you discovered with your sister, it is something that alumnae hold dear. And in the beginning, it was, apparently, almost benign." Sarah explained that it had started when the first female students enrolled, at the end of the 1970s. "The name was meant to be a joke of sorts. Something that showed how smart and serious they were that they could use a reference connected to the French Revolution. To them, it was obvious that the real Reign of Terror existed among the boys and the male teachers, with their traditions of hazing. The girls looked after each other those first few years, and the group was supposed to support solidarity among the young women and, ironically, prevent them from losing their heads."

Sarah sighed. "But it changed. There were a few Robespierres who had different ideas about the position, and they begin imitating the boys rather than avoiding their bad habits." They even tried to sponsor a scholarship, to become an alumnae group, though that effort got squashed, fortunately. And then, one year, Sarah said, in the mid-eighties, a new girl was driven to a suicide attempt that did not succeed, and at that point, the head took on the task of trying to banish all traditions. Sarah looked at Madeline and said, "It might be hard to believe, but the backlash came not only from alumni but from faculty, who saw the traditions as holding together something sacred at the school. The kids were smart about it. In the middle of all the brouhaha, they just went underground. The last couple of years, Porter and I have been gathering evidence about what's really going on. But we had no idea that Claire was a voice of reason on this front."

Madeline asked her, "Did you know about Rosalie? About how she'd been harassed?"

Sarah's face grew more pinched. "I suspected it, yes, and pressed both her and her parents about it, but they would have nothing to do with the school. We failed that child. We failed her utterly." Sarah looked tired enough to collapse on Madeline's shabby armchair. She was taking all of this personally. She saw it as her duty to admit where Armitage had gone wrong. "And Rich Girls?" She repeated the website's name as if she'd discovered a morsel of rotten food in her mouth. "That one we didn't or at least I didn't know about. There are lots of others, Madeline. Lots of them. And we keep tabs on them, to protect the kids, to try and block what they have access to. But there's a lot of leakage nonetheless." Sometimes, Sarah said, she wished it was fifty years ago, when it was hard to take airplanes, make phone calls, do any of the million things kids took for granted now. Technology was supposed to be this fantastic boon, and then its abuse showed you it was just another way to draw out the darkness in people.

Madeline said then, "I looked at it, Sarah. It was blocked on my school computer, but not on my laptop, for some reason. But I wanted to see if Rosalie was telling the truth." Madeline almost had to close her eyes as she told Sarah this part of the story. "I felt ashamed even typing in the name of the site," she said, stumbling over herself. The images of the girls' lush curves had been both horrifying and erotic at the same time, and she had experienced a thrill of recognition when she saw the bodies of the four girls who had slept like children on the floor of her living room. Rosalie had been right. If you knew who they were, you could recognize them from the curl of a lip, the angle of an arm. They hadn't entirely disguised themselves. They were mostly nude, and in poses with one another, arms wrapped around one another, legs lifted high. There was a crudeness about the entire series of images and shadowed expressions that was utterly at odds with how they presented themselves at the academy, but as Rosalie said, they had even used their school's name for the titles of the pictures: Armitage Babes, they called themselves. The shot that purported to be of Rosalie revealed nothing but a girl's naked body, up to her mouth and chin. The eyes were absent, and it might have been any barely developed child. For some reason, they had yet to terrorize Maggie by posting a similar image. Madeline had felt an intense wave of nausea pass through her, and she had turned off the computer with a rough snap. "But it's real," she said now to Sarah. "They're there. And almost proudly, barely disguised. Anyone could find them there. Why would they do it? What could possess them?"

Sarah was looking out the window as she spoke. "It's something I've thought about a lot, Madeline. Why did Claire have her baby here? Why did Lee Hastings post pornographic pictures of herself on the Web? Why did any of these children do such damage to themselves? And I know I don't have a definite answer, and the one I've come up with might be woefully partial." Her hands locked together, she looked at Madeline again and said, "I have to keep reminding myself that they are children. They don't talk like kids, dress like them, want to be treated like them, but they are. Don't think I'm saying that they're naïve or should be condescended to simply because they're young. What I mean is that they are inexperienced. Impulsive. Unable to foresee consequences with brains that aren't in any sense fully developed. What I mean is that it is understandable that they make mistakes, sometimes ones that change their lives."

Madeline thought about what Sarah was saying. She remembered with shame some of her own teenage missteps. Crawling through the window of a boy she liked only to discover she was in his parents' bedroom. Intemperate e-mails that had gone astray. "Maybe," she told the assistant head, "maybe that's a part of it. But I wondered if it was more cynical than that. Sometimes I think they just don't care what people think. Not us, their parents, no one but their peers. There's some bravado and disdain in what they do that makes me wonder who they are. And it's so unfathomable to me. They sit there in front of you all excited to read Milton, for God's sakes, and then they do things like this."

"You might be right, too," Sarah said sadly. "But even so, it doesn't mean they shouldn't have the chance to learn from serious errors in judgment. It doesn't mean they don't have the capacity to change. Thanks for telling me, Madeline."

"What happens now?" Madeline asked. "Do you tell the parents?"

Sarah said, yes, they had to, come what may. And there were usually disciplinary actions taken, as discreetly as possible but still pursued. Last year, a boy had been kicked out. Others were suspended and required to seek therapy. Parents always went berserk. "Every time it's the same. Lawyers, threats to sue, all the rest. But yes, we tell the parents, even if it reflects badly on us. This year, given everything that's happened, it's harder to say what the consequences will be." She paused then, clearly gathering herself for something else. Sarah, a small woman, took a deep breath and seemed to straighten her spine in an effort to appear taller. "All of which makes what I'm about to ask you now seem almost farcical. But I would like to offer you a full-time faculty position for next year. As a rule," Sarah continued, "we don't offer positions to interns, no matter how good. But I think you're a real teacher. I think you've got tremendous potential. Everyone's seen it, and we'd like to ask you to stay."

"Really?" Even with my messy hair and being late to chapel? Madeline wanted to ask. Even though I don't entirely believe in what's on offer here? Even though I've been quite vocal about that? She couldn't help herself then and said, "But Sarah, I'm, well, very un-Armitage. And that's a polite way of putting it."

For the first time in what Madeline suspected was a while, Sarah laughed. "And maybe that's exactly what we need, Madeline. Someone who doesn't take everything we do entirely seriously, who remembers that what we're supposed to do is keep teaching."

Madeline looked at the assistant head's clear eyes. Her fierce expression and her taut posture. She was committed to her work, no matter what happened. She was committed to her school, no matter its blemishes. She was committed to trying to understand students, even when they engaged in activities she didn't countenance. Her lack of sure footing didn't steer her away from her appointed tasks. Suddenly, Madeline wanted badly to be someone like Sarah, someone that confident and poised. But just then, her hair still dripping, her brain still grappling with what Kate had told her and the pictures of the girls, she knew she couldn't yet give a definitive answer. She thought about the cramped Boston apartment that otherwise awaited her. The afternoons in rich kids' homes, stuffing them full of ways to ace the SAT. Armitage, even in its current state, was certainly a more appealing option, even if it did leave you a spinster stranded in the middle of woody Massachusetts. But still, she had to think about the offer more coherently and make sure she wasn't leaving her roommates or employer in the lurch. "Sarah, I want to say yes. But I want to be sure that yes is a real one. Can I take a day to think about it and then can we talk?"

"Absolutely," Sarah said and started to rise.

"But one thing is for sure," Madeline added hastily. "If I stay, can I switch dorms? I'd love a slightly bigger place."

Sarah said she was certain they could work something out. Madeline saw her to the door and said she'd call her office to make an official appointment early next week. "Thank you, Madeline," Sarah said, and Madeline said, "Actually, it's you I have to thank, for thinking I might be good at something."

Madeline liked Sarah, genuinely liked her. But she realized, as she stood at the door, she hadn't said a word about Claire being up in Maine when Porter was. Was it that she didn't trust Sarah with the information? she wondered, as she saw the upright woman make her way across the Quad and past James Armitage's resolute bronze presence. No, Madeline thought, it's because I don't want to believe something like that is true. She knew she had to tell Matt, and she knew she'd call him in a few minutes, but all she could do for that moment was stand there at the threshold and breathe the clean, rich air, what she needed after these encounters with Kate and Sarah.

And after all the endless meetings that had crammed the week. Nothing like a crisis to bring out the administrators and their shuffling stacks of papers. At one yesterday, the head of admissions had announced that almost half of the new students had reneged on their decision to attend Armitage next year. No one wanted to come to a school where a desperate scandal had struck so decisively. With almost languid fatigue, the dean had also said that it wasn't really a problem; he could make a trip to Shanghai, Hong Kong, Seoul, and Taipei, and fill the dorms to bursting with kids whose parents were more practical about this sort of thing. Armitage was still Armitage, and soon enough its domestic audience would remember its reputation. A couple of years from now, one of its diplomas would still have its strangely powerful currency. Thinking about this, Madeline felt a renewal of her vigor. She wasn't going to abandon this place because it was injured, because its name was sullied. Her intention was to stay. You could almost turn Armitage into an underdog at this moment in its history; Madeline had never felt as good rooting for the Red Sox since their two World Series wins finally shifted their long, sad streak of ill fortune. Her sympathies had covertly turned toward Chicago, though she hadn't admitted that yet to Fred.

She was going to need some coffee to stay awake enough for Last Tea. The machine gurgled and released a comforting scent into her kitchen, a generous term for the compact space. If she got enough of a raise, she might be able to afford an actual sofa and not merely her sister's cast-off futon. She slumped on a tall stool and looked out the window. It was shockingly sunny at the moment, but the clouds lay in a low pad over the river, a sure sign of more bad weather. The Quad was deserted. There were about four events and one more day of classes to limp through until Madeline was released for the summer for good.

Early this evening was Last Tea. On Sunday, they were holding Claire's memorial service, which in spite of everything, the parents were insisting on. Grace had said that it was because they couldn't agree on an alternate venue and that, charged as it was, Armitage was the best available compromise. Madeline shivered a little thinking about that; only students, the family, and faculty would attend, but it was still going to be dreadful. Why couldn't they wait? Because, Madeline knew, it was a way to appease the grieving parents, to stave off or at least delay the filing of the inevitable lawsuit for wrongful death, because Claire's class was a captive audience here, because Porter had said it was the right thing to do. It was hard, but they had to face it.

Porter. He had pared down everything. There would be no baccalaureate service, a quasi-awards ceremony at which prizes for everything from best Latin essay to finest moral fiber were given away. No hokey, jokey dinner before graduation, and then a very modest ceremony itself. Reunion had been canceled altogether. Even the development people, normally willing to forgo all matters of etiquette when it came to money, had agreed that this was not the year to wring the alumni dry. The coffee was ready. Madeline poured in a lot of cream and sat down again to drink it.

She had been counting on Fred to guide her through this last series of obligations. Her heart thumped a little painfully as she thought about him. He had been such a good counselor across the highly coded terrain of Armitage. But equally strong was her recognition that this was a potential relationship with few prospects; he was launching himself into another world. She knew better than to let her hopes run away with her. This was what it meant to be grown up, to see things within their correct proportions. It was sobering, it was sad. She really liked Fred, but she was almost positive he was heading out of her range, off to New York, following the scent of his ambitions. What do I believe in that is larger than love? Madeline thought, absently polishing the counter. Is there anything? Teaching might exert that kind of gravity for her. She hadn't, after all, offered to visit Fred in New York or followed Owen to North Carolina. She had, however reluctantly, been responsible only to her own sloppy self, her own future, which was, oddly, resolving itself at her sister's alma mater, this place where something truly unsettling had happened and where students led lives that the adults around them could not fathom. As she sat there, Madeline realized it was Porter she was thinking about. His ability to ride through unbearable events with grace and humanity intact.

None of it made sense. Even now, sitting in her kitchen, hands wrapped around her favorite coffee mug—commemorating Prince Charles and Princess Diana's wedding, salvaged from a Somerville stoop—she couldn't weave the events into a coherent narrative. Narrative had to make some kind of sense; that's what she had spent the bulk of the year trying to teach her students. There was such a thing as a fictional or poetic truth, but this story was resisting that. It didn't have any kind of logic, intuitive or otherwise, and stories had to, they had to have motive, underpinning, their own peculiar patterning. She couldn't for the life of her see the whole. At that moment, she burned her lip on her hot drink and blotted the pain away with a napkin. A beautiful, rich girl dead, her baby missing. Her former boyfriend questioned and released, several times. Her former boyfriend who refused to leave.

There was something important in Scotty's determination to stick through his time at Armitage. She had seen him yesterday walking across the Quad and been struck by his affect. He had looked older, his shoulders hunched. He'd looked like a man with many cares. He'd looked, she thought, like he had been working hard, and he never looked that way.

Madeline picked up her mug and wandered to her computer and opened her Armitage account. An e-mail marked urgent told her that Tamsin Lovell had been arrested for the assault of Jim

French. Tamsin? Jim? What did they have to do with each other? Madeline stared at the note on her screen and felt energy siphon from her body. Right now, there was no digesting that news. Thank God she hadn't gone to lunch, where she would have been caught in a swirl of rabid chatter: faculty would have been tearing through that bit of news like a ravenous dog at a roast chicken. She was going to stay focused on her own worry, Madeline decided, and she logged in then to student records.

A few years ago, Porter had put student files online, and as usual, Fred had said, the old guard had protested. Privacy issues; hacking; why did every last thing have to be computerized? Fred remembered some of them had used the debate to chew on their worry that they would have to stop writing comments by hand and start typing them. But Porter had prevailed, arguing that greater access, carefully protected, increased awareness about students and provided teachers with highly useful information.

What it meant was that, with special passwords, teachers could open current student records and schedules. It was indeed helpful, Madeline had discovered through the year, to find out how kids had done in other classes, who their advisers were, and other pertinent information. You couldn't change grades or alter pages, but you could quite easily view a student's entire history at the school. What was Scotty studying this semester that had so taxed him? Madeline wondered. A bio class with Harvey—ugh, she thought; calculus with sweet old Alice; an English class; and Special Topics in Physics. Madeline looked at what that array of courses boiled down to, and it was almost immediately transparent why he'd chosen them. Nothing started before 9:30, and he was almost always done by 1:30, a senior's crafty use of timing to determine academic load. Something jiggled in Madeline's memory as she looked at

Scotty's last class of the week. The science course. What was it? Where had she recently seen that course mentioned? None of her advisees was taking it; only seniors could enroll. Then she remembered. Claire had been enrolled in it, too. Special Topics in Physics, taught by the myopic Bruce Benton. Maybe that's why Claire had selected it; Mr. Benton was renowned for his gentle spaciness, though he was as hard a grader as anyone. Still, he would have been unlikely to notice Claire's condition, apparently having chosen some astral realm over the earthly many years ago. And what was the class's special topic? That would take a moment to find, but again, because of Porter's innovation, it was possible. The entire curriculum was online, for the perusal of prospective students, parents, other teachers. A way of maintaining transparency and encouraging high standards.

The computer flashed away, and then the page she wanted appeared on the screen. Optics. Claire and Scotty and a handful of other seniors had chosen to spend their last semester studying the properties of sight. From fibers to satellites, but starting, Bruce wrote on his rather short but elegant syllabus, with the simplest form of twisting light, which involved mirrors.

Madeline moved so quickly she knocked Charles and Diana to the floor, where the mug promptly broke into several jagged pieces. Well, it had ended that way for them, hadn't it? she thought rather sadly. But she was in so much of a rush that she didn't even bother to clean up the pieces or stop the flow of coffee. What she did, after jamming flip-flops on her feet, was rush at a breakneck pace to Claire's room.

She hadn't been there since the girl's parents had visited. The entire dorm felt hushed and empty as she stormed up the staircase, but that was, Madeline thought, because it was. It even felt dusty, though the custodians came through all the time, mopping, cleaning, putting small details to rights. All the doors along the corridors, usually festive and bristling with decorations and pronouncements of individuality, were empty, blond rectangles of wood. Her running feet echoed hugely down the halls. Finally, Madeline slowed as she reached the third floor and opened Claire's door.

On its back was the mirror that had triggered her memory. A full-length mirror, not standard issue for the rooms—no one wanted to encourage teenagers to look at themselves more than they already did—but easily and often bought at the Wal-Mart in Greenville. It had been off the door when Madeline first saw Claire's room, propped near the window. She had come back later that day, she recalled, to see if it was still there, and it hadn't been. A custodian, she'd assumed then, or the person dispatched by the family to pack Claire's belongings had returned it to its proper place. But what if someone else had wanted it returned to its usual spot?

Madeline lifted the mirror off the back of the door and, in her mind's eye, tried to remember where she had seen it. She stuck it by the window now, to the right of the net curtain hanging in front of the sash, and then she lifted the curtain and angled it closer to the glass. No, that still wasn't right. She moved it to the left side and angled it again and looked out. What she saw astonished her. Even though the day was starting to cloud over, the flash of light that traveled from the mirror's surface across the Quad was as vivid as lightning. It had channeled the refraction from another reflective surface, in a window on the third floor of a building across the lawn. Greaves, Scotty Johnston's dorm. The corresponding mirror was still there to answer a signal sent from

Portland. And although Madeline wasn't sure, she could guess that the room across the Quad belonged to Scotty.

Shaking slightly, trying to get this new piece of data to fit inside the jumbled story, Madeline moved to rehang Claire's mirror on the door. As she carried the heavy object back, she could glimpse her own face working in its surface and knew that what she saw there was sheer adult worry. But she hadn't needed a mirror to determine that.

She ran as fast as she could back to her apartment and paused to throw a dish towel on the tan puddle that her coffee had created. Her hands were shaking as she pounded on Matt Corelli's highlighted name on her cell. He answered on the first ring and said immediately and with concern that he couldn't or didn't mask and that she heard, as directly as that beam of light that had traveled between the two mirrors, "Madeline? What's wrong?"

He was on campus, near Greaves as it happened, and Madeline watched him walk with quick, sure steps across the lawn, his hair tossing in the wind. She had just managed to put the pieces of the broken mug in the trash when he knocked on her door, but her hands were still covered in coffee.

"Sit down," he told her and helped her to the futon. "Tell me everything," and she did. She told him about Kate seeing Claire at Porter's in Maine in August. She told him about the flash of light traveling between Claire's and Scotty's rooms. He listened, made a brief phone call, and within minutes, he had men in Scotty's room. Moments after that, yet more of them led Scotty back to the station.

Matt had left as soon as Madeline finished speaking. When he was gone, she gathered the bits of broken ceramic from the trash. Although it seemed unlikely, she was going to be able to repair Charles and Diana. It would be a bit dinged, but it would be whole again. Her fingertips sticky with epoxy, she remembered watching the tall boy getting crammed into a squad car. He was shaking his head and smiling, with a kind of fierce irony, an expression of contempt. A look that even at a distance said nothing other than You just don't get it, do you?

"No," Madeline said softly, gluing in the last large chip and staring at the cracks that warped their way now through the handle. "No, I don't."

CHAPTER 21

Saturday morning, Fred walked into his sun-spangled studio to greet his first-period class. These were the same students Malcolm Smith had visited, and Fred reflected that they had made a lot of progress since that foggy day in April. He had brought with him the file, his letter, and a wide envelope, and placed them on a canvas-covered table marked with the ghosts of hundreds of hand-pinched clay pots and vases. When he was through with teaching, he would head to the post office and send the whole ugly package off. Quinn Foster peered at him and said, "You look rocky, Mr. Naylor. Are you all right?"

"Just a tough night, Quinn," he said, "nothing to worry about."

The girl settled back at her easel, clearly not reassured, and Fred turned around to see what the rest of the students were doing. They had thrown themselves into their work with energy, and their wobbly drawings of the chapel and the Armitage statue and one another had grown steadily surer and more competent. Only one or two of them had a real feel for the materials and process of making art, but all of them had improved at rendering the world around them more convincingly. They had had fun. They had learned something. They had functioned well as a group. And he saw now that they, too, were tired and frightened, listless and ready to end the horrible year. He had lost three kids from this class since Claire died, but the twelve left were some of the kindest and best adjusted he had taught in a while.

He watched Quinn struggling with her pastels and thought for a moment about how much he would miss his students' serious expressions and steady industry next year. He liked teaching. He liked feeling that he had a role, a reason to occupy the earth. It had been one of Llewellan's grand themes. To find work that sustained an individual but provided the world with something useful. Fred knew that his grandfather had looked askance at the making of art—he wondered now if Llewellan had considered it the province of "nancy boys"—but that Fred's choice to teach, and at Armitage, had been deeply reassuring to the old man. Fred had to admit, as he started to wander the studio and examine what the kids were shaping on the pads in front of them, he had done it for Llewellan's grudging approval, for his love. Which made it all the more important to take this break, to test himself against his own judgments.

None of the students was making any headway today. Llewellan had always encouraged steeling oneself against self-indulgence, and given his own son's terrific propensity for just that—Harrison drank, talked, and spent too much—this attitude, though palpably Victorian, had appealed to Fred. But today, he stood in the middle of the studio, the place he had first felt paint come alive in his hands, and said, "Stop, everyone. Just stop for a minute." They all looked up at him.

"We have one day left of class, on Monday, but you know what I'm thinking? I'm thinking we need to go outside, bring a few pieces of paper with us, and mess around. We only have forty minutes anyway. And I want to find out what kind of trouble you're going to be getting into this summer." The kids looked relieved, one whistled, and within moments, they were stationed in the shade of a maple tree, chattering about camp and internships, trips to Africa and boring summers at home in Westport. He did the same thing with the next class, and told both not to bother coming on Monday. They had done well, he told his students. They had worked hard and improved. It was time to free them for the year.

Finished with classes, he strode to the post office and, with only a moment's hesitation, sent his package first class to Malcolm Smith. He imagined it bumping through the mail with all the other letters and boxes to Rhode Island, and he imagined, too, the man's spotted hands fumbling at the envelope, then spreading Fred's harsh discovery before him. For a moment, in the cool of the corridor where the P.O. was located, Fred stood still. He wanted nothing more than to go curl up in his bed and sleep away the next few days. But there was something else left to do.

She proved, especially compared to Edward Smith, remarkably easy to find. A yearbook from 1954 showed him that Naomi Beardsley had been Llewellan's secretary—and that had been her title; the administrative assistant hadn't been invented until the eighties. From the photo with the other office staff (prim, bespectacled women in dresses that might easily have passed for nuns' habits, they were that black and unrevealing), it was impossible to say what sort of person she was. She looked quite grim with her cat's-eye glasses, neatly pinned hair, and unsmiling mouth, all of which distinguished her from none of her colleagues.

The Internet even spat out her current location, about fifteen miles away, in an assisted living place called Fox Marsh, where, if the information on the screen was to be believed, she edited the community's monthly newsletter, signing herself quite often as Old Fox on Thin Ice.

On the drive over, he called his mother in Connecticut illegally, no headset involved, and told her everything: the discovery about Llewellan, his decision to leave Armitage, the move to Brooklyn. His mother, sensitive, serious, a potter and an elementary school teacher, at first said nothing. He drove along, listening to her long pause, before she said, "Fred, you are doing the right thing. At every level," and in her words, Fred heard the release of years of frustration. "Come home before you go to New York," she said. "There's lots more to talk about."

Pulling in to Fox Marsh, he wondered what stories his mother might have to share. Reserved, collected in the face of her husband's excesses, Fred's mother had raised him and his younger brother with grace and care. But she had done so at a cost. Marrying a Naylor had brought drama into her life, and more than a certain amount of difficulty. He was looking forward to seeing her. Now there was Naomi to deal with.

A pleasant woman at the front desk told him Mrs. Beardsley could be found in the dining hall, but as he scanned the group of white-haired men and women, he saw no one who reminded him of that secretary in her black, enveloping clothes. He was conscious, too, of a kind of collapsed humanity that he noticed when groups of old people were gathered in one spot. It wasn't only the bent backs and wandering minds that gave him this feeling but the compression of all their abilities and the need for the culture of the young to herd them into one place and pretend that they, diminished, weren't really there. But the smell of institutional food was the same as that which floated through the Armitage Commons: cooking for too many at once bled out flavor and spice, no matter the age of those eating. Llewellan had had the luxury of avoiding this kind of residence; he had died in his own bed, of pneumonia, at ninety-two. But his mother's parents had been less fortunate, and Fred remembered dutiful visits to see them at what had then been called a nursing home, trailing down corridors of gray carpets.

Then all of a sudden, a tiny woman was at his elbow and she was saying, "My goodness, you look exactly like him. You must be his grandson."

She barely came to his chest, and she still wore dark, shapeless clothes. Her hands trembled and her voice as well, but her eyes were a clear hazel and awake. She leaned on a wooden cane and looked sharply at him. Fred startled and tried to explain what he was there for, but Naomi stopped him. "I can hazard a guess as to why you're here. There's probably only one reason. Just tell me your name, and we can go and talk somewhere that's a bit more private. These old bats listen to everything." She was right, Fred saw. Every head had turned in his direction and was busy now trading some speculation about who the new young man might be and what he had to do with Naomi Beardsley.

"I don't much like it here," Naomi said as she walked him, quite briskly given her cane, out of the dining hall and toward a garden generously dotted with benches no more than twenty feet apart. "But I didn't want to smash my hip and wind up being a burden to my son. And if I don't have privacy, as least I have the knowledge I've spared him that." She had been at the Swamp, as she called Fox Marsh, for two years, "long enough so that if I have some ghastly stroke, they have to take care of me." It wasn't far from what family she had, and she admitted the staff were friendly sorts. No drinking allowed in the dining room, but it didn't mean you couldn't have your peg of Canadian Club in your own apartment.

She settled herself on a bench below a linden tree. She gave off no smell of the old, nothing mentholated or medicinal, just a fragrance of soap and health. Fred sat next to her, trying to guess her age. Given her general forthrightness, he didn't think she'd mind if he asked. "I'm eighty-seven," she said, "but everyone in my family lives to be about a million years old, so I'm not ready to buy the farm just yet." She looked at him more closely. "You're here of course about Edward Smith. I wondered if anyone would ever find that file. I didn't destroy it, but I didn't make it easy to locate, either. It really is striking how much you look like your grandfather."

Fred thought of what he might say, but he reflected that he owed Naomi this moment to describe what had happened, what she had seen, and what she had done. "I always regretted not being more forthcoming about that poor boy. But I tried to convince myself that I'd done what I could," she said simply. She was a widow with two children when she worked for Llewellan Naylor, she explained. Her husband had been killed in Europe, a member of a U.S. engineering team that had gone to France to implement the Marshall Plan. "Run over by a French truck. Not even a casualty of war," she told Fred. But whether he had died through glory or mere happenstance, she still had the children to take care of. She had needed that job, she explained, and at the time, Armitage had paid better than anything else in the area. She had also looked after her aging parents. Her father had been a laborer in the Greenville mills, her mother a finisher of seams in a Westerfield factory.

She talked rather haltingly but with some small pleasure. Fred didn't think she had the chance to speak much about her past and to discuss how she had spent her life. He was struck, too, with the sober acceptance of her fate. The dedication with which she had earned her living. Her evident devotion to family. Her decision to eschew ambition in favor of doing what she needed to to protect and sustain those closest to her.

"But he fired me anyway," Naomi continued, almost as if Fred weren't there, "because I'd typed those letters and seen what he had done, and he could tell, though I said nothing, that I disapproved." And she had, she said. She didn't know if any of the allegations were true. It was such murky territory. Unimaginable in those days that someone would do that to a child and, even more, bring it to light. But given what had been revealed about the Catholic Church the last few years, abuse might have been rampant for all she knew. She had been acquainted and worked with all three of the men Edward's father named in the letter. "And to be honest, I never liked them. But the masters were like gods then. What they said had to happen, did. No one rebelled against them." She paused for a moment. "So even having a feeling about them one way or another wasn't tolerated, and certainly your grandfather wasn't one to stand for that kind of independence." Even now, more than fifty years after the event, she was evidently still bitter about what had happened, in somewhat the same way, Fred thought, as Malcolm Smith, though his loss was surely the more devastating.

Llewellan, whom she called Mr. Naylor even now, had sacked her in March 1955, and she had gotten a job as a manager at an electric plant in Greenville and never seen him again, though for the rest of their working lives they had resided no more than three miles apart. She had been ejected from that universe, and Armitage had closed its gates against her. "He wasn't always like that," she told Fred. "I worked for him for seven years. He was usually honest when dealing with problems. He could admit that things didn't go as planned, that people didn't always behave as you'd hoped. But this stung him. He couldn't accept it." She appeared to have finished, Fred thought. But he was wrong. "So on the day he fired me, I gathered up what I could of Edward's records, which were all in our office, and I got the carbon of the letter I typed and then I filed the entire packet in the archives, with one small card in the old catalog for someone to discover years from then. A time capsule of secrets, I saw it as. I decided I'd let history do the work for me. And it did."

They sat for a moment without speaking. The linden released its honey-sweet smell, and bees buzzed among its leaves. A few of the other residents of Fox Marsh were shuffling through the grounds. Clouds were gathering for another burst of rain.

Then, slowly, Fred told her what had prompted his search. He told her how Malcolm had come to find him and how, at first, he had wanted nothing more than to ignore him. Naomi listened, her hands quivering. He told her that she had made it difficult to find the papers, but that eventually he had. "What are you going to do with them?" she asked.

"I've already sent the whole file to Malcolm. And I'm going to resign, too." He started to shift, ready to leave now. He needed to find Porter immediately.

"Well, if you'd like to stay in touch, I would appreciate knowing if anything happens." She pulled a pen from a pocket and asked if he had a scrap of paper. He offered her the back of an ATM receipt and noticed that the handwriting whose faint trace he had followed was almost the same. Not quite as firm, but just as distinct. She stood and steadied herself and then said, "Yes, that's wise to leave. I should think you need time out of his shadow. It was very long." He walked her back to the entrance. He had one last question, he said. Why did she sign her editorials for the newsletter Old Fox?

She smiled then, the first time she had, he realized. "You're forgetting the second part. On Thin Ice," she said. "It's from the *I Ching*, a symbol that means walk carefully. Exercise caution." She turned then, wished him a quick good-bye, and walked back to the Marsh where she now presided.

Fred drove to campus quickly. He had to see Porter before Last Tea, which was where announcements about faculty departures were always made. He also, he confessed to himself, needed to tell the head he was leaving before he changed his mind.

He was in luck. He parked his car and saw Porter striding across the Quad. He looked wrung out, but that distinguishes him from no one right now, Fred thought. Appropriately enough, Fred asked if he could talk with him about next year in the shadow of the statue of the school's founder, the old warlord. Porter said, "Well, at least you don't want to talk to me about Tamsin." Why would he need to do that? Fred asked, surprised, and Porter said, "I don't have time to explain. Check your e-mail, and tell me what's going on. You look like you've seen a ghost, Fred."

"I'm resigning, Porter. I'm moving to Brooklyn to paint again," Fred told him, and he explained that he had an unprecedented opportunity and he was going to take it. As he spoke, he noticed how the season had ripened into luscious fullness: the leaves had turned a thick green, the lawns were dense as horses' manes. Every twig, blade of grass, and rock seemed outlined in rich, tender light. Fred had never felt so attached to the academy. And *attached* was the word his mind selected because it had to settle on one, but his body felt the loss of his connection to this world in a hundred places.

Below a gray layer of fatigue, Porter looked as he always did: at ease in his height and handsomeness, his voice as full and

round and soothing as it had always been. "What the hell is going on, Fred?" he asked gently. Was it this investigation and the
situation Armitage was facing? Was it his load of courses? He
launched in on ways that he might keep Fred at the academy. A
reduced teaching schedule, support for his work during the summer. A new dorm? Fewer advisees? He deployed all the usual
blandishments: the excellence of Fred's teaching, the art program
couldn't sustain his loss, did Fred know how many students and
parents had identified him as the teacher who had made the most
difference to their or their children's education at Armitage? Fred
did know, because Porter had assiduously made sure to pass on
praise, knowing how useful it was to feel known and visible in what
one did.

But as Porter wheedled and badgered, Fred observed two
things. The first was that none of the lures Porter dangled reached
him anywhere that mattered. It was when he thought about painting that he actually felt alive, and the feeling wasn't precisely a
good one: it was a tingle, close to pain and a near relation to
panic. It made his skin crawl and his heart thrash in his chest, and
it was as vibrant as he had felt in years.

He knew, too, that it wasn't only the thought of painting
again. He had the discovery of Llewellan's hatefulness to thank
as well, and that he couldn't face discussing with Porter. He kept
saying, "Porter, I really appreciate your concern and I am sorry to
leave you and the department in the lurch, but I have made up
my mind." He was done with this institution and with institutions like this.

The second thing he noticed about Porter was that his heart
wasn't in the coaxing. He sounded and looked the same; he was
as articulate as always. He looked Fred earnestly in the eye. But

he doesn't mean it, Fred thought and felt a burst of pity for the man. Was this hesitation new? Had Claire's death revealed Porter to be as human as the rest of them? Was it, Fred thought, just that we needed him to be better than we were so we stopped being able to see what was actually there?

Then all of a sudden, Porter stopped talking. He peered a little more closely at Fred and said, with some surprise, "I'm not making one bit of difference, am I? You just don't want to do this anymore. I could offer you two years off and a chance to come back at double the pay and you wouldn't take it. You're done, aren't you, Fred?" And as he said this, he stood to his full, patrician height and shook his head, not with amazement or scorn, Fred saw, but with envy. Porter, too, wanted to be done with Armitage, with the life he had made for himself and his family. He, too, yearned for something different. Fred was nearly as tall as Porter, he realized all of a sudden. How funny, he thought, he had always assumed Porter was so much bigger than he was.

He went back to his apartment and collapsed on his bed. When he woke, it was 5:45. He had only a short time before he had to get ready. He buttoned his shirt slowly and dragged a comb across his unruly hair and pulled on a battered blue sport coat, reserved exclusively for events like this and the Christmas concert. Just as the clock in the chapel struck six, he walked out the door. He'd be slightly late. When he had been a student, and in Llewellan's time as well, Last Tea had taken place at three and was literally that, a decorous tea party complete with the wife of the headmaster serving as mother over a heavy Victorian set and greasy petits fours. Fred's grandmother said her wrist used to ache after Last Tea, the pot was so heavy. The thought of Lucinda serving in that capacity was ridiculous. And it might well have been her suggestion that

Porter shift the ritual's tone. He had scheduled it three hours later and added alcohol and decent hors d'oeuvres to the offerings, and everyone had enjoyed themselves a great deal more. The tea set had vanished into a storage room, replaced by tall, utilitarian urns of coffee.

The party was held in the Head's House, and Fred joined the stream of his colleagues at the tall white door. Usually, Lucinda presided over this part of the gathering, but it was Porter this year who took each faculty member's hand and shook it warmly. Glad you could make it, he kept saying. So glad to see you. Wonderful of you to come. Such a terrible way to end the year. So confusing. But it's important to honor certain traditions. He was just as warm with Fred as all the others and, Fred thought, just as distant as before.

Fred immediately poured himself a large glass of Merlot and glanced around for Madeline. He had avoided her since he'd returned from New York. He wasn't proud of that, but she had done just as good a job of sidestepping him. Still, over the past two days, he'd half-hoped to find a note or message or e-mail from her, but there had been nothing.

Then, all of a sudden, she arrived. Long, tangly hair, bright cheeks, mildly, sexily unkempt. She was pumping Porter's hand enthusiastically and taking just a little too long to talk to him. Right behind her, Marie-France Maillot stood there impatiently in her narrow gray skirt and prim white blouse, her face pruning up even more than usual. Everyone knew she harbored a huge and harmless crush on Porter, who almost always spoke his more than serviceable French with her. Marie-France loved correcting his mistakes in gender. Fred smiled but was dismayed to find his stomach contracting heavily at the sight of Madeline.

Then she saw him, too, and on her face was her usual un-guarded expression: Fred could see that today it combined anger, attraction, impatience, irritation. And he smiled because even though those angular New Yorkers had her beaten hands down in terms of sophistication, Madeline was ten times more alive than they would ever be. A brimming handful of energy and warmth. And he was leaving her here, where someone was going to scoop her up in a matter of minutes.

She strode over to him, but not before pouring herself a large glass of Merlot, too. "Hey," she said, "you know what Emily James just told me? 'Miss Christopher, you look as bad as I feel.'" Fred laughed. She did look tired, it was true, but he said to her impul-sively, and it made her cheeks flare red, "Madeline, you could be dressed like Marie-France and you would still look good." She took a sip of her wine and dribbled a little on her skirt. "Oh, damn," she muttered happily. "Are you going?" she asked, clearly not able to help herself. When he told her he was, she said "damn" again and whispered "of course," because she had just been of-fered a chance to stay.

Then neither of them felt they could say much, and they stood together in nervous, companionable silence. The room filled with their colleagues, some of them well past usefulness in the class-room but most of them dedicated, bright, orderly people with tidy minds, truly engaged with their subjects and students. Many of them he would miss; some he'd forget altogether, and others he'd be actively happy to leave behind. Harvey Fuller, reptilian as ever, had just poured himself a glass of juice.

And then there was this shadow of loss. It lay across every-thing. Despite his own uneasy elation, Fred was able to recognize just how deflated, frightened, and undone the community of teachers was. Madeline got dragged off by Grace to the other side of the room, but conversation was muted, although he could hear people muttering about Tamsin and Scotty and poor Jim French's banged-up head. Most people drank coffee and lemonade instead of alcohol. An anxious murmur had replaced the usual end-of-year giddiness. And where was Lucinda? She ought to be here helping Porter out. Regal, stylish, straightforward, she was formidable, and her invisibility made a difference in the event. But just then, Porter cleared his throat, and his colleagues stilled themselves. Most people had to take a fork and clank away at the stem of a wineglass to command attention. All Porter had to do was stand up straighter.

"It's time for the hard part now," he said. "Saying good-bye to those we know and care about, the ones who have had the audacity to find a job somewhere other than Armitage. And this year, we have more than just that sort of loss to deal with. Before we start, I want to thank you all for your grace and hard work in an absolutely horrifying time. I have never felt closer to you and more blessed to have you as colleagues." This was more effusive than Porter usually allowed himself to be. Madeline had unhooked herself from Grace and come back to join Fred; they both noticed Porter's voice and looked more closely at him. Then, as if recognizing that his tone was slipping, however slightly, he turned over the event to the chair of the math department, who did his best to sound sad about losing Marcus Lyle, off to pursue his love of fly-fishing. Next came a couple who taught history and had taken positions to be nearer their families in Georgia. Known, expected departures, announced early in the spring, which was the season for change in this world. A couple of advancement people were wished well next, off to do their necessary, grubby work at salaries close to three times what the faculty were paid.

Madeline had sneaked off to fill up her and Fred's glasses and secure a napkinful of goodies. She came back just in time to see Porter claim the room's attention again. "We have a bit more business to attend to," he said, "other rather unforeseen developments." Fred looked at the head more closely and knew the man must be referring to him, but who were the others? Could Roddy the Shoddy finally have gotten the ax? "The first is Fred Naylor, our fantastic art teacher," Porter said and waited to go on as surprise settled over the room. And then he began to speak about Fred, to Fred. What he said and how he said it made Fred blush, and he noticed that Madeline was smiling crazily. She even punched him in the arm, Porter's praise got her so excited. And no one missed Porter's resounding finale: "Art does matter, art may matter more than schools, and Fred, despite his heritage, despite the safety his life here has held for him, has made the harder choice to leave, to find out what he is really good at, to find out who he is." Fred could barely glance at Porter. Colleagues came up and congratulated him, honestly pleased at his news. "Great opportunity, Fred," said Forrest Thompson. Even Marcus Lyle gave him a smile. Slowly the hubbub subsided and they composed themselves for the next announcement.

At last, Porter cleared his throat and started again. "After thirty-two years of service," he said, "Marie-France Maillot has decided to return to Marseilles." No one had known, and all eyes turned to watch the slender, stiff woman, her eyes trained on the carpet, her fingers taut around the handle of her teacup. "Thirty-two years of being our most treasured emblem of France. Thirty-two years of reminding us every May Day how to sing the 'Internationale.'" He spoke about the Mustang, the way she carved her fruit, and the herbs in her windows that thrived despite all the, ahem, cigarette smoke in her apartment. He spoke about the trips she took with kids back in the eighties and the time they all escaped from her and went to the casino in Monaco. He made people laugh, and even more, Fred noticed, he made them see Marie-France as more than the stick-figure caricature of a grammar-mincing Frenchwoman. She emerged in his words as a passionate person, someone worth knowing. And then he did a lovely thing. He had memorized a short poem by Apollinaire, and he spoke it aloud to her. He then gave her a first edition of the poems, found a few years ago in Paris and waiting for this occasion, which he knew had to come sooner or later. Her family would reclaim her, and why not? She was eminently worth reclaiming. Then he leaned to kiss her, once, twice, three times, four. The kiss of the South, the placing of the cheeks on one another, *les bises*. "*Tu me manqueras*, Marie-France," he said as he leaned in the last time. "*Tu me manqueras*." I will miss you, in the familiar form. I will miss you.

Then Porter released the frail woman and looked round the room. "I wish I were done, but I am afraid I have to ask for a few more moments of your time." He gathered in another breath. He looked, Fred realized abruptly, incredibly sad. "I have nothing but the simplest words for it. I must resign from Armitage. This is my last day. I can do nothing but thank you for all you have been to me, done for me, done for the school. You have meant more to me than you could ever know." Marie-France fell to the ground, and Forrest Thompson bent stiffly to revive her. Stan Lowery spilled his Chardonnay on Porter's dog. Several women screamed. At last, Fred saw Lucinda, who stood as cold and dry as a dead tree in the threshold of the door that led from the foyer to this stiff and stately room. She had twisted a sweater around herself, and she could not look at her husband. "Why, Porter?" asked Stan, for all of them.

Porter shook his head and said, "Stan, I owe you an explanation. I am more than aware of that. It will all become clear very soon." Fred was too shocked to speak. He wanted only to get himself and Madeline out of there. But she was rooted to the floor. She was whispering, "He did it. He was the one who killed Claire. She told the girls about an older man. It must be Porter." Fred looked at her. "Madeline, that's not possible," he hissed. Lucinda was still standing there, though she watched the room of teachers with unconcealed contempt and then started to walk quickly up the stairs.

Porter turned to follow her and stopped once, to look around the crowd, but he said nothing. Fred said to Madeline, "We have to get out of here," and grabbed her hand. He wanted to believe she was wrong. He wanted more than anything to know that the fine man who had made those speeches was innocent. But he thought instantly of his grandfather and knew it was impossible to say what people were really like, to know motives fully, to be aware of all the layers that constituted human beings.

The last thing Fred saw as he steered Madeline out the far door and through an exit in the kitchen—he knew this house, after all; he had grown up in it partly—was Marie-France sobbing in Forrest's arms. Finally, they were outside. The air was cool on their faces, and it was starting to rain, and Fred couldn't tell if Madeline was crying or not in the suddenly steady downpour.

He didn't care who saw them. He didn't care what anyone thought. He opened the door to his apartment and unplugged the phone and planned not to turn on any computer or any device that might tell him one scrap of what was going on. He settled Madeline on the sofa and poured her some Scotch. He took off his jacket and tie and poured himself a drink, too, and sat next to her. She was still shaking and on the verge of tears.

"He was in Castine with Claire. I think he must have raped her or gotten involved with her somehow. He was the father of the baby," Madeline said, gulping the Scotch. "God, that's strong. That's why she stayed. She was going to humiliate him, humiliate the school. Show everyone that his beautiful family wasn't what they thought. But then Porter killed her and took the baby, or someone did. Fred, it doesn't make sense." She told him then about the mirrors between Scotty's room and Claire's, and that she thought it was a signal the girl could send to him if she were in trouble.

"Porter? Rape a student? And why wouldn't't Scotty and Claire just call each other? Madeline, it's all insane," Fred said, but as he said it, he thought again of Llewellan and how intensely unknowable people were.

Madeline was crying now. "I don't want to believe it's true," she said. "He's a good man, I know he's a good man." And in spite of himself, of his imminent departure, Fred folded her in his arms and found himself kissing away her tears.

"Fred," she said and pushed him slightly away. "You have to stop that. It feels way too nice and then you'll be gone and painting away and going on dates with girls named Ilsa and I'll be up here grading papers and spilling cranberry juice on myself and missing you." She smacked him on the arm quite hard and smiled, even as the tears kept rolling.

"Ilsa?" he asked and kissed her cheek again.

"Yes. Or Simone or Vanessa. And they'll be video-installation artists and half-Brazilian, half-Norwegian, and—" She was clearly going to continue in this vein for some time so he was forced to kiss her mouth, just to keep her from talking, which was effective for a while.

But after a minute, she went on just where she'd stopped, though she also said, "That was even nicer, Fred, in fact I've been dying for that to happen for some time, but those girls won't have straggly hair or talk too much."

He kissed her again, and it was indeed the best thing that had happened in a long time. It felt both incredibly new and wonderful— she tasted like honey with some Scotch in it—and also just as he'd known it would: she was so darling, this woman, and he liked her immensely. It was so delightful to show her that. But she was right, even though she was kissing him back with passion and surprise and pleasure. There was no predicting the Ilsas, Simones, or Vanessas he might encounter.

"Madeline," he said as he delicately pulled her hair back in order to gain access to the buttons on her shirt, "what about you and all the Andrews and Jakes and Peters who are going to be lining up in front of your door? What are we going to do about them?"

She snorted. "My door? Here at the convent of Armitage? Do you think it's an accident that Marie-France is leaving a virgin, Fred?" But she helped with the buttons and got her own fingers working on his. Her hands were cool and her fingers lean and nimble and delicious on his warm skin.

"But that won't be your fate, will it?" Fred asked as he pulled her shirt away to reveal round shoulders and a plain bra and Madeline's sudden shyness at being half-naked in the room of her closest friend on campus.

"No," she said as she pulled his own shirt free from his body and began tracing her fingers across his chest. "But that wasn't the state that I arrived in, either." And then, thank God, she stopped talking altogether.

At one point in the night, Madeline had woken up and said, "Fred? Porter didn't do it, did he?" and Fred had said, "No, he's not capable of that," and they had both gone back to sleep, reassured and wrapped around each other. When he woke up again, it was fully dark in his bedroom. He lay there and listened to Madeline breathing deeply, snuggled below the covers. He had no idea if it was midnight or three in the morning. All he knew was that he was ravenously hungry and torn with more than a little misgiving. Making love with Madeline had been, his body told him, total pleasure. She was as passionate a lover as she was a talker, generous and full of humor and sweetly curved in exactly the right proportions. Careful not to wake her, he wondered at the edge of anxiety, almost fear that followed him as he tiptoed into the kitchen to find something to eat.

His hand on the refrigerator door, he remembered. Porter. His resignation. The utter trouble the academy was in. What a dark note on which to start a relationship. Was that what had happened? Yes, he thought, as he looked at the rather bare shelves. That was exactly what had happened. Then he felt rather than heard Madeline behind him, and he turned to find her warm and naked in his arms again and saying, unsurprisingly, "I am starved. Can you cook? And aren't you never supposed to spoil a friendship with sex?"

"Yes, to both, absolutely. And especially about the friendship part. Except when you should and it turns out to be a great decision." They made a plate of eggs and sausages slathered in ketchup for Madeline and hot sauce for Fred and sat in his bed to eat it. "This is great, Fred," she said, and he knew she meant the whole thing. The lovemaking, the food, the unexpected joy of it amid the sadness. "You're a great kisser, Madeline," he said and kissed her some more. "Thanks, Fred," she said.

Which led to more time below the covers and another long nap, after which they woke to find it was dawn. "I should go," she said. "It's Claire's service this morning. And I bet there are a thousand e-mails and announcements, and all of it will come crashing down today."

"Not yet," he said. "Don't go yet." He wanted, he realized, to tell her why he was leaving Armitage for good. He wanted to tell her about Llewellan. "I know it's been a bad week for revelations," he said and held her hand, "but there's more." To her credit, she sat and listened to the entire story. To Malcolm Smith coming into the studio. To Fred's search in the archives and Scotty's sudden appearance there. To the eventual discovery of the file and of Naomi Beardsley's note. He ended with his visit to Fox Marsh. "I can't," he finished, "come back. I have to find out what it's like to live outside this place," and he gestured around the room, which was strewn with clothes, some of which were, he was happy to note, Madeline's.

She looked at him and said, "You know, there's no way to be sure what happened. Edward's family blamed the school, blamed your grandfather. But who knows what those masters did or what sort of state that boy was in. Is it possible to judge him so clearly? It's disgusting that people thought that way about kids, that they could judge a boy who was probably gay so harshly, but wasn't it the way of the world then?"

Fred sat up straighter. He was surprised, but he kept listening. "I'm not apologizing for him or excusing him. It is creepy and irrevocable and all those things, and maybe, hopefully, it's a little better now. But isn't it easier to look at it today and cast all that harsh criticism his way? Isn't he also the same man who taught you how to fish and swim? Wasn't he beloved by all those people for real reasons? All I'm saying, Fred, is that people are complex. It doesn't mean he wasn't responsible for what happened to Edward, but it doesn't mean that the good pieces of him weren't real, too."

"You're also saying that I can't use him as an excuse to leave," he said. How smart she was. Just stepping on the high-mindedness of it and grounding him more firmly in what his leaving really amounted to, which was doing what he desired.

She smiled. "That's right, sweetie. It's your choice. Own up to it. It's what you want, no matter what your grandfather did. But what you did, sending the file to the family. That was the right thing to do. Now they have to deal with it or not. It's up to them. That was brave, since anything could happen," she finished. "They could file a suit, make it all public, create a huge stink. I think you did the right thing, but I would have wanted to burn it." She told him then that her own sister had been part of the Reign and had refused to talk about it with her, protecting something evil even years past necessity. "And I wanted to pretend for a minute that I was going to stay here to root it out and make things better at Armitage, to make up for Kate's sins. If you think about it, the Reign's just an extension of the kind of terror that was probably inflicted on poor Edward. But if I were really truthful, I'd have to say I want to stay because I like teaching." You have to be honest in the end, she said, if you even want to try to sleep through the night.

"I thought about not sending on the file," Fred told her, extremely close to kissing her neck again. "But Malcolm chose me for a reason. He bided his time. He made a very precise shot. And he had no idea what we had our hands on. What was lurking in the basement."

"But I know," Madeline said and edged herself out of his range. "And we don't have time. And I need to make myself presentable."

She dressed quickly and leaned over to give him a long, happy kiss. "Bye, Fred. See you later," and she was out the door with a loud bang, neither of them caring what the kids or teachers saw, heard, knew. He leaned back, aware he should follow suit, get showered, dressed, roused for another impossible series of events. But he lay there thinking about this lovely woman, her warmth and spirit still on his body, in the room. She hadn't said a word about what was next, how they were going to manage. Madeline, stinted on love as a child, took affection where she found it, gratefully. Or perhaps he was underestimating her, he thought as he made his way to the shower. She was grown-up enough to know that you couldn't predict what was going to happen next and that staking claims or making commitments when every element of her life was in transition was something it was wiser to avoid. All he knew as he turned the shower to the hottest possible temperature was that he couldn't wait to see her again. My girl, he thought, and then, Not yet. Haven't earned her, and he washed himself clean.

CHAPTER 22

The call had come in at 6:25 on Saturday morning. A man claiming Tamsin Lovell had attacked him in Nicholson House had dialed 911. Would someone please go and arrest her, and by the way, could an ambulance be sent to the academy? And quickly? His cell phone was low on batteries. Matt and Vernon had just arrived at the station, disheveled, in foul moods, and in a moment, Vernon was racing to go and try to find Tamsin and Matt had sped immediately to Jim French.

Vernon had been lucky. He knew the make and model of Tamsin's car and had seen it speeding away from Armitage as he lurched onto Main Street. "Made it easy," he said. "She was thirty miles over the limit." She was still wearing her jogging gear and ponytail, and had bent her head in apparent awareness of the futility of her situation. Vernon said he'd experienced a rough and uncomfortable pleasure seeing her there in her diminutive car. He had spent much of the last two days having her dodge his questions about what she'd had in the bag. Yes, she had argued with Mrs. McLellan, but "everyone knew she was a stroppy sort." Which made Tamsin what? Vernon had asked. "Discreet," she had answered and more or less kicked him out of her office. Since her arrest, she had maintained a glassy silence, despite five interrogations, all of which she had sat through with a rough smile and utter disdain. Her lawyer, more expensive than she might have been expected to come up with, had stood by with a mixture of professional cool and mystification. No one seemed to understand her complete refusal to cooperate despite ample evidence of assault and the threat of more charges coming. The documents she'd been shredding were slowly being pieced together. Vernon was trying to trace the call she'd been making. Porter claimed to know nothing, a stance that was becoming increasingly hard to fathom or believe. By four that afternoon, Angell had said, "Put her in the holding cell for a few hours. See what happens when she gets a load of her new room-mates," and there, among some drug addicts and a few drunk driv-ers, she sat in hostile stillness while her lawyer scurried about trying to secure bail.

By six thirty that evening, Matt had needed to go outside and assume a horizontal position on the seat of the picnic bench. He lay there and noticed it was about to rain and couldn't care about an imminent drenching. Scotty Johnston's lawyer had just sprung him, and the boy had managed to leave yet again without saying anything about the mirrors, Claire, or the whereabouts of her baby. The warrant to search Harvey Fuller's apartment had been delayed. Jim French was hazy about the entire assault. He remembered that Tamsin had been talking on the phone and loudly, but he had no idea to whom. At least he was out of the hospital and nursing noth-ing more than a mild concussion and a bad headache. At least no one else was dead. It was soothing in the semidark below the table, with the heavy air about to slide into rain, and the only element marring the very temporary peace the acrid smell of a cigarette. Matt sat up and, to his surprise, saw Vernon creeping out of the scraggly woods that edged the station's parking lot. He was grinding a butt beneath his sole and obviously hadn't spotted Matt prone on the bench. Spying him now, he lifted both hands in surrender.

"Just don't blow my cover," he said. "It's this whole thing. It's that Englishwoman who will not explain what she was up to.

It's that Scotty kid. It's the whole damn thing. I just couldn't be good anymore."

"But why not a cheeseburger or some fries, Vernon? As far as sins go, aren't they a little more comforting?"

"I don't really like smoking. Could never get addicted. But a good burger? One bite and I'd be gone." He sat down opposite Matt. "It's raining," he said.

"That it is," said Matt, but neither of them moved. Drops began to spatter the warm tarmac in the parking lot and sink into the dark fabric of their jackets.

"Do we go and arrest him now?" Vernon asked. "We're not even sure where he is."

"Soon," said Matt, "but it's not going to be smooth. Not one bit of it will be smooth."

"And still no baby," Vernon said.

"No baby," Matt said, and then they turned around. A car had rolled into the parking lot. A Volvo station wagon. He and Vernon both stood. "So it's going to start like this," Vernon said. "That's not what I would have predicted." They watched as Porter McLellan unfolded himself from the car. He turned, not seeing them, and instead of walking toward the station, he stood there for a moment and appeared to watch the water beading on the hoods of all the squad cars. Porter was not wearing a raincoat, either, and seemed as immune as they were to the dampness. He didn't move for a moment and appeared merely to be breathing in the spring air. But then he did something that was both strange and oddly beautiful. He lifted his face to the sky and let the rain pelt down on his skin. He turned his hands palm up and let the water, falling harder now, gather there.

"Shall we?" Matt said to Vernon, and together they walked over to the man in the rain, who by this time had lowered his hands and was standing there, looking at the policemen come toward him. "Let's go inside, Mr. McLellan," Matt said, and the tall man followed him. The station was silent as they walked in, three tall, dripping men. Uniformed officers, secretaries, ubiquitous FBI watched the shining puddles they left in their wake. Matt opened the door to his office, and Vernon gave Porter a seat. Matt sat at his desk. None of them spoke. Rain lashed the window. Vernon clicked on a small light, but otherwise, the room was almost dark.

"I have a letter here," Porter said at last and pulled out an envelope from the inside pocket of his jacket. "This is my confession, Detective. I am sorry I did not make it right away." His face was ashen, his words robotic. "I cannot apologize enough for having prolonged this horrible time." His voice was growing thinner, frayed like an old cloth.

"Does your wife know you're here, Mr. McLellan?" Matt asked.

Porter shook his head. "No." He appeared to be about to add something, then caught himself, and shrank back into his chair. He stared at his own hands.

Matt removed the letter and read it aloud. "It is with profound guilt and regret that I confess to murdering Claire Harkness in her room on the morning of May 22, 2009. She was planning to implicate me as the father of her baby. I went to reason with her and found myself carried away with rage. My crime was unintentional, but nonetheless I bear full responsibility. There are no limits to my regret. I will add, however, that I do not know what happened to her child, who was gone by the time I reached her room."

"Mr. McLellan, would you like to call your wife?" Porter shook his head. Matt continued, "I would also suggest you call your lawyer." Again, Porter shook his head. "How did you find out that Claire had had a baby and that she was planning this accusation?" Matt asked.

"A girl in her dorm came to tell me," Porter said and stared out the window, apparently unable to meet anyone's eyes.

"Mr. McLellan, I don't think the baby is dead. I think he's nearby. But I need to know what you saw. What you did."

"I wish I could help, but I can't." Porter was almost whispering. "He was gone. Claire wouldn't say where he was. Someone had taken him away."

Matt said then, "The reason you can't help us, Mr. McLellan, is because none of this is true, is it? It wasn't you who was there. You had nothing to do with Claire's death or the disappearance of the baby. But you know who did. And that's what we need to talk about."

But Porter again said nothing and kept staring at his hands, his jaw slack and his head low. It was then that Matt heard shouting in the hallway, an intense reversal of volume given Porter's deadened silence. Porter shrank further in his chair, clearly recognizing the voice. The next moment, Matt's door flew open, and Lucinda almost tumbled into his office, followed by two spluttering officers. The young men hadn't stood a chance of containing the headmaster's wife. "Porter, say nothing. Stop now." Her eyes flew to the paper that Matt was still holding and said, "Let Robert handle this. You have to, for all of us." She was commanding him, also pleading with him. "Let Robert take over, Porter," she begged, holding her husband by his limp arm. He would not meet her eye, either.

There was something dulled and cooling in Porter, some loss of essential heat.

He continued to sit in the chair. He could barely breathe, much less move. And then another person burst into the room. In the commotion Lucinda was making, Matt hadn't heard what must have been the rush of his footsteps down the hall. It was a boy, a tall, dark boy, in jeans and a button-down shirt. So this is how it ends, Matt thought. They had never met him though they had been on the brink of arresting him before his father had arrived at the station. Miles McLellan. Porter's youngest son and a senior at Armitage. Who else could he be? He looked exactly like his father.

Matt watched the soaked and shivering boy, the raging wife, and the broken man over whom she towered, and knew he'd guessed correctly. It had been Miles who had fathered the baby last August in Castine. Claire had seduced the boy and then hidden the resulting pregnancy. It had been Miles who had gone to Claire and argued with her about their son. It had been Miles who had pushed her against the bedstead. It had been Miles, crying, in his father's disreputable old jacket, whom Betsy Lowery had mistaken for his father.

The boy had run or, more likely, biked from the academy or wherever he had been hiding. Admittedly, it was all downhill, but he must have cycled with incredible speed to have followed his mother so closely. He had decided to step forward. What a beautiful child, Matt thought. High cheekbones, dark, clear skin, and glowing eyes. Tall and well built. The son he and Claire had made could have been astonishing. "You can't do it, Dad," the boy said softly now. "It was my fault. It was all my fault." His parents turned to him then, and as he watched their faces, Matt moved toward them. "Miles," Matt heard himself say. Porter's son looked at him, his cheeks flushed, his chest heaving. He started to speak, but Matt said again, "Miles, don't say a word. Wait for your lawyer. Listen to your parents." Matt felt Vernon rise beside him, and what his feeling was, Matt couldn't say without turning to look at him, but his partner chose to stay silent. He didn't interrupt what Matt was doing.

Lucinda and Porter stared at Matt, not quite grasping what it was he was offering them, not quite believing this stroke of good fortune. Miles rushed to his parents and broke down in sobs. Matt couldn't stop looking at them, their arms twisted around one another, a knot of self-protection, grief, and humiliation. Lucinda and Porter tried to soothe their boy as they must have done when he was small. They stroked his hair and paid attention to no one but him.

But he wasn't a young child. He was old enough to have gotten a girl pregnant. He was strong enough to have killed her. Matt remembered the bruises that had ringed Claire's wrists and dotted her neck. Her death could easily have been accidental, as the pregnancy must have been, too. But then Claire had made the momentous decision not to have an abortion. Claire had planned to use the scandal as an elaborate attempt to shame her family, her school, her entire heritage. She was the one who had lost. She was the one they had all lost sight of, the person whose rage and abandonment they had mismeasured. Her gamble hadn't worked, had folded back on her with irrevocable consequences. To think of her anger, her frustration, and her misguided calculation almost made Matt weak. He felt sick and empty. Vernon, too, looked washed of the capacity to act.

There was so much to do, Matt thought, watching them, and in his mind, the scenario played itself out. Through the sly manipulations of a lawyer, most likely the Robert whom Lucinda had invoked, Miles would most likely be convicted, if he were even formally accused, of manslaughter or the like. He might not even serve time. Kids of his kind went to New Zealand to work on sheep farms for a couple of years then off to college, their names not untarnished, but their lives more or less back on track.

It was his father who would suffer most. He would have to leave not only a world to which he was born but a world in which he had wielded a high degree of power and control, influence and importance. But he had been willing to forfeit it all for that boy weeping in his arms. Everything for a son. Matt turned to leave the room, Vernon close behind him, bumping into Angell as they left. "Corelli? Cates? Where are you going?" But neither of them could talk. They walked through the station, which was still close to entirely silent. Vernon stole a couple of umbrellas from a bin by the door, and together, they went out in the rain. "Friendly's?" Vernon asked. "Ali's," Matt answered. "This situation is not worth reigniting a cheeseburger addiction, Vernon."

But Ali's was closed, and they wound up with pizza in Matt's car, parked near the train tracks that separated Greenville from Armitage, unable to face a restaurant, cheer, smiling waitresses.

"This bites," said Vernon.

"At least you didn't get the pepperoni," Matt said. His car would smell forever of tomato sauce and stale crust. He couldn't care at the moment. "Roll down the window. It's hot in here." It was better with the windows open; the cool rain washed from time to time over the greasy food.

"I'm not talking about the pizza," said Vernon, inhaling most of a slice.

"Clearly," said Matt.

"She gets pregnant by the son of the headmaster, and she's going to spring it on the whole school. Then she gets scared. It's actually real. It happens and she's got to deal with it. So she sets up a system with Scotty; he's going to get the baby out if she can't handle it, and she can't. And then Miles hears and goes to talk to her. But the baby's gone and he gets mad and knocks her down and at some point runs to Dad."

"Most likely," Matt said. "I cannot get over how young they all are." Crouched in his car, rain pelting the windshield, he felt fantastically old.

"Manslaughter?" Vernon was pulling the cheese up from the pizza and watching the stretchy web it made between his fingers.

"That's revolting. Stop playing with your food. Maybe. Depends on forensics, the lawyer, the judge, venue, all of it. Miles is a minor." Matt sighed. They both knew the answer was probably no.

"I just don't spend a lot of time with cheese. It's a novelty. Well, obstruction of justice at least. All the way around. And that English girl."

Matt said that those charges would probably stick. And as for Tamsin, they had traced her call to Colson Trowbridge, and she had admitted having an affair with the chair of the board, which was why she'd even accepted a job at that ridiculous school in the first place. Porter had found out and was going to fire her, but then he needed her help when the whole debacle with Claire exploded. She had hidden Miles for several days, to keep his face out of view of the police, a stupid, desperate move that Lucinda, Tamsin claimed, had hatched. She'd removed the photos from Porter's desk for the same reason: they were panicked that someone would remark on the incredible resemblance between father and son and put it together that Betsy Lowery saw Miles, not Porter, that morning. The papers she'd been shredding had been photographs as well, but of Claire and Miles sitting together near a harbor, probably in Castine. She had no idea where they had come from. "Who took them?" Vernon wondered, then answered his own question. "Who cares?" he said, rummaging for napkins. "She's the one who's going to do time."

Vernon still believed in the cleansing powers of time in the pen. Matt had dealt with ex-cons too long in Philadelphia to think of jail as much more than a training ground for further disaffection and rage. He also didn't think imprisonment would add that much suffering to what Porter was going through already. His ruin was complete.

Matt tried to breathe deeply, but something kept catching in his chest. "I also figured out one of the things old Fuller was lying about. He has a house in Castine. I saw a watercolor in his apartment, and the title finally clicked. *Castine Harbor at Sunset*. He was up there when Porter and Claire and Miles were. He must have seen them. He knew all along the family was involved. But there's something else, too. We'll get the warrant tomorrow."

"Bastard," Vernon said mildly. "Any pizza left?"

"He is, and yes, there's some left."

Vernon mulled all this over as he indulged in another slice. "And we don't know about the baby. But Scotty does."

"Indeed," said Matt and reached for the car keys. "And that's who we're going to go and see now."

"You okay?" Vernon asked as he crumpled the pizza box and stuffed it in the back of Matt's car.

"No, Vernon," Matt said. "I am most decidedly not okay." They drove fast through the rain, back to the school on the hill.

"God, I hate this rain," Vernon muttered. "Been thinking about taking the kids and Kathy to a serious beach for a few days."

"Really?" Matt asked as he turned onto the long drive leading to the campus. "Won't that enlarge your carbon footprint?"

"Ipanema," said Vernon, almost sheepishly. "I've always wanted to go."

But Scotty wasn't in his dorm. Scotty wasn't anywhere on campus. Scotty had, so it appeared, hastily packed some belongings and left Armitage without telling his dorm head, parents, or anyone else. In the hard rain that covered the campus, he had simply disappeared.

CHAPTER 23

Returning to her apartment Sunday morning, Madeline found what she'd been dreading. Another note slid under her door, as always in lurid red pen. At least there were no more threatening quotations, but the contents more than made up for it. "We have pictures of you from last night. We know where you were and what you were doing." At first, Madeline's heart seized. Pictures of her and Fred on the Internet or YouTube? It would be the end of their careers. Slowly, she calmed herself. Fred's bedroom had no windows. There was no way they could have gotten a camera in there. The worst they could have done was to take photos of her entering and leaving his apartment. And that, though frowned on, was not illegal. And, she reminded herself, she'd been fully clothed both times. Still, she was furious.

Just when she was stomping around her living room in rage, she heard a knock at the door. Of course it was Grace. The classics teacher looked at her in scorn and was close, Madeline knew, to asking her where she'd been. It was her reflex with people even a couple of years younger to treat them as if they were teenagers on the brink of malfeasance. Then she couldn't help herself and sputtered, "Were you out for a jog?"

"Not without my Nikes, Grace." Madeline was wearing ballet flats.

Grace was already dressed for the memorial service, in a long brown skirt and a jacket of some somber material. "I tried to reach you last night and early this morning, but you didn't answer your phone. I wanted to be sure you knew that Miles McLellan had been arrested. That's why Porter resigned." Although clearly still rattled by the outcome, she was savoring the triumph of her surprise.

Madeline sank abruptly to her futon. "Miles? Miles was the father?" she asked, and relief ran through her. Her instincts had been accurate. Porter could not have killed that girl.

Grace gave a firm nod, and Madeline saw at once that underneath the grim colors and the crisp, imperious tone, the woman looked undone and in her own way was seeking comfort. Madeline understood. Given the immediate options—Marie-France and Harvey—she would have chosen the intern, too. "Do you want to come in, Grace? Have some coffee? I've got to eat before I get ready for the service." She also wanted to call Fred to be sure he knew. A wash of pleasure ran through her body at thinking his name, but it was tinged with something close to shame. They had been, well, the word was the old, silly one—*disporting* themselves—as Armitage imploded around them.

Grace peered cautiously across the threshold, wanting to accept. "It's fairly clean," Madeline said, "and my coffee's the best in town." Grace came in and sat at the very edge of the futon while Madeline ran water and fetched the beans. "They're still having the service? In spite of it all?" she asked, grateful for the dark scent of the roast spilling out across her fingers. Her sleep the night before had been spotty at best.

"You obviously didn't read your e-mail," Grace said. Madeline put the coffee on the stove and popped a bagel in the toaster.

"No," she said, "I was too busy not jogging." It was quite liberating to speak so saucily to Grace, who even asked, quite timidly, if Madeline had an extra bagel she was willing to part with.

Which was how Madeline found herself sharing breakfast with her dorm head and discussing issues like graduation and who would now run Armitage. They assumed that a formal ceremony would be canceled and that Sarah Talmadge would be appointed to an interim position. And then Grace put down her coffee cup and with no warning burst into tears. "Madeline, it's so shameful. I really didn't see that Claire was pregnant. I really didn't know. And to think of everything that's happened because of that, it's just so distressing."

Which was how Madeline found herself comforting the distraught woman, wrapping an arm around her small shoulders and telling Grace that she herself was just as responsible, had been just as blind. And that it was probably nothing they would ever forgive themselves for. But it didn't mean they had to run, did it? They could be brave and try to undo whatever bit was theirs to undo.

"So you're staying?" Grace sniffed. "Well, I'm glad. It takes courage not to leave when a situation looks bleak. But we'll come back," she said, meaning the academy and its reputation. Then her face clouded, and Madeline thought they were both thinking that that kind of return might be possible for them but not, of course, for Claire, her baby, Porter McLellan, who though still alive, might well have wished himself dead.

"I'm sorry to unburden myself on you. I'll let you get dressed now," Grace said, scarlet in the cheeks as she brushed bagel crumbs from her skirt to her palm.

"It's okay, Grace. I'm happy to help," Madeline said, and she let her colleague out the door. Her colleague. This was what it meant to have them. They weren't your friends necessarily. They were people you worked with, often rather closely and on rather intimate issues. And now and then, they revealed themselves to you, and through those revelations you might begin to earn a mutual respect. "Thank you, Madeline," Grace said and sniffed.

Once Grace was out the door, Madeline called Fred, but he didn't answer. He was probably in the shower or on his way to breakfast. He'd hear the news soon enough. Besides, she needed to get ready. How pathetic that such sad circumstances could devolve into such petty questions: who cared what anyone wore at a time like this? There was nothing for it; she still had to face her closet, and out of respect for Claire's youth, she refused black. But the heat was going to be powerful today and the limes and oranges of her summer clothing were far too festive. Madeline settled finally on a navy cotton skirt, a white blouse, and sensible flat shoes. She tried and at last succeeded in making her hair stick on the top of her head in the semblance of a chignon.

The service was called for 9:00, but it was just 8:15 and she was terribly restless. What was going to happen to Armitage? What was going to happen with Fred? Should she stay here at the academy as she'd agreed? There was time for a walk around campus, and as she crossed the Quad, she thought about Sarah Talmadge. Would she eventually apply for Porter's job? He had trained her well. She did her job with an efficiency and a compassion that everyone said reminded them of Porter. If appearances could be believed.

Madeline made her way down to the Bluestone, which was high with all the rain of the last week. It was Lucinda's elegant face she kept imagining. The way it had frozen at Last Tea as she watched the world she and Porter had created vanish with a few words. The destruction in front of her, all the hard work, all the years of service, ending in this disaster. Even if Miles wasn't convicted and Porter managed to stay out of jail—they could, after all, afford the most expensive legal help—it was a life in ruins. There was no way they wouldn't be drastically changed. There was no place they could move where the story wouldn't twist itself around them, dark, tarnishing.

The river was brown and running swiftly. Madeline threw in her last message from the Reign, balled into a crumpled sphere, and watched it bob almost instantly out of sight downstream. She turned around and went back up the bank, seeing the wide expanse of the campus sweep out before her.

There it was. The trees, the brick, the gleaming glass. A whole beautiful, well-oiled world. Its proportions lovely, its aims quite high, it spread there in the light before her. Armitage, like a castle that had survived a bomb, turrets and towers and buttresses still standing in spite of the smoke that swirled around it. As she walked back, Madeline knew with a not entirely positive certainty that Armitage would weather the disruptions of Claire's death and her baby's disappearance. The trustees would find another taker, another head, eager to be known as the one who pulled the school together after this blow. Its endowment was healthy enough to withstand the students who left, the students who protested, the parents and alumni who wouldn't give money. It was Armitage: there would always be people who wanted to come here and have a little of its glory conferred on them, a scrap of its reputation. Classes and dormitories would fill again. The shame and excitement of the crimes would eventually dissipate. It was what was meant by the idea of an institution. The school was larger and sturdier and more deeply rooted than anyone who lived, worked, or studied here. It had its own separate life.

Madeline took a deep breath as she walked under the elm tree in full, arching leaf near her apartment. She had never gone to a school where the trees grew that tall, the buildings were that grand, a place that confident of itself. Where she'd gone, bake sales made a difference. Here, a gift under five million could barely get your name on a plaque, much less a building. She stopped to look up at the saw-toothed edges of the trees and the gentle sway of the limbs.

Some of those inside this heady and entitled realm would also stay and stay, living off the school's sap. Harvey Fuller was going to die here, Madeline predicted; he'd have a stroke in the middle of the *Drosophila* lab and crush his skull on a microscope. Rob Barlow. Grace Peters. People whose identities were so wound into being teachers, and teachers at this very school, that they couldn't survive outside it. Like certain New Yorkers, whom you could never imagine off the island of Manhattan, more than a half block from a sushi bar and a dry cleaner. Some of these teachers grew so twisted into the place you couldn't tell when Armitage stopped and they started. But wasn't that precisely what the school said it didn't want? Wasn't the ethic supposed to be one of individual triumph and the ability to take risks? If the teachers didn't embody that ideal, then why should the students? Fred, in leaving, was doing what every student was encouraged to do: take a step beyond security and experiment. What Madeline was doing by staying was not exactly clear.

Across the Quad, a few faculty members were out walking their dogs. Madeline gave everyone a brief wave, which was returned just as briefly. No one wanted to reveal too much right now. It was still too sad, too raw, and nothing anyone could say could buffer the shock. Madeline could almost see Fred's dorm from where she stood. She was glad he was going, in spite of everything that had just happened between them.

Madeline noticed then that she had sweat through her white blouse and realized that she had just enough time to go back and change before heading over to the chapel. She knew, too, that she would honor her agreement to return and that she would try to stay for a few years. Then, who knew, she might go back and get a degree in writing and actually finish a collection for real. Or she might meet someone and get married and have a baby. Or study for a Ph.D. in literature and teach kids at college. She liked classes, she liked homework, she liked trying to make kids write clearer sentences. So what if irony were dead and this was earnest work done earnestly? She enjoyed it. She was going to push to move to a bigger apartment and get a slightly better coaching assignment and then the next crop of interns would come in and get the short end of the stick. Or the raw end of the deal. She could never get those expressions right. And that was how the system worked. But she would ask Sarah if she could be a mentor for the interns, if that could be part of her package. They should have someone they could talk to, someone to drink with at Mackey's.

In a shirt that was a little wrinkled, Madeline arrived at the chapel, which looked like it had been transported intact from a Norman village and deposited right here in the middle of New England. But it had had a face-lift on the way: every crenellation, every gargoyle was perfectly intact. Centuries of rain and angry mobs hadn't damaged this building, which was only about eighty-five years old, though the details that it strove to copy would have been at home in the thirteenth century.

It was almost full, though the service was still ten minutes off. The students and faculty had been required to attend, but what seemed to be the entire staff was also there: the housekeepers, the cafeteria workers, the landscapers. Everyone had dressed for the event. Sarah was at the lectern, looking drawn but composed. The glossy heads in the front row belonged, Madeline guessed, to Flora Duval and her former husband. She looked around for Fred, who was on the far side of the chapel, between another art teacher and his dorm head. He was busy studying the program and not distractible at the moment. Madeline slipped into a pew almost at the back and was startled when the man to her left turned toward her: it was Matt Corelli. He was wearing neatly pressed khakis and a navy jacket of heavy linen. His tie was also dark blue. He smiled at her and said, "I was hoping I'd see you here. Good thing you got in late." He looked tired, as if he'd been up late, and he, like Sarah, also looked sad. Madeline doubted very much that he had wanted to arrest Miles and Porter. But he also looked very handsome: his dark hair combed back from his forehead, his large, square hand holding a creamy pamphlet, the program for Claire's service.

"I'm not late," Madeline protested. "It doesn't start for ten more minutes." She noticed that his partner was next to him. He also said hello.

"You're right," Matt said and then looked away and said, so quietly she almost didn't hear him, "but I'm still glad to see you." She didn't think that she was imagining the grin his partner broke into, either. Just then the music started, sonorous pumpings from the organ. A subdued fanfare of Bach. Henry Granding was an organist of the old school—was there any other kind? Madeline wondered—and he gave his renditions an athleticism that perhaps their composers did not intend.

It was a bit distracting to have the detective right next to her, but she was trying hard to take in the scene around her. The pews were filled to bursting, but with whom? The parents were in the front row as well as several handsome, blond children who must have been Claire's half siblings. Clearly, there were other members of her family in the rows behind Flora and William, too. Madeline could see only the back of Flora's golden head, but when she turned, Madeline saw she wore the same huge dark glasses as she had before. After the family came an array of the teachers. Almost seventy of them, heads dipped, hands folded. Every single one of them looked drained, and most had their eyes closed, in prayer, Madeline guessed, that this year would finally end.

It was almost medieval, this seating by ranks. First the aristocratic Harknesses, then the faculty, then the remaining students. Madeline saw Sally Jansen, her parents perched on either side of her. Even Maggie Fitzgerald was present, limp and wan as ever. Somewhere, Lee and Olu were lurking, Madeline was sure, but she couldn't spot them from her seat. Then came the staff. Madeline saw Jim French with a bandage on his head and a frail, elegant woman next to him who had to be his mother, they looked so much alike. Past the staff, she saw a few men with gelled hair and women in jewel-toned jackets and bright lipstick—media, though the television crews had been denied access. But who were these several dozen kids? Not Armitage students, certainly. They were much more reminiscent of Greenville's population, where the girls wore clothing so tight it made them shorten their strides while the boys almost tripped in their wide pant legs. If it hadn't been a memorial service, they would have worn baseball caps popped up at an angle, Madeline suspected. How did they know Claire? Why were they here? Was it curiosity? Had there been another connection?

One of them, a boy with a shaved head and a Boston Red Sox T-shirt, lifted his chin in recognition of someone he spotted. There was also in this segment of the crowd a suppressed energy, a kind of tense excitement that had nothing to do with death.

Wisely, Sarah kept her comments very short. She said, "We are here to commemorate Claire Harkness. While the circumstances of her death and the disappearance of her child are still unclear, what we can say and know for a certainty is that they are a tragedy. Her parents, her relatives, her brothers and sisters have lost a beautiful member of their family. The school has lost one of its most treasured students and now faces a crisis that will test it absolutely. We have not much to lean on in this drastic time. And in that humility, may we come together." She was brief, she was honest, she reminded everyone of Porter, though she did not, of course, mention his name. The parents had not wanted to speak, and no one had burst into tears, though a few of Claire's classmates had seemed on the brink of an outbreak. Matt and his partner kept their heads bowed throughout. We'll survive it, Madeline thought. We will get through it. Wide strips of light ran through the stained glass and twisted into bright knots on the stone floor, the shifting pages of the programs, in an almost unseemly glory of red and blue.

But just as the choir had begun to sing "A Mighty Fortress Is Our God," something happened at the back of the chapel. Someone was opening the doors, which had been firmly closed once the service started. They were solid oak, studded with metal, and a considerable barrier to anyone trying to sneak in. It was a joke that the hinges were kept unoiled on purpose to make it impossible for anyone to creep past when he or she was late. Madeline wasn't imagining it. Someone was opening the doors, and the sound of metal grinding metal made the entire congregation turn to look.

Then another noise threaded through the church, and at first Madeline couldn't locate its source. What is it? she thought, and was suddenly reminded of Tadeo, but Tadeo at birth, with that reedy screech only newborns produce. A baby, Madeline knew, her heart rising. A baby. Claire's baby; it had to be. She stood, and so did Matt and the rest of the congregation, in a rustle of linen and astonishment. Matt reached for his phone and pressed a number urgently. His partner rose, too, swearing softly.

In the central aisle, a girl held the baby, a girl with long brown hair, the one Madeline had seen at Mackey's, the one who had been so frightened. Madeline heard a voice call suddenly, "Kayla!" and saw that the cry came from Mrs. French. She had to be restrained by her son, who was looking at Kayla with wonderment and pride. Then Madeline saw another person she had not expected to: Scotty Johnston was following the girl. He was the one who must have opened the doors as she held the tiny, crying baby. But while she kept walking, he melted into the crowd on the far side of the chapel.

Matt placed his hand on Madeline's shoulder and excused himself as he and his partner slipped out from the pew and moved swiftly to the girl's side. She looked up at them and said something. Matt answered, held her elbow, and steered her toward the Harknesses, who had, along with everyone else, turned to see what was happening. The partner started to search the crowd, apparently for Scotty. The choir broke off abruptly. The organ gave up in midbleat, and instead of shapely chords and voices, a wave of awe ran through the chapel. The baby wailed and wailed, high and piercing above the soft, perplexed whispers of the crowd.

Claire's baby, alive, in this strong, proud girl's arms. The teenagers who clearly didn't belong started to whistle and call her name. "Yo, Kayla," someone shouted, but not even that dissuaded the girl from her task. With Matt at her side, she kept walking, heading, Madeline saw, for Flora.

Flora had understood instantly. She had pulled her sunglasses from her face and was moving as fast as she could to find Kayla. The two met almost at the top of the aisle, and Kayla, her face streaming with tears, handed the baby to Flora, waiting there with her own arms held wide.

Matt held the girl then, and Madeline watched her crumple. He held her close and ushered her away. She saw nothing but the purest relief on his face, nothing but release. Flora stood uncertainly at the head of the aisle, looking at the tiny child in her arms, as her former husband moved toward her and Sarah Talmadge released her grip on the lectern. Only then did Flora begin to rock the child. It was that motion, that gesture of tentative tenderness, that unleashed the applause. The kids from Greenville began it, kids who must have known and helped Kayla; it was not the decorous response that greeted the Christmas concert or the violin recital or any of the other polite and well-heeled events for which the chapel served as stage. It was loud and rhythmic and full of cheers and whistles and a kind of raucous joy. A hooting, something untrammeled that everyone—the teachers, the staff, the students—gave way to.

"He's alive," Madeline kept saying and found herself hugging Grace, who was hugging Alice Grassley. She looked for Fred, but he was caught in the tumult on the other side of the aisle. The children's applause had freed them all and somehow pressed them outside. The stern gray building was simply too small for the relief and wonder they were feeling. Out on the curve of lawn in front of the chapel, grateful for the hot sun, everyone who had attended the service could not stop reveling at the baby's return.

Then, in the midst of the confusion, Madeline saw something almost as unexpected start to happen. The pack of kids from Greenville edged by cautious steps toward the children who constituted the rather shattered remains of Armitage's student body. Not toward Olu and Lee and the rest of the oligarchy, who remained aloof, and always would, Madeline thought sadly. Some of Armitage's graduates would never really feel that they quite belonged to the rest of the population. But most of the others weren't that blind or provincial. Those were the ones who walked awkwardly forward to meet these new arrivals. The teenagers stood there, not in separate clumps but overlapping, the kids with the sweatshirts talking to the boys in the blazers, the kids from town and the kids on the hill. Madeline grasped nothing—how the baby had been kept alive; how that long-haired girl had been involved—but she stood there, transfixed, amazed at how much all those young people had to say to one another.

CHAPTER 24

Kayla *sat opposite Matt and stared out the window of his of-fice,* which provided little more than a very dispiriting view of concrete and cars. Even so, she did not shift her gaze. Her father stood behind her, not quite hovering, but not touching her, either. For once in this case, no lawyer perched on every word, throwing a protective mantle over his client. Kayla's family didn't have enough money to afford a good attorney and appeared ready to deal with whatever happened themselves, not used to paying anyone for the privilege of representing them. The girl had immediately agreed to come to the station and called her father on the way. The man was pacing in the reception area when they arrived, in spotless clothes, silent, obviously wretched with concern. Now she said something to him in rushed, forceful Portuguese. He looked at Matt. "She wants to talk to you by herself. She won't say anything if I'm here." He spoke to his daughter, again in Portuguese. She said, "Pie, they tape it. You can listen to every word if you want to." The man kissed Kayla's head, glared at the digital recorder on Matt's desk, and told them both he would be right outside the door if she changed her mind.

But even with her father gone, Vernon off dealing with Scotty and the search of Harvey Fuller's apartment, and the door firmly shut, Kayla remained silent. Matt had guessed that she would want to tell the story without an audience, but perhaps, having been discreet for a critical time, she was having difficulty finding words that could capture what she had done. Which was, apparently, tend with remarkable gentleness to the needs of a newborn for an entire week with little adult intervention. Even as she sat there, tearstained and worn-out, her shoulders were back and her spine was straight.

"My father said, 'Just tell the story.' But there are a lot of parts to it and you could start in a lot of different places," she said softly, but this was as good a spot as any. Kayla had met Scotty and Claire at the Greenville animal shelter early this spring. "They didn't need to do their community service anymore. They just liked getting off campus and seeing the dogs, and I did, too. My dad says we have too many kids to have a pet, so I started going there to be with animals. They were on the same shift. We walked the dogs together. I thought, stuck-up rich kids, all Ivy League, but they were okay. And they were good with even the mean strays."

They had gone when they hadn't needed to. That was why that information hadn't shown up as something people mentioned about them. Nor had it appeared on their schedules. But we forgot to look into that part of Claire's life, Matt thought. No one mentioned it, but we forgot even so. We assumed every aspect of the case took place up there, inside the gates.

Kayla said by the third week of walking the dogs, she had realized Claire was pregnant. "How?" Matt asked. "I'm interested because no one else seemed to. What did you see?"

Kayla looked at him directly then and said, "It was how Scotty treated her. Wouldn't let her walk the big animals. Carried her book bag. And she was wearing these boys' shirts, which skinny girls usually don't do. Then I noticed how she was walking." She had six younger brothers, she explained. She had seen her mother. And girls at her school got pregnant all the time. "She barely showed. It was hard to believe she was at seven months."

She leaned forward then and said, "What I am going to tell you is true. I'm bad at lying. Ask anyone at my school. Ask my father. I can't do it. I just blurt things out. I always get myself into trouble because I can't hide what I've done." When she realized that Claire was having a baby, she couldn't help herself. "I said to her, 'What are you doing at school? Why aren't you home? Why aren't your parents helping you?'" And they looked at me like I was some alien who couldn't speak English."

Matt could imagine it. The Portuguese girl with the large, close family, sly and haughty Armitage kids, the strays and the barking. Kayla stopped looking directly at him and again stared out the window, the story breaking from her more quickly now. "So I asked them, Is Scotty the father? And he got red in the face and looked kind of mad and embarrassed at the same time. No, Claire said, he's not and I haven't told him who is. You could tell it was this huge, suppressed thing between them, so I didn't say anything more about it. But I asked what they were going to do when the baby came. Did they have a plan? And they didn't. They didn't have a clue. All they said was Don't tell anyone. They were totally frightened that I would go to their teachers or something. But I didn't want to get mixed up with them. I nearly stopped going to the shelter and I tried to switch my times, and then something happened." She paused to take a sip of water.

Matt guessed what was next. Claire and Scotty had seen the answer to their problem in practical, experienced Kayla. "They got nice to me. They asked me questions about my family. I felt sorry for the girl. For Claire. I thought she was brave to have the baby. Most girls like that, they get rid of it," Kayla said, and she made a fast, slashing motion at her belly. She stopped again, looked at Matt sharply, and asked, "Where are you from?"

"From Greenville. Born here, but I went to school up there," he said.

"You did? And you're a cop?" The words flew out of her mouth. He had already believed her when she said she was bad at lying, but this just reinforced that impression. He laughed and said, "You know what? That's what everybody thinks but almost no one has the guts to say."

She shrugged. "It's just that those people, the ones up there, they do money jobs, they work in banks. Or they marry other rich people and don't work at all. Being a cop is a real job, like the kind my dad has." Her father had worked in the mills for seventeen years, and he was a foreman now. Pride lined her voice when she told him that. But when Matt asked her what her mother did, she bent her head. "That's when it got complicated with them."

When Claire and Scotty figured out that she had all these younger brothers, they asked her what she knew about babies. Kayla snorted and said she had said to them, "What don't I know about babies?" Matt saw her ambivalence now. She'd been showing off, parading her real-world knowledge in front of those shiny kids, who in spite of it all, intimidated her with their money, their education, their curious cool. So she told them that her mother had had all of her kids at home. And that was when she knew she had told them too much.

Matt finally understood the hold Claire and Scotty had on Kayla. The mother must not have any papers. Her father, Kayla explained, was from the Canaries, and he was still waiting after all these years for a green card. Her mother didn't have legal status at all. She was from Brazil, where she had grown up with nothing. She had saved enough twenty years ago for a plane ticket and had come to Greenville, where she had a cousin. She met Kayla's dad and they got married. Then the laws kept changing, and always she was on the other side of them. She'd had her babies at home, not wanting to risk hospitals and deportation, separation from her children. "We're legal, my brothers and me, because we're born here. We can stay. But my mom, she's vulnerable. And they figured it out. Those two figured it out." Scotty said his father was a lawyer. Claire said her family knew people in the government. And Kayla believed them. And then they told her they wouldn't let anyone know if she agreed to help them out with the baby.

"First, he offered me money." Her disdain was total, Matt saw. She might be grudgingly in awe of them, but Kayla would accept nothing from people like Scotty and Claire. "I told him I would help because it was the right thing to do and they couldn't go to the cops about my mom because I would go to the hospital with the baby and turn them in. We each had something on the other." She had been satisfied with this part of the negotiation, holding her own against Scotty and Claire. They knew nothing, she said, nothing about birth or what it could be like. She paused then, collecting herself for the rest.

"Were you there when Claire had the baby?" Matt asked.

Kayla shook her head. "She was late, but it happened fast. She wasn't expecting it. Scotty was with her, in the tunnels, I think. I don't know how they managed." They communicated by a dial-up computer he had rigged up down there. Kayla had an account that she checked every day on an old laptop a friend had given her dad. No cells. Scotty said they were too easy to trace. Then late Sunday night, early Monday morning, he showed up at her house. He banged on her window, which was on the first floor. She was the only girl, and she had her own tiny room, the only one in the family with that privilege. She must have told him that, but she had no idea how he'd found out where her family lived. "He had the baby with him, and he just said, 'Take him. He's in danger,' and he gave me all this formula and diapers and blankets, and then he ran."

She stayed up with the infant, feeding him and holding him. At this point, Kayla stopped talking, clearly thinking about that night. Matt, too, marveled at it and imagined the tiny child, the girl's intense focus, the audacity of these young people in crisis. When Kayla started to speak again, she did so more slowly and was more subdued. The first morning she'd been lucky. Her mom had a job cleaning houses, her brothers and father left early for school and work, and she could stay at home and have nobody figure it out. The next day, Kayla said, she had heard about Claire and she got even more frightened. All Scotty wrote on the computer was "I didn't do it."

"Did you believe him?" Matt asked.

"Yes," Kayla said quite forcefully. "He loved her. He's a jerk, but he loved that girl." She looked down at her hands and went on. It was all really confusing, but her luck had continued to hold. Her father had been away part of the week, at a conference for new foremen for the plant; her mother was busy with a new job. "I set up a nursery in the garage." No one used it, Kayla said. "It was full of old boxes and bikes, but there was this attic that I set up to make it nice for the baby." She had claimed to be sick for three days, and she'd gotten her best girlfriend and her boyfriend to help her. That was how the story got out at school. Not everyone, Kayla said, was good at keeping secrets, which explained how all those kids had heard about the service. She and her friends had rotated nights, but she'd been with the little boy most of the time.

She'd had to give up her job with Mrs. French. "I didn't want to do that, but it was the only way I could manage to stay with the baby.

"But then on Wednesday night, he started to cry and cry, and my girlfriend and I couldn't figure it out. We were worried he had a fever, and we wanted to take him to a hospital. That was when we decided we had to tell my mom and dad. My mom took care of the baby, and I went to this bar where my dad goes with his friends to watch baseball. We don't keep a lot of secrets in my family, and I felt bad. But with everything going on up there, my father said we couldn't get mixed up with the police. We didn't want to expose my mom." She was looking now at Matt with a combination of worry and pride. She had held up her end of the agreement. She had taken care of her family. She had taken care of that child.

Fortunately, the baby started to eat again and was fine, but that was it, Kayla said. They had all had it, and they were terrified about what was going to happen. She hadn't heard from Scotty since Tuesday, and so on Thursday night, she stole onto campus and threw a large rock into his window. "If he could figure out where I lived, I could figure out where he lived," she said with some degree of satisfaction. "Even with security, it was pretty easy to get in by the river. No gates there." Kayla told Scotty that she was going to the police and she was going to hand over the baby. His mother was dead, but he had grandparents and a father somewhere, and it was over, even if it meant her own mother was going to jail. But Scotty said no. Two more days, maybe three. It was all going to come down very soon, and the baby would go right where he should. "He was scared, Mr. Corelli. Even he was scared. So I agreed. I said Sunday, latest, and he said okay. And then we heard that the arrests had happened." She sipped some more water and wiped off the moisture with the back of her hand, looking for once, Matt thought, like a child. "Then Scotty showed up on Saturday night. He looked bad. His eyes were red, his clothes weren't clean. He said he had to stay with me, he had to see the baby. He kept looking at him, but he didn't want to hold him. He barely slept. He just sat there, watching us. He said we would go up to the school the next morning." She stopped again.

"It was creepy the way he and Claire talked about their parents, like they weren't there, like they weren't important. But I didn't think they could be totally right. I didn't think you could bring a kid into the world and not care what happened to her. So I agreed, but I wanted to do it in the church. Because Claire's mother would be there, and I would give her back her grandson."

Kayla was crying now. She pulled a Kleenex from the box on Matt's desk. "Did you see him? We called him Pablo. I know they won't keep that name, but who cares? It's funny, but even when a person is really little, he needs a name." She blew her nose and crumpled the tissue. "Is he okay?"

Matt said she had taken excellent care of him. She had done beautifully. The baby was at the hospital now with his grand-mother, getting a checkup, but everything was looking fine. He had an officer with Flora, and after he was finished with Kayla, he was going to see her. He turned off the recorder. "Thank you, Kayla." He meant that gratitude to encompass everything she had done: for being the kind of person who at sixteen could take care of a newborn, for being as strong as she knew how to be in difficult circumstances. For being someone who expected to solve her own problems.

The girl stood up. "I've got a lot of homework to catch up on," she said. "I should go." But she hesitated. "My mom . . . ," she said, and it was the first time since he'd met her that Matt had seen her look truly frightened. Her face tightened, and she couldn't meet his eye.

He stood as well. "I have to be honest. I don't know what will happen. It's up to the immigration people. But Kayla, if I can, I will help you."

She looked at him and said, "Thanks," without much hope but without irony, too. She was too worldly to believe what any bureaucrat said, but she hadn't entirely given up on him. Still, she wasn't quite done. "What's going to happen to that boy, the one who killed her? Is he going to go to jail?"

"Maybe, Kayla. It's still too early to say." He looked at her and felt she understood that, for people like Miles, there were nearly endless permutations to that possibility, and they depended on money, judges, the vagaries of courts and juries. It would take months if not years to sort out the public punishments. Matt hadn't seen Miles since that moment in his office with Lucinda and Porter; the lawyers had swooped down with ferocious speed. The DA was nervously appeasing them all.

Kayla leaned down. "Scotty brought this bag with him when he gave me Pablo. It looks expensive, like she went out and bought it from some fancy store. I forgot to give it to her mother. Could you do that for me?" She placed the tote on his desk, and Matt was struck by it, too. It looked like the sort of present people gave at baby showers, a crisp little blue sack with compartments for bottles and wipes. Claire must have gotten it for herself, a small badge of motherhood, of preparedness for an experience that had in fact entirely overwhelmed her.

Kayla stuck out her hand. He took it and was impressed with both the delicacy of her bones and the strength of her grip. "A cop who went to school up there," she said, shaking her head and opening the door to meet her father, who'd been standing there the whole time, waiting for his daughter. Matt watched them walk down the corridor, the man's arm wrapped around his girl's shoulder, both of them murmuring in Portuguese.

In his office, he called Vernon, who said that he had no idea where Scotty was but that most of his gear was still in his room and he wasn't at home. His parents, naturally, were frantic, but Vernon had a feeling he hadn't taken off anywhere. His wallet was on his desk, complete with credit and bank cards. Matt told Vernon where he thought he should look for the boy, then asked what was going on with the search of Fuller's apartment.

"Almost done," Vernon said. "We did find something, but I want you to see it. I don't want to talk about it on the phone." His partner sounded oddly morose and somewhat chastened.

"Vernon?" Matt asked.

"Later, Matt," Vernon said and clicked off.

Another quick call confirmed that the police officer had accompanied the baby and Flora back to her hotel. "I'm on my way," Matt said, but as he spoke, he'd begun rifling through the contents of Claire's fancy bag. A gruesome habit of cops, he thought, licensed snooping. Our fingers always moving through people's drawers and pockets, trawling for news. It was an activity he could engage in almost absentmindedly, the blunt search and display of personal effects. Claire had tried, he thought, as he probed the bag's contents. She had tried. There were a few diapers for infants. A pacifier still in its plastic wrapping. Some talcum powder and a tiny yellow shirt. These items made a forlorn clump on his desk, and again, he cursed himself for having focused so doggedly on Armitage, for having forgotten that Greenville could so easily have been involved. Of all people, he should have known better. But at least the baby wasn't dead. At least they had picked Kayla. Someone competent, someone careful. Claire and Scotty had chosen well; he wondered if they had known how lucky they were.

He tugged along an inside zipper. He really ought to stop and go to see Claire's mother, who had a certain amount of explaining to do about why she hadn't seen fit to mention that she had seen Porter at a critical moment this summer. But Matt's fingers felt the outline of some object in this part of the bag. He discovered a notebook, much like the one that had held Claire's brief journal entries. European, he thought, expecting whatever notes he found inside to be in French. But the pages held not words but images.

She had started with photos, mostly of her mother when she was younger. The resemblance to Claire was uncanny. The father had left no apparent trace. The pictures, fading now, were of Flora in dresses and on sailboats, an incredibly pretty young woman savoring her beauty. Then Matt saw one that made his chest clench. A man who looked astonishingly like Miles McLellan sat on a bench, his arm around the young Flora. They couldn't have made a better-looking couple, and there was something heated and convincing about the way he held her shoulders. She was turned toward him, and her hair was a blond cloud that seemed to wrap about them both. It was Porter, of course, and Madeline's rushed story about how her sister thought that Flora and Porter had once been a couple began to make sense. It was the only picture in Claire's book that featured the two together, and it held pride of place in the center of the page.

Then everything shifted. On the next pages, all Claire had gathered were images of Porter, first alone, and then with Lucinda and his growing family. Some were taken from newspapers. Some were ones that Matt recognized from the alumni magazine. An album of obsession. An album, he realized, of the family that might have been hers, of what she had so badly wanted. Parents who stayed together. Parents who loved their children. Who did what they said they would do. But Porter wasn't her father. Some feckless banker who had no time for her was. Yet, Matt thought, turning over the pages, it was probably a lot easier to blame Porter. To be at Armitage year after year getting more and more jealous of what he had built and what he had and then, in Miles, a very convenient way to get back at them. For what, precisely? Matt wondered. For merely existing, he guessed. For being so palpably happy and successful. For having what she never could: a circle of loving care that surrounded them. People who would do anything for each other.

He packed the notebook and the few items the bag had held and decided on impulse to bring them to Flora, who was staying in the area's best hotel, which still wasn't much more than a glorified Best Western.

When she opened the door to her room, he was struck by its resemblance to Claire's: expensive disorder everywhere—silk and shoes and scarves draped casually on every surface, all of it lightly wreathed in a scent of cologne. He noticed, too, bags lined with tissue paper, full to the brim with small blue shirts and sweaters. All the proper clothes. A brand-new crib, white and draped in flounces of green gingham, was tucked in the corner next to the bed. Flora had worked quickly to get the right accoutrements in place. And inside the small, soft palace slept the tiny child. Flora herself looked composed if tired.

She stood by the crib and watched the baby. "We're going to call him Nicholas, for my father," she said. He had died, she said, when she was quite young, as had her mother. But he had been the kindest man, she added, and tugged a blue blanket around the child's shoulders. Matt came to look at the little boy. He still had that newborn pucker to his face and that mat of black hair, but it was clear, even fast asleep, that he was a beautiful child. "Kayla called him Pablo. She said even when people are very small, they still need a name."

"That was sweet of her, wasn't it? Though of course that's not a name we would ever keep," said Flora. She was returning to Paris as soon as the baby's passport came through, probably late this week. How funny that even little babies needed all the proper documents before they could travel. They had some friends in Washington who were going to expedite the process for them. And then there were a few legal hurdles, questions of custody, that had to be handled. But they had a lawyer working on that. Of course they did, Matt thought. Expedience and instant, expert help were of the utmost importance to people like Flora Duval. Matt said then, still standing, a cold line of anger threading into his voice in spite of himself, "Mrs. Duval, I'm aware you and Claire's father aren't interested in pressing charges against Scotty and Kayla, but there are several questions I'd still like an answer to. They may prove helpful in understanding why Claire died. Were you and Porter McLellan ever involved with each other? I can be blunter. Did you have a romantic relationship with Mr. McLellan, and did Claire know about it?"

If she was surprised, she didn't show it. She merely said, "Yes, in college. Porter and I were together for three years. Everyone thought we were going to get married. My parents adored him." She pulled a chair from the desk and sat down next to the crib, as if taking her eyes off the baby for even a moment might be dangerous.

"But you left him?" Matt asked. It was another facet of police life that made him deeply uncomfortable: the very infrequent desire to press a witness extremely hard. Right now, he was quite content to make Flora Duval incredibly uncomfortable. It would change nothing, what she said. It wouldn't bring her daughter back or restore Porter's reputation, but it was still what he was going to do.

"No," she said, sadly. "I didn't. He broke up with me the spring of our senior year. It was something I had said in passing, something I'd mentioned at a party. Something about not being able to imagine life as a schoolteacher. How dull, I said, and he had taken it to heart and realized that his ambition to be part of schools, to lead them, would make me dreadfully unhappy." Soon after, he had taken up with Lucinda, who Flora noted rather scornfully, "had grown up the daughter of a head in some godforsaken part of Vermont."

The baby began to stir and stretch. Flora reached toward him, but then he settled again. In the hall, Matt heard the rhythmic drone of a vacuum cleaner. "Why didn't you mention that you and Claire had seen the McLellans this summer? You must have known the timing was crucial."

"I was there for a day. What could possibly happen in a day?" She was shaking her head now, as if Matt were an insect she wanted to shoo off.

"But Claire was there for slightly longer. I'm still interested in knowing if she was aware of your relationship with Mr. McLellan. And if so, how much did she know?" This sensation, an actual pleasure in having the right to badger someone, was something he was going to need to discuss with Vernon. But for right now, he planned to let himself savor it.

"Why does this matter, Mr. Corelli? What does that piece of my history have to do with why Claire was killed?" It was the first time she bristled. A frown line appeared between her eyes, and something close to a pout shadowed her mouth. "To answer your question, however, she knew a few things. She'd stumbled on a photo of us taken years ago, and she needled me all about it. Why hadn't I told her when she was applying to Armitage, the usual teenage silliness." Flora's hands had tightened around the bars of the crib.

"And what did you say, Mrs. Duval?" His own rage, at himself for not seeing all this earlier, at her for having not known her daughter, was beginning to twist through his jaw.

She looked at him then and said simply, "That he could have been her father. And that, in some ways, it was a pity he hadn't been."

Matt unzipped the diaper bag, took out the notebook, and gave it to her mother. Flora said, "What's this?" then began to look at the pictures Claire had painstakingly gathered and glued to the pages. "But I didn't mean it seriously. It was just something I said." Her voice was breaking, and the baby was beginning to rouse himself below his gossamer-soft blanket.

"I know," Matt said. "I understand that. But Claire was paying close attention."

He left as the baby woke and started to cry and nearly ran into the small woman manhandling the heavy vacuum in the hall. He apologized, and she smiled at him. Seeing where he'd come from, she said, "Pobrecito." Matt hoped she wasn't right, that Flora would provide more than intermittent attention and excellent clothing while she raised this child.

He had to sit in his car for a few minutes, with the windows rolled down, before he dared to call Vernon. He was remembering what his father did when he had been accused of cheating at the academy. He had kept saying, "I didn't do it, I promise I didn't do it, Dad," as his father paced back and forth across their small living room. His mother had sat in an armchair saying nothing, her face heavy with disappointment. Joseph had stopped then and come over to him, and Matt hadn't been sure what was going to happen next, whether his father was going to hit him, hold him, shove him out of the house. Joseph had a fearsome temper, and Matt and Barbara had at times cowered before him. But that afternoon his father had stood in front of him and taken his face in his hands and said, "My son, my beautiful boy, I believe you. I just can't stand it that I couldn't protect you. That I wasn't there."

Protection. The delay or avoidance of harm. All Claire had wanted was something resembling a family. Something whole and solid that might offer a shield against the hardest pieces of growing up. And when she couldn't fashion one of her own that made any sort of sense, she was going to hurt the one that she most envied as much as possible. His phone rang then. Vernon, with Scotty found, he hoped. "He's at the shelter. Won't move. You better get down here."

When Matt arrived, a worried man in blue surgical scrubs met him at the entrance. "Are you the other police officer? Mr. Cates told me to tell you to meet him out back." Matt went around the building, following the sounds and smells of dogs, and saw in the yard with the waist-high, chain-link fence, Scotty sitting on the ground, three or four dogs of various breeds and sizes lapping at his hands. Vernon was leaning against the fence and watching. Matt opened the gate and joined them. The dogs took little notice of him and Vernon, intent on greeting Scotty, who was bending toward them and speaking to them softly. Mostly pit bull mixes from the looks of them, ribs visible, with those jaws and scarred heads, tattered ears.

"Scotty doesn't want to answer my question," Vernon told Matt.

"What did you ask him?" Matt looked around the enclosure, a space of about forty by sixty feet. Tufts of grass sprouted along the fence. Water tubs stood by the door. Mostly, the area was covered with dirt and holes where the animals had dug. Matt understood the holes. Any dog in its right mind would want to tunnel out of here.

"Why he thought it was okay to kidnap a newborn and spend a few million taxpayer dollars on a nationwide search," said Vernon. He and Matt were on either side of the gate.

"You fucking assholes," Scotty said, almost conversationally, glancing up for the first time since Matt had come inside the enclosure. He looked nothing like the boy they'd first seen in the station. His hair was unwashed, a spray of acne was sprouting along a high cheekbone. His fingers were lost in the scruff of a wide-necked mutt at his feet.

"Probably a legitimate question, Vernon," Matt said. "And he is actually very lucky, because Claire's parents don't want a lot of legal hassle. They're not pressing charges. But I think I know some of the answer anyway. And it starts in October or November of last year." He was keeping his voice low and almost neutral, and he wasn't looking at Scotty. One of the dogs came over and gave Matt's pant leg an experimental lick. Why were shelters always in the drabbest parts of town? The answer was obvious. No one wanted to think about abandoned or angry animals. Stashing them somewhere un-appealing, as if they were living toxic waste, made it easier for most people not to have to deal with them.

Matt continued, "Claire went up to Damariscotta for a few days last summer, and somehow she and a friend wound up in Castine. And there was Miles McLellan, ripe for the taking. My guess is he had had a crush on her for years that she had slowly manipulated. Claire knew something that Miles probably did not: her mother and Porter had had a relationship at college and then Porter had left Flora for Lucinda. That information wouldn't be something that Lucinda would want her kids to know about, I'd guess. But when Claire had the chance to hook up with and dump Miles, she took it. Claire thought she could get a kind of revenge, not just on Miles but on Porter. He had a family, three handsome boys, a loving wife, a sterling reputation. He could have been, she fantasized, her own father. But instead, she had a man who rarely saw her, a mother on her third marriage in Europe, and not a sin-gle adult who knew or cared about her in any kind of substantive way." He glanced at Scotty, who was holding one of the pit bulls in his lap.

"But she made a mistake. She got pregnant. And at first, she might not have believed it. When she did, she thought about it and realized what she could do with this baby. She wouldn't just hu-miliate and embarrass Miles: she could destroy his whole family. She could tarnish the whole academy. She could make a really, really big scene, and then somebody might just pay some attention to her." Matt paused again.

"So she set a plan in action. She tied the thread with the girls in the Reign, to keep them off her back. Then she roped some other girls in because basically she didn't like or respect the Reign and she needed more support. She tied the thread with them, too, and they did her bidding because of the tradition and because she was Claire Harkness and it was the biggest story in town. At some point, probably much earlier, Scotty, she let you in."

The boy gave him a quick look and then almost immediately glanced down again. The dogs had wandered off and were chasing one another around. One of them lapped up water. The day gleamed and bathed the small yard in light that revealed every scrape or sore on the dogs' bodies. Matt continued, "I don't know why you let her stay. I'm still trying to figure that piece of it out. Did she threaten to give herself an abortion if you told? That's what she did with the girls in the dorm, even after she'd sworn them to secrecy. And you were worried she would kill herself in the process. Maybe she threatened that, too, when you kept asking her who the father was."

Now Scotty was watching Matt's face, and his color was mounting again. "But you went along with what Claire wanted, Scotty. And you helped her with her homework, and covered for her in class, and organized the girls to get her food and whatever she needed. You pounced on Kayla when you saw what she could offer: someone who could deal with babies, actual babies, not just pregnancy.

"And it almost worked. You had set up the mirrors so if Claire needed you, you could be there. You had Kayla in place. But then Claire had the baby much faster than she or you or anyone could have expected. And it was terrifying. And you were both unprepared. Where did it happen, Scotty? In the tunnels, in the computer room?"

The boy leaned back on the door that led to the shelter and said in a voice they could barely hear, "The tunnels. We met down there because Claire said she was feeling sick. And then she bent over and started to scream." He stopped then, but as with Kayla, Matt sensed it was something of a relief to finally say what had happened. He could do so only here, where he and Claire had met Kayla and spent time with animals. One of the dogs trotted over and pawed at him, though for the first time since they had been here, Scotty ignored the animal's overture. "It was so fast. She just kept screaming, saying it was tearing her up. And then there was water everywhere, and blood. And then we saw the head. This little head. And she pushed him out. But when he came out, the cord was all twisted around his neck and he wasn't breathing. He was blue and I thought he was dead. But then I unwound it and I started to rub his back and he gave this cough and started to cry. I nearly dropped him, he was so slippery. Like a fish. But even then, the blood kept coming. I had a Swiss Army knife with me. I don't know why. I don't carry one mostly. But I had it in my pocket." He stared again at his fingers, as if amazed at what they had done. Like all rowers' hands, they were raw with blisters. He looked up at them, eyes red. "I did some reading. I knew you had to wait to cut the cord. In the pictures, it looks blue and wide. But it's not. It's kind of red and gray."

Vernon and Matt looked at each other. Watching two dogs scuffle, Scotty said, in a voice that was softer than they'd ever heard him use, that he had gotten sheets from a laundry room in a nearby dorm. He had wrapped up Claire and the baby. He had taken her back to the dorm, and she had told him to find Sally. He had gone back with cleaning supplies he'd found in the tunnels and mopped up the whole mess. Then he'd burned it all in the furnace below Nicholson. He didn't know how it worked; he just kept pushing levers and buttons until it fired up, and then he shoved everything in. "My clothes and Claire's, too. They were ruined."

Neither Matt nor Vernon said anything in the silence that followed. One of the dogs gave a low howl and then abruptly broke off. It must have been hellish. In the dark, with an infant, Claire in agony, blood everywhere. Vernon was studiously examining his nails, something he did, Matt knew, only when he was feeling sympathy for someone. At last, Matt said, "You were very brave to manage it alone. You realized Claire could have died, and the baby, too. But something else happened during the birth, Scott. I think Claire told you who the father was and why she'd done what she'd done. Then once you'd gotten her back to the dorm and gotten everything taken care of, you couldn't help yourself. You went to Miles McLellan and you told him what you thought of him, and you probably would have beaten him up except that he said his father would get you expelled and your acceptance retracted from Harvard. But before you told him, he didn't know. I don't think he even knew Claire was pregnant until quite late in the spring, and he was too ashamed to tell his parents. I'm still wondering who sprang it on him. One of the girls, one of the Reign most likely, but he had no idea that he was the father because Claire had confessed to no one. And Claire was furious, wasn't she, and she was scared when she found out what you'd done. Miles had fallen hard for her. She had dumped him with no qualms. He wasn't predictable. He had a temper.

"So early Monday morning, she signals you to come over and she gives you the baby. She says, Take him to Kayla, I don't want Miles to find him here. And you do. But then something happens you can't predict. Miles does go to see Claire, soon after you've left with the baby, and he is incredibly distraught. He is terrified. He begs her to tell him where the baby is and to explain why she has done what she's done. Why has she broken his heart this way? And he holds her and shakes her and she is exhausted and weak and he pushes her a fraction too hard and she hits her head in exactly the wrong spot and she's dead."

Three of the dogs had discovered something interesting in a patch of dirt by the door and were scrabbling fiercely to find it. From inside the building came a volley of barking. Vernon shifted next to him, still unwilling to look up from his nails. It was a fantastic day in early summer, an exact balance achieved between humidity and temperature, and a light wind swept through the small yard.

Scotty was standing now and trembling, as if a wave of electricity were passing through his body. "You loved her, Scotty. So did Miles, in his way. She had the misfortune to be someone you only have to look at to love." He wanted to keep talking, to say, But it started earlier. Her beauty and how she used it was one of the roots of this whole, sad mess. It started with someone not loving her for anything other than that hair and face. People just didn't want to peer beneath that elegant surface. How could anyone who looked like Claire not be happy? They didn't want to take the time. But Matt didn't say more. Scotty knew already.

The boy was surrounded again by a group of dogs, whining and tugging at his pants. He was sobbing now, ragged sounds that might well have come from one of the unfortunate animals. He knelt down again and let them lick him and offer him their comfort. Vernon walked over to the boy and crouched next to him. A feat, Matt knew, since Vernon didn't like dogs and had resisted for years the entreaties of his wife and children to get a puppy. "I'm sorry, Scott," he said. "I'm sorry I treated you like an asshole. But you need to go home now. Your parents are worried. You need to go home." The boy slowly gathered himself, though he still sat there, surrounded by the worried dogs. "We can drive you back, Scott," Vernon said. "Let us drive you back."

The boy got to his feet, and for all his height and strength, he looked like he might fall over. Matt wondered when he'd last eaten or slept. Scotty steadied himself against the cinder blocks of the building and slowly, leaning down to give the dogs a last caress, came with them. He didn't say a word the whole trip back or when they reached his dorm, where they saw his parents standing on the steps, ready to charge at the cops, faces tight with fury. The boy got out of Matt's car and faced his parents. "Leave them alone," Scotty said, "they didn't do anything." He turned back to Matt and Vernon, and seemed to try to say something. His face was splotched and his mouth was working, but no words came out.

Vernon and Matt drove away. They, too, seemed unable to speak, and Matt felt a terrible heaviness descend on him as he walked back through the station. They sat at their desks, still in silence, until Matt put his head on the smooth surface and said, "Vernon, do you ever feel like you will never recover from being a cop? That you're as bad or worse than anyone you ever arrested? Vernon, I am so fucking tired."

Vernon sighed. "Enough with the melodrama. I'll be right back," he said, and in a few minutes, he was, holding two mugs full of something scalding. Lines of steam rose upward in lazy spirals. It was the most relaxing thing Matt had seen in days, that steady kink of vapor. Vernon sat down and pushed one toward him. "Drink it. You'll feel better."

Matt sat up long enough to take a slow sip and let the flavor seep into his mouth. "Vernon, you finally did it. You got me to drink green tea."

"Like it?" his partner asked quite hopefully.

Matt took another sip. "I know what it tastes like now. I know what it reminds me of," he said, "and I don't know if it's good or bad."

"Yeah?"

Matt watched his partner. "What are you going to do tonight, Vernon?"

"Go home and see my kids and talk to them until they're sick of me. And then I'm going to do the same with my wife."

"Exactly," Matt said. "And the tea. It tastes like gunpowder."

EPILOGUE

What a long, freakish summer it had been. It had started with what Vernon discovered in Harvey's apartment. Camera equipment and a minuscule darkroom converted from a half-bath. Vernon said, "I saw that stuff and I wanted to be sick. I was sure it was little boys." But it wasn't. It was years of portraits of girls. All of them clothed. All taken without their subjects' knowledge. Candid pictures from soccer games. At theater performances. Always chaste. All of them taken in places where no one would have remarked on Harvey's cameras, which were uniformly small, though fitted with long lenses. The files were meticulous, begun about a decade earlier, and they cataloged obsessions with various students throughout their Armitage years. But only by their first names: Mary, Lily, Alex, Rebecca. Each would graduate and he would have to choose a new muse. His last had been Claire. What struck Matt was that Harvey had captured some of her loneliness, some of her fear. They were head shots, the last series, which dated from April. There was no way, looking at that face, you would have guessed she was pregnant. But Harvey had also shot pictures in Castine, and those were the photos that Tamsin had been shredding. Harvey, knowing a warrant would discover his obsession, had panicked and taken the pictures to Porter in a desperate measure to blackmail him. How pleased he must have been to discover her there so unexpectedly. Even pieced back together with tape, Claire looked gloriously pretty in those summer photographs, but not happy. Not once in any of his pictures did she look happy. Tanned, lithe, intelligent. But never relaxed, contented, open. It was a face that knew, well before Harvey's documented interest, that it was watched.

Of course, Matt and Vernon told Sarah Talmadge. Of course, Harvey abruptly lost his job. Harvey had been purple with outrage and had threatened all kinds of lawsuits. But Matt advised Sarah to tell him that withholding evidence in a possible murder case could earn you quite a jail sentence, and he was gone within two days, Sarah said, the apartment looking as if no one had ever lived there.

All of July was mired in depositions needed from the rafts of lawyers every individual involved in the case had hired. Then Vernon got so cranky, he said he was going to take every speck of comp time ever owed him and that would mean he would be unavailable until November. At that point, they had a few pitiful cases of embezzlement on their desks and not much else to occupy their days except avoiding attorneys and the journalists intent on tracking down scraps of the Armitage case. What was upsetting, Matt thought, was that, after something so wrenching, it was hard to get excited about less vivid transgressions. This realization was harder on Vernon than it was on Matt. Vernon had spent so much time keeping his job within manageable proportions, eminently easy to put aside at the end of the day. When it turned out he had an appetite for excitement, it made him almost unbearable. At that point, Angell ordered them both out of the office for two whole weeks. Vernon grumpily packed up his Prius, and he and Kathy and the girls sped off to a cabin on a lake. They might, Vernon confessed, be getting a dog on the way back.

Matt spent four days with Barbara and Inge in Connecticut, taking walks, cooking, drinking, and talking through what sort of

sperm donor they should pursue. They'd worked out their disagreement, Barbara had told him, and were ready to pursue par-
enthood. The two women were thrilled and scared and all the
things you ought to be before embarking on such an adventure,
such a duty. They were ready to have their lives revolutionized,
which Matt thought was probably an appropriate response to something as small but complex as a baby. He still had not quite gotten
over the minute perfection of Claire's child. He had so rarely met
someone so new. In his mind, he called the baby Pablo, the name
Kayla had given him. "We should just ask Matt," Inge said one
night after a bottle or two of wine. "Barb, he's smart, he's handsome, he's as close to you as we're going to get genetically. And if
you carry the next baby, then they're really related." Matt felt a
flush of intensely complicated feelings at that moment. Fear,
closer to terror, a tentative hopefulness that they would ask him,
and a fervent wish that they really would not. Barbara looked at
him closely, gently. "He would do it if we asked, Inge. He would.
He's that good a brother. But maybe he's not ready to be a father.
Give him a little time."

The next day, before he left, Barbara said to him, "She was
serious. She was drinking, but she meant it. She wants you in the
baby's life. Me, too." They were on the porch of Barbara's pretty
house. Inge was a demon gardener, and the window boxes were
flowing over with sweet potato vine and white geraniums. They
could hear her in the house, humming. She was a brilliant carpenter, too, and an excellent cook. Barbara had been incredibly
lucky to find her. She'd never had a girlfriend before, calling herself a lesbian of circumstance for falling in love with Inge. "But,"
as she had told Matt, "if someone who looked like Inge told you
she liked you, wouldn't you change your orientation?" Matt had

had to agree. The Swedish woman was six feet tall and had had a career as a model before becoming an art restorer. That she was smart and kind and emotionally balanced were additional reasons to welcome Inge into his sister's life.

Matt looked at his feet, which were in running shoes, and he wondered how fast he could actually go if he really wanted to avoid this conversation. "Barb, if you want me to, I will." He contemplated the doctor's visits, the room with the tawdry pornography; he'd had friends go through the process and he knew some of what was involved. "But no matter what, I'll be in the baby's life. That's a given." She kissed him, and Inge gave him a huge basket of food to take on his drive to Maine. He waved to them as they stood on their porch, blond and brunette, arms twined around each other's shoulders, to wish him good-bye. He was on his way to Acadia, where he had rented a cabin for a week of total peace.

He was going to hike, fish, read, sleep. No telephone, no computer. His car was full of tackle and books, fleece jackets and food. He couldn't wait.

And the week was everything he had hoped for. He barely spoke to a soul except for a few other people on the trails he walked. He woke at chilly dawn and drank coffee in the mist on the small porch. He prowled the glorious rocks and tide pools and made a couple of very quick forays into icy water. He caught a few fish and cooked a few good meals. And throughout, he thought about whether or not he should help out Inge and Barbara and, more to the point, become a kind of father before he found his own partner. When he had his own children, if he had his own children, would the existence of this child blur the lines of paternity in useful or destructive ways? He thought about his own parents and their stern devotion, and he thought about Vernon's abject adoration of his wild twins. It seemed quite clear that having kids required an absolute yielding to responsibility blended with a help-less love. It seemed to tap into something deeply human and im-possibly burdensome at the same time. He wanted to be sure. He wasn't sure he was. A week of solitude produced deep bodily relax-ation and an emotional readiness to entertain difficult questions. Barbara and Inge weren't the only people on his mind. He was thinking about Vernon, about committing for another year to Greenville; a conversation with Angell was on the horizon. He was thinking about his father, increasingly frail. He was thinking about a fall full of testimony and a reimmersion in that awful case. And he was thinking about Madeline.

The day he left Acadia, Mount Desert Island was wrapped in fog. He was sad to leave, and a familiar post-vacation dread of the upcoming week shrouded him the same way the dense mist hugged the roads. Gradually it lifted, and he noticed that the gas gauge was low. He figured he could make it to the next exit, which was for Castine. He had noticed the town's location on the way up and wondered if he'd managed to avoid refilling the tank just to make a spontaneous stop in the place where the whole de-bacle had had its start.

After finding a gas station, he was suddenly reluctant to get back on the road. He ought to. He had no call hanging around here. But in spite of himself, he drove downtown, wedged the car in a parking spot, and walked out along the pier. Gracious houses, a harbor the shape of a horseshoe, dotted as he suspected it always was in sum-mer with elegant sloops. Painters and poets lived and worked here. Small cafés and shops lined the waterfront. He could see the town's crisp appeal and wasn't surprised that Porter and his family had re-treated here when their lives collapsed.

He could imagine Harvey here, too. The town had a certain briskness that Matt felt would appeal to the man. He might be here now, up in his cottage, though Matt doubted he would seek out the same place in which Porter and his family had found refuge in the wake of the sensation that the case had caused. Castine was too small and the chances that they would bump into each other too great. Harvey Fuller, bitter and warped, wounded and scorned, had gone to ground elsewhere, Matt suspected.

He should leave himself. It was unseemly, this curiosity, this courting of connection. How many degrees separated him from someone like Harvey? He didn't have a camera. He didn't pretend to be what he was not. But still he shouldn't lurk around here. He turned to go back to his car, and then he saw them. They had just left a coffee shop. Porter, Lucinda, and Miles. The mother and son wore sunglasses though the day was overcast, a habit that had come with their sudden notoriety. Lucinda immediately, instinctively wrapped her arm around Miles and ushered him off. A boy of eighteen, far taller than she, a boy who had killed someone, but to whom she still reacted as if electricity or dangerous surf, barbed wire or a snarling dog might threaten his safety. When would she release her hold? Matt wondered. He had seen the boy only twice since that rainy evening, and he had sat there, slumped and anxious and scolded to near silence by two lawyers, looming like falcons on either side. The boy had appeared beaten, empty. And each time, Lucinda had been waiting outside the room, ready to throw that protective arm around his shoulders. Or was all that care a sign that she was one of the good mothers? One of the ones who watched and counseled, a mother who was always there.

Lucinda barked something at Porter, clearly telling him to come with her. But Porter shook his head and pulled himself away from his wife and son. For a moment, he stood there. And then he walked toward Matt, one hand lifted in a motion that wasn't so much a greeting as an acknowledgment. Behind him, Matt heard the halyards of the boats moored in the harbor start to clank in the rising wind.

"I was just about to go," Matt said as he shook Porter's hand. The day was starting to darken further. "I don't mean to keep you."

"If you're headed back to Armitage, it's a long drive," Porter said, almost wistfully. He would of course know the way intimately.

"I'll take it slowly," Matt said, glancing at the sky. He was suddenly very embarrassed, as if he'd been caught snooping, as unabashed as any reporter from a tabloid, which was not an inaccurate analogy. It was also certainly unwise, given that nothing about the case was resolved, and sooner or later, he would see Porter in a courtroom. "I shouldn't be bothering you, but I'll admit I was curious to see this place. I was coming down from Acadia."

Porter stood next to him, and together they looked out at the ruffled water. "I'm spending a lot of time up there these days. There's a lot of solace in those woods. Lucinda's worried I'm turning into a hermit. She wouldn't let me take *Walden* on my last trip." He tried to grin. Matt watched him looking out at the neat white boats tugging at their moorings. Porter was altered. He'd grown smaller, more wizened.

They were besieged right now, he said to Matt, but that was still no excuse for not trying to do your best. "I'm most worried about Lucinda, who is treating all this like a war, girding herself for some ultimate battle." But Miles concerned him, too. He was spending too much time in his room. He refused to be coaxed out.

"What about you?" Matt asked him.

Porter shrugged. "I watch birds. I am trying to write. I'm reading or rereading. Thoreau, Emerson, Melville. Dostoevsky. I don't think more hours spent poring over testimony and being coached by lawyers will ultimately make much difference." Those weren't the lessons he was prepared to draw from what had happened. Literature was a more useful guide. "I should go now," he told Matt. "But I am glad to see you. It gives me a chance to say thank you for helping us at a critical moment."

Matt could say nothing in response. That he'd been young once would sound callow. That he wanted to help preserve what he could of what had been an honorable man was even worse. He took Porter's offered hand and remembered that one of the comments people had always made about Porter McLellan was that he was very good at remembering to offer gratitude. And although the trip back to Massachusetts would take another eight hours, Matt sat in his car for a long time and looked at the storm preparing to blow into the small harbor.

BY THE END OF AUGUST, the green of Armitage's maples had dulled to a color that looked better on old lizards than on trees, Madeline thought. She was sitting on a lawn chair outside her dorm collecting herself with a tall glass of ice water. She had just moved into her new apartment, and it was a vast improvement over her original digs. With the futon foisted on an old friend, she had bought herself a small sofa with a brown velvet cover, which now sat looking rather natty in the middle of her living room. She had some sharp new clothes in her closet, a haircut she liked, and a mind bustling with new tricks to try in the classroom. Sarah had called her in late June to ask if she wanted to attend a new-teacher institute, and it had been excellent.

Even so, she was hot, dusty, and a little confused by the welter of feelings that returning to Armitage was calling up in her. A sudden breeze ruffled the canopy of trees around the Quad, and abruptly, the leaves flipped to reveal the chalky gray of their undersides. She had seen Sarah as she'd driven her U-Haul onto campus, and the poor woman had looked even more tired than she had at the end of May. As expected, she had been appointed interim head, and she'd probably earned her salary twice over given the summer she'd had. The scandal had been splashed about the media, parents were in an uproar. Rumors were flying about a huge suit the Harknesses had filed, and she'd had even more faculty departures to contend with. Stunningly, Harvey Fuller had resigned. That, at least, had meant that Betsy Lowery could return to the biology department, a development that spread relief throughout the school. But still, the endowment was down, and even the cynical assessment of the head of admissions had not quite translated into full dormitories. Everyone was giving Armitage a year or so to tend itself, and then they'd see if the wounded beast might be worth the investment again.

Madeline sipped more water and held her hand to the breeze. Sarah's job was a bit like galvanizing war-weary troops, though of course what teachers did was not even remotely as dangerous as soldiering. Most of the time, Madeline amended. She was glad that all the members of the Reign would be gone this year and that Sarah had begun her tenure by announcing that the old traditions would all be ending. Armitage was facing a new era; it did not have time or place for activities that didn't promote the well-being of every student. She'd appointed Madeline to the committee, though Madeline knew it would take more than that to root out something as powerful as the Reign.

Madeline's stomach grumbled, and she realized she'd only had coffee for breakfast. But she was too engrossed thinking about a conversation she and Fred had recently had to deal with finding food. He had heard nothing from Malcolm Smith, the man to whom he'd sent all those incriminating files. "It's freaky," he said. "I was so sure there would be this earthquake, and instead, there's utter silence. Which is more disturbing. He might be hatching some vengeful plot, but I've got no idea about it." Since you can't control it, Madeline had said, the best thing to do is to put it aside. Get lost in what you're doing. If it comes up again, it comes up. He knows how to find you. Fred had smiled and said he was glad he had his painting to devote himself to. He had not said how glad he was that Madeline might provide distraction.

That thought was irritating enough that she rose from her chair and went to get her keys and wallet. It would be good to give herself the treat of a trip to Ali's, to see how his summer had been and to stuff herself with falafel before attacking the files that had to be unpacked and arranged. Activities that would also safely usher Fred away from the front of her mind. She was teaching two classes she had never taught before—The Contemporary Short Story and American Drama—and she had spent the last two weeks on the beach elbow-deep in copies of *True West* and George Saunders collections, and now they were sitting sandy and water-stained in unstable piles around her desk. She had looked at them and thought, This is what teachers do. Carry around dog-eared copies of books they love, underlined and scrawled in as if they held all the meaning in the world. Then we try to shake out whatever is magical or wondrous in them and deposit it like pirate

gold in front of all those minds around the table. It was curious
stuff, teaching. Who knew why it worked when it did and how exactly you could measure its success? But it was fruitful to think
about, and best of all it made Madeline feel purposeful. It was a
feeling she was growing to like.

Ali's had moved from the laundromat to its own stand-alone
place next to a beauty parlor. It was certainly an improvement,
though Madeline missed the scruffiness of the old restaurant. Not
Ali. "Customers are all complaining the new joint doesn't have atmosphere," he said when he saw Madeline. "But who wants the atmosphere of a laundromat? All that fabric softener was driving me
nuts." Madeline took his point, told him she was glad he was happy
and business was going well, and went outside to bask in the sun in
an orange plastic chair, another addition to the new ambience.

She closed her eyes and stretched out her legs. She had been
running a lot, not exactly longer distances, but trying to run a little
faster, to get stronger, and she could feel the results in her tightened muscles. It had been hard work in the heavy heat of the
Cape, but there was something about surviving that horrid spring
that had made her a bit more able to tolerate difficulty. Everyone
had noticed it. Isabelle had said, in a tone that combined both
disapproval and grudging respect, that Madeline wasn't quite such
a pushover as she used to be. When had she gone and developed a
backbone? And Kate, too, hadn't been able to reduce her instantly
to vassal status. Madeline had agreed to look after Tadeo only during certain hours and not on weekends and said that she was off to
her institute for two weeks in July and apologized to no one, a real
first. "Why do you need your weekends free?" Kate had had the gall
to ask. "To see friends," Madeline had answered, for once, evasively.

To go to see Fred in New York from time to time, trips about which she kept quite silent, except that Kate said pointedly, "You go away for the weekend and have sex and I want to know who with," which so mortified Madeline she finally confessed to what was going on. But she still said less than she might have, and that too marked the start of a new confidence, a new continence that stemmed from that week at the end of the year. All summer long, people had invited lurid confessions and speculation about Armitage and what had happened, and she had soon decided that the best course of action was to say as little as possible. If you hadn't lived through it, you couldn't possibly understand it. A girl had died, a stupid and pointless death, and turning it into an item to gossip about just made her feel queasy. Madeline had rarely chosen silence over conversation, but in this instance she felt quite sure she was right to do so.

Ali called her name, and she went inside to retrieve her falafel. She smiled at the tall man and announced, "*Shokran*," "thank you" in Arabic, which she had looked up on the computer to be able to say to him. He smiled and said, "Nice accent."

"I've been meaning to ask him for years how to say that," someone said behind her. She spun around and saw the detective. Dressed not as she had seen him last, in khaki pants and navy blue blazer, but wearing something he might have worn to the beach: a T-shirt and shorts and scuffed sneakers. He looked young and, Madeline thought, disturbingly good.

"Are you on duty?" she asked and fetched a lemonade from the cooler as Matt ordered his meal.

"Thankfully, no," he said. "I've been on vacation and just got back. It all starts tomorrow."

"I know," she said, "me, too, and I'm excited and kind of terrified at once. It's like Labor Day's about to hit and all of a sudden there's all this school rushing at you like an enormous train."

He laughed, and they went outside and sat in the plastic chairs. "Last time I saw you eating falafel, it was pouring."

"As I recall, you were interrogating me and we met here because you were hungry," Madeline said and tore into her sandwich. Her tone was light, but mentioning that deadly week brought some of the feeling back: the constant damp, the frightened students, and the amazement that something so definitively drastic could happen at Armitage.

"That's right. I know cops are only semihuman, but we have to eat sometimes, too. So how was your summer?"

It was surprisingly easy to talk to him now that he wasn't watching all of Armitage with such strict attention. Madeline found herself telling him about her mother and her absurd, show-offy kitchen. Kate's difficulty in adapting to life as a working mother. "Honestly, my sister's better at the 'working' part of that job title," Madeline said. Her own enjoyment in thinking about teaching, about how to get kids to grapple with ideas and make them better writers and not just cynical spinners of tales good enough to earn them entrance to Harvard. Maybe it was a fool's errand, but she was going to try it anyway.

He listened as he had when he was taking notes, with an intensity and focus that might have been unnerving if he hadn't been genuinely interested. He was following, asking questions, responding with pleasure. They were done with their sandwiches, and it would have been easy to crumple the tinfoil in little silver packets and walk off, but neither of them felt like doing that and instead they slowly sipped their drinks, making them last. She thought, He's someone I can talk about it with. He lived through it, too.

She asked him about his summer and what it had been like after everything wound up at the school. He talked about his sister, Barbara, and visiting her and her girlfriend. About his week in Acadia, without phone or radio or news, and how peaceful it had felt. He talked about his father, Joseph, getting crankier by the minute. "At work it was low-key, criminally speaking, almost too much so. Full of lawyers and delays for the stuff that happened in the spring. Lots of technicalities." He looked at her then to see if she minded talking about it. She was grateful. All summer long, people had just plowed ahead, as if the story were theirs to seize.

"It's okay," she told him. "I don't mind. It's sort of a relief to actually discuss it with someone who was there."

So he kept talking, about the motions for change in venue, about the countercharges. And there's this, too, he said. He and his colleagues had missed things. It was galling to feel so less than perfect. That whole crowd was looking only for mistakes. She watched him as he spoke and then said, more in the style of the old Madeline than in that of the new, more circumspect version, "Well, I think two things. We all missed things, and we'll never forgive ourselves at the academy because we were supposed to care for her. Imagine how Claire's parents feel. But the other issue, this interest in perfection. It's because they're so rich. They can afford all that help, all that pursuit of exactness. My father's a lawyer, and he always says justice comes at the same price as the hourly of your attorney."

Matt turned to her and said, "This is an interesting topic, and it's getting hot here. Want to walk by the river?" Which seemed an incredibly nice and natural way to continue the conversation.

The path by the Bluestone wound under oak trees and wil-
lows, and although it was less than ten minutes from campus,
Madeline hadn't even known the path existed, much less walked
along it. In the shade of the dusty trees, Matt prompted, "So you
think it's money. You think that's what protects them."

Watching the sluggish roll of the river and remembering the
way the note she'd tossed in the high froth last spring had disappeared, Madeline said, "Not precisely. It's the habit of money.
The taking for granted you can do what you want. The money
and the confidence and the clothing and the vacations and the
schools all get blurred together in this stew of feeling better than
other people. Special. As if gravity doesn't apply to you. Some of
them wake up. And a lot of them don't. Some of them have
parents who seem ready to protect them their entire lives." She had
picked up a willow switch and was drawing a pattern in the gray
water with it.

"And then, just when you least expect it, they're responsible
or generous or open in a way that is mind-blowing because there's
been no precedent for it at all. I still think there was something
weirdly noble in Claire keeping that baby, even if all she wanted
to do was humiliate everyone around her. She could have so easily done something else."

Matt tossed a stone to the center of the river and weighed another in his hand. A light wind was blowing clouds over the sun,
and the day was at last cooling. "You might be right, Madeline."
She liked the way he said her name, with a softness to it when
most people made the i hard and firm. Some kids whizzed by on
bikes. In the middle of the river, a fish arced and flipped its silver
skin through the hot sky.

"I saw Porter," Matt said. "On the way back from Acadia, I realized I was close to Castine. So I drove through and tried to get a sense of what it was like there. Have you ever been?"

Madeline said no. Her sister went, attracted, she said, like a salmon drawn to the stream where it was spawned, except that prestige and houses were what pulled Kate, not instinct.

Matt smiled and said it was true that that was what was there. But it also had this beautiful harbor, and he'd been standing there, looking at the boats he'd never know how to sail, when he bumped into Porter.

"How is he?" Madeline hadn't quite understood until now that part of her reluctance in returning to Armitage was about working at a place that didn't have Porter in it. They were walking in the direction of Armitage, toward the bridge that marked the outer limits of the crew course where the trees grew more densely.

Matt considered his response. "He's reading, watching birds, though I got this sense that he was smaller. But he seems prepared to do what's necessary." He threw the second stone in the river.

"*Necessary*. It's such a stark word," Madeline mused. "What does that mean in his case?"

Matt shrugged and said, "Tell the truth as best he can, I think. Atone. If possible."

"It's biblical," said Madeline with a shiver.

"You make that sound like a disease," Matt teased her, and she said, "No, no, it's not that. It's just that most people shirk what they've done. They don't admit to it. They find a thousand ways to make it not their fault. So what Porter is doing feels rare. It feels valuable."

They stood there in silence for a minute. A great blue heron winged past, and the wind gathered some force. The day might resolve in a thunderstorm, though none were forecast. "Madeline," Matt asked, hands free of stones, face aimed at the sky, "are you seeing anyone?"

"That is very funny," she said, "because I was wondering the same thing about you, but I didn't have the courage to ask and was feeling stupid after thinking about Porter being so brave." She felt herself turning pinker. "And the honest answer from my perspective is sort of yes, sort of no." She had just returned from seeing Fred, and it had been clear to her that his paintings had already swallowed him whole. They'd made no plans for a next meeting, and she sensed that, despite their mutual delight, they might be returning to an ambiguous state of friendship. They had even agreed that there wasn't anything exclusive about their time together, though Madeline sensed it was less an Ilsa or a Vanessa who would claim Fred than sheer hunger to be painting as much as possible. It was actually a lot harder to compete with an intellectual passion than with a womanly one. People always tripped up, revealed themselves, made themselves rather easily unlovable.

"And the doubly honest answer is no, I am not committed to anyone, but I go to see a friend from Armitage in New York once in a while. I don't think that means I can't ask you for a falafel. But I would have to tell him first."

Matt laughed and looked at her and said, "Could we make it dinner on a Friday night somewhere not in Armitage? After, of course, you've told your friend," and she found herself surprised at how delighted the prospect of a long meal with the detective made her.

They walked back along the river to Ali's, where both of them had parked. "I miss the laundromat," he said. "It had a *je ne sais quoi* of lint to it that just changed everything."

"Me, too," Madeline said, and they agreed that, once school settled down and he got back to work, they'd meet for a meal somewhere definitively out of town, maybe even all the way in Boston. She drove back to the school, through the iron gates, parked her scruffy car, and spent an incredibly productive afternoon and evening pulling together syllabi. Something changed as she was writing those course descriptions. She was concerned, she realized, not so much with making her students smarter as making them more scrupulously honest with the tools they had at hand, with the words and stories with which they surrounded themselves. It could matter what you did with language: it could help to turn you into someone real.

WHEN HE HAD SEEN the backs of Madeline's calves at Ali's, Matt had felt as he had when he'd taken those quick plunges into the fierce Acadian water. Short of breath, quickened, and sharply, cleanly alive. He had no idea how much he had hoped to see her. It made him unbelievably happy that he had, for the moment, edged out the art teacher. Matt strode into the police station whistling. Whistling. He never did that. Joseph had said that the sound made screaming kids sound like Beethoven and that he could make a person wish for deafness. Barbara had said more kindly that his ear was off and he should really leave the music making to the professionals. His mother had said she loved it because once you heard the sound you knew it couldn't be anybody but Matt.

But no one else shared this opinion, especially Vernon, who popped into the hall and looked at his partner. He stood there in his baggy jacket, chewing something that crunched loudly, probably a long stick of jicama. "I thought someone was torturing a cat," he said, "but at least we could arrest him for that. Stop, please stop." Then he looked more closely at Matt, swallowed, and said, "So what happened? You win Sox tickets? Get Christmas off this year?" Matt stopped whistling—the noise bothered even him— and found he couldn't stop smiling long enough to answer Vernon. "Nope," he finally answered as he swung past his partner into their office. "Far better. I asked Madeline out and she said yes." Turning in the threshold, Vernon threw his hands in the air and said, "Finally! A life!"

ACKNOWLEDGMENTS

I would like to thank everyone at Voice, in particular Sarah Landis and Barbara Jones, for their advocacy of my work and their support of this book as it took shape. Jennifer Rudolph Walsh and Claudia Ballard also have my gratitude. And I am very grateful to Jim Rutman for his good advice and assistance as the novel evolved.

A CONVERSATION WITH
CHARLOTTE BACON

Q. *The Twisted Thread* is a departure from the tone of your previous work—what inspired you to write a mystery? How did the experience of writing it compare to your other books?

A. I am one of those omnivorous readers—milk cartons, circulars from Sears, Russian novels, comics—a habit that stems from early childhood. Every summer, my family went to our small house in upstate New York and spent long stretches of hot days lying in a field with some kind of book propped over our noses. Often, I read mysteries. Josephine Tey. Dick Francis. Maj Sjöwall and Per Wahlöö. John le Carré. In college, I immersed myself in a different kind of literature and then began to write, propelled by an interest in character and the murky forces that inform even ordinary choices. But I still found myself drawn to mysteries, and when I was struggling with a long novel about three years ago, I let myself get distracted by an image that arrived unbidden one morning: a beautiful blond girl, dead on the floor of her dormitory. I then wrote the first one hundred pages of what became *The Twisted Thread*. Of all my work, I would say *The Twisted Thread* was the most fun to create, the easiest draft to turn to day after day.

Q. Did you attend a boarding school like Armitage Academy? How much, and what kind of research did you have to do to make the New England setting so authentic?

A. I did attend a boarding school in New England and have lived or worked at several others. I would say that it's a setting that I know quite intimately, and bringing it to life on the page didn't require a great deal of archival research. Even so, working with memories is its own variety of investigation. My own boarding school was the place where I worked hardest in my life and with the most earnest of intentions. I had wonderful teachers and friends and encountered none of the harassment that I depict in the novel. Creating darkness of motive and cruelty where I had not experienced it was the hardest part of writing *The Twisted Thread*.

Q. Do you identify with any of the characters in the book? Do you believe you would have investigated Claire's murder in the way Madeline does?

A. Well, my hair flies around like Madeline's, and I am a runner, though a slow one. She has my enjoyment of teaching and habit of spilling on herself, and I like Guinness, in moderation, of course. I am curious the way she is, too, but a lot older, and no, I don't think I would be brave enough to take on something as frightening and alien as a murder investigation. But what I love most about writing is the way it forces me to identify with all my characters. People have such various skills, habits, and interests. I identify with Porter's desire to create order and his love of his children. I understand Matt's ambivalence about privilege. I wish I had Jim's way with tools, and more of Kayla's practicality. On certain mornings without adequate coffee, I have Vernon's prickliness, or so my family says. And I know the struggle that Fred lives through, torn between a desire for a steady life and one devoted to making art. For me, characters can't come to life on the page without my willingness to see a shard of my own personality in them, no matter how vulnerable that makes me.